Olivia's Bliss

Olivia's Bliss

Deborah Wright

POOLBEG

Published 2000
by Poolbeg Press Ltd
123 Baldoyle Industrial Estate
Dublin 13, Ireland
E-mail: poolbeg@iol.ie
www.poolbeg.com

Copyright for typesetting, layout, design
© Poolbeg Press Ltd

The moral right of the author has been asserted.

A catalogue record for this book is available from the British Library.

Great Britain: ISBN 1 85371 903 X
Ireland: ISBN 1 84223 040 9

Set by Phoenix Typesetting
Cover design by Slatter-Anderson
Printed and bound by Omnia Books Limited, Glasgow.

About the Author

Deborah Wright graduated from Lincoln College, Oxford University with a 2:1 in English Literature. After her degree, she worked briefly as a PA and sang in a rock band, then spent two years avoiding gainful employment in order to write full-time. In 1999, she won the *Ireland on Sunday*/Poolbeg 'Write A Bestseller' competition with her first novel, *Olivia's Bliss*. She lives in Sutton, England with her family and two cats.

Acknowledgements

Thank you to my family, especially my mum, my best friend, who has always been so supportive & enthusiastic about my writing, my brothers, Paul (thanks for the printer!) and Stephen, and my dad.

Thanks to: Alexander Hewitt, for all his inspiration, advice and support (especially concerning the T Mac and the Cream Bun), for the Haagen Dazs & Pizza Express trips, for all his hysterical wit, for his astute daily commentary on *The Big Breakfast* – the list is endless. To 'Uncle' Geoffrey for his kind loan of the Toshiba, and equally to 'Uncle' Alex who at times practically became my literary patron. To my 'sister' Sarah P, to Alistair Shearer for his expert tips and comments on the India chapters; to Nick and Pauline Greathead, Bernard & Jane, and, of course, 'Uncle' Brian for all the lifts. And to my new friends *oop* North – particularly Nicky & John Collins for the loan of their lovely quiet house.

To my friends in North Carolina, especially Lewis, Paul D-R, Chris & all the others for all the bliss you bring. To Eleanor Lee, who has put so much selfless energy into New Deal. Also to my bank managers at

Lloyds for being so kind about all my begging letters.

Thanks to my superlative agent, Simon Trewin, and to the great team at Poolbeg: Philip MacDermott, Kieran Devlin, my wonderful editor Gaye Shortland, Valerie Shortland & the brilliant marketing team – Paula, Lucy & Suzanne.

A sincere thank-you to Ali for her advice on my contracts.

Bravo & hi to my 'brother' King Of Metamorphoses, who became 'Ricky' in this book – 1000 hugs & kisses & tootle pips from POF.

Most of all, I cannot express my love and infinite gratitude for my dearest S.L.K. who organised everything so perfectly . . .

Dedicated with
All my Love
For
S.L.K.

PART ONE: RICKY
1. This Is Your Life

"Olivia Bliss, this is your life!"

Michael Aspel strode across the stage, brandishing his fat red book like a waiter with a wine list.

I was perched on the edge of a squashy brown settee. I looked up, blushed, and waved at the audience.

"Well, Olivia, let's begin with when you were born . . ." Michael opened up his book and looked inside.

I waited expectantly. Oh God, I prayed silently, please don't let him have spoken a word to my mother. And please, no mention of the Dracula teeth, setting fire to the living-room, the rock band etc etc etc.

Something was wrong. Aspel was frowning and swallowing. The audience, at first hushed, started to fidget and whisper.

I looked down at my crumpled red T-shirt and ripped jeans with hearts painted on with dayglo pens. Why the hell am I wearing these? I panicked. I never meant to put these on. No wonder everyone was pointing at me. Josephine was right, I should have borrowed her smart lilac suit.

Aspel's mouth was still opening and closing. Then,

with a sigh, he snapped his book shut. He shook his head.

"I'm sorry, Olivia," he said in a voice of doom, like a judge pronouncing a verdict, "but there's nothing to say. You must have the most boring life we've ever come across . . ."

"But – but – what about –" I stuttered, but my words were lost in boos and catcalls from the audience. A cameraman collapsed into a chair in disgust.

"But – but – but – please!" I cried.

Then Michael Aspel did the strangest thing. He came and sat down next to me on the sofa. And started to kiss me! I sat there, frozen, not knowing what to do. If I got up and walked away would I make even more a prat of myself? Was it new *This Is Your Life* protocol to bump up ratings with a bit of raunch? Then, when I gently turned my head away, he started to lick my neck.

"Hey, *getoff!*"

I woke up with sweat pouring down my forehead. Where am I who am I? I panicked, gazing up at the poster of Brad Pitt on my ceiling, grinning down at me reassuringly.

I looked at my Minnie Mouse clock. It read 7: 45.

Roberta, my Red Setter, was bounding all over the bed, pink tongue lolling, begging to be fed. Leonardo, my tabby, also ravenous, jumped up and started to purr in my ear, rubbing his face against my cheek.

Monday morning. No *This Is Your Life*. Just a nightmare. Thank God.

Still, something felt wrong. There was somewhere I ought to be . . . somewhere . . . appointment . . . interview . . .

"Argh!"

I was going to be late. Oh well.

"I just had this dream! I was on *This Is Your Life!*"

In the kitchen, Leila, my flatmate, was sitting reading a footie magazine, more for the glossy pictures of Dave Beckham (woof woof!) than for rules of the game, eating a bowl of cornflakes with vodka because we had run out of milk as usual, much too engrossed in bleached blonde hair and sarongs to look up.

"Here, darling." I offered Leonardo some cornflakes. He flicked his tail in a huff and then miaowed nastily at Roberta who cringed away nervously.

I put a piece of very stale bread in the toaster as Josephine strolled in. As ever, she looked fantastic even first thing in the morning, as though she'd spent the night in a beauty salon. Not one fine Milky-Bar-blonde hair was out of place. She narrowed her blue eyes, then yawned elegantly and plugged in the kettle.

Josephine would understand, I thought. Josephine was rather a fan of psychology and was always pouncing on Freudian slips or getting us to draw pictures of trees and telling us it meant we liked men with big penises (like we really needed to draw a tree to work that one out) and telling us if we dreamt of rain we were going to get married and so on.

"I had this dream!" I cried. "I got off with Michael Aspel —"

"Oh God, nightmare," said Josephine.

"No, the problem was, I was on *This is Your Life* only there was nothing to say. What does it mean, what does it mean?"

"Simple," said Josephine, arching a perfectly plucked eyebrow. "You don't have a life."

"Oh thanks very much!"

Josephine removed some melon from the fridge.

"Well, look at *Cosmopolitan*," she said (*Cosmo* is Josephine's Bible). "The two fundamentals you need in life are career and love. Your love life is non-existent. You've been using a denial-defence mechanism for the last three years by saying that you're going to finish your book but you never do."

I couldn't launch an effective protest, so I turned to Leila, short, round, jolly like a teddy bear, the eternal mummy and peacemaker.

"Leila, do I or do I not have a life?" I demanded, whipping away her magazine.

Leila pushed her short dark curls out of her blood-shot eyes and looked from me to Josephine uncertainly.

"Aren't you going to be late for your interview?" she changed the subject.

"Oh, thanks so much," I said, and walked out. Huh, huh, huh, I thought as I stomped up the stairs. I'd asked Josephine a perfectly straight question. It was obvious I'd wanted her to lie to me and she'd told me the truth – what kind of friend was she?

Besides – what could be said for *her* love life? She hated men. And could you call three days' modelling work a year a career?

I brushed my fair hair furiously until I realised I was looking like a poodle on Viagra. I was frantically spraying on anti-frizz when Josephine knocked on the door and came in looking rather sheepish. She sat on

4

the bed and removed a few dog-hairs, looked around my room disdainfully and asked what I was going to wear for my interview. Her way of saying sorry.

"I was thinking about this." I held up an absurdly short skirt – the type of thing workmen fall off roofs for.

"Oh, that's no good!" Josephine declared. "They'll spend the interview looking at your legs – you'll get it for sure. Hang on, I've got the thing." She ran to her room, rifled through the 'jumble' section of her carefully co-ordinated wardrobe, and came back with a pair of ghastly brown and white striped flares. With it I wore a red jumper, and Josephine added a clashing, shocking-pink scarf and a pair of dangly parrot earrings.

"There you go," she said triumphantly. "There's no way they'll employ you now."

As I slunk my way downstairs, she called after me,

"Don't forget, Olivia – the new lodger is coming this afternoon!"

It was one of my worst interviews ever. I apologised for being late by claiming I had to walk my dog as it had a hyperactive personality problem, and they didn't say a word. A nice tanned bloke with balding head and dark fluffy patches of hair sprouting from big ears led me to the back kitchen of the pizza restaurant, sat me on a stool and, despite frowning at my outfit, smiled encouragingly.

Shit, I started to panic. I know – I'll do the 'I can't speak English' routine, I thought. That had been a marvellous success the previous week for a cleaning job at Benhilton Primary School where I had answered every question by cocking my head to one side and mumbling, *"Eh? I Italiano. Comme star bene?"* Perhaps it would now save me from having to spend my entire social life serving pizza to lager louts and screaming children.

"So, you would like to waitress, say – five nights a week?" he asked.

"Comme star bene?"

"Ah!" his face lit up. *"Comme star bene! Si! Si!"* Suddenly we were like a jolly pair of friends on a pasta ad. This was really going horribly wrong.

"So what hours would I be expected to work?" I hastily returned to straight English. "Because, you see, I'm afraid I can only work from six thirty to seven thirty in the evenings because I've just invested in a month's clubbing pass to the Hippodrome and I don't want to waste it."

"Ah," he scratched his head, looking mildly bemused, "so seven thirty to ten thirty" – he coughed delicately, "would be no good?" He looked at me with such soft dark eyes, as though he was frightened of offending me, that I felt a wave of guilt but I ploughed on relentlessly.

"Erm, well, I'm sorry," I said demurely, "but I am committed to getting pissed and pulling men. I just don't think I could work those hours. And I can't really work lunchtimes either because then I'm recovering from my hangover. But afternoons might be alright," I added, knowing the restaurant was shut then.

He paused for a moment's thought.

"Pah!" Suddenly he slammed a fist on the table. "Then that is no good! What are you doing here

wasting my time! Get away!" He picked up a tea towel and flapped at me as though shooing away a pigeon. I hurried away jumpily, through the door, running down the high street until I arrived at a panting giggling halt at the end.

Well, thank goodness for that.

It was the second interview the Job Centre had sent me to that week. For the past year or so I had been doing my very best to sign on for as long as possible but I think they were starting to get rather fed up with me.

Now, I don't want you to form an impression of me as a girl who likes to make a career out of sitting on benches outside McDonald's blowing straw wrappers at people. No, I had spent nearly every minute of every day writing a novel.

I was six years old when I first tried to be a novelist. My first books were on my greatest subject of expertise: chocolate. I think I must have been inspired by reading Mr Men or the Garden Gang because I wrote a series of books about Rowntrees' sweeties, like Kevin The Kit Kat or Polly Fruit Pastilles. Then I sent them to Rowntrees and told them it would generate lots of good publicity. I even did all the drawings in felt-tip. They replied with a very nice fuck-off, but sent me twenty packets of Smarties as a consolation present. They lasted about forty-eight hours.

My primary school teacher always said I'd have my name in lights but of course I didn't really know much about fame then. I just liked writing. During my teenage years I tailed off a bit. My books are just like my love life: great beginnings, disastrous endings. I have so many folders filled with books that explode with a bang and fizzle out at chapter four.

So I applied for a degree in English. At London, because Leila was going there to study Physics, and the nightlife was meant to be so good – after all, I had to live a little, get some research for my books.

"Great writers must have experience before they can really write in depth," I declared to my irked father, who was a domineering chauvinist, saw no point in female education and wanted me to take a secretarial course at the local college where he could keep an eye on me.

I'd been determined to get a First just to prove him wrong, but unfortunately I never really took to my degree. I spent much more time reading Jackie Collins and then my end of year special paper on 'The Hunkiest Men in Shakespeare' hadn't gone down well. I had thought it was incredibly witty. I compared Mark Antony (eight out of ten), yummy but much too involved in his work, with Hamlet (six out of ten), neurotic but hey, you'd have some *deep* post-coital conversations, man . . . but my tutor hadn't quite got the humour. I'd then been horrified to end up with a 2:2.

A 2:2 degree was, as my Mensa-intelligent brother Scott (who had got a First in Mathematics at Cambridge) had pointed out, simply the worst result. Even to have got a Third would at least have been a failure with flying colours, as though you were brainy but couldn't be bothered. A 2:2 looked as though you'd tried for a 2:1 but were too thick.

"Tar very much," I said furiously. "Anyhow, it's not just brains, it's personality too."

I'd then applied and failed to get lots of jobs in publishing and had flitted through a series of dead-end temporary jobs, most of which I was gladly sacked from. Then I had started to sign on and write full-time and send things off to publishers. I was convinced that my masterpieces would be scooped up right away for a six-figure deal.

Instead, about two months later I was receiving a steady stream of standard rejection slips. With each one I grew more and more despondent and now I was just getting to the point where I was suffering a mid-life crisis at the age of twenty-five and was truly about to consider a career path in Pizza Hut.

I took solace in the local Waterstones.

I breathed in the crispy smell of new books, trailing my hands lovingly over the covers.

The latest new book was yet another Jane Austen rip-off, yet another sequel, this time to *Mansfield Park*.

I liked most of Jane Austen but had a vague memory of *Mansfield Park* being the one where the heroine was seen and not heard and fainted all over the place. Judging from the sequel's cover, it looked as though despite being married Fanny was still seen and not heard and was just fainting in a different house on different sofas.

I'd always intended to write a Jane Austen sequel and everyone had beaten me to it. I'd been simply furious the morning that *Bridget Jones' Diary* came out.

I'd just been about to do a modern *Pride and Prejudice*, and now about the only ones which hadn't been done were *Northanger Abbey* (too immature) and *Persuasion* (too Hormone Replacement Therapy).

Then, just as I was browsing through a *Mars Meets Venus*, the idea hit me.

Excitement slowly started to squiggle over me. I must write it down, was my first instinct. And then: this is brilliant, this is brilliant, oh Olivia, you absolute genius. Within a minute the whole life of the book flashed before me – write, finish, agent, publisher, blockbuster, house in Chelsea Harbour –

My eyes were pinned dreamily on the clock. Suddenly the *Mars Meets Venus* slipped from my fingers.

"Not much good?" the assistant asked.

"No!" I cried. "It's the – new lodger – oh God – I should get back – shit – Josephine's going to kill me!"

2. Ricky

I think that Josephine's main reason for acquiring a new lodger was just for the money. There was a spare box of a room on our floor which had ended up as a junk room for Leila's snooker table and golf gear, plus all my boxes of old books and letters since I hate to throw anything away.

"Look, dears, if we charge seventy pounds, which is perfectly reasonable, I can reduce your rent by ten pounds a week, and still make a profit of fifteen a week which can go in the Party Fund, d'you see?"

I didn't fancy the idea of a lodger at all. I'd seen *Single White Female* and knew the nicest people could turn out to be psychos. But Josephine did own the house, so I was in no position to argue.

Josephine had put through her Lodger Bill by calling a House Meeting and a Vote. I always found such meetings total bores. Josephine loved them because she would sit at the head of the table and play queen whilst poor Leila was forced to take minutes and keep the peace while Josephine and I battled it out over rotas / parties / custody of the telephone. Fairly often, the meeting ended in pillow-fights.

*   *   *

We'd finally agreed that the new lodger should be:
   a. tidy
   b. non – smoking
   c. without pets
   d. male (Leila, me) / female (Josephine)

"You can't have three girls living with a bloke. You won't be able to walk naked from your bedroom to the bathroom," said Josephine.

"We will if he's gorgeous," I said, winking at Leila, who giggled and blushed. "Look, here's the compromise: why don't we say that we'd prefer a female, but if he happens to look like Keanu Reeves, there is no contest."

The ad was placed, the calls started to come, the interviews proceeded.

First came Sally. Pretty, twenty stone overweight, bringing cakes.

"Uh uh," said Josephine afterwards. "Too fat. She'll ruin our image. How will I be able to have cheese and wine-tasting with that hippopotamus in the background."

"Josephine!" I couldn't believe her sometimes, especially since she had once been bulimic herself. "You are being so superficial – so – so – fattist!"

"Sizist, Olivia," Josephine corrected me.

Then came Julia, shy, meek and thin, with the awkward grace of a newborn colt.

"So tell me, Julia, what kind of life d'you lead? What, for example, were you doing at ten o'clock last night?"

Josephine asked, giving her a scrutinising blue stare over her cup of tea.

"For goodness sake, Josephine, you're not supposed to be cross-questioning them!" I complained afterwards.

"I was just asking a few questions. Besides, I think she'll just about do."

But Julia, no doubt scarred by Josephine's Gestapo questioning, never called back, which left Ricky.

Ricky Caldwell, Leila and I agreed, had the sexiest voice imaginable, so smoky and drawling and husky, with a hint of Celtic. He was always polite and gentlemanly but there was a lovely teasing undertone to his voice, as though he never took anything quite seriously. Every time he had called to arrange (and subsequently, cancel) a look round, I had felt my stomach turn and for the first time understood the appeal of telephone sex.

Then, after Ricky promised to turn up a third time and never came, and then said he would absolutely, definitely, without a doubt, be there on Friday morning at eleven thirty, Josephine said: "Oh, let's not hold our breath."

The only other possibility had been a late arrival the day before whom I had nicknamed Boring Brigit. Well, maybe it was a little harsh, she'd seemed nice and all that but somehow so smart, so efficient, like the sort who got up at six am to go to the gym and were fantastic at their accountancy or bank job and had a incredibly smooth love life where they fell in love with a guy, dated for three years, had two point four children and lived a simple, happy life.

Oh dear God, I prayed, *please, please make him turn up, please, I swear I'll be really good and instead of buying that bomber jacket from New Look, I'll put the money in the Good Samaritans' envelope but I swear to you, God, if he doesn't turn up I'll be needing them myself . . .*

I ran all the way to the tube, jiggled all the way on the tube, ran all the way to the bus stop, jiggled all the way on the bus, ran all the way up the road . . .

To discover Josephine coming out of the front door, clicking open her umbrella.

"Did he come?" I cried. "Was he really horny? Oh he was, wasn't he, Josephine, we have to let him stay!"

"He came," Josephine sniffed. "He's alright."

Alright! This was strong praise from Josephine!

"Alright!" Leila shrieked, clutching her football against her chest, her puppy eyes wide as though still suffering aftershocks. "He was unbelievable! Oh, you should have seen him, Olivia, he has these amazing come-to-bed eyes, he just looks you right in the eye and you have an orgasm on the spot!"

"Oh my goodness!" I was close to hitting myself over the head with Josephine's umbrella. How could I have missed him?

Ricky: it was though everything was suspended everything was a prelude to life was holding a great big breath until his arrival in five days, four days, three days, two and a half days . . .

He was expected to arrive at ten that Saturday. Josephine was strutting about impatiently, jangling her car keys, impatient to get out before the best sales items went. I had pretended to oversleep and was still wearing my Snoopy nightshirt. There was no way I was getting dragged out shopping. I wasn't even going to so much as go to put the milk bottles out. I felt like one of those birdspotting fanatics who set up stubborn camp and refuse to drop their eyes even while eating, in their determination to catch a precious glimpse of the Lesser Spotted Toad Warbler.

He was not going to escape this time.

By three o'clock, Josephine was in a complete temper. She had tried his answerphone three times but all she got was a jingle from the Blues Brothers and his breezy message *"Do leave me a message, especially if you're sexy"*. She and Leila set off shopping.

"If he turns up," Josephine snarled, "you can tell him to pack up and go!"

Curling up on the sofa, I nibbled my pen and started on my latest masterpiece.

This was the idea for my book: a rewrite of *Pride and Prejudice*, from the point of view of Wickham.

It was total genius. Wickham was by far the sexiest character in the book (Darcy may have had a big house but he was so staid, I reckoned he didn't have a penis to match). Alright, so Wickham was a bit of a lad but only because he was born in such a repressed age – he was merely ahead of his time, a romantic visionary, a Casanova amongst monks. He was also the most tragic character, I felt, because he ended up getting lumbered with Lydia and then fading out altogether, poor bastard . . .

What a wonderfully juicy, Byronic, heart-breaking book it could be. I already had plans for Wickham to rob Jane of her virginity and Mrs Bennet to nurture an unrequited passion for him.

Wickham's Memoirs, that's what I would call it.

The trouble was, writing the first line. I sat down and chewed my pen for a while, doodled on my pad, flicked through *The Radio Times*.

Exercise would make my creativity flow. I pulled off my shoes and trampolined on the sofa until I heard a distinctive twang. Then I decided to put the milk bottles out.

I had just opened the door when a great big roaring fat motorbike came zooming up the road. It charged to a halt outside our house, and a man, dressed in black jeans and brown flying jacket with a sheepskin lining, got off.

Yum yum, I thought, half hiding behind the door in my nightie.

Then he took off his helmet to reveal a beautiful face and mussed-up blonde hair.

Yum yum yum! I watched surreptitiously. Could it be him, could it?

Then, even better, he walked up to the bottom of our peeling black gate and checked the number. Then, like a hero in a *Milk Tray* ad, he vaulted himself over the fence and came bounding up to me.

He was even better close up. For a moment I simply stared, drinking in the sculptured features, chiselled cheekbones, square jaw smattered with fair stubble, effeminate lips, turned-up nose. He had the most amazing eyes, like Rolos, flecked with light hazel, like dints of toffee, which slowly slid over my breasts and down my legs to my feet, where I curled my toes in delicious embarrassment. Then he smiled.

I simply stared and stared. I couldn't speak, only salivate.

"Hi, sorry I'm late, didn't get up till eleven, had an *insane* hangover," he said. He seemed delighted by the effect he was having on me. "I'm Ricky Caldwell."

I was so overcome I dropped the milk bottle.

"There, there," said Ricky soothingly, his lovely (though slightly grubby) long brown fingers caressing my toes.

I lay back on the sofa, moaning with bliss and intense pain, watching him through half-closed eyes.

He was everything I'd expected him not to be. In my fantasies I had pictured him as tall, dark, in a swish suit, purring up in a slinky car – and here he was blonde, car mechanic-ish, but gazing at me with such lovely brown smiley eyes, so real and somehow more attractive than I could ever have imagined.

Then Josephine walked in. I must have been so engrossed in gazing at him, I didn't even hear her key in the lock.

Ricky stood up and said, "Hi," and offered a hand. She shook it very lightly and then looked from me to him to me, suspiciously, incredulously.

"Olivia," she said with that bitchy, territorial ring to her voice, "honestly, he's been here less than an hour.

I know what you're like but this is a bit quick!"

"Don't worry," Ricky clicked, "we're not doing Sarah Fergie toe-sex or anything—"

"Oh no," I said quickly, blushing, sitting up. "I just dropped a milk bottle and I thought I'd got a bit of glass in my foot, but luckily it's only a little cut, you see—"

"That explains the glass outside – I thought it was vandals again," said Josephine coldly. "Well, are you okay?" I guess the question was addressed to me but she looked at Ricky. It was very hard not to.

I waited miserably for her to show him the door but, to my surprise, she swallowed, ahemed, frowned him up and down, and then said,

"Well, I suppose having a male lodger will help to balance and harmonise the masculine and feminine vibrations in the house."

Ricky gave her a look as if to say, *You what?*

"Perhaps I could help you with your things . . ." she offered begrudgingly. He had a rucksack and several carrier bags strapped to his motorcycle.

"If it's not too much trouble," said Ricky, with that slight taking-the-piss edge to his voice again.

Josephine looked at him sharply; he smiled charmingly.

I tried to stand up, then yelped – putting my sore foot down on the carpet was like treading on hot coals. Ricky put an arm around my waist to steady me.

"I think you'd better rest a bit," he said gently.

So I lay down on the sofa, hearing Josephine taking him upstairs, praying "Please God, please don't let him fancy her."

I could tell right away she fancied him, because I could overhear the formal sharpness in her voice. Josephine always goes all posh and la-di-da when she's on the defensive. I don't think she knew quite what to make of him. He wasn't her usual type at all, since Josephine normally only goes for Mr Filofax on fifty thou' a year with a Porsche thrown in.

But as they came down the stairs, Ricky looked in and winked at me. They came into the room and Josephine passed him a contract detailing all his commitments.

"No noise after ten o'clock, clean the bath out after use, take two slots on the rota," Ricky read, looking mildly troubled. "Do I have to ask your permission to breathe at certain times?"

"What job d'you do then, Mr Caldwell?" Josephine asked snidely.

She folded her arms with a triumphant look on her face, waiting to dismiss him as a bimbo, a sex god with the IQ of a potato.

"Oh, I just work in magazines," said Ricky casually. "I do a column for *Vixen.*"

Our jaws dropped. *Vixen* was one of those glossy super-celeb-packed womens' magazines, a sort of cross between *Cosmo* and *Hello*. It was Josephine's dream that she would one day get a modelling job in it but they only included the crème de la crème of supermodels.

Ricky smiled at us and said, "It's really cool, I get to work with twenty women, and have discussions with them about orgasms and PMT all day."

Almost oblivious to our admiration, he slumped

down on the sofa like a big lazy cat. He was so at home and chilled out, it was as if he was the host and we were awkward strangers.

"To be honest with you," he confessed modestly, "I only got it because of my dad, Sir Henry Caldwell. You might have heard of him?"

Heard of him! Sir Henry Caldwell was one of those literary big shots who owned about twenty publishing companies and houses. He had a big Sunday-night show, the sort of thing where gay poets draped themselves over pale blue sofas and discussed the merits of a book consisting of sixty-four blank pages. He wrote 'lit crit' and clever books, the type which people had on their bookshelves though they'd never even read them.

Even Josephine could not fail to look impressed.

"Yeah," said Ricky, "well. . . I was going out with this girl, then she chucked me out and I ended up living with Dad but he's got this big chip on his shoulder about me being independent and *adult*. And you know what parents are like – no matter how old you are they still treat you as though you're twelve. So I got pissed off and decided to get my own place." He reached out his long fingers to Roberta, making kissey-kissey noises. Josephine and I watched in amazement as Roberta, who is a bit of a neurotic dog, came up and sniffed his hand shyly. Then she lay on her back and rolled her brown eyes at him and he rubbed her tummy while she drooled.

"Wow, normally Roberta runs and hides in the wardrobe when strangers come," I said in surprise.

"Roberta, aren't you a sweet little thing?" said Ricky,

fondling her silky ears. Then he grinned winningly at Josephine. Watching them smile at each other, however, my relief was edged with a fresh fear. *No, no, please,* I willed Ricky silently, *don't fancy her. She can have anyone she wants, she'll only use you and abuse you and spit you out like chewing-gum and then you'll have to move out. Okay, I may not have her beautiful cheekbones and my legs are only half the length but at least I have . . . what do I have? Well, well, I'll be nice to you.*

So far the contest had been between me and Leila – but we were more comic comrades than rivals. She was so sweet-natured, God bless her, that even if she won him, I thought she would feel so guilty she'd turn him down.

Josephine, however, was painfully beautiful and she had a very determined Scorpio streak – she always had to have her way, get what she wanted. She was serious competition.

3. A Man About the House

Over the following few days, it was as if we were all competing in some kind of amorous game-show, scoring points off each other to win Ricky–The Star Prize. One evening I came in to find he had left a Milky Way outside my door as a pressie, with a message scrawled on a piece of paper, *For my dearest Chocoholic*. Dearest! *Dearest!* I whirled around the room, reading it over and over, and then tucked the note under my pillow and the Milky Way in a drawer. I didn't actually like Milky Ways (too light and airy, an insipid attempt at a chocolate bar) but that wasn't the point – it was sacred now.

Then Josephine out-did me with a triple letter score when he walked into her room wearing nothing but a pair of silky white boxer shorts ("with lipstick marks!" as Josephine filled us in) and asked tremblingly if she would remove a spider from the shower because, most charmingly, he claimed to be terrified of spiders.

Josephine and I were levelling ahead with ten points and Leila was trailing way back but unexpectedly caught up when she and Ricky discovered they shared a major passion: football. One Saturday they spent the entire afternoon nestling on the sofa, glued to the screen, ploughing their way through Budweiser six-packs.

"I'm great fan of Man United," Josephine purred, much to Ricky's delight.

I gave Josephine a dirty look; she'd obviously done her homework.

We both forced ourselves to stifle yawns over the following half hour as the ball meandered back and forth. Then, finally, a goal was scored. Josephine and I burst into cheers, only to see Ricky scowling at us in disgust.

"It was in our goal!"

"Oh, was it?" I asked.

"Erm, I knew that!" Josephine spluttered, then dragged me out for a shopping trip.

"Urgh, how humiliating!" she moaned as she worked her way through the party-dress section of Top Shop.

Josephine then came up with a genius plan. The main problem with wooing Ricky was that he spent all day at work and most nights partying. Even if he was in, he was invariably on the phone as Mandy and Shelley and Emily and a string of competitors called him up.

Josephine, however, had discovered that one of Ricky's great passions in life was movies. She thus created a compulsory video evening every Wednesday night.

That Wednesday, I was determined to go into battle with as much ammunition as possible. I picked out my best new outfit: white jeans and shirt, because Josephine had declared I was a winter person and should go for light colours. I lay in the bath, luxuriating in Body Shop bubbles and feeling a Galaxy ripple down my throat.

Towelling myself off, I stood naked in front of the mirror, gazing at myself critically. "Thighs too fat, boobs too small, legs too hairy, eyebrows too bushy. Urgh, urgh!" I muttered, then screamed as the door swung open and Ricky walked in, unbuttoning his 501s.

"Oops!" he stopped short and stared at me. I grabbed the towel and held it up. Unfortunately, it was only a facial one.

"Sorry!" Ricky grinned delightedly. "Just came in for a slash." As I pressed myself in shame against the cool steamed tiles, he popped his head back round and added flirtily, "I think your breasts are very nice, Olivia."

I wiped the steam off the mirror in a daze. Oh my God oh my God oh my God.

When I finally came down for the video evening, I simply couldn't look him in the eye. Even more embarrassing, he had recounted the whole story to Josephine and Leila. Leila was blushing shyly and laughing but Josephine prodded me venomously in the knee and whispered, "Very crafty!"

We all snuggled up on the sofa to watch *The Terminator* – Ricky's choice – his revenge, I think, on me for choosing *Mary Poppins* the previous week, which he complained had not been sexually explicit enough.

Josephine and I were baulking at the violence but Ricky seemed to find it all very amusing. I couldn't stop drifting off into fantasies about him; we were sitting so

24

close I was paranoid he could see into my mind, see me lying in the bath, Ricky walking in, Ricky sitting on the edge and rinsing my back, Ricky and I entwined in the shower, kissing as the water trickled over our faces, my hands palming over his back, him licking my eyebrow . . .

I was just reaching the point where it was unbearable to be sitting next to him any longer when the credits rolled up and Ricky cried: "The night is still young! Let's go to the pub!"

So off we went.

I noticed Josephine wrinkling her nose with momentary disgust as Ricky pulled his battered old Beatle up outside The Goat, where cigarette smoke and fighting lads unfurled from doorways, the windows glowed with kaleidoscope lights from fruit-machines, and pop music pounded so loud the walls seemed to vibrate. Hardly the sort of chic little wine bar tinkling with light conversation and champagne glasses that Josephine was so habituated to.

As usual, the moment we entered, all heads turned to Josephine.

A group of builders with crew cuts were playing snooker. One missed his shot and as they looked up, all their jaws dropped simultaneously.

"Alright, darling?" one of them called over and Josephine held her head high.

I suddenly felt awfully plain in my white jeans and shirt.

Ricky was obviously a regular to the bar because absolutely everyone – well, every female there – seemed to know him. They surrounded him like wasps crawling over a hive, flinging their arms around him. I noticed he kissed them all hello right on the mouth as well as giving the customary hug.

Then one girl called Laura took his hand and dragged him over to a crowd of people, again mostly girls, flocking around a table in the corner. Instantly Josephine and Leila swung round to me.

"So what's he like?" Leila begged me.

"Full lips indicate a very sensual kisser," said Josephine, narrowing her eyes dreamily.

"Oh no – hey – no –" It took a great deal of protest to convince them nothing had happened back in the bathroom and I wasn't just covering up out of guilt.

"Hmm," said Josephine, and then she added with amazing generosity, "Still, he seems to like you most out of all of us . . ."

Then Ricky came up to the bar to buy us a round.

"What are you girlies whispering about?" he asked.

We all looked completely blank and giggled.

After that I could barely focus. Josephine had said he liked me best. If Josephine, my oracle, had said it, it had to be true!

Ricky proceeded to get drunker and drunker, more from girls plying him with drinks than deliberate choice.

"Ask me if I'm an orange?" he said, pulling a cigarette out of his packet with shaky hands.

"Are you an orange?" I said, gently turning his cigarette the right way up.

"No!" he yelled and roared with laughter, then nearly set alight to his fringe.

"Ricky, Ricky," Laura chided him, returning,

squeezing back past me and plonking herself in between us, "honestly, naughty boy, not too much to drink!"

Ricky laid his head on her shoulder and agreed, but two pints later he was challenged to a drinking contest by a rather hard-looking Australian girl called Roslyn who embarrassed him by beating him with ease.

"So you guys live with Ricky?" Laura asked me. I could tell she was just trying to be nice to me to impress Ricky.

"They do indeed," Ricky said, "and I think it's about time we had a celebration for my new moving in. How about a party!"

"*A party!*" everyone echoed and Josephine, envisaging drink-rings on her spotless cabinets and stubs on her Axminster carpets, looked distinctly dubious.

"Yeah, a party!" Ricky cried. "We can have one for Olivia's birthday. It's next week!"

Next week? It was January, eight months too early for my birthday.

"Erm, actually my birthday is in September," I tried to protest but I was engulfed in a tidal wave of, "Oh, it's her birthday, how lovely – a birthday party!"

"*Whooppee!*" Ricky yelled, standing up and knocking over his drink. "Must have a slash!"

As he pushed past me, he ruffled my head and mouthed, "Alright?" I nodded and watched him wistfully as he stumbled his way over to the loos, smiling, shaking hands, punching shoulders, calling hellos. He was so funny and friendly and popular, but obviously my competition extended much further than Josephine – we were talking the entire female race. Seeing him accidentally (or perhaps purposefully) go into the ladies', I shook my head and laughed.

By closing time, Ricky was so drunk Josephine and I had to walk him to his car.

"Let me drive!" he mumbled.

"Don't be ridiculous," Josephine said primly, feeling inside his jacket for his keys.

"Hmm, down a bit," said Ricky lecherously.

I stood shivering uncontrollably as Ricky then refused to let Josephine drive his car, *Bertha,* before introducing them to each other.

Then he ushered Leila into the front and climbed into the back next to me. Putting his arm around me, he cuddled me up against his chest and my heart turned over.

"Your teeth are chattering," he said hazily, putting a finger to my lips.

In the front mirror, Josephine gave us a slightly dirty look. She may have decided Ricky likes me more, I realised in increasing alarm, but she's not going to give in without a fight.

Ricky turned the journey back into something like a wild coach trip, making us all join in and sing 'Ten Green Bottles'. The song died away and I rested my head against his chest and he smoothed my hair back from my face. It was a very natural gesture, as though we had already been boyfriend and girlfriend for ages.

Then Ricky roared, *"One thousand green bottles!"* And after that I couldn't stop shaking with laugher all the way home, until even Ricky was murmuring, "It wasn't that funny, I know a funny joke – ask me if I'm an orange . . ." but I was simply high on nervous anticipation. It's going to happen, I thought, gazing up at his profile and the backdrop of the stars outside, it's really going to happen.

Back home, Josephine took firm charge again.

"Come on, let's get you up to bed," she ordered Ricky.

"Let me just hug Leila goodnight," he demanded.

"*Come on*, Ricky," said Josephine, dragging him upstairs to his bedroom.

In my room, I listened to Josephine giving Ricky tomato juice and very strict instructions that he was not to lie on his front in case he was sick. I sat on my bed, stiff and uncertain, listening to the bang of the bathroom door as she undressed and went to bed. Then the yellow patch of light on the landing disappeared, which meant she had switched off her lamp.

I sat there, thinking: shall I, shalln't I, shall I, shalln't I go to his room? *Will I seem like a brazen hussy or could it have happened anyway and will I spend the rest of my life regretting not taking this opportunity?*

Do it, be bold, nothing ventured, I rallied myself, but my legs still remained stuck to the bed.

I tossed a coin. Heads I go, tails I go to sleep.

It came down tails but the disappointed feeling was so huge there was no way I could consider it.

Just get ready for bed, then go. But then it looks really saucy. If I go now in normal clothes, it looks like I'm just checking to see if he's okay. But if I leave it much longer, it will be too late, he'll be asleep.

I was just boiling over in a frenzy of indecision when I heard heavy footsteps on the landing. The toilet door creaked, the peeing seemed to go on forever – it had to be him. Then my bedroom door swung open. My head sprung up. Ricky giggled, "Whoops, wrong bedroom!"

He spread open his arms and I went towards him and he placed a drunken kiss on my head and then collapsed onto my bed, pulling me down beneath him.

He was warm and heavy on top of me. I was shaking with lust, burning for his kiss on my lips.

Then I heard him start to snore.

It couldn't be! He was asleep! I tried to wake him but he was out cold. Finally, in exasperation, I wriggled out from under him and glared down at him furiously, but he looked so beautiful the moonbeams glittering over his hair, caressing his face, as though even the moon was in love with him that it was impossible to be angry with him.

I went to his room and slipped into his bed; it smelt all musky like him, I wanted to roll in his sheets like a cat in cat-nip. I fell into a deep happy slumber. Even if he hadn't got off with me, the point was, he had wanted to. Wrong room – what kind of flimsy excuse was that!? It was going to happen, it was bound to happen, sooner or later.

4. The Spice Girls Meet the Blues Brothers

Monday morning dawned with severe financial crisis. I got a letter from the bank with a bounced check informing me I was over the temporarily extended limit on my overdraft.

An uneasy fear was burning in the pit of my stomach. My grandfather had stomach ulcers and he claimed worry about money directly affected the gut. If I was going to have a mid-life crisis, why not a stomach ulcer too?

When I confided in Ricky, he responded with incredible kindness.

"Hey, tell you what!" he said. "I was thinking maybe I could pass some of your writing on to my dad . . ."

My heart rose; his eyes gleamed.

"But he's such a moody git, there's no way he'd look at it."

My heart fell.

"But," said Ricky excitedly, "he is looking for a new PA. And I said you'd be just the ticket and he's seriously interested!"

I opened my mouth to point out that I had no PA qualifications and besides, I didn't want to work-

Then visions flitted across my mind. Me handing Sir

C a letter with my manuscript tucked accidentally underneath. Or, his agent calling up and Sir C just happening to be in a meeting and me just happening to mention my latest book . . . the possibilities were endless . . .

"Oh thank you!" I cried, flinging my arms around him in my enthusiasm, then drawing back self-consciously. Ricky smiled and cuddled me again, saying I was "irresistibly huggly!"

"Oh, by the way," he added casually, "I said you used to be PA to the Chairman of ICI and your typing speed was eighty words per minute."

Eighty words! More like two words per three fingers per half hour.

"Chill out," said Ricky, seeing my face. "Life is all about bluffing."

That was the lovely thing about Ricky – he never worried about little earthquakes like I did all the time. He was so carefree, as though life was one big joke or a never-ending party.

Speaking of parties, Ricky had talked Josephine into having my premature 'birthday bash' and he'd come up with a great fancy-dress theme: the Spice Girls meet the Blues Brothers.

And even more worrying than money – what Spice Girl should I be?

I should have gone as Baby. Looking back, for months to come, I always fretted that the entire evening would have gone down a totally different course of action if only I had gone as Baby.

But, even though I did have fair hair, it seemed so

presumptuously arrogant to go as Baby since she is the one all the blokes fancy. So I decided to go as Ginger. Alright, so she might have left, but I'd liked the idea of dying my hair for ages; I had a vision of standing in the middle of the living-room, surrounded by doting men, tossing back a mane of tousled red locks like Andie Macdowell in the L'Oreal ad, Ricky watching me *because I'm worth it*.

So: I bought one of those henna dyes from The Body Shop and slapped it on with a great deal of difficulty. The paste kept slipping off the plastic gloves. By the end, the sink, bath, mats, flannels, toothbrushes and floor were all stained red that wouldn't shift no matter how hard I scrubbed.

I also managed to get a reasonable amount of dye in my hair. I was supposed to leave it on for forty-five minutes so I set my Minnie Mouse alarm clock and left it by the sink.

Then my mum called. It was weird – it was the third time that day she'd called. The first time was to tell me she'd just got a new dress super-cheap in the market, the second time was from work to slag off her bastard boss who always rang just when she was going for lunch. And now again, to tell me nothing much in particular . . .

Something was up, I could tell, but when I suggested this she held back, all defensive.

"I was just telephoning to see if you were okay, darling, and what you were going to wear tonight. I almost wish I could come too, I'd love to be Ginger and get all dressed up in a sexy suit –"

"Mum, please, no," I protested, horrified visions flitting through my mind.

"Oh, don't worry, I shall stay in and watch TV on my own," she said sulkily, and then I felt really mean and tried to think of something nice to say, but she said, "Oh God, he's" (her boss) "back again," and put the phone down.

I stared at the phone for a moment, trying to work out what was wrong. Maybe Jed had broken up with her – but she'd never seemed to like him much.

"Olivia!" Josephine yelled from upstairs. "Will you come and turn off your fucking alarm clock!"

I ran upstairs and switched it off. Oh goodness, how long had I left the henna on for? Maybe an hour.

I rinsed my hair like mad, but even after fifteen minutes the water was still like blood. I gazed up at the mirror – my face was smeared with red as though I was a vampire who'd just over-indulged. I dabbed it with a flannel but still my face looked blotchy, as though I was developing a queer skin complaint.

I combed out my hair – it turned my brush and nails red but it was too wet to see how red it would be.

I could hear footsteps and voices outside, the thump of Leila and Josephine moving furniture around and their groans as they chipped paint off corners.

"Where's Ricky?" Leila wheezed.

"Olivia!" Josephine hammered on my door. "I know you're in there. Don't try and get out of helping!"

I remained silent, locked in a tight ball, scissors in one hand – in my other, the henna packet, those deadly words glaring up at me: *Washes out after two months*.

They knocked several more times, then gave up, no

doubt assuming I was just being lazy and unhelpful. The house quietened. I heard the spray from the shower, then a curse from Josephine to discover all the hot water had gone because I had now washed my hair a total of five times.

I heard Leila getting ready (she was going as Sporty Spice – albeit a slightly plump one – so she hardly needed to worry about doing anything except pulling on her usual trainers and jogging bottoms), and Josephine's sing-song voice, "Do I look okay?"

Which of course, she did, because she was going as Baby and would not have hair the colour of tomato soup.

Half an hour later, I finally let Josephine slip in. She was looking absolutely fantastic as Baby, in a white dress with white boots, her pale, smooth hair swishing in two ponytails. For a moment I was reminded of primary school, when Josephine always had bunches that the boys chased her around the playground to pull and she was teacher's pet of every staff member.

I yanked her in and shut the bedroom door and cried, "Josephine, it's a major crisis!" and threw off my towel and showed her.

"Yeah? What?"

"What?"

"But you're supposed to go as Ginger, stupid!"

"Oh." Maybe it was just my paranoia. Josephine hugged me and told me to hurry up and get dressed.

Oh, I thought, maybe I look okay after all.

Downstairs, the living-room had been transformed. The furniture was covered with plastic; balloons and streamers hung from curtains and picture frames.

In the kitchen, Ricky was making a cocktail. Somehow, that disappointed me. I didn't want him to get drunk. Ricky sober was enough – when he was pissed he was too much, like a caricature of himself. Besides falling asleep at very inconvenient moments.

"What the hell did you do to your hair?" he cried.

I paled.

"Oh no, you look great," he said quickly, looking at my short dress. "But Ginger's left the Spice Girls anyway – why didn't you go as Baby?"

The party had kicked off by ten. By twelve, empty plastic cups and bodies (either unconscious or entwined) littered the hallway; the living-room was crammed with sweaty jiving bodies, streamers were thrown, corks and balloons popped. Ricky went around popping balloons in necking couples' ears.

The crazy thing was, everyone thought it was my birthday. It was absurd – complete strangers kept giving me chocolates and Body Shop baskets and writing paper and cards. When I complained to Ricky, he said, "Hey, cool, you can have two birthdays, like the Queen!"

Billy, an old friend who I used to temp with, turned up with a petite blonde, yet another Baby, and a mug with a picture of Garfield with the slogan *I'm a mug for chocolate.*

"Olivia!" he cried. "Happy Birthday!" He leaned over to kiss me full on the lips. Hmm, Billy was nice but much too much of a flirt.

"Who's your new girlfriend?" I asked, watching the blonde now talking to Ricky.

"Fuck knows what her name is. I woke up in bed with her last Saturday and we've been going out ever since and it would be really embarrassing to ask now."

Franny turned up.

Franny is Josephine's cousin. She is very Sloaney. The sort of person you can't miss, due to her size, shrieky voice, hyena laugh and obsessive desire to be the centre of attention. But all the same, I couldn't help liking her, she was so bustly and gossipy.

"Olivia, Happy Birthday! Goodness, you're looking not so much Ginger as *Paprika!*" she boomed, handing me a silver-wrapped gift. "Josey, darling!" They kissed the air.

Franny was just taking off her coat when she spotted Ricky.

"Now that," she said, her eyes lighting up, "is what I call *Crumpet.*"

She then went off to join the rest of the females gathered around him. Oh bugger, my heart twisted inside, is it ever going to happen? Every time I get close to getting him, he gets whisked away like a carrot on a stick. If only I had gone as Baby.

An old ex called Elvis came. He had the wilting air of a dwarfish sunflower, and looked very awkward, so I tried to be nice and talk to him. Then he started following me everywhere.

"Your hair looks lovely, it goes so well with your

pink dress," he simpered with complete sincerity and I wanted to punch him.

I was saved by the neighbours who came to complain. Ricky was pushed forward and he was very charming and cooey.

"It's not a proper party unless the neighbours complain at least six times!" he then declared, and went bounding into the living-room.

A group of tweedy, thin druggie types, their bony ribs sticking out of tight T-shirts, had invaded and put on some music with a monotonous dance beat where a single female voice kept chanting over and over again, "Let's get high . . ." Everyone had stopped dancing except the ravers.

Ricky grabbed the CD and threw it out of the window like a frisbee, and put on The Beatles and roused everyone up to start dancing.

Oh please ask me to dance, I begged, standing in the doorway, but Franny got there first. Her bosom shook violently as they jived to *Twist and Shout*, her long hair flying everywhere, practically garrotting people. I had to admire her guts. Here I was, standing all foolish at my own party, fretting that everyone was pointing at my red hair. I must be sociable and talk to people and look confident and self-sufficient, I decided, and, seeing one of the ravers catching my eye, went over and gave him a welcoming smile.

"Hi, I'm Jason." He was the thinnest, probably the ringleader. He had very pale blue eyes and was wearing a T-shirt with a picture of the Mona Lisa smoking a joint.

Hmm, I thought, perhaps here is an opportunity to make Ricky jealous.

"Hey, we gatecrashed this party, man, we heard it was going to be real wild but it's just a low-key suburban rumble," Jason murmured. "How about kicking off together?"

"Erm, well, I live here," I said.

"Oh," Jason blinked in confusion. "Hey, cool . . . man . . . yeah, real, suburban . . . erm . . ."

"I'm Olivia," I said, for lack of anything else to say.

"Olive? Hey, cool, man, back to nature, back to the plants . . ."

"Er, no, Olivia," I corrected him gently.

"Yeah, cool . . ."

A pause. Jason squinted down into his drink as though it held the answer to the meaning of life.

"So what kind of music are you into?" I asked, to fill up the silence.

"Er, hey, man, cool, Glastonbury is great, yeah, you should, yeah, get tickets before they sell out . . ."

At which point I gave up and sipped my drink and tapped my foot as though I was really concentrating on the music.

Then Ricky saved me.

"*Olivia*, why aren't you dancing?" He came galloping over, grabbing my hands and pulling me into the throng. Then he said in a low voice, "You have to protect me from the Shrieky Sloane!"

I laughed and danced and suddenly felt glorious – the stomach ulcer healed in seconds. He took me in his arms and spun me round and sang, "Yeah, shake it shake it on, baby" in a wonderfully out of tune way.

Then Josephine came stalking up.

"Ricky, Ricky, it's a disaster!" she cried.

Oh yeah, I thought?

Ricky, never one to refuse a damsel in distress, followed her out to the hallway. Then he shot straight backwards. It appeared that some Hell's Angels had turned up and were trying to gatecrash. Poor old Leila, who was playing bouncer, was trying to negotiate with them.

"It's part of our insurance policy that we can't make claims for a party with uninvited guests," she was saying, sweat beading on her round forehead. A big DM boot was wedged firmly in between the door and the step.

"Oh Ricky, what shall I do, call the police?' Josephine wrung her hands.

"Hey, I know," said Ricky, suddenly bouncing up. "Never fear, Ricky is here!"

He bounded upstairs and we followed him in bewilderment into the bathroom. Ripping open a packet of ribbed condoms, he started to fill them up with water.

"Here!" he ordered, handing one to me.

"Ricky, what are you doing?" Josephine wailed.

Ricky ignored her and carried on filling them up, then hurried into her bedroom. He was dripping water everywhere but Josephine seemed drunk enough to have gone beyond panicking about the wreck the house was being transformed into.

Ricky opened the window, sat with one leg in / one leg out and chucked the condoms down on the Hell's Angels, totally drenching them. He's mad, I thought, they'll burn our house down. But to my relief and amazement they only bellowed a few swear words, then shook their fists and zoomed off on their motor-bikes. I hoped they weren't going to get reinforcements.

We cheered and Ricky took a bow. Across the road one of our neighbours tweaked the curtains and glared.

"Hey!" Ricky suddenly said, picking up a bottle and swinging it between his forefinger and thumb. "Let's play Spin the Bottle!"

There was a chorus of 'no's' but Ricky rallied us all round, roaring at us for being such bores. Josephine crossed her arms and shook her head rather drunkenly.

"Spin the Bottle is for kids."

"And who wants to grow up?' Ricky cried, grabbing her hand and pulling her down beside him. Which was perfect, as far as I was concerned, because I then plonked myself down oh-so-casually opposite him.

Franny, booming, "Golly, Spin the Bottle was when I had my first kiss!" sat down beside me, and Billy with his one-track radar for anything sexy popped his head round the door.

"Come in, the more the merrier!" Ricky shouted, and Billy entered, followed by Elvis, who then strategically placed himself next to Ricky, and opposite me, horror of horrors.

Josephine turned out the lights and lit up a few little pink candles and placed them around to create an eerie effect and it was all rather exciting. I'd never played Spin the Bottle and it's one of those things one feels one ought to have played, like Strip Poker or

Knock Ginger, in order to have had a proper child-hood.

We were all a bit sheepish and giggly at first. Ricky took charge and spun the bottle so that it came to rest between James (shy, gay bloke) and Melissa (shy, sweet girl). There was a chorus of wolf whistles and baying led by Billy. Then James leaned across and whispered something in Melissa's ear and she nodded in relief. Then she gave him a quick peck on the cheek and that was that.

"Hey, that's cheating!" Ricky shook his head in mock disgust and spun the bottle again.

It came to rest opposite Josephine and Franny.

"Oh well, let's try again," said Josephine shrugging.

"Wait!" Ricky protested. The pink candles flicked two wicked flames in his eyes. "We never made any rules about heterosexuality."

"Ricky, that's disgusting!" Josephine put a hand over her mouth and burst into shocked laughter. Ricky and Billy exchanged rather excited glances, but their hopes of lesbian voyeurism were dashed when Franny, splut-tering with disgust, yanked hold of the bottle and spun it round firmly again.

It came to rest opposite me – and Ricky – no, Ricky and Elvis, or Elvis and Ricky? Then Ricky, my angel, tweaked the bottle so that it faced him and everyone laughed.

"You'll have to do it again," Josephine started to protest but thankfully Billy overrode her.

"As an impartial judge, I believe it came to rest between the two and therefore," he shouted with glee, "Olivia must get off with both of them and she must do it properly, none of this kiss on the cheek cop-out!"

There was a chorus of 'here here's' and I shrugged and said, okay, a game was a game.

"You go first," said Ricky to Elvis. "She'll want to save the best for last."

It was like doing my penance before going to heaven, I thought – still we all have to make sacrifices.

I closed my eyes and decided to pretend he was Ricky, which was extremely hard because he was the worst kisser in the world. A total washing machine. His lips were pale and cold and somehow emitted enough dribble to shower my chin so when I pulled away I desperately wanted to wipe it off for Ricky's sake but I didn't want to embarrass poor old Elvis, who was sitting there grinning inanely at me and making me feel rather ill. So I pretended to run my hand through my hair and wiped my chin on my sleeve.

Ricky sat up on his haunches. I licked my lips, trying to bite back a smile of elation. As he leaned forwards and I leaned forwards, everyone fell silent, as if sensing the tension between us and I was sure they could hear my heart boom-booming against my chest. I could feel Josephine's narrowed stare, Ricky's hand was in my hair, then tilting my chin. Our lips brushed-

"*Olivia!*" Leila cried.

We both jumped so violently that Billy fell over backwards and knocked over a candle, thus setting fire to Josephine's beautiful purple and orange Indian rug.

Hysterics ensued: Ricky threw his cocktail over the rug, Josephine slapped him and said he'd have to pay for it, the brief flames had already gone out but

43

everyone was frantically trying to stamp them out in the communal panic.

And in the midst of all this, Leila was pulling my arm and making frantic signals at me. At first I was furious with her, then I thought she was saying the gate-crashers had returned.

Then I deduced that Mum was on the phone and it was an emergency.

I dashed down the stairs, visions of her lying attacked and dying flitting through my mind. I picked up the phone and my heart went cold because I could hear that she was crying, but she was sobbing too much and the music was too loud so I just said:

"I'll be right over."

I ran out of the house, jumped into my little red mini and, as I put the keys in the ignition, a wild, crazy impulse came to run back upstairs and grab Ricky and demand my kiss. Then I shook myself and quickly put the car into first gear.

5. Mum

My mum had become a very different person since divorcing Dad.

I was eighteen when he had walked out on her. Back then she was very much like the archetypal vicar's wife: tweed skirts and neat grey-blonde hair and organising lots of car-boot sales and church fetes, though she was very scatty and always muddling dates and I remember Dad always snapping at her for burning cakes or losing Brownie badges. He was such a fastidious man, he used to get in a temper if his service was as much as a minute late. As he expounded from the pulpit, you could almost feel a collective shudder passing through the god-fearing congregation.

Dad then shocked us all by suddenly moving out on 23 September 1990 and going to live with Ms Trim, the Girl Guide leader, slim, blonde, twenty-four years old and very efficient. Apparently they had been having an affair for the previous four years.

Mum grieved for years.

Scott, who had graduated from Cambridge and was working nine to nine at some investment bank in the city, had little time to visit her so every evening I tried to give her a call from uni or pop down to visit her and cheer her up.

For the first few years, she seemed to be worrying like an OAP, as though she was suffering from early senility, her hair turning almost entirely grey, her hems unstitching, lines carving into her unmade-up face. She would wear shoes on the wrong feet and bumble around the house refusing to put the central heating on because Dad wouldn't have liked the cost, pulling cardigans around herself and mumbling about what a terrible wife she had been. Then, when Dad, despite Scott's reasoning and my histironics, kicked her out of our family house and 'supported' her in a very grotty little flat in Carshalton, it was like the final stake in her heart.

But, about a year ago, I had started to notice a change coming over my mother.

I think I first noticed the warning signs when I popped over one Sunday and found her painting her toe-nails blue and humming away to Capital Gold (in the past it had always been Classic FM, because that was what Dad liked to listen to).

Slowly, subtly, like the change of the seasons, the metamorphosis occurred: a new perm, a blonde rinse, highlights, high heels, a new black Gucci handbag, a new job working as a secretary at a doctor's surgery.

"I'm not going to accept a single penny of your father's money anymore," she announced and from then on we were never allowed to mention his name again. It was like a swearword.

Soon she even started popping over to my house and pinching my clothes and I had to go and reclaim them and find them smelling of beer and smoke and once I even found a suspicious white stain on one of my skirts.

"Just talcum powder," said Mum airily.

But when I came in one morning to find a strange man with sideburns sitting at the breakfast table, I knew things really had started to change.

The strange man, David, was followed by several more strange men, and the last one had been a cocky American called Jed who kept giving me money every time I went over, as though he wanted to buy my approval, which was totally unnecessary since I thought he was rather charming, and as long as he made Mum happy, that was all that mattered.

I squealed into the carpark, ran up several flights of graffitied steps and, panting madly, rang the bell. No reply. I rang again.

Finally Mum appeared, undoing all the locks which were installed to keep muggers and rapists and old boyfriends out.

She collapsed into my arms and sobbed like a child and I stroked her hair and felt very awkward. Her mascara was streaming all over her face in black rivulets and I could smell that she had been drinking.

I took her inside and finally, after a lot of stuttering, she confessed that she was pregnant.

Pregnant!

"Are you sure?"

She was quite sure, she had done a test. She showed me.

"Oh my God!"

Then she started to rant on about how she was going

to give up her job and she bet Dad wouldn't give her penny and . . .

"What, what!" I said, holding my head as though it might fall off with shock if I took my hands away. "Who's the father? Surely he can support you?"

"That's just the point!" she wrung her hands, "I don't know, it might be Jed, it might be Mike."

"Mike?"

"The boy from the Ritz. Bell-boy, with the little earring in his ear -"

"Yes, yes," I said irritably, "but, but -"

Mum stared aimlessly into space; she had stopped crying now and seemed more relieved. As she talked on, I couldn't help sensing a lurking triumph, as though she had somehow got her own back on Dad – she kept telling me not to tell him, she wanted to break the news to him herself.

"Of course, it might be John," she said vaguely.

"John!" I exploded. "Mum, how many possibilities are there!"

I'd forgotten how sensitive she was; she started to weep again and so I gently led her to bed and then went to the kitchen to make a cup of hot sweet tea. As the kettle boiled, I stared blearily out at the sky, black and flat as tar. Somehow the party seemed years ago. It was now five in the morning and lack of sleep made my mind floaty and fuzzy; thoughts were weird and abstract, like broken dreams.

I took the cup to her room and plumped up her pillows and she held my hand and said wouldn't be lovely for me to have another little brother or sister.

I tried to smile and say I was very happy.

*   *   *

It was awful, it was clearly one of the most crucial moments in my mother's life and all I could think about was getting back to the party to get off with a bloke I'd only known for a month. Perhaps it was just a defense mechanism to avoid accepting the dreadful truth.

I felt so mean. I waited at least an hour after she had fallen asleep, tidying up her flat and then leaving my last ten-pound note beside the bed for her with a note saying I would be back the following afternoon.

On the way back, my car broke down, then I realised I had run out of petrol but I had no money left to buy any. Since the car was slipping all over the place due to the frost and my bad driving, maybe it was a godsend to prevent me from killing myself. I wasn't a member of the AA or anything equally sensible so I just decided to walk it.

It was now around seven in the morning and bloody freezing. The weather couldn't make up its mind whether it was going to get it together to snow or not – the odd aimless flake trickled from the reluctantly lightening sky.

My breath created will-o-the-wisps, I kept blowing on my hands but my fingers were like strawberry ice-pops.

Only the thought of Ricky prevented my worry about Mum from meglamating into sheer panic. If she had a baby, she would never be able to survive. Blair had it in for single mothers . . . I'd have to support her. Get some grotty job selling oven gloves for 50p an hour at the local ASDA or something equally dire. There would be no time for writing anymore: *Wickham's Memoirs* would die a death, remain an unfinished masterpiece . . . it was a complete nightmare.

But beneath all of this was a glow of hope at the thought of Ricky at home waiting for me. I pictured him taking me in his warm arms and kissing away my tears and saying he would support us both.

I was so lost in thought, suddenly I was home much sooner than I'd expected.

Two police cars were outside the house; the police were questioning Jason.

"Did you acquire your drugs from a dealer at the party or previous to arriving here?"

Jason looked very confused.

"Erm, yeah, hey man . . . Glastonbury . . . yeah, cool place, man, groovy bands, yeah, get the ticket now, though, they sell out fast . . ."

This sounded worrying. I hid behind the privet hedge next door and remembered a time I'd gone clubbing in Kingston and the police had started arresting youths randomly, just to fill up cells.

So I crept round the back of the house and crunched over the frosty grass. In the kitchen there was a group of people I didn't recognise having a jolly, rowdy breakfast. A black guy with dreads and shades offered me some bacon and eggs, which I declined politely. Roberta, meanwhile, was sniffing eagerly, rolling her brown eyes and whimpering for titbits, as though I had starved her for the last month.

I went into the wasteland of the hallway, kicking

aside beer cans. The living-room was empty. I climbed over a body on the stairs (Elvis, obviously no longer teetotal) up, up, up, to Ricky's room but his door was wide open and his bed was empty and unmade.

A horrible fear chilled my heart that he had gone home with another girl.

Josephine's door was shut – maybe the Spin the Bottle had degenerated into an orgy and I would walk in to find a mass of couples, I thought somewhat hazily, and so I knocked and walked in. She was in bed with Billy – Billy! – giving him a blow job. She looked up at me through a waterfall of blonde hair.

"Hey, Olivia, do come and join us!" Billy cried cheekily. Josephine slapped him; I retreated quickly.

I tried Leila's door. No reply. She wouldn't be with a guy, so she had to be asleep. I knew it was selfish to wake her but I just had to find out where Ricky was. It was an emergency. So I knocked and went in.

She was in bed with someone. I was shocked: Leila hadn't been with a bloke for years. Then a muffled voice from under the covers murmured, "I can't get them off with my teeth!" I started to back away, then the sheets wriggled and a blonde head popped out at the other end of the bed. It was Ricky, hair falling in his bloodshot eyes, grinning up at me. Leila let out a nervous giggle.

I tried to speak but at first no words would come.

"Erm, I'm really sorry, excuse me," I stuttered at last and shut the door.

Outside in the hallway I skidded on a balloon and nearly went flying down the stairs.

There was a white mark on my wrist but I was so blank I didn't acknowledge the pain. I ran into my bedroom and shut and locked the door.

I went numbly to the mirror, gazing at my reflection. I looked utterly shocked and deathly pale, my veins standing out like frozen rivers. It was as if I was staring at someone else. Who was I... was I me... was I in some weird parallel universe where Bill Clinton was celibate and Mother Teresa owned a brothel and Josephine slept with Billy and what the *hell* was *Ricky* doing in *bed* with *Leila* he didn't even *fancy* her-it didn't make sense, it should have been me, what the hell was going on?

With terrible timing, the telephone started to ring. I picked it up, my shellshocked brain suddenly convinced it was Ricky.

It was my father.

"What the hell is your mother doing getting herself pregnant!" he shouted, as though I was personally responsible. "And how does she mean to support herself?"

"I'm going to support her," I said stoutly, and he laughed and said he'd never known me to hold down a job for more than five minutes.

He then proceeded to rant on about the sins of sex outside marriage and other utterly hypocritical things that made me so furious I couldn't even begin to fathom how to answer him back.

I couldn't bear to listen to another word. I put down the telephone, and then, so that he couldn't call back, threw it off the hook.

I lay down on my bed, buried myself under the

covers and started to cry. My nose started to run but I couldn't be bothered to get up even though it was cold under the covers. I cried for too long and started to give myself a firm lecture – Olivia, you stupid cow, obviously he never fancied you, you were utterly deluded, Josephine is right, you've been living in a fantasy world – but still I cried.

I just felt so alone. Where the hell was Roberta? Normally when I cried she licked my tears away. But no, even my dog had deserted me in favour of food, in my greatest hour of need.

I tried to do that thing in *The Sound of Music* where Julie Andrews says don't be worried about storms, just think about all the things that make you happy. I thought of sunsets, kittens, Roberta, Green & Blacks, Top Shop, good books – Jilly Cooper, good films – *Four Weddings*, Christmas, Ricky – no, not Ricky – Leila, friends, my friends were nice, Leila was nice, maybe that's why he liked her, for her personality – and still I cried.

I didn't understand why Ricky hadn't come rushing out of the bedroom to say, "Oh Olivia, I was just pissed, it was all a mistake!"

I'm going to move out, I thought, I shall move into some crummy bed-sit in some horrible housing estate stinking of cats' piss and Ricky will try and call but he won't be able to get through because the phone will be vandalised and then he'll feel awful – and – and . . .

Five minutes. I set my Minnie Mouse alarm clock. If he doesn't come in five minutes, then I really will go.

Five minutes later: still no Ricky.

I yanked open my drawer and tore up the note he'd first given me. I found the first Milky Way he'd given me, which I'd preserved, then I gobbled it all up with a vengeance and only felt much worse.

PART TWO: WEDDING BELLS
6. Angst

"Olivia Bliss, *this your life!*"

I sat on the black wooden settee, gazing up in terror at Michael Aspel. Only somehow he didn't look quite like Aspel. He was dressed entirely in black, a cape rippling down his back. He had dyed his hair black and there was an eerie Mephistophelean glint in his eye.

"Let's begin with your best friend, Leila Adamson," Aspel purred.

I sighed with relief as Leila walked on; Aspel was seriously giving me the creeps. She was looking lovely, wearing Josephine's lilac suit with a green cardigan which I had seen in Ricky's wardrobe. She kept nervously looping the buttons in and out of the holes.

Then, to my shock, in front of zillions of viewers, she broke down crying.

"Leila, Leila, what is it?" I begged her. "Why are you so upset?"

"I just don't want to hurt you, Olivia," she said between choked sobs. "I love Ricky so much but your friendship means everything, and if it's hurting for us to be together, then I'd rather break up with h-him than have you move out —"

"Oh, Leila, don't be absurd," I put my arm around her and waved Aspel away. He was grinning evilly, the parasite. "Of course I don't like Ricky, I'm really happy for you."

"Or is she?" said Aspel.

"What?" I snapped.

"Or is she?" Aspel said, drawing out each syllable like Jeremy Beadle, rubbing his hands together wickedly. "Let's take a look at what Olivia has really been feeling over the past few weeks."

I drew in a gasp as a beautiful Goth girl, grinning like a game-show hostess to reveal vampire teeth, yanked a huge black veil to reveal rows and rows and rows of television screens. And on each and every screen, was me.

Me sobbing miserably after discovering Ricky and Leila together.

Me attempting to write but merely doodling Ricky's name all over my pad.

Me glumly attempting to fill in a *How Sexy Are You?* quiz in *Cosmo*, then throwing down my pen in despair because basically I had no sex life.

Me going to Waitrose and filling up my shopping basket with mountains of Haagen Dazs ice cream.

I felt Leila drawing away from me in shock.

"Let's face it, Olivia," Aspel concluded. "You haven't exactly handled your break-up well, have you? Let's face it, your love life has been a disaster from start to finish and Ricky is just the cherry on top."

"No, it hasn't." I leaned back as he approached me

sneeringly. His face was pitted and bumpy as though there were snakes writhing beneath his skin; any minute I expected him to erupt like something out of *Alien*. "No it hasn't," I whimpered.

I turned to Leila in despair but she shook my arm away and stalked off in disgust.

The last thing I heard before I woke up was Aspel's cackles of eerie laughter ringing in my ears . . . turning into my ringing alarm clock . . . somewhere I was supposed to be . . .

Oh, just another interview, I thought, burying my head under my pillow, the nightmare still leaving images like a horror movie, an uneasy, dirty, clinging film of disease. Why, I fretted, why these recurring dreams about Aspel? Some karmic connection in a past life?

Interview!

"My God!" I sat up. *Interview*. With Ricky's father. Sir Henry Caldwell. Big shot. PA Interview! *Argh!*

On the bus I sat watching the second needle whizz around my watch. I flicked desperately though the book Ricky had given me, which I had been meaning to get round to reading for the last ten days: *Fink Frog* by Sir Henry Caldwell;

For a moment I wondered if it had been written in Japanese:

Khruch khruch krutch I saw I saw the bird flew white roll kruch krutch home sweet home flew sweet night gale

On

The roof

: . . . ?

      Ha, so they swear in Finland . . .

What the hell was this? I nearly had a nervous break-down. Was it another one of Ricky's stupid jokes? Why arrange the interview in the first place if he was only going to mess it up for me? Maybe the Aspel dream was some terrible forewarning omen.

Then I flicked through and realised it was supposed to be like this. All eight hundred pages of it. I checked the dust jacket and discovered it was supposed to be about love in the Second World War. There was a twenty-page introduction by some git Professor who raved on about breaking the boundaries of prose and idiom, uniting poetry and prose, plus two lengthy paragraphs on the symbolic genius of page 57, which was blank except for the word 'the' three-quarters of the way down.

How on earth was I going to make it through the interview? Oh God, I prayed desperately, I need a miracle.

Sir Henry Caldwell lived and worked in a huge white house in Primrose Hill. We sat in his downstairs office, the clock ticking, the sound of a crying child in the room above piercing the silence.

I swallowed and tried to study the Job Description but I couldn't take in a word. Opposite me Sir Henry Caldwell was ploughing through my CV, reading every bloody line with painstaking concentration, frowns grided across his forehead, drawing out the torture.

"Don't worry, he'll just flip through it," Josephine had assured me gaily as we typed up that I liked to spend my spare time absailing and working for Cancer Research.

He hadn't seemed angry that I was late. Rather, he had kept me waiting outside in the large white hall for nearly half an hour until curls drooped over my face with nervous sweat and every other minute I had to pin my feet to the floor to stop myself from running out. Then he had come striding out of his office, extending a large hand, giving me a firm handshake.

I still couldn't get over how different he looked from his son. Ricky was tall and blonde and lean; his father was stocky and dark. I estimated he was in his early fifties, but he looked at least ten years younger, with a strong, broad physique, marred by a hint of a swelling belly and heavy character lines carved around a surprisingly sensitive face – I could see where Ricky got his lovely cheekbones from. Probably Sir C had been very handsome in his youth, a bit of a Jeremy Irons.

"I see here you enjoy rock-climbing."

"Sorry?" I jumped.

"I see you like rock-climbing," he said, with interest. "It's a sport I enjoy occasionally myself."

"Oh well, I'm just an amateur," I said.

"Where d'you like to go?" he asked.

"Uh, Wales, stuff."

"Whereabouts in Wales?" There was pleasant interest on his face but he was firing the questions like bullets. He had the most disturbing eyes, the same almond shape as Ricky's but harder, the colour of blackberries, probing, demanding, stripping.

"Erm, Snowdon," I said quickly. "I once scaled the whole mountain."

For a moment he stared at me, his eyes like a loaded

gun. I felt my heart crashing against my chest. How tall was Snowdon? The closest I'd been to Wales was eating lamb. Oh God.

"Interesting, most interesting," he murmured softly. Those midnight eyes ran very slowly over me, from my head to my toes. It wasn't a sexual stripping, more a scientific, analytical scrutiny, but I found myself squirming and pulling down the hem of Josephine's Chanel suit.

"Well?" he asked. "Is that okay?"

"What? Oh?" I flapped the Job Description. "Great. Super."

He snapped my CV shut and laid it on the desk. I waited for the next stage of torture to begin.

"So, d'you have any further questions?"

Questions? Of course, one must ask questions to appear intelligent and interested. I was so used to screwing interviews up, I hadn't prepared anything. For a moment I racked my brains wildly. The only thing I could think of was whether there was a toilet as I was desperate for the loo–

Like a godsend, the door flipped open and the woman who'd answered the door stuck her head round. It was interesting to see how he bristled instantly, like a hedgehog putting up spines.

"Darling, I'm doing an interview."

"I know, darling, but when you've finished, Alicia and I are waiting for a walk in the park."

"Darling, I'm working this afternoon."

"Yes, darling, but your daughter would like to see you." She gave him a very wide smile which clearly said, "Do it or I'll divorce you, *darling*".

Sir Henry looked at me with furious embarrassment. I quickly looked away as though I hadn't caught a word.

"We'll discuss it later," he said, with a firmness that frightened me, but had no effect on his wife who merely *tssched* and slammed the door with a petulant bang.

"Frightfully sorry," he was all briskness again. "Yes. So, when would you be ready to start?"

For a moment I froze in amazement. Did he mean start – as in start? Work? Oh wow! Oh wow! Just wait till I tell Ricky! Oh! I wanted to swing round lampposts, reach across the table and kiss him thank you thank you thank you.

"Right away," I shrugged joyously.

Seeing my delight, he smiled for the first time that day.

"Well, I shall see you tomorrow at nine o'clock," he said.

I planned to be cool and casual when I got home but the moment I saw Ricky my news spilled out of me. Ricky whooped and ballroom-danced me up and down the living-room.

Josephine entered, holding hands with Billy, her new beau since the party.

"Oh well done," she said, looking mildly surprised. I think she had secretly doubted my chances and now I felt wonderfully smug and talented.

And even more so when Ricky kept shaking his head and saying, "You must have been so good – Dad is just such a perfectionist, you must have made such an impression."

"I guess so," I said, the interview growing more rosy in my mind by the minute.

"Come out with us tonight and celebrate!" Josephine cried.

"Oh no, I'll be okay," I said, ignoring her pointed look. After the party Josephine had consoled me about Ricky with surprising tenderness. But she was also determined to stop me sitting at home and pining.

But I had no desire to play gooseberry, sitting in a cinema wedged between Leila and Ricky on one side and Josephine and Billy on the other.

I watched, or rather channel-hopped for a few hours, then retreated under my thick duvets. Since the party the best part of my day was always sleep – shutting out reality until morning bit me awake with that gnawing feeling that I had lost him, that he was lying just a few bedrooms away in someone else's arms.

I found myself crying myself to sleep. What did the best PA job in the world matter when I couldn't have Ricky?

7. A New Job

The first morning for my new job, I was late as ever. I woke up feeling bleary with exhaustion. Dear me, I'd forgotten how disgustingly early one had to get up to go to work. I'd also forgotten how cold it was waiting for a bus in the early morning sunlight with schoolkids chewing gum and throwing ice-pops at passing cars. And how grimy the Northern line was, how suffocating it was inside the tube, how often the train would grind to a halt with all the lights going out and a dry BR voice making up some excuse about a leaf on the line.

By the time I reached Primrose Hill, my aching legs felt quite ready to go home and go to bed. Oh well, I consoled myself, hopefully I'll be able to sneak in a bit of writing today. Writing would heal my Ricky wounds. I'd seen the Toshiba laptop I'd be working on, the inspiration was flowing and I could barely wait to get going.

Sir Henry Caldwell, however, had other ideas. I arrived to find him on the telephone, barking at some journalist over his column being excluded from this week's *Sunday Times* to make way for the witticisms of A A Gill. Feeling self-conscious, I got up and went to the kitchen to make him a cup of tea, just to prove

I could use my own initiative. The trick with a new job was always to perform well – or at least look as though you were performing well – for the first few weeks. First impressions were crucial. Once a good impression had been formed, you could get away with surreptitious murder for months before the boss started to notice you weren't quite the office angel he'd envisaged.

"You're late," he snapped, and then frowned at my DM boots, "and if you come dressed like that tomorrow, I'm sending you home." He took a mouthful of tea and nearly spat it out. "What the hell is this?"

"PG Tips," I stammered.

"I drink Earl Grey tea. I like the tea bag strained for three minutes, no milk, one sugar." He paused and I paused, nodding and forcing a smile. "Well?" he said. "Don't you think you'd better make a note of that?" Disgusted to find me unequipped, he passed me a pen and sighed as I scrawled it out sulkily.

"Right," he said briskly. "Now the things I need typed today are . . ." He then proceeded to give me about ten thousand letters to reply to, besides typing up part of a manuscript and a column. As I left the office with my arms piled with papers, I was sure I saw a hint of a smile on his face. Was he trying to crush me and prove he was master, or was he just taking the piss? In revenge I strained his tea bag for ten minutes until it looked like black coffee but he didn't say a word, much too engrossed in his papers to even notice.

Huh.

What he needs, I decided, is a sense of humour. If

he carries on like this he'll end up having a heart attack. So I played an old trick that had endeared me to bosses before, which was to make some really comic typo. Finally I found the perfect opening: *Dear Mrs Winterton, I would be delighted to meet with you and your guests on . . .*

Dear Mrs Winterton, I typed with a wicked smile, I would be delighted to come and see your breasts on . . .

That would crack him up, I giggled, picturing him roaring with laughter. Then the tension would be dissolved and we might have a good laugh and a chat and he'd be utterly charmed and let me go home early.

I went into his office and handed the letters over, biting back a giggle. He read over the letters with an impassive face, sniffed, drew out his fountain-pen and covered them with blue ink slashes.

"Again," was all he said.

I stood up and walked out, feeling like a naughty schoolgirl who'd just been given lines. God, I thought, does this guy have any sense of humour?

By the end of the day I'd managed to work through about one centimetre of my six-inch-high In-Tray. I had calluses on the forefingers of each hand and a throbbing headache. And not one word of my book was written. I went home feeling tremendously cheated.

At home, I spent nearly all evening moaning to Ricky and Leila, who were curled up on the sofa feeding each other Haagen Dazs ice cream.

"I'm really sorry," Ricky said, "I should have warned

you. He was just the same with my A levels. It didn't matter if I got an A plus, it was still never high enough. No article I've ever written has ever impressed him."

The next Monday, I seriously considered not turning up but Josephine shook me awake and told me not to be so pathetic. So I allowed myself to be shepherded along in the flow of other weary commuters and managed to turn up only five minutes late.

I rapped my knuckles on his door but there was no reply. Then, to my joy oh joy, I remembered Sir C was only around to dispense work on Thursdays and Fridays because he was writing full-time the rest of the week.

Monday and Tuesday were great: I sat with my feet up, chattering away on his phone bill to my mum and my friends and taking a three-hour lunch break to go shopping in Top Shop. I splurged my entire week's salary on a new suit with a short skirt and trim jacket. There, that would impress him, I thought, handing my credit card to the assistant. That would shut him up.

Wednesday came and I sat in my office flipping through my phone book because there was nobody else to ring. Suddenly the office seemed very big and lonely. Maybe I should work on my book. But my inspiration seemed to have deserted me – it seemed like Sod's Law that, whenever he was around, I was frustrated with brilliant ideas and now he was gone I had nothing to write. Five o'clock came. As I switched off the light, I passed by his study and suddenly realised with a jolt of shock that I actually missed him. Missed his arguments, his fury over the tea, someone to clash up against. How perverse, I found myself thinking. Oh well, he'll be back tomorrow.

He did indeed return, in an absolutely filthy mood. Disgusted by the amount of work I had done, he thrust an enormous manuscript into my hands.

"Just focus on this for now," he said. "And I don't want you to show this to anyone, okay? It's my new piece and it's strictly confidential. Now I want you to make this the priority for the next few days, forget all the other stuff. I'm working to a deadline."

As he turned his back, I made a 'Heil Hitler' sign and he whipped back round.

"I saw that!" he said.

"What?" I feigned innocence. "I was just doing my hair."

Slumping back to my office, I frowned over the pages, wondering how on earth I was supposed to decipher his spidery handwriting. He should have become a doctor, not a writer. Oh how the hell could I have imagined that I was missing him?

I typed laboriously until lunchtime; I was then interrupted by his wife, Agatha, and her horror of a daughter. The young Alicia's brown hair was awkwardly curled into ringlets and she was dressed up in a pink dress that puffed out like a fuchsia rose and seemed at odds with her scowling face.

"Oh, goodness, Olivia, what a week we've had!" Agatha gabbled and gossiped. I grinned, chattering back. How can such a pleasant woman put up with such a horrible man? I wondered. I was growing to like her more and more by the minute. Though she was in her early fifties, she dressed with a kind of expensive

Ascot grace, all gold bracelets and polka-dots, that made her look much younger. Her brown eyes had a girlish twinkle to them, as if she was conspiring to share a naughty joke with you. Goodness knows why Ricky was always so mean about her behind her back to me; she was his mother, after all.

"Now," she said, "I was hoping that you might do me a few errands, darling." She burrowed in her handbag. "I was just hoping that you might pick up my coat from Sketchleys."

"Sure," I said, keen to do anything to help. Her husband could learn from her, I thought darkly, on how praise and charm are the best motivators.

In the dry cleaners, there was such a long queue that I barely had time to have lunch. I arrived late back at the office to find Sir C hopping mad, not even giving me a chance to explain. I ignored my rumbling stomach and put my sandwich to one side, tapping away resentfully.

Ten minutes later Agatha appeared again, with Alicia, gushing thanks for picking up her cashmere coat.

"I don't suppose you could watch Alicia for me, could you?" she pleaded, wringing her hands, her bracelets tinkling. "It's just that I've got a lovely man coming to give me a vacuum demonstration and she'll only get in the way."

"Well, I've got a heck of a lot to do –"

"It will just be for ten minutes," she said with slightly more bossiness, flipping back her hair and pulling her daughter forwards. "Now you'll just sit here and be well behaved, won't you, darling?"

Her darling looked as though she would do nothing of the sort. She refused to sit down and went to the window, folding her arms crossly. Then she started to blow hot patches on the window and pencil in swear-words.

I ignored her and carried on typing.

Upset perhaps at not being told off, she wandered up to my desk with bolshy curiosity.

"What's this?" she demanded, picking up a stapler.

"It's a stapler," I said in a gay voice, showing her how to punch in a staple. She had a few goes and looked unimpressed.

"My mummy said you're not much good in the office," she cocked her head to one side, punching a staple like an exclamation mark. "She said Daddy only hired you because you've got nice legs." She poked her naughty head under the table, inspecting them thoroughly, then popped it back out. "I don't think they're that amazing," she concluded.

"Alicia, you shouldn't repeat such things," I said, my face flushed, my fingers stumbling over my keys.

"My mummy has a lot of trouble with her legs," Alicia added darkly. "She's always rubbing weird plastic things over them." She paused, her intelligent eyes flitting over the office as if assessing what other damage could be done. "Could I staple some more, please?"

I handed her some scrap-paper and gave her a seat behind me and for a while she seemed content to sit and staple away. Five minutes later, Agatha returned, gushing 'thank you's. Somehow I couldn't quite look her in the eye.

A few minutes later Sir C stormed back in.

"How much?" he demanded.

I turned to hand him my proud pile. That was strange, I was sure I'd put them there. Then my jaw dropped in horror.

"What is it?" he came up behind me. Then his face clenched in anger when he saw me trying to hide them. Pushing past me, he picked them up, scowling in disbelief at the staples pitted all over them. "What the fuck are you doing?" he howled. "Are you insane? D'you think this is a joke?"

My temper snapped. I couldn't bear to be shouted at for one more time.

"No, I don't think it's a joke," I screamed back, my voice catching with tears. "I don't think it's a joke that you give me way too much to do and then your wife swans in and sends me off to the cleaners and then makes me babysit as well as everything else – well, I'm sorry, it's too much, I don't want to do this job anymore!" And flinging my bag over my shoulder, I ran out of the house.

I kept running until I came to the park, where I finally collapsed onto a bench, sniffing and burrowing desperately in my bag for a tissue, wiping away my tears, black smudges of mascara staining the Kleenex. The argument kept repeating itself over and over in my head, blowing out of all proportions, until he was hitting me and I was giving him a good whacking back and my fists were clenching the tissue in my fantasy.

Gradually the tears subsided and I sat there for some time, watching a few boys gleefully kicking a football around. Birds were singing in the trees; March blossom was caressing the freshly cut grass. I didn't want to go back, I didn't want to go home. I didn't know what I wanted to do. I wished Ricky was there with me to hug me and say everything would be alright.

Finally I drew in a deep breath, flipped open my compact, repaired my face, and returned very slowly to the house. When I knocked on the door, I heard instant footsteps and for a moment I nearly considered fleeing away. Then the door swung open and there stood Sir C. To my amazement, he beckoned me in, asking if I was okay, his face full of remorse.

He took me into his office, sat me down, and then – and I really couldn't believe this one – he actually *made me a cup of tea*. For some reason the kindness of the gesture made me want to burst into tears. Had I been in the wrong? I was racked with sudden guilt. Over the last few hours, I had blown him up into some kind of demon. Now I was wondering if maybe I had overreacted.

He sat down opposite me and chewed his lip anxiously.

"Look, I'm terribly sorry," he said, "please don't go. I had no idea my wife was putting upon you, I have no idea why, we have enough staff running around after her. I'll speak to her about it. It won't happen again. You will stay, won't you?"

I took a shaky gulp of tea, scalding my tongue.

"Well, you see," I gazed down at my tea, "I – you see – well, I'm just not sure that I want to be a PA." I took a deep breath. "To be honest, you see, I'm a writer."

"A writer?" he asked in surprise, leaning back in his chair. "How interesting. What d'you write?"

"Well, novels, and stuff. But the thing is, I mean, that's what I really want to be doing. I mean, I've never got anything published, but it is what I want to do . . ."

"I see," his tone hardened slightly, "and so you thought it might be convenient to come and work for me."

I looked up, spluttering some kind of guilty defense, but he shook his head, with a slightly contorted smile.

"No, it's alright. I don't blame you. It took me a very long time to break in, too."

"Really?" I looked at him with new hope.

He paused for a few minutes, tapping his ruler against the desk.

"Well, why don't you show me some of your stuff?" he offered at last.

"Oh really? Oh, would you?" I cried joyfully.

"Look, I can't promise anything-"

"No, of course not-"

"But we'll see what we can do."

I sat there, marvelling at the extraordinary turn of events and what an odd mixed-up mish-mash of a day it had been. Then I looked up and caught his eyes. He didn't look away. I didn't look away. And suddenly something, I don't know what, some spark, something passed between us.

It was so unexpected that when Agatha burst in, fussing over me, for a moment I had to shake and compose myself.

"I'm so frightfully sorry," she said. "Are you alright? I hope my terrible husband hasn't been bullying you too much. His bark is worse than his bite."

The husband rolled his eyes and grimaced slightly as she came to his side, stroking his hair, smoothing down his crumpled collar.

"Anyway," she said gaily, "I suppose it's time for you to be getting home?"

And so it was. Time had rushed by and it was now five o'clock. I picked up my bag, said a cheery goodbye, turning again to try to catch his eye, to share some secret Morse-code signal, but he stared out of the window, shutting me out.

8. Fifth Gear Fancy

But the next day, he was back to his bad mood again. Nothing I did was right. My letters were all wrong, he declared. There were no typos, they were simply full of *the wrong sort of words*. I knew they were just as he had dictated on the tape but he refused to acquiesce.

"Hmm, I shall bloody buy him a copy of Edward De Bono's *I am Right You Are Wrong*," I declared to my Snoopy mascot, slumped on my desk. "Thank goodness I'm getting out of here at five." Ricky had invited me to go clubbing; somehow playing the gooseberry to him and Leila didn't seem to bother me as much; after all, I might well meet a nice bloke myself, catching eyes across the dance-floor, swaying up to each other . . .

I was just walking out at 4:59 when Sir C's voice stopped me:

"Where are you going?"

"Sorry?" I asked, turning back.

"I need you to work tonight. We've got a ton of stuff to do and I'm booked in for golf tomorrow."

"But, but – it's *Friday* night!" I cried.

Sir C looked up, his blue fountain-pen spitting angry flecks across his page.

"It stipulated in your job description that you might have to work Friday nights. Now I need you tonight!"

So I went back to my office and told Ricky it was off.

"Oh, just tell him where to go," Ricky assured me. "Dad's ego gets so big sometimes, he forgets other people have a life too."

Which was all very well for Ricky to say, he was his son.

As the evening went on, my irritation started to bubble beneath the surface like water on the boil. I mean, it wasn't even as if there was much to be done. Sir C was such a control freak he had to dictate every single stupid letter, even responses to absurd fan mail like a warning about a forthcoming alien abduction which we both laughed up replies for (though the final polite result was 'I do thank you for your kind information and I shall do my best to take heed'). I wasn't allowed to 'pp' a thing.

Six o'clock came and the telephone rang.

"Yeah?" I snapped sulkily.

"Is that the office of Sir Henry Caldwell?" a posh English accent enquired.

"Yeah," I sighed. "I'm afraid so."

"Well, this is Anthony Minghella on the line. Look, I'm most interested in making a film out of *Solitude*, d'you think you could put me through to Sir Henry right away?"

"Oh sure, sure," I cried, sitting up, picking up a pencil. Anthony Minghella! Oh my God, he was the one who made *The English Patient* with yummy Ralph

Fiennes (sorry, Rafe Fines), which had won all those lashings of Oscars, oh wow.

Typically, Sir C's red light had to be flashing, indicating he was engaged. Every few seconds, I kept asking Minghella if he would hold, and he said fine, but eventually his time and patience ran out.

"Look, what kind of office are you running over there, can't you tell him it's urgent!" he barked.

"I'm trying! I'm trying!" I sweated, then, to my relief, suddenly Sir C's crisp English accent was on the line:

"Olivia, you silly girl! I can't believe you fell for it!"

"What!" I cried, my head still buzzing, "Sir C – I mean, Henry, I mean, Anthony Minghella's on the line. He wants to speak to you right away!"

"It's me."

"What?"

"Me." Suddenly he switched on his ultra-posh-oh-yar accent again, "Well, I couldn't believe how long I managed to pull that one off."

Then I clicked.

"Oh you bastard!" I cried in outrage. I slammed down the phone and burst into his office, where his laughter was booming off the filing cabinets. I sat down on the chair, folded my arms, laughed, scowled, and then cried: "Just you wait! Next week Stephen Spielberg or someone really will phone up and I'll tell him where to go and you'll lose a million-pound contract, then you'll be sorry!"

Sir C wiped his tears from his eyes.

"Dear me, I am sorry, I couldn't resist," he said. "Now, now, where were we?"

He signed his letters, mimicking his posh accent all

the time. I rolled my eyes and tried very hard not to laugh.

"Now," he said, suddenly brisk again, pressing his hands into a steeple, "I've got something urgent which needs dealing with."

Oh yeah? I thought. Another thousand letters to be typed? Throughout the city, you could feel that buzzy Friday-night feeling of tooting horns and pop music as the whole of London prepared to party. At this rate I would be stuck here till midnight.

Then he reached into his drawer and, to my amazement, brought out a bottle of whiskey and a box of chocolates.

"Well," he said, "I thought with the evening ahead of us we needed some light refreshments . . ."

In the end, not one single more letter was typed or signed. We sat there, sipping and drinking, me pretending to like the whiskey to please him, and trying not to pinch all the chocolates, which my fingers kept creeping up to like spiders and he kept pushing towards me, saying he didn't have much of a sweet tooth. We talked about the latest Booker Prize winner and Nicole Kidman's new play. He asked me what I thought of Ricky's new girlfriend and I said loyally that Leila was quite lovely and he said Ricky needed to settle down, if he hadn't got him that job at *Vixen* he didn't know what sort of mischief he'd be in . . .

By the time we had finished gossiping, Sir C had pulled practically my whole life story out of me and I had missed the last train back. He put on his coat and his driving spectacles and very kindly offered to drive me all the way home, declaring a young girl like me shouldn't be walking the streets alone. At the end he waved me off and said a cheery, "Have a good weekend!" I let myself in and discovered it was now one in the morning. The others weren't back yet, but somehow I didn't mind. It really had been a lovely evening.

The memory stayed with me throughout the weekend, as I drifted around the house, replaying our conversations like looking back on old photo albums, rewording them as if refining a novel, until Josephine, catching me talking to myself about six times, put a hand on my forehead and asked if the stress of my job was getting to me.

Monday morning came. I fought with Josephine for the bathroom; I was determined to make myself look as fantastic as possible. After all, I was PA to a very important man. I put on my new pink suit, mildly dismayed to find the skirt shorter than I'd realised, with a slit up the side that I hadn't noticed in the shop. I had a sudden vision of Sir C's eyes sliding up the pink lips of the slit and quickly shook myself, applying some coral lipstick.

On the tube, I was pleased to see my outfit seemed to be waking up the city boys, who fought to give up their seats for me, peering surreptitiously over their *Financial Times*.

Sir C, however, did not give my outfit a second glance. He sent me off without so much as a 'How are you?' I returned to my office, smarting, wondering what I had done wrong. It was as if Friday night had never happened.

Suddenly his wife came flurrying in with Alicia, who

was blaring her hands around her lips making imaginary trumpet noises.

"Surprise! Surprise for Daddy!" Alicia announced excitedly.

"Quiet!" Agatha shushed her, pulling the door shut with a conspiratorial smile. "Now, Olivia, I want to let you in on a little secret . . ."

As planned, at the end of the day, I left work slightly early and caught the bus to Cafe Rouge. The entire top section had been reserved for us. As I entered, I discovered Ricky fastening balloons into a corner. Seeing me, he nearly fell off his step-ladder.

"Olivia!" he cried, coming up and taking my hand. "This is a nice surprise, I didn't know you were in on it too."

"Well, I – well, Agatha said . . ." I trailed off awkwardly because to be honest I had been quite surprised to be invited too.

Ricky opened his mouth, then clamped it shut, his eyes widening as he heard his father's footsteps on the stairs. He squeezed my hand excitedly as we waited for him to laugh or at least manage a smile. Instead he merely scowled.

"I didn't ask for this," he said at last and then glared accusingly at Ricky.

I stiffened with indignation but Ricky merely rolled his eyes. Sir C, however, softened palpably when his daughter came pounding up the stairs, flinging her arms around him, crying *"Happy Birthday, Daddy!"*

"Thank you, darling," he said. "Now can I have my leg back, please?'

Alicia grinned cheekily and coiled her anaconda grip around his thigh. "No, Daddy, no." Then she sprung up and grabbed his hand. "Come and see the placemat I made for you."

"Hmm, very nice, darling," said her father, swiping her head gently, and she burst into ostentatious giggles. I had expected some pretty picture with crayon trees but instead she had put a mischievous: '*Only 75 today and you still look so young!*'

"Seventy-five indeed," Sir C muttered, sitting down and pulling her onto his lap whilst she chattered and tried to pull his fountain-pens out of his breast pocket.

Last but not least Agatha made her grand entrance, in a cloud of perfume and fur, pausing to let the waiters slip off her coat, waltzing up to Sir C and kissing the air by his cheek.

"Happy Birthday, darling," she said.

"You did all this?" he asked, and she shrugged girlishly, which made me prickle with indignation. I had, after all, been the one sent out to buy all the presents, and then again when Agatha had realised we had no wrapping paper, and then again for cards, and then to look after Alicia whilst Agatha made herself up and got me to zip up the back of her dress as though I was her bloody maid, leaving me no time to get ready. Then I shook myself – it was so trivial, what did it matter? It just would have been nice for Sir C to know.

We all sat down to eat in high spirits. Agatha took charge, charming the waiter, ordering for all of us, arguing with Henry over whether he was allowed his favourite with chillies which she claimed would not help his recently healed stomach ulcer.

"Honestly, Mum," Alicia rolled her eyes, "you're already arguing and you've only just got here."

Only children can get away with speaking the truth. Everyone laughed and the waiter patted her head.

"Can I have Coke?" Alicia demanded, kicking her heels.

"No, dear," Agatha browsed through the menu, "you know it's bad for your teeth and if you have too many E's it makes you hyperactive."

"No, Mum, you just snort it up your nose, it doesn't hurt your teeth."

"Alicia!" Agatha snapped. "Really, with the fees we pay for your school, and this is all you come home with!"

Sir C and Ricky and I exchanged repressed smiles and Alicia, pleased to have caused a stir, momentarily shut up, then demanded that Daddy should open all his presents while we waited for the food.

The presents spilled across the table, gold and pink wrapping paper shredded on the floor: a selection of silk ties, a pair of gold cufflinks, the inevitable bottle of whiskey, some Earl Grey tea, Polo aftershave. Seeing my package, he frowned and said I needn't have got him anything. As he fingered the olive green cravat, I thought of what a stupid present it was: all he wore was black and brown and navy. It was much too fussy, too garish, too foppish, more the sort of thing Agatha would have worn, but I had been in a rush and men were so impossible to buy for, what else was there except ties and socks and hankies – only this had looked a little more unusual at the time . . .

"Thank you," he smiled up at me, "thank you very much."

My heart was just turning an unexpected flip-flop when Alicia pushed her present into his hands: a box of Belgian chocolates, with a few missing.

"Well, I just had to check they weren't poisoned," she explained as her mother looked incensed again.

Ricky had bought him some personalised notepaper and a fountain-pen.

The meal grew more and more lively as the food and wine flowed. I couldn't help noticing that Ricky, though having an ice fight with Alicia under the table, seemed slightly subdued. I noticed that he and Agatha managed to avoid saying one word to each other.

At the end, a waiter appeared with a birthday cake drenched in white icing, complete with spitting and fizzing fireworks. Sir C looked so cross that I knew he was secretly overcome.

After cake, Ricky went over to sit with his dad while they drunkenly argued over politics and novelists. It must be so nice, I watched them with dreamy affection, to get on so well with your dad like that. Agatha kept trying to interrupt, but it was obvious she had no idea what she was talking about, so she gossiped loudly to me about 'silly mens' talk' as though wishing they would overhear, and then dragged me off to the ladies'.

I was feeling tipsy and high-hearted with happiness. I'd had such a lovely evening; I'd been half-dreading it all day, repeatedly asking Agatha if she was sure I should come but they had made me feel like one of the family.

"Thank you so much for inviting me," I cried to her.

"I'm so glad you came," said Agatha, gently removing an eyelash from my cheek. She frowned down at my skirt, and added, "You know, dear, you don't need to wear quite such short skirts in the office. I know they're the fashion but I can't help thinking they look tarty. I've got heaps of stuff I want to throw out for jumble – you must come up and take your pick."

Nearly everything Agatha wore was garish, covered with spots or trimmed with fur. I felt slightly deflated.

Back in the restaurant, I nearly stumbled onto my chair, and Ricky grabbed my arm with a teasing, "Whoa – there!"

Sir C caught my eye with a smile. As he helped me to pull my coat on, I felt the faint brush of his huge hands on my shoulder blades.

Agatha left a generous tip. She scooped up all the presents into a large cream carrier bag. As I checked under the table, I noticed my cravat had fallen to the floor and, somehow upset that he hadn't put it straight on, I stuffed it into my pocket to give to him later.

Outside, we all bundled into a taxi. I was squashed up between Ricky on one side and his father on the other, stiff and awkward. His daughter had plonked herself on his lap and (I think having stolen some of his wine) was rubbing her head lovingly against his neck, purring and pretending to be a pussycat. She demanded to play I-Spy, and her daddy patiently chose 'G'. She managed about two tries before giving up in boredom.

"'G' for my Gorgeous Daughter," he said fondly.

"Oh Dad, that's cheating," she complained, but after that she settled with a quiet peace on his lap and by the time we were home she had fallen asleep and he carried her off upstairs to bed. Ricky and I went into the kitchen to make tea. Outside in the corridor, I heard his wife entreating him to come upstairs with her but he was adamant that he wanted to stay up and write a few more hours. I heard her wail like a little girl and clatter off up the stairs in a huff.

"Parents," Ricky muttered, stuffing his hands in his pockets. "Fancy going for a quick walk?"

"Sure," I said, but as we reached the door I felt myself being pulled back to Sir C like an elastic band. Suddenly I suffered a terrific sense of anticlimax, as if the evening had gone nowhere.

"Erm, you wait outside," I said. "I just have to go to the loo."

Ricky waited outside in the moonlight. I pushed the front door nearly shut, and tip-toed down the passage to Sir C's study.

I came to a nervous halt outside the office. I felt as though I was outside a headmaster's study waiting for the cane. When I touched the handle I got an electric shock and paused, waiting for my heaving breath to quieten. It didn't. Holding my hands behind my back, I nudged open the door with my foot.

"Hello?" He was sorting through a sheaf of papers. He did not seem surprised to see me.

I shifted from foot to foot. He looked up enquiringly.

"I'm terribly sorry to disturb you, but, I've . . . er . . . got another little present for you," I said. As I hurried awkwardly around the side of the desk, crossing that line of barrier which normally set us apart as boss and secretary, he flinched, then blinked, quickly concealing his surprise. I had wanted to place the little gold-wrapped box in his hand but he instinctively crossed his arms defensively. My fingers dropped it clumsily onto his papers. Blushing furiously, I leant over and kissed him on the cheek. "Oh, s-sorry," I stuttered. "Now, look, you've got lipstick, now that won't do." I licked a finger and tried to rub it off, feeling his sandpaper stubble, then took a cautious step backwards.

Sir C looked down at the present, then slowly opened the top drawer of his desk, slotting it between a bottle of Tippex and a packet of the Extra Strong Mints he was always sucking.

"Thank you," he said quietly, "thank you very much."

I paused awkwardly. Wasn't he going to open it? This was not how I had played the scene out in my head; he was like an actor saying all the wrong lines. Or was I the one playing the wrong role?

"Well, I just wanted to say thank you," I said quickly. "I mean, you really are very lovely to work for."

"Thanks," Sir C nodded, "I'll open it later."

"Yes, yes," I spluttered, "open it with your wife, of course." There was still a faint smudge of pink on his cheek and I couldn't stop staring at it and feeling I ought to inform him. "Well, erm, I guess I should go back. Thanks . . . once again." Desperate to get out before I made a total prat of myself, I turned and was stumbling towards the door, his cravat still knotted between my fingers, when he called out in a soft sing-song, almost tauntingly:

"Olivia."

"Yes?" I caught my breath.

When I swung back, he had pushed his chair away from the desk and was sitting with his legs apart, arms behind his head, hands cupping the back of his head.

"Come here," he said.

I felt a thrill of desire helter-skelter down my spine. Slowly, I edged forwards towards him but, when I was about a foot away, his voice stopped me.

"I want you to sing me 'Happy Birthday'," he said.

"What? Here? Now?" I asked.

He nodded his head, a smile playing his lips, like a king commanding a dancing girl.

I took a deep breath and started to sing. My nerves made it sound Marilyn Monroe breathy, though I was convinced I was squeaking out of tune in all the wrong places. Gradually my weak voice, like a newly flying bird, gained grace and started to soar – then I stumbled:

"Happy Birthday, dear . . . dear . . . Sir C–" I paused; Josephine had kept emphasising to me that the correct form of address was Sir Henry Caldwell but that sounded such a mouthful.

"You can call me Henry," he said gently, and we both looked at each other and started to laugh. Every time I started the final line, I burst into giggles again. Then I saw him close his eyes, waiting patiently, and I gulped, and sang the last two lines very softly and sweetly. When I opened my eyes I saw that his were still closed and there was a peaceful look on his face, a question mark of a smile. Then his heavy lids lifted and he gazed at me, almost dreamily.

"Thank you," he said quietly. "That was beautiful."

"Well, I guess I should go."

He did not reply. He merely looked at me. His eyes were fully open now and there was a funny expression in them.

"So, goodnight," I gasped.

Sir C did not reply. Still he looked, unblinking, unflinching.

"Goodnight," I repeated, rubbing my sweaty palms together.

"Goodnight," said Sir C lightly.

"Goodnight," I said, then turned and ran all the way back down the stairs and out into the dark erotic night. It was only as I shut the door that I realised I was holding the cravat and I quickly balled it and stuffed it into my pocket, so that Ricky wouldn't notice.

Outside Ricky and I walked along past the birthday-cake houses, beneath the streetlamps and budding trees, meandering down to a graveyard. I noticed Ricky's face tighten as he picked a few daisies and then put them on a grave. Squinting in the darkness, my heart shivered uneasily as I caught the fading words: *Here lies Mary Susan Caldwell, died aged 45, 15 January 1985*.

Ricky sat himself down on the grass, resting his chin on his knees and looking over the lights of London. I sat down, awkwardly twiddling blades of grass. Somehow some pain was tangible; I wanted to reach out and comfort him, but I didn't understand, I didn't know what to do or say.

"Is she your grandma?" I asked at last.

"What!" Ricky almost spat out. "She's my mother."

"Your mother . . . ?" I asked in shock. "But I thought Agatha . . ."

"That witch? You must be kidding. No, he was married to my mother long before Agatha got her claws into him." Ricky snapped off a piece of grass and chewed it fiercely.

"Oh. Oh." So that explained why he and Agatha bristled like electric fences.

Ricky stayed silent for a moment longer, irritably brushing away a fly. Then he reached into his shirt and drew out a locket, flicking it open. He flicked on his lighter so that I see the picture of his mother inside. She was blonde and girlish, with his dimples in her cheeks. I could see at once that Ricky took after her – she was so soft and sweet, the complete antithesis of his father.

He rubbed his thumb affectionately around the aura of her head. "She died when I was fifteen. Cancer."

I lay in bed that night listening to the sound of Leila and Ricky making love and it suddenly struck me that I didn't love Ricky anymore. Well, I did love him – but as a friend. In the graveyard, I had listened and comforted him and I had told him a bit about the problems with my father. We had come away closer, feeling the sweet friendship between us, easy, comfortable, innocent.

The trouble was, like a dieter who starves herself and then takes up smoking instead, I was now in love with his father. His forty-seven-year-old-enough-to-be-my-father father who was also married with a six-year-old child.

I tossed and turned with uneasy, unsettled desire, trying to work out how and when it could have happened.

Somehow it had crept up on me. It seems ironic and odd that first-gear fancies i.e. men that grab your attention like a red hot Porsche swerving down a road, and reduce you to instantaneous orgasm the moment you meet, never seem to last long. Maybe it's because you're fooled into thinking it's love at first sight and pin a perfect personality onto them, then realism smashes through the idealism and the charm wears off as quickly as it came.

But then there are fifth-gear fancies: men who, when you first met them, you fancy about as much as cold fish-finger, and then five weeks on they are suddenly the next best thing since sliced bread. Men who grow on you, slowly snake their way into your awareness, creep on you like a mist . . . men like Sir C . . . oh God, I wanted him. But what the hell would Ricky say? He was still in love with his mother's ghost. Look how he hated Agatha. And yet he had almost implied Sir C had just married her on the rebound, so . . . perhaps.

Oh come on, Olivia, I hugged my pillow to my chest. There was no way anything would ever happen. I mean, even if he did fancy me, and what a big "if" it was, he would never make a move. But then, again, hadn't he nearly made a move on me just now? Or was he just flirting? Or?

9. Anticipation

I stood in front of the mirror, frowning uncertainly at my reflection. It had taken two days of near starvation and then two hours of nearly fainting due to restricted blood supply to finally squeeze into the dress, which still looked as though it might burst at any moment. The material was white silk, decorated with splurges of pale pink, cerise and plum, rather like someone had dipped a great big fat paintbrush in some watercolours and splashed them on.

"What d'you think they're supposed to be?"

"Flowers?" Leila suggested.

"I don't know if I like them. You don't think I look like an expensive sofa in Harrods?"

Leila shrugged uneasily and went back to sewing up the hem on her little black dress. She wasn't really paying attention – Leila was getting jittery because famous people made her nervous and she was so used to slopping about in tracksuits, she hated getting dressed up.

I was equally uncertain about my dress. If I examined it from behind, it looked much better. If the pattern was dubious, the fit was lovely – clingy, toe-length and backless, tying at the nape of my neck in a tight knot.

The thing was, with Agatha there tonight, I couldn't very well not wear it. She had forced the dress onto me, insisted I borrow it. I couldn't tell if she was being genuinely charming, or wickedly bitchy, but in either case she was impossible to refuse. So I had put the dress on, and Leila had said it looked lovely, and Josephine had said it looked lovely and I was just coming round to it when Ricky walked in, burst into shocked laughter and told me I looked as though I belonged in the Harrods sale, in the expensive-sofa department.

"Shut up," I hissed.

"Just ignore him," said Josephine.

Which was all very well for her to say when she was looking like Gwyneth Paltrow, shimmering in pink silk, tiny white pearls at her throat and ears, her fair hair coiled at the top of her head giving her a swan-like grace. Huh.

The party (which Sir C had promised me was going to be *the* literary party of the year: Amis, Bragg, Trollope et al attending) was being held in yet another of Sir C's houses, which seemed to be dotted all over the country like sheep. This time the location was Farmingham, Kent.

Ricky's battered Beatle looked somewhat out of place beside all the sleek Mercedes. As we veered up to the huge sky-blue gates, the guard in the sentinel box peered at us suspiciously through the twilight gloom.

"Who are you?" he asked, picking up the guest lists.

"The Spanish Inquisition," said Ricky impatiently and zoomed on ahead.

We purred on up a grove of sycamores to the colossal mansion. Painted entirely white, it looked like a big birthday cake, each of the windows lit a different colour, like a row of birthday candles. In keeping with the tropical theme, the porch was decked with palm-trees draped with winking fairy lights.

As we stepped out, flashbulbs blinded our eyes, then all the photographers frowned at us when they realised we were nobodies. Then, as Melvyn Bragg and his wife rolled up, they started clicking frantically again.

"Christ," said Ricky, "this is more of a press conference than a party. Trust Dad."

Josephine looked rather affronted. I think she had been expecting them to recognise her from the Tampax commercial she had just filmed.

Inside the hallway, a cloakroom attendant took our coats and purses. We surged forwards into the pulsating living-room. The wall between the living-room and parlour had recently been knocked down to form a long, narrow room painted entirely white. The rice-matting floor was splattered with confetti; in the corners, more palm-trees wilted and Taiwanese girls dressed in mauve bikinis shimmied here and there offering silver trays loaded with fruit cocktails. There were even a few scarlet macaws which, unnerved by the crowds, were annoying everyone with raucous squawks, and it was not long before a butler approached their equally nervous keeper and suggested he take them back to London Zoo.

* * *

As I watched Sir C weaving through circles, shaking hands, kissing women hello, I felt somewhat stupid that I should have wasted so much time fretting hopefully. He probably had no interest in bothering with me anyway. I was just his PA. A nobody. But God, what is it that black tie does for men? He suddenly looked as distinguished and delectable as a box of After Eights. The suit made his eyes look so dark the pupils were barely discernible, giving him a slightly Machiavellian air; it showed off his broad back, making him taller, not so much Sir Henry as King Henry.

Beside me, Leila and Josephine were far too busy gaping at all the celebs to notice him. Suddenly, Josephine spotted someone in Sir C's circle that she knew: a tall guy wearing a shiny purple suit, with a shock of dark hair and sideburns. She tapped him on the shoulder.

"Oh Rupert, darling." They kissed the air and he drew her into his charmed circle. "How long's it been since we filmed *Planet*, how long . . ."

Ricky returned with some drinks. He followed my gaze.

"SCG," said Ricky, sipping his drink.

"What?" I snapped, my eyes still on Sir C, watching his eyes light up as he was introduced to Josephine. She offered him her hand and he leaned down to kiss it.

"SCG," said Ricky. "They're known as Sir Henry Caldwell's groupies. All these young girls hanging around him, hoping for a bit of his money or fame or attention, just because of that 'Six Degrees of Caldwell' theory."

"What's that?" I spluttered.

"The 'Six Degrees of Caldwell'. It's like that theory in Hollywood that Kevin Bacon is linked to everyone by six degrees and is thus somehow quietly pulling all the strings. My father is supposedly the literary equivalent." Ricky took another slug of his drink. "All they want is to sell their story to *The Sun* and get ten thou', but," he added with a touch of pride, "my dad's far too sharp to fall for them."

He seemed innocently oblivious to the fact that an equal number of women were just as interested in him, eyes swivelling across the room to caress his greyhound frame, a passing waitress pressing drinks on him with an inviting smile.

When I glanced back, Sir C was looking over at me. I smiled and gave a shy wave. Then he started coming over towards me!

He was on top smoothie social form.

"Ricky," he grinned at his son, giving him a faint punch on the shoulder. "And darling Olivia – you look simply divine," he said, giving me a kiss on the temple. I tried to keep cool and introduced him to Leila, but I was quite taken aback by how rude he was to her. He gave her a quick once-over, then turned away abruptly, ignoring her question as to how many people he'd invited.

Leila looked mildly offended. Ricky put his arm around her and gave her a slightly apologetic smile as if to say, "Well, that's my dad . . ."

"There's tons of important people I want you to meet," said Sir C, drawing me away. I looked back at

Ricky, who nodded and shrugged, turning back to talk to Leila.

As we snaked our way through the crowds, heads kept turning, chorusing 'Hello's' and giving me slightly appraising glances. I kept getting paranoid that they were thinking, "SCG – the latest and youngest member?" Bugger Ricky.

Sir C murmured that his wife was unable to attend – she had ME – she was feeling poorly that evening – but she sent her best wishes.

"She has ME! But she seems so lively!" I had always pictured ME sufferers as being so weak they could only just about to sit up in bed and feign enough energy to sip some water.

"Well, it goes in cycles – she rests and then goes wild and rushes around and exhausts herself – ah, here's Alan Titschmarsh."

A thin, sallow man, who was looking rather odd in a cream jacket with a green kilt, wire horn-rimmed spectacles and a shorn head with a ponytail at the back, was chatting away to Alan, non-stop, tiny flecks of spit popping out of his mouth. Alan was looking rather caged, as though he rather wished he could be back potting tomatoes in his garden shed . . .

"Boris Ameldon," Sir C whispered, his breath warm on my ear, "famous for his arthouse films." Then he turned to Titschmarsh. "This is Olivia, one of our next generation's great up-and-coming authors," he said, showering me in flattery like confetti.

I was terribly excited. My mother was a great fan of Alan Titschmarsh ("Oo, whenever I watch him manhandle his barrow,' makes me tingle all over") so I immediately asked for an autograph for her, much to his pleasure, and Sir C's bewildered surprise. Titschmarsh gave me the autograph and a wink that would have made my mother faint. Then the two men started to chatter away, so I turned to Boris and asked him what films he had made. He looked so taken aback that I quickly corrected myself.

"Ar, have you won many awards for your films?"

"Ah, yes," Boris said in a clipped German accent, "many, many, many. As far back as 1983, I was trying to get my arts – I prefer to call them so, 'movie' is such a vulgar word – I was trying to get my arts distributed, albeit with little success. Finally, I went to Cannes where *The Greenhouse* won the award for Best Animated Film."

"That sounds nice," I said brightly. "I just love *Wallace and Grommit.*"

Boris's pebble eyes blinked behind his glasses.

"Yes, yes, yes, but my film was more serious, hey? It took me two years to make the various vegetables that made the greenhouse their abode. My time setting was post-millennium, pre-World War Seven, where the only surviving species were a few genetically engineered vegetables, following a computer riot that wiped out the human race and left only machines. Thus, a carrot and a potato debate their existence in the fashion of Plato and Socrates."

I burst into fits of laughter, then, seeing Boris's estranged expression, realised that this was not the anticipated reaction.

"I am sorry," I apologised. "I was just thinking, you

know, how much humour there is in tragedy, how much bathos in pathos."

Boris's face relaxed again; there, I thought, with a giggly triumph, I can do this intellectual wank just as well. As Boris continued to drone on and on, I drank my cocktail as quickly as possible so I could have an excuse to get away. Then, seeing my empty glass, a smiling Taiwanese waitress immediately approached me with a fresh one.

Oh God, I thought, why is it I attract wierdos like magnets? It's just the same on buses: why am I always the one who has a nutter sitting next to me, ranting on about alien abduction while I try to nod and smile and the whole bus falls silent, listening and smirking at me questioningly, as if we might be related. Perhaps I was too soft, perhaps like Josephine I should have been an ice-bitch, but there you have it – within five minutes, I was making polite chit-chat to Boris, trying not to cringe as his eyes roved over me, my neck aching from looking down at him.

"And then in autumn 1987, no – 1989," said Boris, "for it took me three years to make *Isolation* – ah yes, that was one of my most innovative works, a two-hour piece where the camera rests solidly on a piece of wallpaper."

Fortunately at this point, Boris was thankfully interrupted by a Taiwanese girl bashing a huge gong. Blushing, she took a deep breath and managed to pronounce shakily:

"Dinner is served."

By now it was nearly nine o'clock and everyone was raring to eat. I grabbed my chance, declared I was starving and hurried off into the impatient swirls of the crowds leaving Boris gaping indignantly.

"Save me, save me!" I ran giggling to Leila and Ricky, who begged me to point out Boris and then proceeded to take the piss out of him until I was begging them to shut up, fearing he might see.

We gaped in appreciation as we entered the drawing-room.

It was a large room with a very high ceiling, filled with rows of long mahogany tables laid for a five-course meal. It had been lit with grass-green light, long trails of green crepe paper hanging from the skirting board. Green, turquoise and navy balloons littered the floors; along the walls were lined colossal James Bond style fish tanks filled with flitting tropical fish. Dried seaweed curled around the candelabra, and there were little bowls heaped with oysters and coral-encrusted silver tongs. In the corner a girl dressed as a mermaid, her long fair hair flowing over her naked breasts, plucked at a harp, nodding and smiling at the *oohs* and *ahhs* of the guests.

I sat down next to Ricky. Instantly, a hoard of women converged to sit on his other side.

In fear of Boris, I saved the seat on my other side with a paper napkin. Just then, however, Boris came back like a boomerang, plonking himself down beside me, sending the napkin fluttering to my feet.

"Sir Caldwell was going to sit there," I said.

"Ah, ah, ah, but Mr Caldwell is over there," Boris pointed out slyly and I leaned forwards to see him greeting a French supermodel who kissed him ecstatically on either cheek and then pulled him down beside her.

I was shocked at the barb of jealousy that pierced me inside. On one hand, I felt like picking up a bowl of bloody oysters and flinging them over the bloody Frog's head; on the other, an indignant voice cried: can't he just resist anything in a skirt for one minute?

"Olivia, Olivia, what are you doing?" Boris teased me, and I looked down to see I had shredded my napkin with my fork.

"Nothing," I said irritably, with a gay laugh, tossing back my hair and composing myself.

I cheered up tremendously when Sir C, seeing me, moved to sit opposite me, though the Froggie supermodel moved with him.

The waiters, all dressed in fluorescent shorts and T-shirts which looked wildly incongruous with their slicked-back hair and elegant manner, came round with the first course, silver glasses filled with a light pink salmon mousse. I wished Ricky and Boris would lower their voices a bit; I was sure I could detect the French supermodel gabbling to Sir C in French, and Sir C, surprisingly enough, seemed to be conversing back with reasonable fluency.

I tried not to stare at the pink moustache glistening above Boris's thin, twitching lips as he described his production of *Hamlet* using an all-female cast. Then he was collared by a man on the other side of him, and at last I had a moment's fresh air. Then I caught Sir C's eyes and repressed a giggle.

"Boris Ameldon," Sir C reassured me in a whisper

across the table, "is a total case. He's having a crisis of sexuality at the moment, he's considering having a sex change, maybe that's why he's wearing his kilt."

Clearly Boris was not one of the Someone Importants Sir C was so keen to charm. It was almost refreshing to hear him slag someone off for once.

We all tried to suffocate our guffaws as Boris turned back suspiciously.

"When I was at school," I shot back in a wicked whisper, "the bursar there had a sex change, so we all used to take the mickey by writing letters that went 'Dear sir / madam . . .'"

Boris, looking rather inflamed, hurriedly reverted to the cosy subject of his 'arts' again:

"My latest project is entitled *The Beauty Myth* about a girl who sells her soul in order to remain eternally beautiful. The lead we plan to be played by a robot as a symbol of the superficiality of our society in adoring beautiful women."

Down the table, Josephine reddened and looked slightly huffy and several men at the table raised their eyebrows. Ricky snorted, chucked a bread roll in Boris's direction, missed. Boris, unaware of the offense he was causing, continued to jabber on.

"Well, I don't know about you," Sir C bulldozed over him raucously, "but I love having pretty girls around me and I've no complaints about my present company."

"Ah, but beauty is a transient thing," Boris persisted. "Remem–"

"If I had to lose my looks or my brains, I would most certainly lose my looks," I said, then waited in paranoia for someone to say, 'What looks?' but luckily nobody did.

"Me too," Boris conceded.

"Some of us have neither looks nor brains to lose," Sir C added in a low voice, winking at me.

"Yes, yes, yes," Boris carried on, "but remem –"

"Hey," Ricky interrupted him loudly, "why don't you tell your joke about the Typical Man, Olivia?"

"Fine, I shall not quote my quote," said Boris tightly.

"Go on," Ricky egged me on. For a few minutes I hissed 'no' and he tickled me and said 'yes' until nearly the whole table was looking over at us in bemused curiosity.

"Do tell," said Sir C, his eyes on Ricky's hands on my waist.

A few seats away, Josephine shook her head frantically and closed her eyes in disbelief. I don't normally tell my my Typical Man joke unless I'm drunk. Very drunk.

"Well, once upon a time, there was Typical Man. One day he won the lottery, and being such a generous bloke, he decided to give away five hundred pounds to his favourite girl. But he had three girlfriends and he didn't know which one to choose. His first girl was so intelligent she was a member of Mensa, his second was had high-flying PR job, and his third was the editor of a glossy magazine. So which one did the Typical Man give it to?" I bit back a smile as everyone looked at me questioningly. "The one with the biggest tits!"

Ricky screamed with laughter. But several gentlemen gave me disapproving glances and the

French supermodel looked pained. For a moment Sir C seemed to be scowling. Then he threw back his head and roared with volcanic laughter, causing the chandelier above to give a tinkling tremble. Boris looked rather confused and started to tuck into a white roll, heaping it with crab paste.

"Priceless, simply priceless," said Sir C wiping his eyes. "You are naughty, Olivia." He gazed at me affectionately and I smiled back, feeling my insides turning to absolute *squiggles*.

"Eat up," said Ricky, watching me push away my lobster barely touched.

"No, I'm not hungry," I said, looking over at his father.

I went to the loo and by the time I had returned to the table, Sir C had already drifted off, flowing through the room like oil between cogs, shaking hands, introducing. It was fascinating to see this Public Sir C, compared to the irritable recluse I was so used to working with. It was as if he was on stage. Now I understood why he was so successful. I was sure he must have read up on everyone's details in *Who's Who* beforehand so he could flatter them with personal details. He never stayed with anyone for longer than five minutes, and yet those five minutes were enough to make his guest feel completely special, as though they were someone more important to Sir C than all the others, I noted, watching the mens' respectful glances, the ladies' doting looks. Too many doting looks, I thought sourly.

I wanted to approach him but suddenly I had lost my nerve. I looked around for Leila for moral support, to ask her advice, but she was nowhere to be seen.

Ricky, meanwhile, was telling a raucous joke to a group of women. Then I caught the words, "And he gave the money to the one with the biggest tits" and I felt utterly indignant – he had stolen my joke, the one I'd told at dinner – and they were all laughing a lot harder than when I'd told it.

Suddenly feeling petulant and sulky again, I curled up on a sofa at the end of the room and ignored Germaine Kirk's polite but enraged protest when I picked up the remote control and switched on *Eastenders*, so that the pitter-patter of delicate conversation was occasionally interrupted by Cindy's coarse Cockney accent, "Kathy, you couldn't look after me kids for me, could ya?" or Phil screeching, "You dirty little cow, you tell one on me and you'll live to regret it."

Eventually Boris, glass in hand, watched a few minutes, frowned and muttered, "Yar, very twee, very twee." I shushed him noisily and to my relief he wandered away, looking for new targets.

Then I jumped as a very familiar voice floated above my head: "Really, Olivia, why come to a party and watch TV? Come and meet some more people."

It was Sir C. He was nursing a glass of brandy in his hands and smiling down at me.

"Erm, I think I need some fresh air," I said hurriedly, pressing the 'Off' switch on the remote control. My fingers were shaking so much it took three goes.

"Good idea," said Sir C. "Mind if I join you?" He held my eyes for a moment too long.

I looked back to see Ricky safe over the other side of the room, cornered by women.

"Sure," I shrugged, catching my breath.

10. Seduction

We squeezed through the crowds out onto the lawn, receiving an icy blast of April air. Sir C strolled along, swigging from his brandy glass, relaxed as ever.

The cold clear sky was studded with stars, the impassive moon galactic-white. Silver frost had trailed its wand over the trees and grass. A few crocuses and snowdrops were flourishing here and there, promising that the slow spring hadn't forgotten about us . . .

Sir C suddenly quoted a few poetic lines about spring which I didn't quite catch, giving an extravagant sigh. "Ah, isn't it beautiful?"

"Beautiful," I echoed nervously, pulling my stole around my shoulders. Despite being alone together, our conversation seemed to be skating on a surface level. As though he was still in Polite Host mode and I was another one of his guests to be charmed and pleased.

"Of course," he went on, "if Donne had been alive today, he'd have had no chance. He probably would have submitted them to all the publishing houses and been told to bugger off. You can imagine it landing on an editor's desk – 'Who the fuck wants to read a poem about a fly?'"

"Ah, yes," I said, feeling slightly lost as to where this conversation was heading, as though I had switched on a TV programme halfway through and hadn't quite got the gist. "Still," I said, more brightly, "it might well have been an unexpected success. They might have made a Hollywood film – get the mug, get the T-shirt sort of thing."

I thought I sounded rather clever and amusing but Sir C smiled only faintly, guiding my elbow as I picked myself over the minimal paving stones, leading us down beneath a cane arch.

"Most unlikely, though, sadly, Olivia. Donne would probably have penned poetry for a few years, then given up in despair. My point is, Olivia, publishing is a very commercial business and it's very competitive. Every other person you meet is writing a novel . . . low sales . . . net agreement . . . blah blah . . . almost impossible for a first-timer . . . blah blah . . ."

Yes, yes, I thought, I've heard all this before, but where are you leading to . . . ?

Then he came out with it.

"The point is, Olivia, I've read the piece you gave me."

"Oh? Have you?" I gasped, stopping, and then walking again as he nodded his head forwards.

"Yes. I read it last night."

There was something about the tone of his voice that suggested he was not exactly happy with it. I felt my heart twist. I had a sudden illogical paranoia that he was going to sack me.

"To be honest, I'm not at all convinced that your *Wickham's Memoirs* thingummy, though novel and charming, is going to sell. You see, Olivia, writing is a business. You need to consider your markets. Now, this is just a suggestion, but I think you should write a historical romance. They're selling tremendously well at the moment."

"Well – well – yes . . ." I said, thinking: but surely *Wickham's Memoirs* is both historical and romantic? Maybe I was missing something . . .

He paused as we passed by thick hedgerow leading into a mini-maze; white statues depicting Greek gods and goddesses gleamed in the moonlight. I almost expected to see fairies and elves dancing round the pond at the bottom, the atmosphere was so magical and enchanting.

"I have a friend at Cromwells who I could put you in touch with. They have come up with a very snazzy new idea for a set of titles called *X His,* historical romances which are more than just romances."

I waited silently as he continued to build up to his finale.

"So what they're planning is to cross-breed two genres: the classical historical romance with the *X Libris* and go for something romantic but steamy, historical but hot – keep going," Sir C guided me, and I lifted up my skirts as we came to a path caked with wet leaves and overgrown briars.

"Sorry," he apologised, "I told Jefferson to clear this, but–"

I yelped as my dress got caught in the zig-zag teeth of a bramble. Sir C put down his brandy glass and bent down to untangle me but in the end he had to rip the bramble off from its stem, and set me up on the stone wall of a wishing-well to try and unsnag it.

He seemed quite distressed about the dress but all I could think was: thank God, at least he'll never make me wear this again. Then I felt the warm hand that brushed against my ankle suddenly shift so that his palm was on my bare skin.

Then he ran his forefinger down the back of my leg.

An absolute shiver of desire rippled through me. I felt my nipples and the hair on the back of my neck standing on end.

Slowly, his warm palms pushed the skirt upwards. He started to massage my calves, then rubbing circles over my knee. What the hell was he doing?

"Oh, look at all the coins in the well, what a lot of wishes, er, so what were you saying about the um, e-erotic, historical romance?" I said in a high voice, looking back at the fountain, anywhere but those eyes, fixed on me like two black pools of wine. Then I drew in my breath sharply as one hand inched above my knee to the bottom of my thigh, gently kneading and stroking and massaging. A slow, oddly affectionate smile spread over Sir C's face. It was now quite clear what he was doing: I was being seduced.

It seemed to go on for hours, me sitting there in an uneasy, embarrassed ecstasy, eyes squeezed shut, cheeks burning, breath ragged, him staring at me, and those measured, clever hands slowly slipping over my knee and thigh, as I inwardly whimpered inside up, up, up, oh please, up.

Then all of a sudden, they did shoot up and I nearly fell back into the well.

He caught me in his arms, squashing me against his

chest and I tried to wriggle away, suddenly overcome with an unexpected shame and fear.

"Your wife —" was the first line of protest I thought of.

"At home." Sir C didn't blink. Now those black eyes were only a few inches away, scanning my face, assessing fast. "Look, Olivia, "our marriage is on the rocks." I'm sure Ricky told you."

"You're not?"

"No. We've been separated for years, we both see other people. We stay together for the sake of my little girl."

"Really?" I asked disbelievingly.

"We live at opposite ends of the house. You have no idea of how much time and money divorce costs, and what with Alicià . . . come on, Olivia," he ran a leisurely hand over my breast, then downwards. "I know you want me too. You know how it's been for the last few weeks, every time you walked into my office – oh God – I wanted you so much, so much –"

He started to bruise my neck with kisses and I felt lust exploding inside like a Catherine Wheel, but somehow it was all wrong, wrong.

"Agatha, I can't do this to Agatha," I found myself murmuring lamely, and yet Agatha seemed insignificant – I just couldn't help picturing us going back to some seedy hotel and getting turfed out in a taxi. And the next morning I'd come in and he'd pass me a bundle of typing as though nothing had ever happened. After a whole evening of yearning impatience, I found myself thinking: I don't want this, it's too much, too soon . . .

I looked up at the moon, frowning down at me like a disapproving judge.

"I'm sorry," I pushed him away, "but I can't, it's not that I don't like you, I just can't be another SCG."

"S – C what?" he spat out in bewilderment.

He stepped back, looking very angry indeed. I expect he was used to having women strip for him at the click of a finger. In a flash I caught a glimpse of that big demanding ego again and I wondered why I had found him so attractive. Suddenly I found myself wishing I had stayed by Ricky's side.

"Please –" I tried to step forwards but he wouldn't budge.

I panicked, I rushed forwards and he blocked my path, then I knocked over his brandy glass from the bench and it smashed against the wood, splinters showering over the grass.

I bent down instinctively to pick it up.

"Leave it."

"But there might be a dog –"

"I said, leave it. Leave it." Snarling with exasperation, he bent down beside me.

I pretended to pick up a piece under the bench, then I jumped to my feet and made a run for it.

"Olivia! – Shit!" he cursed, cutting his hand on the glass. "Get back here! Olivia!"

Gasping for breath, terrified that he would follow, I looked back to see him by the wishing-well, stamping his foot like a Rumplestiltskin. I was reminded of my father. Being a little girl and being told off for smashing a cricket ball through the kitchen window, making a 'magic potion' out of all the ingredients in the kitchen cupboards and all the other naughty things I used to do, and back then there had been nothing I hated more than being shouted at, so I would sprint off with him calling after me, just like Sir C was doing now, *"Olivia, will you get back here now!"*

Back at the party, I ran slap-bang into Ricky.

"Are you okay?"

"I, I," I caught my breath, looking back, half expecting to see Sir C coming after me like a shadow. I gazed up at Ricky, suddenly hit with a blow of guilt. If he knew . . .

I suddenly clung to him, buried my head in his chest. His arms were around me like a cave and I felt reassured as though he was my older brother helping me down from a tree I had climbed too high.

"Oh, Ricky, let's go home," I pleaded.

"Oh, let's," he said brightly. "Leila already went off in a taxi and I'm totally bored and there's this ghastly woman who looks just like Ivana Trump who keeps following me around and pretending to pick fluff off the front of my trousers."

I laughed at him, tears filling my eyes again. After Sir C's brutal pushiness, his son was as soft and sweet as a marshmallow.

"D'you mind," I stammered nervously, seeing Sir C at the French windows, scanning the crowds for me, "d'you mind if we escape out the back? It's just that Boris is, erm, well, getting a bit over-eager again."

We wove through the crowds; then I realised I had forgotten my coat.

"I'll get it," said Ricky, hurrying off like a true gentleman.

I stood in the hallway, biting my lip, scuffing the mat, thinking hurry up, hurry up, as I watched him get waylaid by a supermodel smothering him with kisses goodbye.

Then Sir C appeared with narrowed eyes.

"Going anywhere, Olivia?" he asked coolly.

God, he was scary.

"I'm going back with Ricky."

"I don't want you to go," said Sir C. He locked a surreptitious hand around my wrist, nodding across the room as a celeb waved him hello, beckoning him over.

"He's just giving me a ride home." I stared out across the room, unable to bear to meet those dark eyes, knowing I would not be able to refuse him. Just the feel of his hands massaging mine, the intensity of his gaze, already erupted such a lava of lust that I felt so weak, I would have let him take me there and then if he wanted.

"Look at me."

"No."

"Look at me!"

I raised my eyes unwillingly.

"I'm going," I said petulantly, trying to pull my wrist away, then yelping as he bruised me with a Chinese burn.

"You're going," he said a very tight, low voice, in my ear, still nodding and smiling as celebs swirled past like a merry-go-round, "but you're going with me. Go to my car. I'll meet you in ten minutes."

I paused, scowling as he tightened the pressure. I had a sudden horrible and naughty desire to spit in his face. "Is that an order?"

His eyes caressed my face, my lips, and gently he released the grip.

"Yes."

"Alright," I said weakly, "ten minutes."

We had to climb a wall to get out and, as I sat at the top, I looked back wistfully at the party, the silhouette of party shapes, thinking: oh Sir C, I'm so sorry, so sorry . . . perhaps I even paused in the hope that he would come running out after me.

"Come on, Olivia," Ricky spread out his arms gallantly, "don't be afraid, I'll catch you."

Ricky did not catch me in his arms but broke my fall. We toppled onto the gravel, then there was a sickening rip of cloth as Ricky helped me to my feet.

"Oh shit!" I said. "Agatha's dress!" It had already been torn before, but now it was positively shredded.

"Don't worry, we can say it was all my fault. It was horrible anyway," Ricky laughed as I tried to arrange the tatters over my knees.

Ricky was very sweet; it was the first time in ages that we weren't bickering.

"I'm glad you're being normal again – for a while recently you've been really mean to me all the time," he accused me.

"Me! Huh! Must have been my PMT," I said ironically.

We continued to chatter and laugh but my mind was still on the party like a stuck record.

". . . and so I don't think I do like Leila anymore. To be honest, I think we're coming to an end."

"What?" I sat up in my seat as Ricky's words suddenly trickled through my brain. Ricky breaking up with Leila! And why was he looking at me like that! Surely . . . not. Wow, not two men in one evening! It never rains but it pours.

"The truth is," Ricky blurted out, his eyes fixed intently on the flare of his headlights, "I think I'm starting to fancy Josephine . . ."

"Oh." I sat back down on the seat. Poor Leila, my heart went out to her for a moment, then my mind snaked back inevitably to Sir C Sir C Sir C.

Back home I sat up in bed, drawing my nightdress over my knees, thinking: why, why WHY, Olivia, why didn't you get off with him? His marriage is over. He wants you. Nobody would even have had to know. It could have just been a one-off, an end to spending all those hours sitting in your office, hearing him moving about next door, fantasising about him pushing you up against the filing cabinet, pulling you down on the floor . . .

Oh God. The thought was nearly enough to give me an orgasm. Why hadn't I got off with him? I picked up a pair of scissors and viciously started to trim my split ends. It was bloody Ricky's fault, I decided, dragging me away like that. Bastard.

Suddenly, like a hologram in a *Star Wars* movie, my old 'A' English teacher, the wild-grey-haired but liberated Ms Watts appeared before me, embarrassing me as she had done many years ago, when she used to catch me looking out of the window and boom across the room, *"Oliv-ia,* why do you think Heathcliff doesn't, if indeed he doesn't, have sex with Cathy before she dies?" Or, "Olivia – don't look at the clock – do you think Jane Eyre would have been capable of having an orgasm?" How she had loved sex – medieval sex in Chaucer, repressed sex in Austen, a sexless Lady Macbeth; she got very upset when we had to study something boring like Wordsworth where trying to find innuendo was like trying to wring water out of a dry cloth.

Now she put her hands on her hips and narrowed her eyes at me like a fairy godmother whose Cinderella had made a thorough cock-up. "Olivia, you are a Nineties girl. You live in a society where you are not allowed to eat ice cream, read a book, go to the movies or wear a pair of Levis without having sex. Why did you not have sex with Sir C when you've spent the last three weeks gagging to? What's this? Hmm? An excuse note." She unfolded it and read it in disgust. "'Dear Ms Watts, I do apologise but Olivia did not have sex with Sir C because she had a sudden fit of nerves and guilt!' What's this – nerves! Poppycock! You have read every issue of *Cosmo* since you were thirteen years, you cannot claim that you have not been thoroughly educated. Guilt! Guilt! Bah, the only excuse note I accept is that Olivia did not have sex with Sir C because neither party had a condom . . . Olivia, you are condemned to a detention, a sleepless night of miserable masturbation and worry that Sir C will think you a tease, as turn-off-and-on-able as British Gas and for the next six months your sex life will continue to be as boring as Thomas the Tank Engine's . . ."

I shook myself: Olivia, you're going insane. Just calm down, take a cold shower.

But as I lay back in bed, I could feel my body throbbing with energy as though it was filled with fluttering moths.

Right, I vowed to Ms Watts, tomorrow I shall cast all morals aside. I shall get up in the morning, I shall drape myself in my slinkiest dress, that velvety one the colour of wine, and sway up to him and put my tongue in his mouth and say I'm sorry and I love you and he'll pull me down onto his lap and oh –

11. Over

The following morning, the moment I walked into my office, I could feel something was wrong. The sunlight was stagnating in pools on the floor; a bluebottle was thrashing angrily against the window.

My desk was bare. The pile of paperclips and staples and rubber bands that I kept in lakes around the desk were now all tucked away in the drawers. My yellow plastic In-Tray was empty. On my chair was a plastic bag filled with familiar things: my Snoopy address book and mascot, a can of Coke, a nail-file, my CV now encased in a new burgundy folder.

Then I heard his footsteps behind me.

"What's going on?" I stammered, even though the awful realisation was already dawning.

He wouldn't even look at me. He shoved his hands in his pockets and scowled past me to the garden. Though his voice was cool I could catch an under-current of fury.

"You can collect your things and go."

"I'm s-sorry?" I shook my head. I felt as though my ribcage was closing in, clenching in on my stomach in disbelief. "You're giving me the sack?"

"Yes," he said, with a faint note of uncertainty as if

questioning himself. Then he flicked his eyes at me as if pouring silent insults over my face. "Yes, I'm giving you the sack," he mimicked my high voice. "Get out. You're fired."

"But – but why?"

He blinked and then laughed incredulously until I felt about the size of the bluebottle at the window fighting to fly free. Then he turned to go towards the door.

"But why?" I persisted, hearing the emotion in my voice and trying to squeeze it out of it just the way he was doing. "I mean, I haven't done anything wrong. What, are you going to sack me because I won't sleep with you?"

He froze, swallowed, and took a minute or two to leash his anger. When he turned back his voice was so dangerously quiet I felt as though my body was being pricked all over with pins.

"Your services have not been satisfactory. Now, I'd like you to please leave."

"You can't do this!" I burst out, feeling tears filling my eyes. "You can't do this! I mean, it's just – it's out of order, it's sexual harassment."

"Sexual harassment!" his voice was like a whip. "How dare you! How dare you! What, with you coming in here – dressed the way you do –" instantly I pulled at the hem of my skirt, wishing I could stretch it to the ground. "Leading me on – until I..." he paused, collecting himself. "Listen, Ms Bliss," he spat out my name in sarcastic disgust, "you have nothing on me, nothing, d'you understand?" Suddenly he came towards me and I cringed, for a moment thinking he was going to hit me. Instead he grabbed my CV. "And this," he tried to thrust it into my hand but I wouldn't take it so he flipped it open, "this is total shit. Rock-climbing, Mount Snowdon, PA to Chairman of ICI. For goodness sake, d'you really think I was convinced by a word of this?"

I recoiled in shock. And there was I, thinking I'd been so clever. Oh God.

I had only ever seen him this angry with other people and had shuddered with smug relief to think that even if he snapped at me all the time, he liked me too much to get seriously mad at me. And now it was me and it was worse than any temper I'd ever seen him in.

"You really hate me, don't you?" I whimpered pathetically, unable to help myself.

He paused, taken aback, then scuffed his shoe awkwardly against the desk leg.

"I don't – no. I simply do not appreciate being lied to."

"Well, why did you take me on in the first place?" I said, trembling now because he was so close to me his suit was nearly brushing my skirt.

"Because –" he looked away, biting his teeth into his lower lip. Then suddenly he slammed the CV down on the desk, making me jump. "Look, Olivia, you had your chance and it's over, okay?"

"No," I moaned, "it's not okay. No."

"I'm sorry?" he asked incredulously. "I said, you were fired, there is no 'not okay' –"

"Well, you just asked me if I was okay –"

"You are fired, what's the matter with you?" He

119

raked his fingers through his hair as though he was dealing with a total looney.

"No," I repeated, "it's not okay." I was becoming hysterical now, and I didn't care, I just had to make him see how he was so wrong, how much I loved him, to explain everything, somehow, only the words sounded wrong, like mixed up Scrabble letters forming nonsense in a bag. "I do like you, I do like you, I just didn't know what to do, I mean I wanted you but with your wife and I love Ricky too only I was never sure I mean I wanted to write too but then I started, I mean, what did you expect me to do, and I never meant – I mean, it just happened and –" My voice was starting to rise like a banshee and we suddenly jumped at the creak of floorboards above our heads, the sound of Alicia wailing.

"Will you shut up, before my wife hears?" he demanded.

"No, but I have to explain, I mean I just didn't know what I was supposed to be I mean if you knew I was lying why didn't you fire me, I mean did you want a mistress –"

"Will you *shut up*!" He clamped his hand over my mouth and I shut up. He was standing so close to me my thighs were pressed up against his. They felt hard and muscular. Suddenly I felt turned inside out with longing. His eyes, almost weary now, travelled over my face and mouth, his hand slackening until there was just the tip of his thumb caressing the outline of my lips, the cleft of my chin. Then he frowned and pulled away, shaking away his hand as though it was polluted. He walked to the door, kicked it open, muttered, "Get out" and walked off. I started to cry, loudly, so that he would come back and say I was forgiven, but all I heard was the thunderous slam as he retreated to the cave of his office.

Back home, I managed to pretend for three days that I was just taking leave off work because I had been so efficient.

I wrote him letters. Apologies. A thank-you letter for such a delightful party. I did about twenty drafts – different coloured paper, Biro or fountain-pen, a hundred different openings (Sir C, Sir Henry Caldwell, Dear Henry) and a hundred different endings (Love, Olivia, With very best wishes, Olivia, Thanking you so much, Olivia Bliss). Finally, I sent it to his office and put on the envelope, '*Urgent*', then added '*Private*', then thought it looked totally stupid so I Tippex-ed it out and wrote '*Confidential*' over the top.

But I never received a reply.

Then, on Saturday morning, I broke down. I tried to call him, only to hear a crisp female voice on the end:

"Good morning, Sir Henry Caldwell's office?"

Oh my God! Four days, just four days and he had replaced me! I could just tell from the clipped syllables that she was marvellously efficient.

She said he was too busy to speak to me, so I tried again, but he was in a meeting, and then again, but it was engaged, and then again, but he was still in a meeting.

"It must be a very long meeting," I said sourly, and slammed down the phone and burst into tears just as Ricky and Josephine walked into the living-room, arguing over whether to videotape *Gladiators* or *Blind Date* that evening.

"Olivia?" Ricky came bounding over to cuddle me. "Whatever is it?"

"I've been fired," I said in a dull voice, gripping the cushion.

"What? But, why? Only the other week, he told me you were the best PA he's ever had."

"I – he – I –" my voice cracked, "I – I dropped a whole bottle of Tippex over the floor, and it went e – everywhere, and so he fired me . . ."

"What!" Ricky proceeded to rant on about his dad having a mad temper, but his bark was far worse than his bite. He was just on the horrific verge of calling Sir C up to sort it all out, when Josephine, who had been watching me with quiet, narrowed eyes, suddenly tugged me up off the sofa.

"Olivia and I are going to Haagen Dazs," she said, pulling me outside to her Ford. "We need to have a little chat."

I wept and wept all the way to Haagen Dazs. Even Josephine's wild driving, which averages a usual ninety miles per hour down a suburban street, failed to cheer and exhilarate me. We sat in the cafe, ordering huge chocolate sundaes with lots of extra chocolate sauce and chocolate bits and chocolate brownie lumps. Josephine licked her spoon, sighed, and said,

"So how long have you been fucking?"

"What?" A huge lump of ice cream slid down me, my shocked stomach clenching at the melting cold.

"Olivia, it's so obvious. The skirts you wore – you – working *late* on *Fridays*."

"Oh God, d'you think Ricky's guessed! He'd kill me, Josephine, he has this thing about how his mother was so ideal and nobody can replace her."

"Oh no, Ricky would never even think . . . funny," Josephine sucked thoughtfully, "how men with such a drive for success have such big sex drives. Look at Bill Clinton. Must all be linked with testosterone."

"I'm not . . . sleeping with him, though," I wailed. "This is the whole problem."

I then poured out the whole story to Josephine, who didn't look nearly as surprised as I'd expected her to, not even when I told her about the sacking.

"So now what do I do?" I sobbed into my sundae. "How do I get him back?"

"You don't," said Josephine. "You just leave it. Come on, Olivia, it's a complete mess. Anyway, you should never chase men, you should let them chase you, and then run, only not so fast that they can't catch you... No, Olivia, once you fall off a horse, you have to get right back up or you'll never regain your confidence."

"But–"

"No buts. We're going to the Hippodrome."

The next morning, after a complete failure of a night where Josephine pulled everything in sight and I ended up being chatted up by a dwarf because I felt sorry for him ("I told you to get back on a horse, not a pony!" Josephine had hissed) she gave me another frightful telling off and then flung me a newspaper.

"Thought you should see this," she said, with a sigh.

My fingers tightened around the newspaper. It was a picture of Sir C – Sir C! Looking all grim and serious in black tie, the flashbulb blinding his eyes. Looking closer, I saw Alan Titschmarsh behind him and realised it had been taken at the party.

Caldwell's Latest Publishing Protégéé, screamed the headlines.

Lily Knife was eighteen years old, a juvenile delinquent from Ireland who had written a book called *Bitch Addict* about a heroine who suffered from nymphomania, alcoholism and heroin addiction. In the photos, she looked dangerous and beautiful, with long strawberry-coloured hair and slanting green cat eyes. Sir C had given her a £200,000 advance.

I felt my heart seize up in pain. Behind Josephine, I could see Ms Watts sailing in with a shaking head.

"I told you so . . ." Ms Watts cooed. "Balls in the hand are worth two in the bush. Let a man fly away and he may never return . . ."

12. Arrested

Then I came up with a plan. One last go. One last chance to get him.

I enlisted Josephine as my partner in crime.

"Alright," she finally gave in, in exasperation, "but if we don't get in, then you have to promise we can go to the Hippodrome."

Instead of putting on something smart and sensible like my white linen suit, I found myself randomly throwing on a white sleeveless T-shirt and a tasselled skirt I normally only reserve for when I am doing painting or gardening, since it is covered with weird red and yellow blotches from a failed attempt at tie-dyeing it with beetroot and turnips.

I looked at myself in the mirror and I looked awful, but I just didn't care. I was feeling in a funny mood that night. Somehow reckless and naughty. It was as though everything I was doing was motivated by an inexplicable desire to really wind Sir Caldwell up.

"Oh, you can't wear that!" said Josephine in shock. She was wearing a floaty white dress that made her look like a water nymph.

"I can wear whatever I like," I said, wondering whether to spray rainbow streaks in my hair, or was that taking it too far? "Come on, let's go down to the pub and get pissed."

Josephine gave me a very funny look.

"From the way you're behaving, I would have thought you'd been at the booze already."

The launch party was being held at a posh hotel in Leicester Square. By the time we got there, we were both fairly drunk, though I was much worse than Josephine. We hovered at the end of the road, watching swanky couples emerge from swish cars, dripping gold jewellery and cuff links. The women looked very Ivana Trump.

We crept forwards and then knelt down on the kerb behind a Jaguar to confer and size up the bouncer. He was dark, very good-looking and looked as though he knew it. We overheard him chatting and his accent was Italian.

"Hey, cool," I whispered, or thought I whispered to Josephine, "you know what Italians are like, they can never resist women."

"Shut up, Olivia!" said Josephine. "No need to shout it out all over the place."

"So this is the plan," I said. "You say you're going to sleep with him and then you tell him to go away and get a condom and we run in –"

"I'm not going to say I'm going to sleep with him, you say you're going to sleep with him –"

At which point the Jaguar in front of us rolled away and we nearly fell off the kerb in shock. Quickly assembling ourselves, we approached the bouncer, smiling sweetly and batting our eyelids. He looked us up and down very sleazily and I gave him a come-hither smile.

Then Josephine did the pretending to rummage through her handbag trick.

"Oh, gosh," she said in a very posh voice, forcing him to take hold of her tubs of Oil of Ulay and Revlon mascara while she searched the dark depths of her Gucci, "goodness knows where I've put them . . ."

"Oh Josephine, you haven't lost the invites, have you?" I chided her, rolling my eyes and tut-tutting at the bouncer, who merely raised a very disbelieving eyebrow.

The bouncer handed back Josephine her tubs without blinking a lid.

"No tickets, no in," he said.

"But we can't go all the way back and get them," I wailed. I saw Josephine making frantic signals but I was utterly indignant.

"Oh come on," I said drunkenly, "you're Italian, aren't you? I mean, what's the point of being Italian if you're not going to give in to female charms. What's the matter with you, you're letting your entire race down, it's a travesty!" I felt someone looming up behind me and I turned to see a very beautiful red-haired girl, in purple velvet, giving me a very smirky look. Her partner, who was a tall, dark sex-god shared a nasty smile with her.

Then I realised who she was: Lily Knife.

"Olivia, let's get out of here." Josephine yanked me away.

"I don't believe I'm doing this!" Josephine moaned two minutes later.

Then,

"Ow, be careful with my dress, it will rip!"

Then,

"I've got stuck, I've got stuck!"

"No, just pull your stomach in. You shouldn't have had so much dinner."

"Olivia, my waist is twenty-three inches – according to *Cosmo* –"

She let out a slight shriek as I gave her a last pull and she nearly ended up falling into the toilet, but thankfully I broke her fall. As she grabbed me to sustain her balance, however, she ripped my tie-dye skirt.

"Oh shit, I'm sorry," she murmured.

"S'alright," I shrugged. "It looks quite sexy, like a slit up the side."

We put our ears to the toilet door for a moment to see if we could catch any voices in the ladies'. The door swung and then there was only running water: the coast seemed to be clear.

We walked out of the toilet and Josephine let out a scream.

We were in the mens', and two middle-aged men in suits were relieving themselves opposite us. One of them was Sir C.

Josephine started to go quickly into reverse, but I hurried her forwards. As we ran out in a flurry of giggles, Sir C caught my eye in the mirror and gave me a very dangerous look.

"Oh, Olivia, let's go to the Hippodrome," Josephine moaned as we stood on the outskirts, nibbling chocolate animal biscuits and downing glasses of raspberry punch.

Lily Knife was standing in the centre of a large crowd of journalistic and literary admirers, humming carelessly to a Tori Amos song in the background. I noticed that though they hung onto her every word, they also maintained a slightly nervous distance, like tourists fascinated by a tiger but not wanting to get too near the cage.

"What do you say to the accusation that *Bitch Addict* was written for you by a ghost writer?" asked one chap ultra-casually, munching on a canapé.

"I say shit to any cunt who made such an accusation, I'd cut off their balls and sue them for every fucking last penny," Lily delivered in a silky voice, with the most syrupy of feminine smiles, as the poor bloke nearly choked on his canapé.

I noticed Sir C emerging from the toilets and joining the throngs of Lily fans. Noticing me, he shot me a glance so cold it was amazing I didn't freeze into an ice statue like the victims of the White Witch in Narnia. I downed my punch defiantly.

"Oh, Olivia," Josephine said urgently, "can't we go to the Hippodrome? I'm going. I mean it. I'll go without you."

"Hang on." I turned unsteadily, hearing a distinctive voice, fuzzy at first, then growing more fine-tuned, like a TV aerial coming into focus.

"Oh, Calvin, you naughty man, not in front of everyone!"

I had to be hallucinating. But no, it wasn't the drink. It was *my mother.*

She was looking sensational. She was squashed, albeit somewhat too tightly, into a red taffeta dress with a ra-ra skirt, her hair, now dyed black, piled up on her head, fastened with red and gold combs, gypsy earrings dangling from her ears. And she was hanging onto the arm of the Italian bouncer.

Every head turned to look at her, while I tried to hide behind Josephine who (the disloyal moo), refusing to play any part in the inevitable social embarrassment, hissed, "I'm going to the Hippo!" and ran off.

Lily looked rather pissed off that the spotlight had swung away from her. Then a slow, triumphant smile crept across her face as Mum, who had clearly had as much to drink as me, tripped up over her partner's foot and practically threw herself into Sir C's arms.

As she fell to the floor, her skirt rucked up to reveal a pair of very sexy leopardskin knickers. I noticed the bouncer paused for a good ogle before helping her to her feet.

"Oh dear oh me, oh my . . ." Mum drew in her breath, fluffing her dark curls that were now exploding all over the place like springs from an old mattress. "I *am* sorry, darling," she said to Sir C, who seemed to draw back into his suit like a tortoise in its shell.

She was just taking off her shoes and plonking them into Sir C's hands, complaining that she'd made the silly mistake of buying them a size too small, when she spotted me.

"*Olivia!* What are you doing here!"

I was about to ask the same, but had my mouth full of chocolate biscuit, so all I could do was smile sweetly.

She promptly introduced me to her new beau who gave me a slimy smile.

"This is Calvin and he is a bouncer."

"What do you bounce?"

"Now, don't be silly, Olivia, now, look, this couldn't be better, you *must* talk to Leila about your book."

For a moment I was confused: I thought Leila was at home with Ricky watching the World Cup. Then I cringed as Mum pulled Lily Knife's arm and practically yanked her over into our circle.

"Leila, this is my daughter, Olivia, and she's dying to get published. You must hobnob and share secrets. Maybe Leila can give you some tips!" my mother cried.

Lily looked me up and down and said charmingly,

"You and your mother are so alike."

"Olivia used to write the most lovely childrens' books when she was a little girl," my mother fluttered on. "D'you remember those little books about Polly Fruit Pastilles and Kevin the Kit Kat and she did all the little pictures in felt-tip too."

"Really, what a prodigy," said Lily. Ugh, how I ached to grab one of her stupid books and ram it down her smug swan's throat. "Well, must mingle," she added, and swirled off, rolling her eyes incredulously.

Mum did not stop there. I had only just got her under control from chasing back after Lily, when she set her sights on Sir C.

"Goodness, he does look like Jeremy Irons, doesn't he?" she murmured throatily, much to my and Calvin's horror. Then, before I could do a thing, she was purring in his direction, and as I heard the distinct phrases, "Olivia . . . writer . . . Polly Fruit Pastilles . . .

did all her own coloured pictures . . ." the raspberry punch swirled uneasily in my stomach.

I turned to Calvin, who was nibbling desperately on a chocolate animal monkey biscuit. Right, I thought, in inebriated fury, if my mum is going to try and nick my man, then I am nicking hers. Tit for tat.

Then I saw my mum beckoning me over and mouthing, "Stop monopolising Calvin." I pretended not to notice. Then she suddenly grabbed Sir C's hands and tried to get him to ballroom dance with her – singularly inappropriate in any case, with *Bolero* playing in the background – and the way she was wiggling, she looked as though she was doing the Birdy Song. Sir C simply looked incredulous.

I couldn't take anymore – I fled to the toilets, ignoring her calls as I passed her.

After twenty minutes of trying to splash water on my face and sober up enough so that I could take control of the situation and get Mum home, edging towards the door and then bolting back in dread of having to go out there and face everyone, I came out of the ladies' and ran slap-bang into Sir C.

For a moment, he stared down at me. Then he grabbed my hand and I found myself being dragged down a maze of corridors.

"What are you doing?" I murmured. "Am I going to be taken to your office and caned?" Or something equally inappropriate and cringeful, but luckily he didn't seem to hear.

I was so hammered I tripped over his shoe, pulling out his shoelace, and nearly brought him down to the floor with me. He paused, glaring down at me.

"You're drunk and making a complete idiot out of yourself, you look a complete state, what the hell are you wearing that skirt for? Your crazy friend isn't helping either."

"She's my mum. Now you see where I get it from."

I hung my head. I simply couldn't bear him to be so angry with me. Lurching forwards, I curled my arms around his waist and pressed up against his chest, feeling the wiry cage of his back, but his body remained taut, unyielding.

"Olivia, take your hands off me," he ordered.

"No," I mumbled sulkily into his chest. I was aware that I was behaving like a small kid, like the way Alicia would sit on her dad's foot and refuse to let him move, begging him not to go to work but play with her instead.

A couple came running into the corridor and, seeing us, quickly backed out again. Sir C, as red as a tomato, prised my hands angrily away. Then he grabbed my elbow and called for his driver. Within seconds a large meaty black guy with a bristly black goatee beard came striding down the corridor. Sir C handed me over to him as though I was a piece of old meat. Hearing him barking instructions, I hung my head in misery again. God, this was turning out to be the most embarrassing night of my life.

Sir C strode back into the hall without looking back. The driver eyed me up. Despite his hulkish build, he had the softest chocolate-brown eyes, and he clucked his tongue and said lightly,

"Come then, honey, let's get you out of here without any fuss."

He strolled down the corridor and I followed meekly behind. Passing by the party, I caught a glimpse of my mother, now safely back with Calvin again, giggling her drunk hyena laugh.

Outside, the driver opened up the door of a long Mercedes.

"Has it got a swimming-pool in the back?" I asked cheekily. He rolled his eyes and gently pushed me in. Then he got into the front and the car rolled away.

Fraught with nerves, I flicked on the small TV and watched *Beavis and Butthead* without taking in a word. I was seriously considering jumping out halfway but, when I tried the door, all the locks were firmly shoved down. I started giggling again, almost hysterical. In the front mirror, I saw the driver eyeing me up uneasily, perhaps worried I was so drunk I would spew across his plush black seats.

The car came to a halt. The road seemed blurrily familiar. Then, as he opened the door, I gasped with surprise: it was Sir C's Primrose Hill house and office. I had expected to be turfed out at the nearest tube station.

"What's going on?" I asked the driver as we went into the house, but he merely pushed me down the hallway and into Sir C's office and told me to sit still.

Shit, I thought, sitting down on the same chair I had once curled up on while taking dictation, this is serious stuff. I felt as though I had been taken to a police station and Sir C was a high court judge, about to sweep in and pronounce a thirty-year sentence at any moment. Oh, why the hell had I gate-crashed? I wondered if he really might have me arrested and tried to form excuses in my mind, like I was feeling emotionally fraught because my mother was pregnant. Perhaps I should pretend my father had died and I was drinking away my sorrows and could take no responsibility for a temporary moment of insanity . . .

Hearing a car roll up outside, I leapt to the blinds but it was another neighbour.

I threw myself back down on the desk, anger starting to steamroll over my fear. What right did he have to bring me here and lock me up like this? I'd been here, what, half an hour already. I knew perfectly well it was one of his torturous waiting games, but that still didn't stop my stomach fluttering with nerves.

On the desk was a brand new shiny diary. I flipped through, examining Ms French's neat, primary school-teacher pencil marks. Christ, she was organised. I'd never managed to have a diary. Feeling a spurt of jealous anger, I couldn't resist scribbling 'Vasectomy, 12pm' under 12th December. Giggling again, my eyes wandered over the desk, assessing what other damage I could do.

I was just trying on a few of Sir C's smart hats and doing a Groucho impression in the mirror, when the door opened and he walked in. Instantly I took off the hat and stood upright, like a solider being brought to attention. He walked towards me and stopped, feet apart, slowly pulling off his gloves, thwacking them nastily against each other.

"I'm really sorry," I blurted out. "Please forgive me?"

"You've been very bad. I don't know if I can."

Then, as my eyes travelled reluctantly upwards, I saw exasperation in his eyes – but it was affectionate, he was laughing, not frowning, and before I knew it his mouth was hard on mine and his knee was prising open my legs and we were kissing as though we wanted to gobble each other up for breakfast, lunch and supper. Still, I couldn't quite take it in, couldn't even feel a twinge of desire, just the blankness of shock.

"I'm sorry about gate-crashing – and Agatha – and everything –" I blurted out nervously as he slipped his hands around my wrists like handcuffs.

"You are a naughty girl," he said with frightening severity. "But I shall tell you off later."

Nearly crying with relief, I pressed my forehead against the comforting white starch of his shirt, breathing in the familiar smell of his expensive cologne, a black chest-hair poking through, tickling my eyelash. His hands travelled over my head, my neck, my back. I felt his body stiffening with desire, heard the raggedness of his breath and looked up and then my face was in his hands and he was kissing me again.

He kissed me and kissed me and kissed me and then pulled me against him, groaning and holding me so tightly I could hardly breathe. I stared at a photograph of Sir C shaking hands with Maggie Thatcher. The figures kept swimming in and out of drunken focus.

Sir C bent down and put his tongue in my ear, breathing, "Oh God, I want to fuck you, I could take you here and now."

Then he pulled away, snapped, "Wait here!" and I heard him dismissing the driver.

I collapsed into the chair, shaking with disbelief. I

still couldn't quite compute. I'd given up all hope after rejecting him at the party. I'd never even expected him to speak to me again, and yet only a week later to the very day, here we were, and it was happening, it was *really* happening. Wow.

Then the bliss hit me and I spun round in the chair, giggling as, through my already double vision, the room swirled into a grey blur. I whooped with delight. I was about to become a fully fledged member of SCG and it was the most wonderful night of my life.

Tomorrow would be a day to regret everything.

But tonight was time to give into temptation, and Sir C was just so delicious and he had said his wife was disloyal and he was just so macho and fierce and hurrah – after so many awful gropings and washing-machine snogs in nightclubs, I was finally going to be made love to by surely one of the most virile and exciting and powerful men I'd met in my entire life, oh God, what was he doing out there, come on, come on.

Hearing footsteps, I jumped up and there he was in the doorway, tall and broad and brutal.

He stood there for a moment, staring at me with such a searing, hot-blooded gaze that I felt my insides turn to mush and my thighs burn with longing.

There was a funny look in his eyes. Somehow triumphant, a bit *veni vidi vici*. He'd got me at last.

He turned and shut the door, turning the key, and went to pull down the blinds. I leaned awkwardly against the desk as he came towards me, his eyes glinting in the elderberry darkness. He paused veeringly, like a cobra waiting to strike.

Then he cupped my chin in his hands and leaned

down and kissed me with brutal force, plunging his tongue into my mouth, pinning his heavy body against me. Then those huge hands were going everywhere, slipping up my roll-neck, his lovely wet groping mouth on my neck as I arched back in ecstasy. Used to gradual foreplay and gentle caresses, I had never been so half-thrilled, half-frightened or evoked such raging lust. He pulled back, his breathing hoarse and ragged as though he was about to climax then and there.

"Undress for me," he ordered.

My inebriated striptease came to an abrupt halt when the roll-neck got caught around my head and I had to murmur for help through a mouthful of wool. As he laughed hoarsely and tugged it off, his hands caressed the undersides of my arms, then delved into the lace of my bra, dragging down the straps. Picking me up by the waist, he hitched me up on the desk, his teeth and tongue grazing my nipples as he pushed up the tie-dye skirt and then yanked down my tights.

Crash! went an entire box of filing as he pushed me down onto the desk. I sat up in alarm but he pushed me back down, undoing his trousers with desperate, shaking hands.

Crash! went a pile of proposals as he pushed my legs apart and then plunged inside. I normally liked a long build-up but I had never been made love to so vehemently that I found my breathing quickening and my mind swimming as desire tidal-waved over me.

"Don't close your eyes, I want to see you come," he ordered. His dark wolf eyes, turned yellow by a passing car's headlamps, bored into mine as I opened my mouth in a helpless 'O' of pleasure.

I took it as a great sign of his esteem that he didn't even care when, in the final flourishes of our orgasm, his beloved Japanese paperweight went flying off and smashed into a thousand silver smithereens.

The next morning, I woke up feeling dire.

My head felt like a shattered mirror. My eyes burned as though filled with sand and my stomach was jumping like a bullfrog on heat. The first thing I did was to rush to the toilet and throw up.

"Bit too much to drink?" Leila said slyly. Then she offered, quite nicely, to make some tomato juice but I just shook my head.

I dragged myself back to my bedroom and pulled the covers up over my head, willing the world to disappear. Oh hell. The events of the night before reasserted themselves like the pieces of a jigsaw puzzle. My mother. Climbing into the toilet. And sleeping with Sir Henry Caldwell!

A thrill of erotic shock jolted me as I remembered the heat of his mouth on mine.

After our lovemaking, we had nestled up beside each other on the carpet. He had finally woken me with a kiss at four in the morning, massaging my stiff cramped limbs, and called up his driver to take me home. The London streets had been deserted, pale blue in the pre-dawn light. It had all been like a dream as he kissed me goodbye and then held me tight to his chest with surprising affection. As the car had driven away I had waved him goodbye until he was a forlorn silhouette in the distance.

But there could be no way that he could be serious

about me. I was just another chocolate in his box of female delights. He was probably waking up in Lily's bed that very minute.

"Well, Ms Watts, what do you have to say to that?" I tried to summon my hologram for advice but she obstinately refused to materialise.

I punched the pillow miserably and went down to seek Josephine out for reassurance.

She was not very reassuring at all.

"Well," she concluded, after agreeing with me that I had been used and abused and he would never call and even if he did I would only end up no better than a mistress, "just consider it as a great sexual experience which may never be repeated again in your remaining sixty or so years on this planet."

"Oh, thanks for making me feel so optimistic about my future, Josephine," I said suicidally, as she went back to filling out a *Cosmo* beauty quiz on *How Sexy Are You?*

"No problem," said Josephine, triumphantly concluding from a predominance of a's that she was very sexy indeed.

Then the phone rang.

My insides turned to sunshine. I recognised that deep, brisk, gruff voice right away. Suddenly the whole of the rest of my life was worth living after all.

"What the fuck is going on?"

"What?" I jumped.

"It's now nine fifteen. You're fifteen minutes late." Now there was a faint humour playing in his voice.

I laughed in weak relief.

"But – but what about Ms French?"

"I fired her."

"But – but, surely you can't do that . . . ?"

"I can do anything I want – now I suggest you get over here – before I dock your pay."

13. Dirty Weekend

A week later, as Sir C had threatened, I received a package through the post. It was naughty underwear packed in plush purple crushed velvet, with a few individually wrapped praline chocolates and a single red rose with a note attached.

"Goodness, real silk!" Josephine picked up the knickers, red with black lace, holding them up to the light.

I jumped, quickly trying to fold the wings of the box back down, as she picked up the note and read, "'Wear them for me this weekend'. Oh I see, going on a dirty weekend, are we?"

"Don't say that!" I said furiously. "We're going away, to cover some work, and – and – also, if there's time left, to do some sight-seeing too." I looked down, fingering the underwear uneasily. Normally I just wore cotton stuff from M&S and this silky stuff seemed to be severely lacking in material – there were low cuts and gaps where presumably one should bulge sexily but I was sure it would just sag unbecomingly.

Josephine cocked her head to one side and gave me an *as if* smile.

"So?" she whispered. "How's it going?"

"Okay." I paused. Sir C had made me swear not to

tell a single soul, but I was bursting to tell someone. "Actually, brill! He said he's going to leave his wife!"

"Really?" Josephine didn't look quite as impressed as I'd imagined. "When?"

"Well. Soon. I mean, it's not such a good time now, with his wife being ill, and his daughter and everything, and he's in the middle of a publishing deal. But there's no hurry," I echoed his words.

"Oh, that old chestnut!" Josephine said, shaking her fringe out of her beautiful eyes. "Really, Olivia, that line is becoming more of a cliché than 'D'you come here often?'"

"No – but – he said, he would, he meant it, he promised me."

"When?"

"Soon."

"Olivia, married men are like politicians. They make promises, and the likelihood of them happening are slim, and if they do, it's normally near election time i.e. much too late in the day."

I frowned in confusion. Trust Josephine to pour her oil of cynicism all over my sea of bliss. She was always doing this with my boyfriends. I would build up my feelings like a precarious house of cards and just when I was putting the last one on, labelled '*I think this is Love*', she would drop lightly, '*I think he has big ears*' or, '*Was it me, or does he smell?*' and blow the whole lot toppling down.

"If he doesn't come out soon I'm going to have to go," she snapped irritably, her scarlet nails tapping impatiently against her briefcase.

"I'm really sorry, I'll just try him again," I said with a syrupy apologetic smile, though inwardly I was seething as much as the journalist. Finally, he picked up. "Er, Jennifer Apsley from *The Sunday Times* is still waiting, and, er, I think she's quite keen to get moving," I said.

"Okay, be along shortly," he said easily.

"But I think –" But he had cut me off. I smiled at Ms Apsley and assured her that he would be along shortly. Though by Sir C's standards that could be any time between now and midnight. God, why did he have to keep people waiting like this? I had passed by his office and all he was doing was feeding his silly bird. It was just another one of his petty games, just as he would have me turn up at seven thirty one morning for 'urgent' business and then not come in till ten himself. Just to prove he was boss.

"Ah, Jennifer." He suddenly appeared in the doorway, reaching forward to shake her hand, simply oozing polite charm and apologies. Suddenly Jennifer became all fluttery, silking back her coiffeured blonde hair and saying it was quite all right, she knew he must be a very busy man.

Sir C took her into the study and buzzed me for tea. I tried hard not to bang the teacups but he still scowled pointedly at me, and then found an invisible chip in Jennifer's cup and sent me back for a replacement. Returning, I banged it down so hard he snapped lightly,

"Careful, or you'll put a chip in that one too."

Jennifer folded her stockinged legs, putting her tape recorder on the table and waited pointedly for me to go. As I went to the door I tapped my watch pointedly at Sir C, with a silent message to hurry up, but he just looked away pretending not to see.

Back in my office, I had a good mind to walk off and desert him. It was supposed to be the start of our dirty weekend and we should have left at lunchtime. Now we would hit the rush hour and turn up too late for dinner and I would be completely bag-eyed and knackered.

I was terrified enough about the dirty weekend as it was. Our first consummation had had a kind of spontaneity, an innocence. Now his expectations would be high. He had probably slept with hundreds of girls. All day my head had whirled: what if I'm not up to his sexual marathons and he thinks the underwear looks dreadful and I can't do position 78 because I'm not flexible and then he steals away in the night leaving me to pay the bill?

Was I really fit for a dirty weekend? I could feel Ms Watts bearing on me again, pinched with disapproval.

"But look," I tried to appeal to her, "other than Sir C I've only ever slept with one other guy. I'm not very good at blowjobs, I always bite too hard – I mean, I'm slightly better at handjobs but my arm always starts to ache and then I have to swop sides but my left arm muscles are even weaker so I have to swop again and oh dear oh dear oh dear . . ."

We finally left at six o'clock. Instantly, we hit the rush hour, jammed in a tooting caterpillar. I could tell at once from the furrowed brow and muscle twitching in his cheek that he was rapidly sinking into a foul mood. He drove very fast and very aggressively, honking and overtaking and swearing, "Get the hell out of the way, you *idiot!*" or, "Move, move," or, "Oh Christ, not a learner, for fuck's sake!" You could almost feel his anger bristling off him like the voltage from an electric fence.

I sat back, just relieved that we had finally got away, winding down the window and feeling the spring breeze in my hair and listening to R4 gardening tips. As the journey went by, the sharp geometric lines of the city softened into the dusky voluptuousness of the countryside, tooting was replaced by mooing and rushing streams, exhaust fumes by dung and blossom perfume.

Sir C seemed to relax too, loosening his tie and propping his elbow up on the window.

We hit another traffic jam in Oxford and he put a hand on my knee and smiled at me.

"Happy?"

I laughed, simply happy now that he was happy again, and then gasped as his hand slipped under my skirt and then up my thigh.

"Just checking to see if you were wearing them," he said lightly, which of course I was.

His black eyes held mine, my stomach dissolved with lust. Then he drew his hand away quickly as car horns honked behind us.

"Oops, don't want to be arrested for indecent exposure," he laughed, and drove on.

Woodstock was a lovely sleepy village with cottagey tea and souvenir shops, cobbled streets and winding lanes and all of those things a country village ought to possess.

Our B & B was an equally lovely red-brick house on the corner, our hostess a warm middle-aged lady who asked if we had had a good journey, said wasn't the traffic a nightmare and she had dinner saved for us in the oven.

Our room was clean, painted soft peach and beige, with a colossal king-size bed with a frilly white counterpane.

We were both ravenous, so we decided to eat before unpacking. The menu looked lovely: Yorkshire pudding, fresh vegetables that you could tell were home-grown and would explode with flavour when you crunched them in your mouth.

But, in the foyer, disaster struck.

"Don't move," Sir C hissed in my neck.

"What!"

"That man," he nudged me gently. "You see the one sitting in the far corner? Over there? I know him."

"So?"

"I *know* him. Get into the car."

"What!"

"Get into the car. We're going somewhere else."

"But who cares if he sees? We can just say we're here on business. I like it here." I could feel my voice rising petulantly and an elderly couple edging down the stairs gave us a curious glance.

Sir C slipped his hand under my elbow and pinched it cruelly. I yelped.

"*Get into the car.* Wait for me there. Right?"

I sat in the car, smouldering, biting my nails, as he came out with the cases and packed them back into the boot.

"So what now? We're going to drive all the way back home?" I tried to keep the tears out of my voice. "Well, I suppose by the time we get back to London, we can be just in time for the morning rush hour."

"No, we're going to find somewhere else," he asserted.

It was easier said than done. We bounced down country lanes, past little cottages where plump sweet ladies shook their heads regretfully; they had only one room, sorry, it was a busy time, they were full, they had one room but no double bed, try down the road, sorry. I folded my arms and bit my lip to stop myself spitting out: *told you so*.

We followed the directions and bumped down a ruckerty lane that came to a dead end with a long, iron gate leading to nowhere but fields upon fields. Sir C chugged to an exasperated halt, slamming his fist on the steering wheel. For a moment we sat in silence. A few cows stirred, mooing curiously and then advanced towards us, poking their heads over the fence, their eyes lolling mockingly at us humans ending up in the middle of nowhere. Sir C sighed, revved up the car. It refused to move. He tried again. The tyres, grinding in the wet mud, merely spat up brown sludge. We were stuck.

"Nice one," I said. "So now what do we do?"

"Don't start," said Sir C. "Everything is under control."

He slammed the door shut and strode on ahead. My thin strappy silver sandals pegged in the mud as I hurried to keep up with him. He marched down a row of ramshackle farmhouses, then finally spotting a B&B

notice, rapped on a door. Instantly there was a tantivy of wild barking and howling. Finally, the door was answered by a little old hag with frizzy black hair, who just about managed to hold back her pack of German Shepherds and terriers, their teeth glinting as they bounded up against her arms.

Sir C gave a polite ahem and bowed his head.

"We want a room," he said. "A double room. And help to carry our cases. Our car's stuck."

"We've got no room." She shook her head, pushing the door, but Sir C stuck his shoe firmly in the gap.

What the hell is he doing? I rolled my eyes, turning away in despair, gazing back down the muddy lane. How could our wonderful dirty weekend feeding each other peaches and champagne on frilly counterpanes have come to this?

To my amazement, Sir C's persistence seemed to be paying off. He had a certain manner of speaking when he was determined to get his way, his voice low, almost hypnotic, his tone polite but refusing to accept the possibility of 'no'.

"Alright," she caved in at last, "you can have the two at the back, but I should warn you they haven't been properly cleaned and there'll be an extra charge of thirty pounds for such short notice."

"Fine," said Sir C, peeling the notes from his brown leather wallet. "You see," he swivelled his head back at me, "we shall still save ourselves at least forty pounds."

We saw why when we got upstairs. The two rooms were like shoeboxes with about enough room to fit the beds and our cases. The beds consisted of metal grids with slim army mattresses. As he sat down on his bed, it caved in until the springs nearly touched the floor. Still, Sir C smiled as though he was lounging on a king-size in the Hilton.

"Well," he said, determined as ever never to be wrong, "not so bad? And it's only for one night. Now why don't you unpack and hang up my suits while I use the bathroom."

I unzipped his navy case. All his clothes were impeccable, expensive, sporting designer labels, everything so perfectly folded that I almost feared Agatha might have done it. Such a contrast to my battered old brown suitcase which as usual I had packed at the last minute, bunging everything in and then making Leila sit on the lid while I did the zip up.

He returned from the bathroom looking relaxed and refreshed. It was the first time I had seen him properly without clothes – well, apart from the white towel slung around his hips. His tan was mahogany, and he was muscly, no doubt from so much tennis, and yet slightly saggy at the same time – just a faint middle-age spread beginning to unfold around his elegant hips.

But gosh, he did look yummy with his dark hair slicked back from his face, accentuating his angular Jeremy Irons cheekbones.

"I need a massage, I'm still achy."

Well, this was copable. In fact, it was all rather fun. He lay down and did his *Daily Telegraph* crossword and I knelt beside him and rubbed my hands all over his smooth scented back, kneading my own aggravation out as well as his. He gave *mmms* and sighs of pleasure, in between snarling, "Left to rot, eight letters, who the hell does these crosswords?" but as ever he bulleted his way to the end, then tossed it aside and buried his face in the pillow and said,

"Harder, pretend I'm a lump of dough."

But I had never baked bread, and besides, I didn't like to hurt him.

"My masseuse Pamela does it much harder," he said, pushing me down beside him.

"I wish I had a masseur, a nice slinky Spanish boy," I said, to annoy him.

He ignored me and picked up my hands, examining them.

"Well, I shall forgive you. You have the most delicate hands, like a nun." He locked them into his big ones. "Do you play the piano?"

"No, I used to play the violin. I failed grade five twice and gave up, I was so crap!"

He gave me a look that nearly blew my skin away.

"Why don't go and get ready for bed?" he said.

In the bathroom, the taps belched out a stream of filthy urine. The toilet did not have a lid; the water was a festering black liquid. I picked up my toothbrush and put it down, my stomach turning. When I went to the loo I had to wipe myself with a few old tissues.

I stared at the fragments of my face in the cracked mirror, and felt those prickles of anger unfolding again, and I thought: this is not funny. How can he treat me like this? As if I'm some hooker to be hidden away out of sight? If we had left on time we could have found somewhere else much nicer. He hadn't given my happiness a second thought. He hadn't even said sorry.

But at the thought of starting an argument at this

time of night, I felt myself wilt. It would be so easy just
to swallow my anger, to pretend I didn't really mind,
and after all I didn't really mind that much, it was just
enough to be with him . . .

"No, Olivia," I hissed to my reflection, "you may as
well lie on your back and write 'Doormat'. You are
going to be assertive."

With a beating heart, I returned to his room and told
him that I was tired and needed to sleep and that I
would see him tomorrow.

"Fine," he said abruptly, switching off his light, but
I could tell by the look on his face that he understood
the point I was making.

I retreated to my room and pulled the thin sheets
over me. Through the scraps of cloth masquerading as
curtains, I gazed out at the soft contours of the hills. I
shivered, feeling my feet start to goose-pimple, and
curled the sheets up underneath them, wrapping
myself up like a mummy. I closed my eyes, and praised
myself for being strong enough to punish him. But my
triumph was as ever bittersweet – whenever I tried to
be assertive I always ended up worrying so much
about the consequences and offences I might have
caused I might just as well have been submissive and
happy . . . locked in his warm arms . . .

Exasperated with myself, I got up and pulled on a
jumper, then retreated back beneath the sheets. The
pillow smelt of smoke. I wondered if I would stink by
the morning.

I was woken up in pitch blackness by a wet blow to
my face. I sat up, feeling the droplets run down my

face and gather dripping from my chin. I felt my hair and the pillow, and they were wet. Outside, rain was slithering across the window-panes and I could hear the distinct sounds of creaking and huffing.

I got up and went to the window. My teeth were chattering like castanets. As I gazed out of the window, my eyes saucered in shock. The landlady was digging a hole in the garden! I watched her heave, fling some earth over her shoulder and then stand up, rubbing her hip. Suddenly, she turned and looked up at the window, and I quickly shot back into bed.

For some time I lay frozen in rigor mortis, like a child terrified by a nightmare, convinced the lurking monster will pounce at any moment. She was burying a dead body; I had seen the black sack; it had to be! Had she seen me? Would I be next? Hearing rattling outside my door, I froze again, squeezing my eyes shut, praying desperately.

The pitter-pattering noise continued; perhaps it was just rats. Or maybe it was a trick to lure me out of bed, where she would be waiting in the hallway with an axe. I remembered the ugly lumps of meat that had been strewn in her dogs' bowls. Maybe I would be chopped up and served for doggie breakfast. Oh God.

Then another thought seized me: *what if the dead body was Henry! What if she had murdered him!*

I jumped out of bed and ran to the door, my toes curling on the dirty cold floorboards. My hand slithered on the handle with sweat. I took a deep breath and opened the door. As a wet furriness brushed my hand, I cried out. Then I gulped with icy relief as I realised it was just one of the dogs, sniffing to see who this new stranger was.

"Martha!" her quavering voice suddenly called from down below. "Martha! You know you're not allowed up there!"

Hearing the stairs creak, I quickly burst into Sir C's bedroom, pushing away the dog as I pressed my back against the door, collapsing back against it in weak relief.

Sir C was just a silent hump beneath the covers. I gently eased his suitcase away and heaved it onto the window-sill so that I could get round to the side. He was lying motionless on his side with the still of the dead. I reached out in terror and touched his throat. His eyelids flickered but he did not wake.

There was hardly room in the bed for a French stick. I peeled back the cover and slipped in beside him with my back to his chest, pressing up on one side to stop myself toppling out. I felt him stir faintly. Oh, what a relief it was to feel his breath on the back of my neck, the warmth of his body against the length of mine. He was alive, thank God, he was alive!

I'm sorry, I whispered silently, I'm so so sorry.

I was so squashed and uncomfortable I thought I would never fall asleep. I was finally just nodding off when I felt his toes curl against mine and my whole body vibrated as though suddenly awaking from a long hibernation. Then his big hands were pulling up the back of my nightshirt and jumper, and I flinched ecstatically at a faint nip at the bottom of my back. He slowly bit his way up the notches of my spine until I was writhing against him, my body one warm liquid pool of lust.

Suddenly he flipped me over so that I was lying beneath him. I let out a shaky gasp.

"Don't be scared," he said tenderly, cupping his huge hands around my chin. Gently he eased his thumb into my mouth and I sucked it nervously, gazing up into his indiscernible eyes as black and soft as olives. Desire fluttered like a baby bird at the back of my throat. The last thing I saw above the curve of his ebony head was a tiny spider scuttling across the cracked map of the ceiling before I squeezed my eyes shut in the ecstasy of our lovemaking . . .

The following morning, as we drove away, I told Sir C about the old woman and the grave and he was soon roaring with laughter. Somehow, last night's disaster seemed almost charming in retrospect, almost binding, something we had shared and survived together.

We drove on for some time. He finally pulled up outside a small, comfortable hotel. I sighed with relief. Sir C only needed about five hours sleep a night but even he was exhausted. We lay on the bed, cuddling and caressing, sleepily discussing all the things we would do that afternoon and the next day . . .

We woke up simultaneously, smiling and stretching like cats. There was only the remains of late afternoon left, so we meandered down to the woods around Blenheim Palace for a late picnic. The countryside was glorious, but the weather was still cold and he made me put his long black coat on before going out. The sleeves drooped in ghostly folds over my wrists. He wrapped me up in his scarf, giving me one glove and keeping one for himself, so we held hands in the middle.

This is so romantic, I thought dreamily, almost honeymoon-ish. As though we had been married for yonks and were taking a Sunday afternoon stroll just like the plethora of middle-aged couples also walking there that afternoon. I kept feeling I should be getting ready to go back for five to put on the tea and then do the ironing or have kids running after us and demanding for Sir C to play tag and nagging me to buy them an ice cream.

"Oh, how lovely!" I cried, as we passed a little stone church where a bride and groom were emerging in a flurry of confetti. As the photographer lifted his camera, they kissed and kissed and kissed and all their friends and family cheered.

"Hmm!" Henry gave a snort, then, seeing my face, sighed and said, "I'm afraid when you get to my age, Olivia, and you've been twice up the aisle, you can't help feeling cynical about marriage." He paused for a bit and then added ponderingly, "The trouble is, I think, we never really love each other, just an ideal in our minds."

"Oh yes," I smiled in automatic agreement, inwardly smarting as we continued to walk in silence. If he didn't want to get married, why did he tell me he was going to leave his wife? Then I reprimanded myself – he'd never actually specifically quite exactly said he'd leave her – I'd just been exaggerating to Josephine. But when I'd gently hinted, he had said, definitely, absolutely, that he was *very fond* of me and didn't know what he'd do without me. And I'd just assumed . . .

"Are you okay?" Sir C suddenly made me jump by looking at me closely and I pushed my lips into another smile and nodded and gulped.

Then, as though prodded by an invisible Josephine, I blurted out, "Oh, I . . . er . . . was wondering if we might have a talk about us?"

I looked up at him, expecting him to yank his glove back and run for it, but his face didn't flicker. He merely lifted a branch out of my path and said casually, "Of course."

"Well. I mean, I just . . . wanted to know . . . well, where we stand."

He stopped and brushed back a stray curl from my face.

"You must know you're very special to me, Olivia."

"Yes. Yes, but —"

He interrupted me with a light kiss.

We continued to walk in silence, until he suddenly spotted a rare species of conifer. We made a long detour to check, only to find that he was mistaken.

"If you don't leave your wife I'm going to resign!" I suddenly burst out.

Sir C blinked.

"Now come on, Olivia, let's not get rash. You know I want to leave her. But we've discussed this before. It isn't the right time, not with Alicia being so young. When you have children of your own you'll understand that you can't always think of yourself."

So patronising!

"I mean, how long are we going to wait!" I burst out again. "Ten years? Twenty years? Our next incarnations!"

Sir C swallowed and said, "Let's talk about this another time, Olivia. Come on, we've had a lovely weekend, let's not spoil it. There's another lovely place in Devon that we can go to next month, and we won't have any problems with B&B, my friend owns the house . . ."

All the way back my mind was ticking like a bomb: marriage, divorce, custody, marriage . . .

We dined together and, despite myself, I started to cheer up. It was impossible not to; he kept relentlessly cracking deadpan jokes and when he said, "In a recent survey, a thousand women were asked if they'd sleep with Bill Clinton and 74% said 'never again'" I very nearly spat my lasagne all over the gingham tablecloth. Upstairs, I hid under the covers while, with his typical fastidiousness, he picked his teeth in the bathroom.

"Boo!" I cried as he emerged.

He started, blinked, muttered, "You mad little girl," then leapt on me, growling, until I was squirming with giggles and desire.

Afterwards we lay side by side, his thick arms around me like a duvet, his huge but infinitely delicate hands trailing gently up and down my body, sending post-orgasmic tremors and little shivers of bliss licking all over me, his breath warm on my neck as we started to whisper confessions as though we'd never told anyone else, peeling through the layers to the core of each other. Normally he avoided talking about himself,

158

always flipping the coin of conversation back to me. But tonight, as though silently apologising for earlier, he told me somewhat sadly how tired he was of writing, he was burning out, running out of ideas, Agatha never liked anything he wrote, she was constantly draining him.

"But you write such wonderful books, you're so clever," I assured him over and over, hugging him fiercely, unnerved to see him dropping his guard, suddenly no longer my invincible hero but vulnerable, human. He smiled and kissed me gratefully and I rubbed the furrow at the top of his nose which always indented when he was angry or upset.

"Somehow it was all so much more fun right in the beginning, when I was struggling and everything I wrote had a kind of urgency. Mary and I were so poor we lived in this tiny house in Fulham. She was only eighteen when she got pregnant with Ricky and things were a bit more old-fashioned then so we decided we had jolly well better get married. Even with the baby, she never pressurised me to get a job, even though I had enough rejection slips to paper a wall. She always had every faith that I would make it. I remember when I had my first article published, in some crummy chess magazine, she went out and bought thirty copies."

"I thought your parents were loaded," I said, fascinated to have this rare moment of insight into this man I could never quite fathom, like a Babushka doll without a centre.

"Yes, but my father didn't like Mary, because he was such a dreadful snob. She was only working in the local Woolworths. I remember going every day for two weeks to buy a quarter pound of bonbons and finally she said, 'How many bonbons is it going to take before you ask me out?'" He paused as I laughed, and he smiled fondly. "Eventually my father got to like her though – it was impossible not too, she was so sweet. You remind me a bit of her, actually." He stroked my collar bone. "You're both very special."

"Oh, really, really, thank you!" I felt as though he had just awarded me a medal. Suddenly I hated myself for pressurising him. He had so many problems and my nagging only made me seem as bad as Agatha . . .

As he started to snore, I turned over and gazed at his face, slack and soft in dreams, and felt so delicate, as though my heart was made of rose petals.

"Oh, I do love you," I whispered into the safe cave of his chest, listening to the confident boom of his heart, "I do love you, Sir C."

14. The End

The next morning, I woke up to see him cleaning his teeth and packing everything away very neatly into his suitcase.

He came over and kissed my forehead.

"Come on now," he said briskly, "I've got a book-signing in Blackwells and you know what the bloody one-way is like. I want you to go back to the office and catch up, I'll travel back later."

I got up, got dressed, and began to throw everything back into my suitcase. He raised an eyebrow but made no comment.

I scrunched dirty underwear in a tight ball, gripped with a horrible hollow feeling inside; that Monday-morning feeling that all the fun is over. I didn't want to travel without him, I'd been looking forward to the long journey back. I felt that nervy mid-life crisis flutter again, a sense of my life skedaddling all over the place with no certainty or direction . . .

It was enough to make me crawl back under the covers, huddling up and pretending it wasn't all really over. Last night seemed so long ago. Now I could hear him humming Frank Sinatra in the shower. Oh God, what if he'd heard me say "I love you" and I'd frightened him off?

Then a wicked thought struck me. No, I can't, I stopped myself. Yes, you can, Ms Watts tugged.

Go on, Olivia, I rallied myself, *if you want to prise him off Agatha, you've got to really go for it . . .*

My fingers were as slippery as butter as I unbuttoned my clothes. I got to my underwear and then lost my nerve. As I slipped into the cloud of steam, I saw his bulky silhouette turn in the shower. As he pulled open the curtain, I ran towards him, then slipped on the wet tiles, knocking him over on top of me, my mouth pressed against the suck of the plug hole.

Sir C pulled me up to my feet.

"Really, Olivia," he said dryly, teasingly, "I'll be through in a min, there's plenty of hot water left for you." Then he looked down and saw my underwear clinging wet against me and I saw his eyes turn starry with lust. He clenched his hand against the back of my head and started to kiss me voraciously, murmuring, "Mmm, we really don't have time for this . . ." I wound my fingers through his hair, tasting the peachy Body Shop shampoo, acidic on his tongue. The water drizzled over our faces. Somehow the pressure of time made it all the more exciting, urgent.

I jumped as I heard the room door click.

"Just the maid," Henry gasped, pulling me hard against his chest, licking my eyebrow.

The maid was starting to sing. Then the door flew open and I felt the cold air sucking up between us as Henry jumped away from me as though burnt.

"Really," said his wife in cool surprise, "now I know

162

why you made so much fuss about not meeting till lunch. So this was your crucial appointment, was it?"

"Mummy!" His daughter, who was standing at the door holding a pair of scissors, cutting out shapes from wrapping paper, started to wail, not understanding but instinctively knowing something was wrong. "Mummy, what are Daddy and Lolly doing?"

Mummy patted her sleek blonde hair and looked at us with an impassive face. Beneath her tawny coat she was wearing pearls and a coffee-coloured blouse.

"I think Daddy and I had better have a little chat in private."

Henry leapt out of the shower, pulling on his blue dressing-gown, flinging one at me. His wife instinctively pulled his child back, flashing her blue eyes at him.

"Look, Agatha, it's not how it looked."

"Darling, it never is."

"Olivia was in the shower and she had cramp. She was calling out for help." He turned and glared at me for verification, and I nodded weakly and muttered, yes, I often suffered cramp, it had been so bad I could hardly move my leg . . .

"Really, Henry," said Agatha, her plucked eyebrows meeting in the middle in disbelief, "your excuses get more ingenious all the time.

Henry's eyes darted back to my shocked face and then he quickly ushered me back into the bed -room.

"Just a little chat," he reassured me, brushing my temple with his lips.

I sat down on the bed in dazed shock, hearing him

declare loudly, as though wanting me to overhear: "Now look, Agatha, you're just being paranoid, it's your illness again, you know what the doctor says about you resting and I expect you've spent the weekend rushing around all over the place . . ."

"Well, yes, darling, because I was preparing to come away with you . . ."

So this was why he had told me he had a 'crucial appointment' this afternoon and I had to go back to sort the office out. Oh God.

"Really, Henry, they get younger and younger!"

"Look, Agatha, would I have fired her if I was having an affair? I fired her because you asked me to! And then I asked you before taking her back on!"

I felt as though a screwdriver was twisting their words deeper and deeper into my heart. I put my hands over my ears. I paced on the rug. I flipped open the book lying by Henry's bedside – one of his own – to find it covered with his pencil scribbles, even though it was being published in its tenth edition. Seeing his perfectionism, so very very Henry, brought tears to my eyes. "Feeling your age, darling?" Agatha was taunting him. "She looks young enough to be doing 'A' levels." I buried my head under the pillow, breathing in the citrus whiff of his aftershave. I should leave, a quiet rational voice said, I should just get up and dress and pick up my case and leave. But a certain masochism, an almost-hunger to feed my misery, made me linger, wait, listen.

The bathroom door creaked open slightly. Unnoticed, Alicia had slipped out. She stood there, her hands twined behind her back, her little mouth puckered and balled up, her eyes slitty beneath hawk brows.

"Well, isn't it a nice day today?" I said in a gay *Blue Peter* voice. "Look at the sunshine there! I'm sure you and Daddy are going to have a lovely time."

Alicia ran over, jumped onto the bed and stabbed me in the cheek with the pair of scissors. I started screaming, and she started screaming, clambering on top of me, stabbing the pillow, just missing my ear. Agatha and Henry came running in. Henry pulled her off, swept her into his arms. The scissors – small, blunt, plastic child ones, rattled to the floor. I sat up, clutching my cheek, feeling the blood warm on my fingers, dribbling down my wrist . . .

"I hate her! She stole Daddy! Hate her!" she kept screaming, punching and clawing him.

"Oh give her to me!" Agatha cried.

"No, she's alright, come on, darling, you're alright, aren't you?" Henry crooned, swinging her away as Agatha tried to pull her back. "Come on, little one, let's go out for a walk." He hurriedly started to pull on a shirt and Agatha ushered me pointedly into the bathroom.

As I stood in the bathroom, I only just became aware of how cold I was, teeth chattering and goose-pimpled. Agatha came back in with a first aid box. I stood still, the folds of his dressing-gown falling over my wrists as she dabbed my cheek with TCP, drawing a plaster over the wound. Despite the trail of blood on the tiles, the wound was almost disappointingly small.

"It will heal in a few weeks," said Agatha dismissively, clicking the box shut smartly, then sighed. "This was the hotel we came to for our honeymoon, you know."

Suddenly I wanted to punch her, to claw her eyes out and scream, "He's mine! Why d'you want him! You don't love him anyway."

Instead I found myself whimpering, "I'm really sorry, it honestly was cramp, I used to have this problem when I went swimming, I can't even wear arm-bands –"

"Really," said Agatha with mild surprise, "please don't bother. I'm almost grateful, you know. I've been waiting for years to divorce him and now I have the perfect excuse."

Sir C drove me back to the station. He flicked on the radio and *A Groovy Kind of Love* crackled and crooned inappropriately through the car. I kept opening my mouth to speak, then snapping it shut. His fury was almost palpable, as though he was reaching out with invisible hands and throttling me.

The train pulled in; Sir C carried my suitcases on for me. He was standing on the platform, I was standing in the doorway of the train. Even here in the quiet country station his head was flicking nervously as though in fear of reporters leaping with cameras from behind the bramble hedges.

"I'm really sorry." As I spoke my cheek throbbed violently.

"Not your fault," he said calmly, drawing away as the door warning started to beep.

"Shall I, shall I come in later?" I begged.

"I don't think so," he said blankly. "We need space. Give us a few weeks, a month or so . . ."

A month! A month was forever.

Seeing my face, he suddenly reached for me, an unexpected sadness in his eyes, but the guard intercepted us, slamming the door shut. As the train pulled away, I couldn't stop myself from squashing my nose up against the window, gazing out at him, willing him to look back as he walked away. I'm sorry, I wanted to scream through the glass, but it wasn't my fault, I love you, I love you so much. If he turns, I willed myself, he'll leave his wife. If he just turns.

But the station was replaced by trees; he was just a dark figure walking into the carpark, and then we turned a corner and he was gone.

"I know just how you feel," said the old lady, sitting down opposite me. "I felt that way when I waved my husband to go off to war. He never came back."

I nearly burst into tears. The thought of losing Sir C was heart-splitting.

All the journey back, the old lady reminisced about the war (the statement about her husband was tarnished slightly when she revealed that a fortnight after he left, she went to a dance and got off with a soldier she'd secretly fancied for ages). I just nodded and fixed a smile on my face until my cheeks nearly split into two.

So that was that. Over.

I couldn't believe she'd turned up! Henry had told me they never went away together anymore, that they always slept in separate rooms, that their sex life had dried up long ago. So what other lies had he told me? Josephine was right. I was just another mistress, a toy for him to take out and play with when it pleased him and pack off when it didn't. That was Henry, I thought dully, that was the way he was with everyone: he sucks out the use, the jelly, charms a journalist, negotiates a deal, and then throws them away like empty shells. How naive and idealistic I'd been to think it was real love. What a prat I'd been to think I was special, I was any different.

15. Confession

At Sutton station, there were no taxis left and it was pouring with rain. I realised that in my shock I had dressed over my wet underwear. I could feel my nose running with the first signs of flu. My ten-ton-elephant wheely suitcase which I was trundling behind me seemed to be getting lighter and lighter . . .

Someone was tapping me on the shoulder.

It was a nice lady with a brown bob. She pointed at my suitcase, which had somehow burst open, and had been spewing clothes all along Sutton High Street. Two teenagers blowing straws around the back entrance of McDonald's were pointing and laughing.

I was ready to scream like a small child. This, I thought, is just not my day.

The nice lady bent down to pick up the scarlet knickers while I splashed up the street, frantically gathering skirts and blouses together and trying to ignore honks and stares from passing drivers. Oh thanks, just drive by, I wanted to snarl at them, then kicked myself because my prayer came true and a very familiar-looking car pulled up. I hugged my soggy bundle defensively to my chest.

Then Ricky got out of the car and gave me such a

surprise I dropped the whole bundle in a puddle.

"Olivia, what the hell are you doing?"

"My suitcase – the clothes –"

After that, we dashed up and down the street, giggling and gathering up clothes, chasing after them as the wind billowed them across the park like ghosts. Ricky even ended up retrieving one from a swing. Finally we bundled them back into the suitcase which the nice lady had been guarding for us, and discovered the zip had broken.

Ricky picked up the case and started carrying it to his car. Oh thank goodness for Ricky. I could almost see the funny side of the situation.

In the back was a little boy about seven or eight years old, with a blonde bowl-cut and soft brown eyes. He was carrying a big rectangular goldfish tank on his knees. How sweet – I'd never pictured Ricky as the babysitting type.

"Hi, I'm Jamie," he said bolshily.

"I'm Olivia." I shook his chubby hand.

For the rest of the journey, Jamie thankfully monopolised me, which was just as well, since Ricky didn't seem in much of a mood for talking. He was in the strangest of moods. I had never seen him so – so – well, careworn, as though life was no longer a joke but a burden, his eyes bleary and blue-shadowed, his hair limp on his forehead, greasy and flecked with dandruff, and there was an irritable, somehow *adult* air about him. He suddenly no longer seemed boyish but old and tired.

After asking me why I was called Olivia and why traffic-lights had green bits, Jamie showed me the contents of his bowl: three giant land snails from Africa.

"This one," he said, holding up one whose shell was so large that it was the size of a golf ball, "is called Mavis, after my Auntie Mavis, this one is called Kerry, after my girlfriend, and this one is called Arnie, after Arnold Swaarsssniggeeer."

"Oh, they're, er, lovely," I said, politely refusing his request that I should hold one on my palm so I could see how 'squishy' it felt.

"We're going to cook them up for dinner tonight," said Ricky, a little cruelly, and Jamie kicked his feet against his seat and yelled,

"No, you meanie, no, Daddy, no!"

Daddy!

I did a double take.

Seeing the surprise on my face, Ricky frowned, then turned away.

"Alright, Jamie boy, home."

He had pulled up outside a small terraced house in Rose Hill. An old lady with grey curls came out and Jamie ran up to her, gushing on about all the exciting things 'Daddy' had done with him over the weekend. Ricky emptied the boot and carried the goldfish tank in. I noticed him exchanging a few tense words with the old lady. Then he said goodbye to Jamie.

He scooped his son up in his arms, so tightly; his face contorted with pain. Then he set him down and patted his head, promised he would be back soon and returned to the car.

We drove on for a few minutes. The windscreen wipers buzzed and clicked. The silence was like a sheet of glass, each of us waiting for the other to break first.

Then Ricky said: "He's my son."

"Oh."

"I'm not married."

"No, I see."

"He lives with his grandmother – her mum."

"Yes."

"She doesn't have much time for him – Lucy, I mean – his mother."

"And I expect you're very busy too," I said sympathetically, just to show him I wasn't judging him in any way, and he snapped back,

"I'd love to pay a nanny so he could live with me all the time but I've got massive debts and he's very happy with her."

"Still, I guess your dad . . ."

"Well, sure my dad helps!" Ricky snapped.

"Yes, yes, of course," I said.

"But only the bare minimum, just enough for Jamie to be with his gran. The thing is with Dad, 'cos he had to work hard to survive when he was young, he's got a chip on his shoulder that I should do the same. It's bloody annoying – Jamie is his grandson and everything but he just gets all heavy on me and gives me one of his lectures," (Ricky feigned a weary Northern accent) "'Me and yer mother, Ricky, survived on three cornflakes a week' sort of thing."

"Well, maybe they did," I defended Henry valiantly.

"Nah, Dad's great but he's a real Scrooge."

Silence, again. I was so taken aback that for a moment I forgot all my heartache. Then the memory jolted me, and I felt that dull stinging feeling hollowing me out again.

"Did you have a good weekend?" Ricky asked casually. "What happened to your face?"

"I'm – I'm –" Suddenly I was desperate to spill over to someone, anyone, everything that I had been through. Ricky would understand. He would give me advice, he would know how Sir C ticked . . .

"I'm having an affair with your father," I burst out.

Ricky promptly crashed the car.

I had never been in a car crash before, even if it was a minor one.

We merely hit a lamppost, which buckled up the bonnet and crunched Ricky's wing mirror to glass ashes.

We both sat so still, I think passers-by thought we had passed out, as they came rushing up.

A woman with a flat white face was mouthing at Ricky's window. More people came, surrounding the car as though we were in a zoo.

Their plate faces suddenly seemed very far away, as though we were encased in a little bubble, outside time, sitting there, staring at each other.

Ricky blinked very hard, blew out a very long breath, and then said in a tight, funny voice,

"I'm going to pretend you didn't just tell me that."

"Are you alright?" A woman banged on the glass.

Then he got out of the car and a police car rolled up and everyone was fussing over me and someone was pressing a hot cup of tea into my hands. Someone tried to drape a blanket around Ricky's shoulders but he shook it off with fierce irritability. He refused to even sit down, he just paced up and down and around in the rubble, staring at me at first with wonder, and then darkening with increasing disgust. I tried to look away, nodding to yet another passer-by who asked if I was okay, but like nervous rabbits my eyes kept flitting back to him across the mangled bonnet. From the way he was looking at me I might just as well have told him that I had murdered his father. Oh God, I thought, why the hell did I say that? What have I done?

We ended up sitting in the ghastly Casualty at St Helier for nearly an hour and a half, stuck in a queue between a girl who'd suffered a minor accident melting biros in a bunsen burner and a little boy who'd stuck a piece of Lego up his nose. Ricky completely refused to speak to me, dabbing his cut forehead with a Kleenex, bristling with fury and completely oblivious to the giggling stares of two admiring teenagers who kept prodding each other and giggling in loud whispers, "No, you ask him!" – "No, you!"

Across the room, the Lego boy was moaning to his mother, who was leafing through *Homes & Gardens*. An old lady smiled at him and told him to be patient.

"Ricky," I said quietly, "look, please don't be mad at me. I'm not trying to replace your mother." As if Henry wanted me to replace her anyway.

"As if you could! My dad is never going to marry again. He made that mistake going on the rebound with Agatha. Nobody can replace my mother."

"It's not that I want to marry him . . ." I lied desperately.

"What do you want to be, his bit of stuff?" said Ricky acidly.

Across the room, the old lady started to wail when she discovered the little boy had stuffed her snuffbox up his other nostril.

"Oh God, I can't stand this anymore," said Ricky, and got up and walked out and left me there.

I sat in churning misery, the little boy's screams going through my ears like knives. I wanted to rattle him and yell *Shut Up*. I wanted to storm out and yell after Ricky, but I just didn't have the energy. So I simply sat and moped in lonesome self-pity: why was it every time I fell in love it was with a bastard? Was it my bad karma for all the blokes I'd mistreated? How ironic that in a perverse way I had been dying for The Wife to catch us together and now it had boomeranged back in my face. My mum had always said be careful what you wish for, or it might come true. Oh, why hadn't I listened to Josephine, learnt from Anthea Turner, realised that a man always goes back to his wife?

I slid deeper and deeper into misery as though I was slowly being sucked into quicksand. My job was over, my writing career was over, my love life was finished, nobody would ever be as witty or wonderful or horny as Sir C, I would end up marrying some half-rate mechanic with a blond perm and having two point four children and working in the local ASDA to make ends meet and all those screamingly boring things –

At last I was led in to see a doctor, only to be told I was fine, just needed to rest and take it easy. Bloody hell! Two hours of waiting – to be told to take it easy!

I came home to find my mum had outdone me, as ever. There were twenty-three tragic answerphone messages on the machine. Jed (whom she had now decided was the father of her baby) had suddenly fled to America after a mysterious crisis at his gym in California. Something about an accident on a trampoline which was going to lead to a big court case and thousands in legal fees and insurance.

I took a deep breath and made my way' round to her place as fast as I could.

"Oh well, maybe if he gets a real good lawyer, he might end up being even more rich," I said, to cheer her up, but she only snapped,

"Oh, don't be silly, Olivia, trampoline my foot! I know he's with that personal trainer, I saw the photo in his wallet. She had a blonde perm, she's a floozy, I know he's with her, I can feel it in my bones. Oh dear God, I've only just resigned from my job . . ."

"Oh look, I'll get a job," I said doubtfully. "Don't worry, Mum, we'll be fine, we'll see it through."

She cheered up a bit after that. I made her her favourite hot chocolate and left her lying on the sofa, reading *Mr MacGregor* and no doubt lamenting that all men were not like Mr Titschmarsh.

16. Sir Wellcald

In my head, I started to write my X-rated historical romance.

Sir Henry Wellcald (hero: powerful, rich, dominating) *strode along the beaten track, his black leather boots crunching sexily on the rocks.*

Instantly, the mill workers stopped their chit-chat and singing and hurriedly hugged their buckets of flour and coal to their chests.

Isobel (heroine: beautiful, vulnerable, destitute) *pushed back a honeydew lock from her face, her hands shaking. How she hated her master, Sir Wellcald, for his vicious words and grim unsmiling looks, harsh pay and cruel temper. Why, only the other day he had sacked one of her brothers for falling asleep in a bucket of coal.*

Hearing his footsteps behind, she started to shake so much she nearly dropped the bucket.

"Isobel!" Sir Wellcald ordered roughly. "Let me see how much coal is in your bucket!"

Isobel turned, swallowing, reluctantly holding it out to him.

She flinched as he yanked it from her, his enormous tanned hands rudely brushing her fair delicate ones.

Sir Wellcald grimaced down at the bucket, then pinned his olive eyes on her. Slowly, they travelled over her face, beautiful despite the coal smears – the fairness of her skin, blue of her eyes, rubiness of her lower lip – and down over her voluptuous figure, her bosom trembling beneath her thin cotton white dress. Oh, how many nights that he longed to throw her down in the hay, strip her bodice from her and make sweet passionate love to her . . . Seeing her lower her eyes shyly, Sir Wellcald drew in a deep shuddering breath, fighting against the torrent of his desire. It was no good, nothing could ever happen between them, not since he had learned of the family secret that hung over Isobel's unknown past . . .

"Here!" He passed the bucket back to her. "Very good."

Isobel had just sighed with trembling relief when Katrina (her wicked older sister, looks just like Agatha, total bitch, struck down by plague at the end) *burst into the mill in a flurry of scarlet swishing skirts.*

"Isobel!" she stormed, for Katrina was jealous of her younger sister for being so much more pretty than she. "You do not appear to have sewn the button onto my bustle!"

I had decided to set my historical romance in the era of the Bubonic Plague, because that was about the only period of history that I remembered from GCSE History.

I was writing it by night to cure my insomnia and cling to one last shred of hope: to send my book to Sir C and for him to be so overwhelmed by my talent that he decided to publish it at once. Or I might even send it in under a false name. I pictured him ringing me up and asking for Florence Rosemary and his surprise when he heard my voice.

"*Oh thank God, Olivia, I've just spent the last few months going out of my head looking for you!*" he might say.

Or might not.

I wasn't exactly sure when the Black Death took place (1400-ish?) or for that matter if they had coal mills, but still it seemed like a great backdrop, as the coal-mill workers, ravaged by sickness, gradually died off, while the hero and heroine remained miraculously un-scathed, though the final scene would hint at danger.

"Isobel, don't move an inch!" Sir Wellcald boomed.

Isobel froze in terror as he pointed to a large black rat slowly approaching. As its whiskers brushed her toes, she fainted in horror. In one swoop, Sir Wellcald crushed the rat beneath his boot, picking up Isobel in his arms at the same time. He carried her up to his Gothic castle, lay her gently on his four-poster bed just as she revived.

"Sir Wellcald?" she asked faintly.

"Isobel," he said, "you have nothing to fear, I am here now." (Sigh sigh – interesting how appealing the idea of a hero smoothing away all cares and protecting heroine.)

He leaned down and placed a kiss –

"Olivia!"

—on her soft lips, slowly opening her shocked mouth, his hand—

"Olivia!"

I jumped and dropped my book on the floor.

It was my new boss, Darren Euston, scowling at me. Euston had all the looks of the romantic hero – tall, dark, nice blue eyes concealed behind thick red-rimmed glasses. But none of the charm.

"Olivia, you have been sitting on that stool for half an hour, staring into space. Now either you kindly assist the two old ladies or I shall have you working overtime this evening."

Bastard.

Ignoring the shocked glances of the old bags, I poked my tongue out at his retreating back.

I had only been working at the local library for forty-eight hours and I hated it already. I hated pushing heavy trolleys. I hated shoving books onto shelves. I hated the customers; there were no arty interesting types, only OAPs and nutters. I hated not being able to write and most of all I hated my boss.

Euston was a new manager at the library, very young at only twenty-four (even younger than me) and fastidiously anxious to make his mark. The only person he fancied more than himself was the other assistant, Mary (far prettier than me), and he had already got it into his head that I was scatty, dreamy and didn't like my job (all true, but so what?). Darren Euston had it in for me.

"Well?" I snapped at the hovering old ladies. "What is it you want?"

"Millie's looking for a Mills and Boon she hasn't read." The bossier one with the pink rinse perm pushed the other forwards. Millie cowered slightly behind the shield of her tartan trolley.

I turned helplessly to the trashy romance section and randomly pulled out a paperback entitled *Forbidden Hearts* with a picture of a hunky man who looked horribly like Sir C threading a frangipani flower into the hair of a helpless fair heroine.

"Oo, that's a good one," said Pink Perm. "She goes to the Caribbean and meets a wealthy business man who sweeps her off her feet."

Millie paused, her frail hands gripping her trolley like bird-claws around a perch, her pale blue eyes fading with disappointment. "That's the one where he has a slight limp and turns out to have had a skiing accident and taken on his twin brother's identity."

Clearly *Forbidden Hearts* was not satisfactory. I scanned the three hundred paperbacks, where the only difference in story was little more than a change in the heroine's name. How the fuck was I supposed to know which one she hadn't read?

Oh, what the hell am I doing here? I fretted, mindlessly flipping through the piles. Still, where else was there to be? Work was hell; home was hell. Home meant Ricky ignoring me or making crude insults all the time, like saying that the gash in my cheek made me look like a Mafia hood and assuring me there would be permanent scarring.

After Millie had thought hard and subsequently rejected *Brazen Feline* and *Maiden of Arc*, and she had very nearly accepted *Country Girl* and then remembered the twist at the end with the lost cow, I gave up and told her she might like to look herself. The two ladies fluffed their perms, looked huffy and retreated to a comfy sofa, no doubt to mutter about the youth of today and our attitude problem. *Well, wouldn't you have an attitude problem?* I wanted to scream at them, *if you'd just fallen in love and he was married and you knew you were never going to have him and yet never stop loving him?*

It was just so bloody, bloody unfair. I felt my temper rising as I smashed another book onto the shelves, not caring that I damaged the spine, then tried to soothe myself by repeating the same old mantra: *remember Olivia, you're doing this for your mother.*

In two weeks' time, I reassured myself, this will all have died down and you'll be sitting back in his office as if there was never any gap. That's what he'd said: *give us two weeks.*

Oh come on, Olivia, I snapped at myself, get real –

"I was wondering if you had any books by Sir Henry Caldwell?" a male voice above me asked.

"No," I muttered, and then did a double take.

And there, standing above me like a shadow in his long black coat, stood the man himself.

There was a thud as the pile of books in my hands slipped to the floor. Sir C sat down on a stool oppo-site me and picked them up, sliding them neatly into their alphabetical places.

I sat there, shaking and gazing at him and wondering if this was another one of my hallucinations which would vapourise at any second. But when he took my hands in his, they felt real enough.

"So," said Sir C, "my wife is divorcing me, she's taking away my little girl and I'm being forced to give her the Kensington house . . ."

"Oh, I'm so sorry," I gasped.

"Don't be," Sir C smiled, "because now I can marry you instead."

He leaned forwards to kiss me but I backed off in shock.

"But – you – can't – marry me."

"Why ever not?" I saw an uncharacteristic panic flash across his face, then his expression moulded back into one of polite, reasoned surprise.

"Because – because – I'm just me – I'm –" I was about to say 'your mistress' but instead blurted out some stumbling excuse. "Because I messed up, I mean, I thought you were mad at me."

"I was never mad at you," he said, slightly sheepishly. "I just – oh, you're so sweet, so innocent." He suddenly pulled me into his arms. "I need someone like you to stop me getting all old and cynical like Victor Meldew."

"Oh, as if!" I laughed up at him.

"So?" he enquired gently. "What is it?" He looked worried again. "You think I'm too old for you?"

"No! No!" A pause. "How old are you?" I blurted out randomly – I don't know why – his date of birth and number plates and Burton's shirt sizes were engraved on my heart.

"Forty-seven."

"Well, it's only . . . twenty-two years."

"Old enough to be your father, I suppose," he said idly, picking the end of a book spine. "Well," he said, a smile on his lips like a label on a bottle. "Maybe you'd like to think it over and then contact me when you reach a decision. You remember the office number? I shall be available between nine to six every day." He delved into his pocket and pulled out a business card and I stared down at it in amazement.

He was backing off, when I shook my head vehemently, curls spilling in my eyes, and cried incredulously, "D'you mean, you're really really serious?"

"Deadly," said Sir C.

"Jeremy Beadle isn't going to jump out from that bookcase and tell me I've Been Framed?"

Sir C looked back and gave me a wry smile. "Doesn't seem to be here, does he?"

"But – I mean, I'm – I'm nobody, and you're – you're big and on TV and wonderful and everything . . ." I trailed off as he frowned and shook his head firmly.

Then he got down on his knees and slipped his wedding ring off his finger and put it onto mine. It was much too big and chunky and slippery, so I had to squash my third and little fingers together to kept it from sliding off.

"Olivia," he said, touching the gash on my cheek still left from his daughter's scissors, "I –

I –" For a moment he stumbled, awkward as ever at showing his feelings, speaking quickly almost as if he wanted this whole thing over and done with. "I do love you very, very much."

"Really, really, really?" I asked incredulously, feeling tears slipping down my cheeks. "You won't change your mind, because if you did, I think I would just die? *Really*?"

"Really," he said, kissing my hand.

"Really really?"

"Really really really. Olivia, I think you're divine. I want to marry you."

"Oh, my God!" I burst into tears and he rose up, kissing my tears away, hugging me against him. In the distance, I heard the faint, automatic call of Darren telling me to get on with my work. Then, hearing applause, we both looked up and saw we had an audience: the two old ladies on the sofa, who were dabbing their eyes and getting out their Tunes, declaring it was the most romantic thing they'd ever seen.

17. The Waiting Game

Sir C (still, even now that we were going to get married, I could not call him Henry) wanted to take me up to The Groucho Club for a glass of champagne, but I made a firm excuse that my mother desperately needed me to be by her side when she went to the doctor's for a pregnancy check-up.

I just had to get away from him.

I felt my heart exploding with love for him. Yet it was too much, like eating an entire box of After Eights in one go, and then being offered a box of liqueurs right away.

I needed to be alone, to digest it, savour it, take in the fact that, just when I had reached the point of almost total lack of faith in romance and love, after Elvis and Peter and James and John & Co, I had finally, most unexpectedly, most suddenly, met the man I wanted to marry.

Outside it was pouring with rain but I didn't care. In fact, it was beautiful. The rain plip-plopped joyously in puddles, slithered and streamed over my face, beaded on my smiling lips. Even when I found a traffic warden writing me a ticket for my car, I just wanted to hug her and kiss her and invite her to the wedding. As I gave her the cheque, she handed me a receipt to sign my name and I stared and then stopped – ah! Ah! I was *Mrs Olivia Caldwell* now. No. Even better. *Lady* Olivia Caldwell.

Oh wow.

"I'm getting married," I sang in giddy giggliness to the kettle, which boiled merrily. Oh wow, oh wow. I picked up the phone to ring Mum but I couldn't even remember her number. I must calm down before I ended up floating up to the ceiling like something out of *Mary Poppins*.

I hurried upstairs, hearing creaky noises and whispers. I burst into Josephine's bedroom, then blurted out "Sorry!" and quickly backed out. I went into my room, slammed the door.

The vision of Josephine and Ricky kissing hungrily, their guilty looks of horror, was imprinted on my mind like a snapshot. What on earth was poor Leila going to say? Still, still, still – I was getting married!

But the euphoria was starting to wear off. I looked into the mirror and felt oddly unhappy. But there was nothing to be unhappy about, I reasoned. Everything was solved – money, writing, love, future, all sewn up for the next sixty-odd years. Yet still my brain searched, as if at a loss for no worry to hang onto. Why did I feel almost *disappointed*? You're only happy when you've got something to worry about, I echoed my mother sharply.

"Maybe it's because you don't really want to get

married. Maybe you just liked the idea of it . . ."

I jumped, seeing Ms Watts blur and form shape like a mirage.

"Come on, Olivia, d'you really want to spend Saturday nights stuck at home doing the ironing?"

"I won't be doing the ironing. He's famous. No ironing necessary," I shot back triumphantly.

"He may be famous but what about *babies*? Dirty nappies. Sleepless nights. Huge stomach, losing your figure . . ."

Babies? I tested myself, squeezing my eyes shut, conjuring up soft-edged visions with *Twinkle Twinkle* on a glockenspiel in the background, while Sir C and I leaned over a cot, smiling down at our little baby, and then lifted our heads and smiled lovingly at each other.

"By the time you reach your sexual peak," Ms Watts continued, "he'll be sipping Horlicks and trundling in a zimmer frame –"

She disintegrated as I threw my hairbrush at her.

"No more! No more Michael Aspel, no more hallucinations! Just normal! Mature, married woman!"

I lifted my curls, currently down to my waist, into a ponytail. Suddenly I knew what to do, I would have it all chopped off. Straightened into a sleek bob, and that, I reprimanded the denim miniskirt hanging over my mirror, will have to go! From now on, suits from Jigsaw, make-up from Estee Lauder. The grown-up Olivia has been born and she is getting married.

Josephine tapped the door and poked a nervous head round.

"Erm, Olivia, you won't say anything to Leila, will you . . ."

*   *   *

The next fortnight was absolute agony.

Sir C flatly refused to see me until he had "sorted everything out". In the meantime, I wasn't allowed to tell anyone – not Ricky, not Josephine, not even my mother. Nor was I allowed to ring him just in case Agatha picked it up, which meant I spent all day wandering around the house, comforting Leila and trying to stop smiling inanely as she ranted tearfully that Josephine and Ricky looked so much better together. I was reaching a point of total 1471 desperation when he finally rang during *Have I Got News for You* and whispered in a conspiratorial voice that he was "just finalising the details" as though we were cementing some top-secret multi-million business deal.

Another week went past.

I was just drooping at the kitchen table over a *Cosmo* stars quiz that cited Sir C (Scorpio) and me (Libra) as being totally incompatible, Josephine sitting on Ricky's lap and feeding him breakfast, when *he called.*

I sat frozen, hearing Ricky cry, "Hi, Dad!" feeling my heart beating in my ears. Josephine slipped her hands inside Ricky's dressing-gown and kept brushing teasing little kisses over his neck to distract him. Ricky pushed her away irritably and chucked the phone onto the table with a snarl on his face: "It's Dad. For you."

Josephine and I exchanged raised-eyebrow glances.

"Oh hi." I waited for him to tell me the whole thing was off, he had changed his mind. Thank goodness I hadn't told anyone; the humiliation would have been life-ending.

"Fancy coming to take a look to see where we'll be living?"

I nearly burst into tears with relief.

We drove down in the peachy sunset, Sir C quoting Keats.

His green jaguar slowed behind a chugging tractor and we rolled gently between sloping fields filled with canary-yellow rapeseed and corn, butterflies fluttering love chases through the poppies and grass, blossom swirly-twirling like confetti. It was the sort of scene that would have inspired a whole volume from Wordsworth.

"Oh, I've always wanted to live in the countryside," I cried, kicking my legs in excitement.

Sir C smiled at me affectionately. "Now, don't get too excited, because Agatha is going to keep the big Primrose Hill house and the one in Kent will have to be sold. This one isn't nearly as grand, I'm afraid – ah – see it?" He pointed out a spire through the curve of the hills but all I saw were the biblical rays of the sun falling through the copse.

Then we turned a corner and rolled up to a pair of very grand blue gates. And there it was – a lovely little cottagey house, where an old man was mowing in the garden. Seeing us pass, he smiled and nodded.

"That's Raymond, the groundsman."

When he had turned off through the large blue gates, I assumed we were just taking a shortcut through some parkland. Then I realised we were rolling down his driveway, and there at the far end, soaring gracefully on the peak of a hill was Rochester

Manor, its gothic spires piercing drifting clouds, hundreds and hundreds of narrow windows stained pink by the sunset.

We got out of the car and I gazed down at the sloping green hills that dived towards a lake, glittering pink sparkles. Ducks rippled peacefully, two swans embraced.

Just wait till I tell Josephine, was all I could think at first.

"Like it?" Sir C stuffed his hands in his pockets and looked rather amused at my reaction.

"Erm, yeah, not bad," I mumbled, and we both caught eyes and laughed. Then I ran to him and flung my arms around him, crying, "I love you, I love you!"

We approached a heavy door with a scowling wolf holding an ancient brass knocker. Sir C tapped in a combination. Inside I gaped at the huge hallway, carpeted pink and gold, staring up at the glass-plated ceiling which seemed miles away. In the banqueting hall there were real gold tapestries and Van Loos painted straight onto the walls: soft cherubs curled around dreamy Madonnas set against gauzy land-scapes. A grand marble staircase led up to a gallery, filled with double bedrooms with real poster beds and lattice windows.

"I bought this one in the early eighties," Sir C explained, "for about £180, 000, when property prices were low. It's worth about ten million now." We reached the servants' wing, where he showed me a case on the wall filled with bells and little painted names: Master George's Bedroom, the Pink Lounge etc.

"Miss Lavinia's bathroom," I read with a giggle. "What help would she need in there? Help, help, I'm drowning in the bath!"

Last but not least, Sir C drew me up to the roof. The view was gorgeous; for miles and miles glorious green hills and valleys dipped and soared, dusky in the sunset. I couldn't believe it, it was like a National Trust property. And I was going to be living here – here! In this grand house with sixty bedrooms, this grand, quiet, cold mansion which possessed the solemn dignity of a church, as though its thick stone walls sighed with serenity.

Henry came up behind me and curled his thick arms around my waist, kissing my head as the wind blew my hair back.

"I've also been thinking about your mother," he said softly. "I'm not having you worrying about her day and night. Now, I've got a little house in Kingston which I'm currently renting out, but the lease finishes in June. There's two bedrooms, one for her, one for the baby . . ."

I was so touched, all I could do was reach over and hold his hand very tightly. Then we both jumped as a car started to roll down the driveway – a very familiar-looking rusty old Beatle.

Ricky.

"Oh, super," said Sir C, taking my hand and leading me down. "Just in time for dinner."

I swallowed nervously. Since announcing our engagement, Ricky had treated me as though I was leper. He even ignored me when I asked him to pass the salt at dinner. I didn't like to say anything to Sir C, not wanting to create any bad feeling between them . . .

But, to our surprise, he came in holding hands with Josephine, who was looked breathlessly flushed, her eyes sparkling like sapphires. Sir C gazed at her classy beige skirt and tan boots appraisingly. There was a funny, oddly triumphant smile on her face. Ricky kept clearing his throat and swallowing. I waited for him to demand us to call the wedding off.

Finally he spat out:

"Dad, we're getting married!"

18. Brides to Be

A fortnight later, I was dragged out on a second dress-shopping expedition by Josephine.

"Tell me again how you know when it's the right one," Melanie begged us. She was lying sprawled across the display sofa, munching at a dripping mint Magnum, oblivious to the disapproving looks from the elegant assistants. Melanie was my sixteen-year-old cousin who was on her fifth boyfriend but still young enough to be enchanted with the idea of love.

"You just know," Josephine asserted, holding a low-cut pink sheath against her and *mmming* critically in the mirror. "I mean, it doesn't matter how long you've known them – with me and Ricky it was just a few weeks. But there was no doubt from the start that there was never going to be anybody but him. You know, it says in *Cosmo* that we're all destined to meet our perfect match, but they could be anywhere in the world – anyone from some monk living in Tibet to the local paperboy."

"Urgh," Melanie moaned, undoubtedly thinking of her spotty local.

"The point is, I was lucky enough to find him living right under our roof. The first day he came, I just knew he was for me – oh, wow, look at this!" She held up a slinky ivory two-piece.

Returning from the changing rooms, she twirled and swirled in front of us. She looked absolutely incredible, her fair hair shimmering over the silk like something out of a Timotei ad.

"Have you got anything matching for Olivia?" she asked the assistant.

Melanie, like a child wanting to hear a favourite bedtime story over and over, licked her stick, proudly displaying a Scary-Spice-style tongue stud. "How did he propose?"

"It was perfect," Josephine sighed. "We were in Regents Park. The sun was setting. We were drinking Cokes, and he just snapped off the ring-pull and slid it onto my finger. Then he got down on the grass and said he had never loved anyone like me."

"Oh wow," Melanie squealed, thumping her DMs excitedly. "What about you, Olivia?"

"Oh, it was just in the local library," I muttered, trying not to wince as the assistant handed me a long ivory dress that looked far too big around the bust. Then, in the changing room, the neck got caught around my head and I had to cry for help through a mouthful of silk.

"Oh, Olivia, it does up at the back," Josephine laughed in exasperation. "Oh wow, you look great," she cried, positioning me in front of the mirror.

The assistant, Melanie and I all looked at the dress uneasily. It was far too loose around the bust and hips, and I wasn't very keen on the frilly neck or cuffs either. It wasn't a patch on the beautiful Cinderella creation Henry had in mind for me.

"Erm, I don't think so," I said. "Henry is already getting something made up for me."

"Oh, but can't you tell him to undo it?" Josephine said in a pained voice. "I mean, if you wear white lace, I can't wear ivory, it will clash, oh come on, Livy!" She put on her extra special wheedling voice. "I can't wear white, my skin is too pale. I'll look like a ghost. D'you want me to look horrible in front of everyone?"

When I refused to give in, she walked out in a real huff. Melanie rolled her eyes and assured me that I had looked crap and had every right to protest. Then, on the bus, Josephine refused to say a word, staring out of the window with a pouty mouth. Oh, why did she have this way of making me feel so guilty?

The idea of having a joint wedding had been really appealing at first. To be honest, I had no idea of how on earth to organise it and my mum would only make a worse mess. It had been such a relief to have my best friend to mooch over catalogues with and pick our invites and quibble over whether to order Twiglets or Ready Salted or both and share all our bliss and nerves together. Henry had also been delighted, tickled with the idea of his son and him being best men for each other, thankful that at last Ricky was going "to grow up and settle down and stop making a pest of himself".

But over the past few days Josephine had been growing increasingly bitchy and edgy. It was just little things that threw her into the most long-lasting strops, like the fact that Henry had bought me a beautiful diamond ring, and Ricky, being broke as ever, had still not come up with anything despite her nagging.

"Oh well, rings are just material symbols, they don't really prove love," she sniffed.

After that I kept finding myself hiding my left hand in my lap, half guilty and half angry. It was becoming all too reminiscent of high-school French tests where I always used to come top and Josephine got so jealous I used to have to fail on purpose before she would speak to me again. Only Josephine, I thought in irritation, could end up turning our marriages into some kind of competition.

Our group meeting the following week was even more traumatic.

I could sense at once that there was going to be trouble. Josephine was in brisk School Captain mode, whereas Sir C was sitting at the head of the table with his hands in a steeple as though he was about to take charge of a board meeting. Ricky meanwhile, who was still ignoring me continually, was looking childishly sullen and tapping away intently at a Nintendo Gameboy, ignoring Josephine's pleas for him to put it away.

"First of all," Josephine announced, pressing her pencil against her pale pink lips, "I think we should have *OK!* magazine rather than *Hello. OK!* are prepared to pay at least twenty thousand more and they want some indoor shoots in the Towers with all four of us."

"Well, we can put a red line through that one," said Sir C, eyeing her clipboard with narrowed eyes, "because there won't be any press there. Now, I suggest we –"

"But – but," Josephine objected, "but we must have press, we must!"

"We must not," said Sir C crisply. "Josephine –" he always called people by their first name when he was trying to charm them – "I have spent my life having lies written about me, I have no wish to personally invite them to write more about me on my own wedding day. I want everything done to keep this as small and private as possible. Just a simple, traditional ceremony, a small reception, twenty or so select guests on either side."

Over the past few weeks I could see that Josephine had been building up some vision of a Charles & Di style occasion at Westminster Abbey with 300 odd friends and all Sir C's celeb contacts waving us away into a stream of Rolls Royces, and clips on SKY TV.

"Now –" said Sir C.

"But – but," Josephine interrupted, biggening her blue eyes in that way that normally melted men into slush on the floor, "surely just a few press might in fact help to keep it more private? Because if we tell them all not to come, they'll only want to come even more."

Henry, however, with all his weakness for women, was not going to be persuaded.

"I suggest we discuss the honeymoon," he said, then frowned as Ricky pushed buttons on the Gameboy in animation, and a series of punch sounds and beeps filled the air. "Ricky, can you turn that thing off?"

"Sure," Ricky mumbled begrudgingly, flinging it to one side and sitting up. "How about India?"

"Oh no," Josephine cried, while, at the same time Sir C's face lit up and he said, "Oh, good idea!"

"We can't go, we can't," Josephine blustered. "I mean, Olivia won't be able to stand the heat, will you, Olivia?"

I ahemed non-committally and twisted my ring in my lap.

"And I mean, we'll end up catching all kinds of funny diseases and they've got epidemics of huge wasps and butterflies –"

"Killer butterflies?" Sir C enquired laughingly, "I think not, Josephine."

Two high spots of colour had formed on her face as though she was a pantomime heroine. I could see her lower lip trembling but Sir C was as solid as rock. There was something almost erotic about his kingly cruelty, his determination to crush her. For a moment they glared at each other.

Then Josephine stood up, threw her clipboard down and said in a choked voice,

"Fine. We'll have separate weddings then."

And walked out.

Sir C blew out a long exasperated breath and rolled his eyes. I smiled awkwardly, wondering whether I should go after her. We both looked at Ricky, who picked up his Gameboy and rattled away half-heartedly for a few minutes, then threw it down and got to his feet, muttering, "I guess I should see if she's okay."

"I guess I should go and see if she's okay," I added after an awkward pause. Henry nodded brusquely and I hurried out to find Josephine passing up and down in the living-room, now having a go at Ricky for not sticking up for her.

"What is it?" she wrung her hands. "Don't you love me? Don't you care about our wedding? I mean, the only contribution you made to the discussion in there was some futile point about making sure we have

Twiglets –" She swung around as I came in.

Josephine folded her arms and scowled as Ricky gently pulled her onto his lap, resting his head wearily against her back. *Tap-tap-tap* went her nails against the armrest. For a moment we all paused in awkward silence.

"Well, how about a compromise?" Josephine offered. "We have a small wedding but we all go to Portugal?"

Like a messenger between diplomats, I rushed back to Sir C to offer him the good news but he was totally unyielding. It was a small wedding and India and that was that.

Josephine was spitting.

"You just rubbed him up the wrong way," Ricky said. "Leave him to cool down and he'll soften. He doesn't like being told what to do."

"Doesn't like being told what to do! How can you be marrying him?" she rounded on me. "Is he like that all the time? He's such a bully!"

"Well, well," I blustered weakly, "I happen to love him, okay?"

"How can he be marrying her?" Sir C complained that evening as we lay in bed together. "She's spoilt, totally uncompromising, completely selfish. I don't know what he sees in her. And they've got engaged in such a rush, I just hope Ricky knows what he's doing."

"Oh, honestly, Henry, she's not normally like this," I stuck up for her lamely, but to be honest I was faintly, meanly relieved. Over the past few weeks Sir C had been marvelling on how beautiful and classy and well-mannered she was. I had been starting to get paranoid that he was beginning to fancy her more than me.

Josephine threw several more tantrums over the next few weeks but Henry remained as cool and hard as granite. He was the one paying for the most of the wedding, he reasoned, so he was going to dictate the rules. Finally Josephine relented, albeit moaning sulkily that she would have to omit hundreds of close friends from her guest list and if she ended up getting skin cancer from the glare of Indian rays, Henry would be entirely responsible.

"I think you must be the first person who's ever managed to get their own way with her," I said to my fiancé with teasing admiration.

Despite complaints from Josephine that I was turning into a boring old housewife, I left our hen party at 10 pm, determined to get a good night's sleep. We had all declared we would have a girlie night out which would be a hundred times wilder, sexier and more inebriated than the boys. But we ended huddled round the table of The Moon On The Hill, Josephine calling Ricky on her mobile every forty minutes to check how many units he'd drunk, in horror of him turning up tomorrow pissed / naked and handcuffed to a stripper / not at all. From the sounds of loud music and rugby chants crackling through her phone, it definitely sounded as though all three might be possible. Thank goodness Sir C was just having a quiet little do with some of his swanky friends. That was one advantage of an older man.

Getting into my thin single bed for the very last time, I tossed and turned for nearly four hours before finally falling asleep, only to suffer a succession of nightmares. In the first, I was walking down the aisle, wondering why everyone was looking at me, only to look down and realise I'd forgotten to put my dress on and I was stark naked. In the second, my alarm didn't go off and I woke up at midday to find the house empty and by the time I reached the church it was too late, the priest just laughed in my face and Sir C drew me away screaming. In the third, when the priest asked if anyone had any objections, in true *Four Weddings* style, Ricky stepped forwards and said that he loved me. He grabbed my hand and we ran down the aisle like something out of *The Graduate*. As we sprinted across the green, I ripped my white Cinderella slippers off, flinging them joyously away, only to discover Ricky had suddenly metamorphosed into Elvis, geeky, spotty, reeking of Walkers prawn-cocktail crisps.

I woke up in a sweat, soothed by the sight of my wedding dress hanging safely from the back of my door.

At 3:13 am, I was sitting up in bed, reading the good bits out of *Pride and Prejudice* in an attempt to exhaust my brain into sleep. Roberta and Leonardo, sensing they were on the move, sniffed restlessly through the cardboard boxes and suitcases containing the last of my possessions which had not been moved to Bucks.

3:30 am.

I turned onto my front. I won't move again, I told my body fiercely. I shall just lie here and do that thing Josephine recommended where you slowly relax each part of your body starting with your feet and moving up your legs and finishing with your head.

4: 15 am.

The house was completely silent. I bet Josephine had dropped off as soon as she got into bed. I could feel a tickle irritating my throat. Oh, Olivia, you must get to sleep, come on, you're running out of time! Hurry up!

4: 25 am.

The tickle was turning into a cough. I padded to the bathroom for a glass of water, only to find Josephine emerging from her room.

"I can't sleep!" I wailed.

"Neither can I, Ricky isn't back, and he's not answering his mobile, and I keep having all these nightmares."

We ended sitting snuggled on her bed, munching After Eights and vying for the worst scenario.

"I have this thing that I'm going to trip over my train and go flying into someone's lap," Josephine wailed.

"I bet someone's going to light a candle and then it gets knocked over and the whole church goes up in flames."

"I bet Ricky won't turn up. Or even if he does, he'll get the time wrong and all those bitches from his work will be laughing at me."

"I have this thing that the priest is just going to ask me to say 'I do' and I sneeze and this big green bogey is hanging from my nose –"

"Oh Olivia, you're disgusting!"

"I'm going to tuck a little tissue up my sleeve, just in case."

"You can't do that, it will bulge! Look, go downstairs and have a Fisherman's Friend, otherwise you'll be coughing over everyone." Josephine shoved me in terror.

I padded down to the kitchen, flicked on the light, and started to see Ricky sitting at the kitchen table. His fair hair was faintly damp and his brown eyes squinted in the fluorescent glare.

"Uh – hi." I tried to think of what I had come down for but I felt so jumpy my mind went completely blank. Even though we were marrying and honeymooning together, Ricky had still being doing his best to pretend I was made of thin air.

"Hi," said Ricky uneasily, chewing his lip.

"Um, Josephine's upstairs, she's worried about your wild stag night," I joked feebly.

"Actually, I didn't stay long. I went for a long walk. I went to lay some flowers on my mother's grave."

Oh, don't, Ricky, I pleaded inwardly, please. Don't lay the guilt trip on me again.

"It kind of reminded me of when I was younger and she was getting weaker. I couldn't understand why she wouldn't play with me anymore. I would jump on her back and yell and then realise she was crying. It was kind of weird, being a mother to my mum . . ."

"I'm really sorry," I bowed my head. I tensed against the sink as Ricky got up and started coming towards me. For one crazy moment I thought he was going to put his hands around my throat and accuse me of murdering her. Instead he reached in the pocket of his jeans and said softly,

"I've got a present for you."

"Oh. Another Milky Way?" I joked awkwardly, then gasped as he unfurled the tissue paper and picked out a long tarnished chain, with a small locket, decorated with a butterfly in jewels. Flipping it open, he showed me the picture of his mother I had seen the night we visited her grave.

"She hardly ever had jewellery, but this was one of the few things she wore. I want you to have it."

"No, but –" before I could protest he was fumbling with the clasp and drawing it around my neck. I reached up to help him with the clasp. "Oh Ricky, that's so lovely!"

"Well," said Ricky a little sheepishly, "I was kind of feeling bad for, you know, being such a git to you over the past few weeks. I know how much Dad loves you, he's mad about you, and I know you'll be so good for him. He's so serious, he needs someone mad like you to make him see the funny side of life –"

"Oh, so I'm mad, am I?" I shot back, still fingering the chain in fond delight.

"No, no – you know what I mean," Ricky cocked his head to one side. "I kind of think I was just uptight about the wedding. You know, making such a big step."

"Oh, tell me about it."

"So we're friends?" Ricky proffered a hand.

"Friends, of course!" I clasped his hand tightly, tearfully, in gratitude.

When I tried to pull away, he carried on shaking, a funny, affectionate smile on his face.

"So I guess we're going to be in-laws. I'll be your son-in-law, I suppose."

"And I'll be your mother-in-law! Well, you'll have to do everything I tell you."

"No way!" Ricky cried. "Anyway, I kind of like to think of you as my little sister."

"Big brother," I smiled up at him, and he suddenly gave me a tight, warm hug, rubbing his cheek against mine, telling me he would always be there for me if I needed him, any time of day, any time of night, I only had to come to him and he would make everything alright . . .

Hearing footsteps, he pulled back.

"Ricky!" Josephine interrupted him. "What time do you call this? How many did you have?" She put her hands on her hips, her eyes narrowed, a helpless smile tugging at her lips as Ricky pretended to ricochet off the mixer and then collapsed into her arms, putting on a slurred voice,

"Well maybe eight or nine and then one forgh the rooad."

Hearing them bicker their way upstairs, I stood in the kitchen for a while longer, watching the first indigo and pink rays of dawn. Climbing into my bed, I cuddled up against my cat, smiling into her fur. Ricky's meanness had been the last pinch on my happiness. Now I felt my heart expand with relief. Tomorrow we would all be married and everything would be wonderful! And how heavenly to think of Ricky as my brother. Of course, I already had Scott but all he had even done was beat me up and hog the TV and take the piss out of me. Ricky was just so sweet! I curled the locket into my palm, weighing the heavy chunky feel of it and fell asleep holding it, only to be woken two hours later by Josephine flicking cold tea onto my forehead. The Big Day had finally come . . .

19. To Be or Not To Be

It was all going horribly wrong.

It was like a nightmare, only it was reality. As the bridal car swung away from the church and we started to crawl around the block for the third time, my father turned to me and said,

"He's not going to turn up."

"He *is*," I retorted angrily, while reminding myself inwardly that Sir C was always fastidiously, hideously punctual.

I was feeling nearly as cheated and angry with my father as with my future husband. After weeks of dithering whether to let him give me away (the only other substitute would have been my brother, Scott, but he said, 'You *must* ask Dad, he'll be so offended'), I had finally let him come and now he had turned up in his worst dove grey suit which had obviously been in the back of his wardrobe for years. It still had coat-hanger creases – he could at least have got his super-efficient floozy to iron them out.

It was obviously a silent revenge for the fact that I was getting married by an agent of the devil in a Catholic Church rather than him in a Church of England. But Sir C was a staunch Catholic and I was a lapsed church-goer, and I liked to go along with whatever Sir C wanted.

I sat back against the leather, irritably holding my head high so the thousand kirby grips Josephine had spent literally three hours sliding in would not be dislodged. I coughed as another tickle came to my throat. Great, just my luck, my wedding day and I start to catch flu.

I knew this was going to happen, it was just much too nice and wonderful to be real. There had been a catch. There was no such thing as a free lunch. There had to be a mistress somewhere. It had to be a joke; I had to walk up an empty aisle to see Jeremy Beadle laughing at me and crying, "Olivia, you don't really believe he would marry someone like you?" Or else he wasn't going to turn up.

Then I felt a hand slipping into mine and Josephine gave me a reassuring squeeze.

"Don't worry," she said with frightened eyes. "If he doesn't come, we'll call ours off too."

"Oh, Joey, no," I protested tearfully, touched by her kindness.

"And to think what I've just forked out for your dress . . ." her father, sitting on the other side of her, muttered, brooding.

As the car approached the church again, I looked down and to my horror realised that in my anxiety I was shredding my bouquet to bits, bruised petals littering my dress.

Then, oh thank God, Ricky gave me the thumbs up – "He's here!" My dad looked disappointed. I coughed with relief.

*   *   *

Walking down the aisle, I suffered an overwhelming sense of deja vu. It really was just like my dream.

I glided down the aisle in my long white dress with Josephine slinky in silk ivory at my side, Leila and Melanie carrying our trains. I had spotted that Leila, who had wanted to wear her rugby gear, was still wearing purple striped trainers beneath her mauve dress but by this point I was beyond caring.

Faces blurred past. A bizarre patchwork of faces and classes. On one side, my ramshackle relatives, Bruce the family hairdresser, his long dark locks now spruce and bleached blonde, my mad Aunt Mary wearing black because she had mistaken the occasion for my funeral, my mother, holding, I swear, Jed's hand on one side and Calvin's on the other. Josephine's beautiful mother dabbing her eyes with a lace hanky and her Sugar Daddy patting his swelling gut proudly as he did when he had just cemented a grand business deal.

On the other side, foreign faces, elegant men in suits, beautiful women with *Vogue* faces and big hats: Sir C's friends and family. Ms French, having replaced me again as his new PA, still looking as super-secretarial as ever in a tweed suit, her shiny brown hair pulled back into a bun, standing awkwardly beside a row of Ricky's twenty-something work colleagues sporting tiny Top Shop dresses, perms and pierced noses. His son Jamie was standing at the front, grinning, his brown hair sticking up sweetly from his head.

But the crowds became black and white as my eyes fixed on Sir C, standing there, waiting for me, face almost grim, but his dark eyes smiling, fluid with love.

He mouthed, "Sorry" to me as I came towards him and I smiled back to let him know everything was alright. And everything was alright. Suddenly I felt tremendously relieved. Here was the man I wanted to spend the rest of my life with. My mid-life crisis was over.

We said our vows and they were effortless, except for my suffering an occasional tickle in my throat and bloody Ms French intervening at one point to offer me a glass of water.

Sir C had said "I do" and I was about to say the same when suddenly I found my head turning instinctively backwards, only to see Ricky and Josephine squashed on the pew, holding hands, smiling, whispering, knowing it would be their turn in five seconds.

When you meet the right man, you know from the start, Josephine's words echoed in my mind, *There's only one right person for each of us out there. I only knew Ricky for just three weeks but I just knew.*

Suddenly my mind whirled with a kaleidoscope of possibilities, my love life flashing before me as though I was falling from a great height: Elvis, Peter, the guy I called up for BR times and ended up talking to for an hour and who then stood me up, James and John (twins), oh and Mark, and Gavin who hadn't believed me when I lost his number (twice), and oh Christ Jefferson who for some reason made me crack up whenever I got off with him so I had to end it before I gave him a life complex . . .

I turned back to Sir C and I saw him holding out the ring and frowning.

How do I know, I scanned his face desperately, as though expecting magic writing to appear across his features, or a halo to shine around his head, *how do I know . . . in ten years' time I won't be on a train in London and suddenly get talking to Mr Right. Or, as soon as that ring is slipped onto my finger, my destiny will fall a different way, all the interrelated criss-cross of life will adjust like rail track switched with signals. Maybe now I'll miss that train, miss my Mr Right, never realising I could have had something better?*

I looked out to the congregation and saw Ms French frowning at me. My mother frowning at me. The vicar nudged me slightly.

Then I looked at Sir C, my husband, and saw the pain in his eyes. Oh, I loved him! The spurt of love was sweet and spontaneous. *I do love you, I do! You are the right man for me!* Bursting with relief, I reached up and suddenly kissed him. Faint laughter rippled through the congregation. Sir C frowned and gently pushed me away but his face slackened with relief. I coughed and closed my eyes. When I opened them I saw a smudge of lipstick on his lips, and he was lovely.

"I do," I whispered in a dry voice, then I coughed again and looked up and repeated with more certainty, "I do."

"We are gathered here today –"

The priest broke off as Josephine unexpectedly let out a high-pitched nervous giggle. An echo of uneasy laughter rippled through the congregation. She clapped her hand over her mouth and Ricky smiled at her fondly. Seeing that smile made my heart wrench.

"We are gathered here today –"

This time, when she started laughing, he just carried

on and she managed to muffle it by practically shoving her fingers into her mouth and biting her laughter into them.

"Do you, Josephine Caroline Wilkinson take Richard Henry Caldwell to be your lawful wedded husband?"

By now she was simply in fits. Her eyes were smudging with panda mascara rings, she had one hand in her mouth and the other clapped over her stomach. Everyone was silent. It wasn't funny anymore.

"I – I –" she made a squeak like a mouse caught in a trap, then spluttered hysterically.

"Shall I say it for her?" Ricky joked. "I do for me, I do for her?"

The priest winced and then reflected as if it wouldn't be a bad idea. Leila and I exchanged incredulous glances. What the hell was going on? Josephine had the finesse and composure of a finishing school graduate; we had all been waiting for her to deliver her sentences in that beautiful graceful voice and yet here she was . . . stepping backwards . . . wringing her hands . . .

"I'm sorry, I can't, I just can't," she wailed, picked up her skirts and ran out of the church.

The silence screamed.

I looked at Sir C. Ricky looked at me. I looked at Leila. Then my mother prodded me rudely in the ribs, her blue-lined eyes wide with shock.

"Well, go after her then!"

I caught up with her in the cool green glade of St Margaret's graveyard, linked to the church across the road. She was sitting on a bench, crying herself sick.

Knowing words were useless, I simply put my arms around her and she clung to me, weeping like a baby, spitting out sentences that made no sense. My eyes flitted uneasily over the gravestones, a ring of daisies, burn marks from an illicit campfire, as the minutes ticked by. Would Ricky run too? What the hell was going on? I felt like an actor in the wrong costume, playing the wrong part. Josephine never, ever fucked up. She was the only person I knew who had passed her driving test first time. If anyone should have messed up, it should have been me.

Finally, she drew away, and I pulled the spare tissue out of my sleeve.

"Oh God, I bet I must look a right state." She sniffed and then blew her nose, twisting the tissue gracefully. Somehow, even when she cried, she was still beautiful. Even with red eyes and nose, she had the fragile, delicate air of a wounded Ophelia.

"Shall we go back?" I asked tentatively.

"No, no, oh God, no!" she wailed. "I can't go back, not in front of everyone. How am I ever going to live it down? They must all think I'm such a bitch. Oh, Olivia, what am I going to do?"

"I don't know." I started to bite my nails and Josephine slapped my fingers gently away. "Well, d'you love him?" I stared straight into her puffy, blue eyes and she looked away guiltily.

"Yes," she snapped defensively. "It's just . . . it's just . . . I just don't think I'm the marrying type. I mean, you know, some people are just so *marriageable*." She looked at me accusingly, as if I had been genetically engineered from birth to form a happy, healthy relationship and actually want to sit at home and cook my husband's meals for him. "I think there must be some marrying gene, it's a personality trait, a kind of weakness where you're happy to just give in to someone else all the time."

I drew in my breath, corking back my insults.

"Well," I said in a measured voice, "it's not about being walked over, it's about making sacrifices for each other because you really care. It's all about compromise."

"Compromise," Josephine muttered, rolling the word like a marble in her mind. "Ricky says that's my bloody problem, I always think I'm right. But the trouble is, I always am. I mean, it was the same when we were looking at suits – I knew the one from Harvey Nichols would be no good, and we got home, and it wasn't. He never listens, he always has to have his way."

For a while we sat in silence. I wondered if Henry and Ricky were having a similar discussion back in the church. It was just so incredible, I thought they got on so well together. I had thought the arguing business was all part of the love-hate-Beatrice-&-Benedict frisson.

"And there are just these things about him that really get under my skin!" Josephine suddenly burst out. "D'you have that with Henry? Just little things, that really start to niggle you?"

"Well," I reflected. I could think of hundreds of faults someone else might list about him, but they were all the things I loved about him. "Well, he does have this disgusting predilection for pickled onions," I said at last. "I mean, I think they're so smelly and disgusting. I said to him, 'Henry, how can you eat those, they're all shrivelled, like jars of old mens' balls' and he gave me such a look."

Josephine gave me a similar look; I had been trying to cheer her up but she was not impressed.

"Don't be silly. I'm talking about, like – I can't sleep with him beside me. You know, I mean, I wear my ear-plugs as it is, but he keeps getting up to go to the loo. And it wakes me up. And then he goes right back to sleep and I lie awake, trying to go back to sleep, and then I'm just going back to sleep, and he starts to snore. And I tell him to drink less, and then he says he gets thirsty, he reckons he gets *dehydrated*. I mean, you tell me about compromise," she said hysterically, "he won't compromise."

Josephine was very neurotic about her sleep. She liked to have at least nine hours a night or she started to get very ratty, and spent all day rubbing anti-wrinkle cream under her eyes. Looking at her closely, I could see she was absolutely exhausted.

"I mean, the last few days were the worst. I just didn't sleep. For three days, I haven't slept!"

"It's just nerves," I assured her.

"No, it's him, lying there. I just feel – so invaded! Knowing that I won't be able to get up in the morning and have a bath or wander around or do my own thing, knowing I have to *talk* to him. I just lie there *hating* him, Olivia, just wanting him to go away and give me back my space. I mean, you know psychologists say we all have our own radius of privacy and I'm more sensitive than most."

"Yes, you are very sensitive," I said soothingly.

"Mine must be about six feet. And what's marriage but the ultimate invasion of privacy? Oh God, Olivia, what am I going to do? I'm going to go through life never meeting Mr Right, I'll end up one of those desperate ageing women chasing after older men who are too busy chasing after younger girls and then I'll just shrivel up into one of those old women who sit and spy on neighbours and won't give little kids back their balls."

"Josephine, Josephine," I cried, taking her hands, "come on, darling, stop stressing out. Just – just try and think of all the positive reasons why you'd like to marry Ricky. I mean, surely you must have wanted to, to begin with?"

"I like all the romance and stuff." She fingered her enormous ring thoughtfully. "I mean, you know, when you first told me you were getting married and I saw all the bridal mags, I felt so – so – well, I just fell in love with the idea. I like the dress and the ceremony and the cake. It's just the bit about living together for seventy odd years that I have a problem with . . ."

"But it's more than just romance. You go through different layers. I mean, to begin with, it's like something out of a Beatles song, and then it fades away and it's a bit less exciting, and the surface layer peels away, but there's a deeper core, a deeper affection."

"I studied that for psychology." Josephine nodded her head vehemently. "Apparently it's a proven physiological state that after five years of marriage the chemicals you produce that make you feel all lovey-dovey run out. And then you get these new ones for another two years that make you feel all married couple and boring. And then they run out. The seven year itch is a scientifically proven fact! I mean, why do we bother! Marriage is redundant, it was never based on love anyway, it was always just a male chauvinist excuse to get a dowry and a free housekeeper, nothing else!" Her voice rose hysterically again and I patted her on the back, trying not to look at my watch, trying not to rush her. Then she dabbed the edges of her eyes and looked back up at me and whispered: "D'you think you might go back and ask Ricky if he'll forgive me?"

"Oh, Jos, of course," I said, and she leaned over and we hugged each other tightly, fiercely.

"Oh, don't," Josephine pushed me away, "you'll make me start to cry again."

"Don't worry," I said, stroking her hair, "it's going to be fine. You're going to be so good together."

We linked arms and hurried back up the sidewalk, smiling now, aware of the excited chatter of birdsong as though they were celebrating the forthcoming wedding. Even the wind blew the grey grumpy clouds away and the sun twinkled and you could almost see Cupid gazing round the corner of a cloud, sighing with a relief that she had at last seen sense. Phew, what a crazy day, I certainly hadn't bargained on all this!

Back in the church, everyone stirred and Josephine managed a shy, brave smile. The vicar, who was sitting behind the altar mopping his face with a hanky, rose, his eyebrows quavering questioningly. I gave him the thumbs up and turned to Leila.

"Can we borrow your make-up set?"

Leila grinned with relief and passed her handbag over.

In the toilets, I tried to repair Josephine's face but she complained that I was doing it all wrong, and, splashing her face, proceeded to reapply blusher and lipstick with slightly shaking hands. I leant against the sink, smiling at her in relief, glad to see the old Josephine back on form.

"I'll just go and make sure Ricky's okay," I said.

I found Ricky in the vestry with Henry. They were sitting on a stone bench, Ricky's head bowed, his father's arm curved lightly around his back. Jamie was crouched in a pew, happily tearing pages out of a hymn-book and turning them into paper aeroplanes.

"It's all okay," I cried breathlessly, nearly jumping for joy. "Josephine changed her mind. She loves you, Ricky, she really wants to marry you."

Henry's tense face broke into a smile and my heart leapt to see how proud he was of me. "Good girl," he mouthed, and I could tell from his eyes he wanted to kiss me in reward.

He patted Ricky on the back and stood up, straightening his suit. Ricky, however, remained seated, his face morose.

"She's changed her mind," I repeated, "honestly, she's out there now, waiting."

Ricky shook his head, then looked up dejectedly.

"I don't want to marry her."

20. Goodbye

Nothing would make him change his mind.

I kept pushing and pulling the argument in every possible direction.

"You make such a beautiful couple!" I cried. "Remember a few days ago – you were mistaken for brother and sister. And you look so right together. And Josephine really loves you, she just had doubts about whether she was good enough for you . . ."

I found the words seemed to be exaggerating themselves as I grew more and more desperate, sitting by his side, pulling his cuff as he sat there like a dummy in Madame Tussauds. Still, he didn't even say a word, just shook his head. Oh, for crying out loud, he wasn't even listening to a word I was saying! Henry was equally quiet, just standing and listening and rubbing the side of his nose uneasily. I glared up at him, mouthing, "Do something!" but Henry, perhaps recognising a stubbornness in his son inherited from himself, shook his head and waved me away.

"Leave him," he said, putting his palm to my shoulder blade and pushing me back into the church, where I caught my aunt gossiping excitedly to the vicar.

"This the first wedding I've ever been to," she said, "and I never thought it would be so dramatic. That's the trouble with young people these days, too much to choose from. And there's a lot of girls about who like other girls now, isn't there, with all these hormones in the water?"

"I'm supposed to have another wedding at six." The vicar checked his watch lamely and rubbed his goatee. "Still, I shall get overtime for this one."

Seeing Henry, he quickly turned away. Henry frowned, clapped his hands and, as always, was wonderful at taking charge.

"If everyone would like to go along to the tent and begin the refreshments, my wife and I –" he smiled at me "will join you shortly." He patted Jamie on the head and bent down. "Why don't you go with Olivia's mummy and have some Coke and crisps, hey?"

Gradually, everyone trailed out, whispering, their bodies moving forwards but their heads swivelled backwards, like twisted dolls. Josephine, who had been sitting at the back, surrounded by sympathetic girl-friends like a queen with subjects, picked up her skirts and came swishing down the aisle; they bustled after her like waiting-women.

"What, what's going on?" she cried.

Ricky emerged from the vestry and, seeing Josephine, looked as though he would like to retreat.

"You – you can't do this to me!" Josephine's face grew hot, the veins standing out like red lines on a map. She turned from me to Henry and we looked away. She looked back at Ricky with narrowed eyes, her voice echoing in the church like a banshee. "You bastard! You never deserved me anyway."

You could hear the collective undercurrent of hissing in the congregation.

"Oh yeah, and what about you?" Ricky stormed menacingly forwards and Josephine stepped backwards uneasily, jumping as he suddenly threw a hymn-book down on the floor. The vicar raised his eyes to heaven and crossed himself. "All you ever wanted was my bloody money!"

"That's not true!" Josephine squealed.

"It is. Give me back the ring."

"What!"

"Give me back the ring." Ricky held out his hand.

"No," Josephine's voice caught with a sob, "it's mine."

"See? All you liked was the ring. You liked the ring a lot more than you liked me."

Seeing everyone recoil again, Josephine twisted it off her finger and flung at him. Ricky caught it deftly.

"Keep your bloody ring!" she cried, bursting into weeping. She stumbled back against the pew and Melanie caught her and within minutes she was surrounded by girls who comforted her and flashed evil glances at Ricky.

He gazed back at them with a set face and said stonily, "I hate the way girls always cluster round each other when they cry."

"Right!" Henry clapped his hands together, moving everyone on like a traffic warden.

Gradually we heard the promising sounds of the orchestra starting up in the tent, a quiet, tentative Mozart piece. You could hear the babble of voices as everyone picked nervously at sausage-rolls and canapés, growing more excited as the Krug started to flow.

Josephine would not stop weeping. I stood on the fringes of her circle, looking anxiously back at Ricky, who was now glaring at me as though somehow it was all my fault. I didn't know who to comfort. I went to my husband's side and felt the comfort of his embrace. Then we pulled apart as Ricky pushed past us, ignoring Henry's calls, storming off into the night . . .

Josephine insisted we carry on and enjoy the reception. Outside we paused to have a few photographs taken, though by now twilight was darkening, and the photographer, a lecherous-looking moustached man, snapped a few half-hearted shots.

As we went into the tent, there was a resounding cheer and a fountain of confetti flew over us. We stopped and laughed, as though suddenly remembering that we had just been married. I smiled up at Henry and he squeezed me against him, kissing my cheek and leading me over to our table, where my mother's proud wedding cake wobbled in five precarious layers. Instantly I blinked as Mum snapped an excited photograph, then waved her Kodak camera with a big grin.

I found my happiness gradually flowing, circling around as though my blood supply had been cut off and was returning. I sat back and ate little, hardly tasting the food, more aware of Henry who had relaxed too, now that Ricky had returned and was tucking voraciously, albeit moodily, into a chicken salad. We held hands lovingly and listened to the music, which grew more vigorous, followed by the speeches.

First came my mother, gulping and emitting a girlish giggle that betrayed the amount of champagne she had had. Jed gave her a slightly derogatory glance, as if disassociating himself, until he caught me gazing coldly at him and quickly flashed on a cheesy American smile.

"Well," she said, "I must say, I did have doubts about whether I would be able to stay for the reception because of course we all know what's on BBC 1 tonight . . . *Eastenders*!"

Everyone laughed faintly, as though uneasy about whether she was serious or not.

"But, I have to say," my mother went on, "tonight has been far more eventful than any episode I've ever seen!"

There was a rumble of slightly more confident laughter. Her tactlessness was almost a relief as she brought the situation out into the open.

"But, I do want to say that I am so very proud of you, Olivia," she said, looking over at me, and I felt my heart melt. "Now, Olivia's always been a bit of a fickle girl . . ."

"Oh Mum," I muttered, shaking my head.

"And she's always had a lot of boyfriends, and her father was always telling her off and not letting her go out with them." Across the table, my father frowned and the floozy pulled a face. "But I've seen my little girl grow up and marry the most wonderful man she could. And I can assure you, Sir Henry Caldwell," she spluttered reverently over the syllables, nearly ready to curtsey, "that my Olivia will make you very very happy, and if she doesn't, you just come to me and I'll sort her out."

"I certainly will." Sir C nodded with wry charm.

"Well, well . . . that's it," she trailed off, spreading open her hands awkwardly like a magician demonstrating his trick is over. Everyone applauded easily.

My father stood up and started to drone out a rather pompous speech that would have made a good Sunday-morning lecture for his congregation but was rather a dampener on the merry May feeling. He had the knack of making people feeling guilty perfected to an art and I was uneasily reminded of being a girl and making up stories for confession just so that I could please him. Thank goodness I was leaving all that behind me now.

My father was thankfully interrupted by Ricky slinking back in. As he shuffled past, Henry patted him lightly on the back. He sat down next to me and under the table I felt him reach for my hand. I felt the easy pressure of his knee against mine and for a moment, through the stroking of our hands, we silently comforted each other.

His nails dug into my palm as everyone clapped limply.

"Erm, I was hoping that I might add a few words," came an upper-class female voice.

At the end of the tent stood Josephine, like a bruised lily, an angel fallen from heaven, still retaining her loveliness . . .

"I was just wanted to say," she said quietly, awkwardly, clasping her hands together almost theatrically, like a chorus finishing the end of play, "that I'm sorry to have let you all down, and I hope Olivia and Henry are very happy together."

Everyone clapped as she came to my side. Henry politely offered her his chair but Ricky instantly stood up, dropped my hand and walked off.

"Have a bread stick," I offered, not knowing what else to say to her.

The band carried on playing. Henry and I swayed against each other across the confetti floor. I wondered how much longer we would have to stay, smiling like robots, before we could finally escape and be alone together. Out of the corner of my eye, I watched Josephine flirting ostentatiously with the photographer, as if hoping Ricky might watch, but he was slumped on a chair, swigging a Budweiser and ignoring the attentions of a voluptuous bridesmaid. For the hundredth time that evening I thanked God that our love was so natural, so uncomplicated.

As soon as Henry whispered "Darling" in that wheedling tone of voice, I almost knew what he was going to suggest – exactly what I had been dreading . . .

"Darling, I spoke to Ricky and he would still like to come with us for the honeymoon. He'll give us plenty of space, and I hate to leave him here . . ."

"But – but – it's our honeymoon, Henry," I tried not to winge like a selfish child, tried to squash that urge to stamp on the confetti. "I mean, it's special, it's our once in a lifetime chance."

"Look, it took me long enough to persuade him . . ."

"Well then, if he doesn't even want to come . . ." I

gulped as Henry gave me a warning look and nudged me as the priest swirled by with a raspberry tart, eyeing us nervously as if expecting another wedding to be dissolved that evening.

Henry and I continued to bristle against each other in silence for a few more minutes.

"But I've been so looking forward to being alone with you," I whispered against his carnation.

"I know, darling, I know . . ." he stroked my hair. "But he's my son . . ."

Well, who d'you love more? I nearly spat out. *Him or me?*

Then I glanced across at Ricky again. He looked absolutely desolate, playing with his penknife as if debating whether to slit his wrists. I tried to put myself in his situation. If I was in his shoes, I would hate to be left home alone with my two best friends away . . .

"Oh okay!" I sighed.

"Good girl," said Henry, leaning down to kiss me. "Don't worry, we'll have plenty of other holidays. We've got our whole lives ahead of us!"

And so all three of us set off, waved by the uncertainly cheering crowds. At the last moment Ricky suddenly leapt out, leaving the car door swinging open, going to Josephine. I saw them exchange something, Ricky bend down to kiss her cheek.

"Oh wow!" I clutched Henry's arm, watching him stroke her face. "They're making up!"

My heart winced as Ricky slid back into the car beside me, squashing my train.

"I gave her back the ring." He looked as though he was about to burst into tears.

The car drove on and I gazed back over the curl of the balloons to see everyone throwing rice and confetti. Josephine was crying again. Oh no, maybe I should have asked her too.

It was only as we rounded the corner that I realised something felt too heavy in my hands and realised that I had forgotten to throw the bouquet.

PART THREE: THE FIRST AFFAIR
21. India

If our wedding had been somewhat shaky, our honeymoon was a total disaster.

One half of me was really sorry for Ricky. As we trailed through the bazaars and temples, I kept buying him little presents, making silly little jokes, and Henry would join in by pointing out sights and scenery with a jovial quote or showing off his general knowledge by reciting passages from all the tourist guides he'd swotted up on.

But the other half of me just wanted to escape from the heavy blanket of the sun that was smattering me with thousands of ugly freckles and slowly turning me the colour of roast pork. Sometimes I just wanted to tell Ricky where to go, and drag Henry into the cool of the hotel and feel him run ice cubes all over my body. We were so lost in love, we couldn't stop touching each other all the time, straightening a button or a hair or an eyebrow, and Ricky would look at us with such a pained envy that I felt guilty for being so happy and then felt unhappy and then felt resentful because it should have been the happiest fortnight of my life.

I was just getting to the point where I was counting the days left before we'd get back to England, when Ricky suddenly came down to breakfast with a backpack.

He told us he was going off to trek around the Himalayas. He said he had met a Brahmin who had told him of saints there, tucked away in the cool caves hidden deep in the woods, who were so freed from physical life they ate only one grain of rice a day. He was determined to find them and discover the secrets of enlightenment. Nothing Henry could say would stop him.

"Oh God," Henry muttered, watching him go with his face wrinkled with worry, "he'll probably end up being sacrificed to the gods, or else come back to England with his head shaved, refusing to eat anything but chickpeas and quoting in Sanskrit."

I giggled and rubbed his knee.

"Oh, he'll be alright," I said, "let's just let him get it out of his system." I had to fight to keep the enthusiasm from my voice, my greedy delight that at last I had my husband all to myself!

That evening, Henry fell sick.

He blamed it on the food they had served us that evening in the hotel.

"Henry, my dear," I said gently, wetting one of his white cotton handkerchiefs with Evian and placing it across his beaded forehead, "you know this is one of the best hotels in Vdaipur – in India." His words.

"I saw the waiter," Henry murmured, "I saw the way he was looking at you." As I reached across to straighten his sheet, he suddenly grabbed my neck, pressing his fingers against my throat. "Are you trying to poison me? You and that waiter?"

"Henry!" I gave a strangled gasp, unable to wrench his vicelike hands away. He stared at me with lunatic eyes. I was close to weeping. "Henry!"

His eyes lost focus. His hands suddenly slackened. He stared at the wall and started to mumble about being a boy at Eton and stealing apples from the housemaster's garden. Cox's Orange Pippins, real crunchy real apples . . .

I nodded and smiled and went to refill his glass with water. It seemed such a long way from the bed to the sink. My legs were so heavy. When I got to the sink, my tired muddled brain realised I could only give him Evian. I paused for a moment, gazing at my reflection, sweaty curls, make-up running in the heat, an irritated rash forming on my cheek.

When I went back to his bedside, he was asleep. I gazed down at him miserably. I hated this gross caricature of him; I wanted my old husband back. I wanted the Henry who two days ago had caught me buying a silk sari for a ridiculously high price and reprimanded me and then laughed and bartered with the shopkeeper, down to half price. I needed him to look after me.

I sat by his beside, the heat all around like a suffocating blanket. I was locked in a sauna; I couldn't sit still; I had to get out of here.

"I'll just be twenty minutes," I whispered to Henry, who carried on sleeping.

Outside, it was dark. I pulled my white scarf tightly over my head, nervously looking over my shoulder. I was convinced someone was following me. I had read in the papers of Indians abducting Westerners, though I had to agree everyone had been sweet and friendly, like the strangers who had given us baskets of flowers and fruit and placed garlands around our necks this morning when we had visited the local temples.

I wandered through twisting alleyways that seemed to lead to a maze of hidden doors and courtyards, leading down to the steps that fronted the tranquil water of Lake Pichola.

A man was sitting by the side of the road, dressed in a silky cloth. I approached him tentatively, narrowing my eyes in the darkness. Up close, I saw that he had a shaven head and his wrinkled skin suggested he was in his late seventies, but his dark eyes twinkled with youth. In his lap he cupped a wooden bowl, waiting but not begging for kindness.

I took some coins from my purse, with no idea of their worth, and shyly put them in his bowl.

"You can have anything you want," he told me, "anything you want."

"Aaaarrr," I was lost for words. All I could think of was chocolate. "Erm, something sweet!" I blurted out.

Out of nowhere, he magicked a brown-paper bag. I looked inside and saw two white pieces of coconut. When I looked up he had vanished.

I really am going mad, I thought as I wandered about in a daze – first Ms Watts, now strange magicians who magic up coconut. I nibbled a little off the corner and it tasted real enough. I almost expected to grow or shrink like Alice in Wonderland. I kept kicking myself for all the things I could have asked for – a satellite dish, a year's supply of chocolate, Chippendales, the island of Majorca.

I was hot and lost and too afraid to ask for help. I let out a sigh of relief when I saw the temple. We had been there a few mornings ago, Henry and I. It was close to the hotel.

Inside, the blue darkness was cool and mysterious, shadows danced against the wink of lamps and little candles. Holy water drip-dripped on the floor. Silence.

Like Henry, my father had always regarded Hindus as heathens and I hadn't been in one of their temples for many, many years. When I was a child, my parents had occasionally taken me on family holidays to India and the pictures of the gods always used to frighten me, their waving arms seeming monstrous. Now they merely unnerved me. I felt awkward and foreign; I found the bright colours garish, the accentuated curves too sensual.

Yet I found myself drawn to the one at the end, a large lifesize picture of Lord Krishna, illuminated by the glow of the lamps. He was seated on a rock, surrounded by adoring animals, a fawn nuzzling against his arm, a peacock fawning at his feet, a *gopi* standing nearby, hiding by a tree and gazing at him with shy bashfulness. He had blue skin and the physique of a warrior but his face had the softness of a baby, soft dark eyes, a radiance. A few mornings ago we had visited this temple, I thought. Or perhaps it had been another, there were so many Krishna *mandirs* I lost track. We had seen an old woman writhe an erotic dance of devotion. Ricky had been rather excited but

Henry had sniffed and said, "Cheap . . ."

I stared up at the picture, mesmerised. I almost felt embraced.

I closed my eyes and let out a light hum. I liked the way it echoed in the pockets of the temple and reverberated back inside my heart.

I looked back up at Lord Krishna. I really should be getting back to Henry, but I felt as though the picture was willing me to stay. It made me feel safe, at ease, suddenly light, without heat or problems.

I closed my eyes and lifted my face and hummed to Krishna, a hum that was too shy to become a song.

Silence. I smiled at Lord Krishna. His nectarine lips seemed to be curving in a smile back at me.

I jumped when I heard a faint humming noise. A continuing echo? Songs outside? My head swivelled in curiosity. Someone was with me. It felt like a huge energy lurking above and all around me, watching me. The hum grew louder, the song took form.

"Ol . . . li . . . vi . . . aaaaaaaaaa . . ."

Were the gods speaking to me?

I turned. The far end of the temple was veiled in darkness. Outside, the headlamps of a passing car flashed through the windows, momentarily lighting up a white face, revealing in a flash-almond-shaped, glittering brown eyes. Then darkness blurred him again. I cried out in shock. Had I seen an angel? Was it a cosmic vision? Then I heard footsteps. Shit, it wasn't an angel, it was a nutter!

The stranger strode forwards across the temple, into the glare of the lamps, and in a second he was holding my hands in his.

"Olivia – it's me – Ricky."

"Ricky what on earth are you doing here!"

"I followed you," he said rather earnestly.

"Oh, you gave me such a shock!" I drew my hands away, pressing them against my thumping heart. "You crept up on me," I accused him, feeling invaded, as though he had caught me changing. "Anyway, I thought you had gone off mountain climbing or whatever."

"I changed my mind. I want you to come back and have some dinner with me and some friends I've made."

"I can't, I have to go back. We've had dinner – Henry's ill."

"I just looked in on him and he's asleep." He paused and stuffed his hands in his pockets. I noticed that the shadowed, pinched look which had indented his face since the wedding seemed to have softened, or perhaps it was just the charm of the dim light.

"You were singing to Krishna," said Ricky. "It was lovely."

We both looked up at the picture again, for some time lost in a joint swoon.

"It's a great picture, isn't?" said Ricky softly. "It makes me think of the end lines of that poem by Eliot – *shantih, shantih, shantih.*"

"'*That peace which passeth all understanding.*'" He had summed it up perfectly.

"I've been saying special prayers to Krishna lately," he said quietly, "for something I really want."

His eyes caressed my face. I smiled supportively and said a little prayer inside that he and Josephine might get back together.

"You must come to dinner," he suddenly insisted. "If you're full up, you can just nibble some *barfi* and it will just be for an hour or so. Henry won't wake up, I just prayed to Krishna to make him better, so we're safe."

I laughed again, shaking my head. Who could say no to Ricky?

As we were leaving, I felt as though my heart was being plucked backwards. I looked over my shoulder at the picture and suddenly pulled away from Ricky and went back to it. I had an overwhelming desire to give something to Krishna, anything, everything. For one crazy moment I nearly took off my wedding ring. Then I gazed down at my pieces of coconut – of course! I laid them down at his feet and bowed my head uncertainly – would Lord Krishna like coconut? I joined my hands together, trying to imitate some Indians I had seen praying. I bowed my head again, apologised to Him for being so clumsy, and then went back to Ricky. There was a softness in his eyes. Suddenly he engulfed me in a hug and a kiss.

"You're so lovely," he cried affectionately.

"The beautiful and intelligent princess, Rukmini, longed to marry Lord Krishna, but her elder brother hated him and opposed the marriage. So instead it was arranged that she would marry Jarasandha. But she only longed to marry Lord Krishna, could only think of his beauty and great deeds, could not think of any other man who matched him in character, age, wealth, property and prowess. She longed that Lord Krishna would come and whisk her away at the

last moment before the wedding ceremony was completed."

I had just eaten the most delicious and joyous meal I'd ever had in my entire life. I could hardly get over their hospitality. They had taken me in as a complete stranger and welcomed me as one of the family, offering me one of the few chairs while they sat on the floor, plying me with *lassi* and sweetmeats. The house had rung with love and laughter. Sweetest of all had been the mother, Jyoti, who fussed over me and Ricky and fed her husband before eating herself, feeding him with her bare hands as they exchanged looks of love.

"As the sun started to set, Rukmini started to fear that Lord Krishna would not come to her . . . She was relieved to hear then that indeed Krishna and Balarama had arrived. Her father welcomed them by sounding a conch and presenting them with garments . . ."

After eating, it had been Ricky's suggestion that we all entertain each other. Five minutes per performance.

So I had told my story of the coconut miracle, expecting derision, but they had all nodded and roared with laughter. Navneet had played a beautiful tune on his *saringi* with Tula Ram, only six, on the *sarod*.

Now I was sitting on the floor with Balaji, their three-year-old son who had taken a fancy to me, sitting on my lap. I liked the feel of his little pudgy brown hands on mine – it almost made me feel broody – as we sat listening to Ricky telling the story of Krishna's marriage to Rukmini.

"It was a royal wedding. There were thousands of women, kings, charioteers singing, musicians playing. You can imagine how many people must have been there. It would have been the Vedic equivalent of Charles and Di." Ricky broke off and smiled as the Indians gave him rather puzzled glances. *"Guarded by followers and soldiers, Rukmini proceeded on her wedding march towards the temple of the goddess Ambika. The wives of the Brahmanas made Rukmimi chant a salutation to the goddess. She made an offering with water and sandalwood and rice and garlands and so on. The kings, seated on their horses, watched the ceremony, and were so moved they were beside themselves with passion."*

Pause. He was standing by the window, lounging against the frame. The smoke from the sandalwood incense curled across the room, misting across his face, winding outwards through the stars, circling the moon. As his story went on, he lowered his voice and fixed his eyes on me, as if there was only the two of us in the room.

He is sweet, I thought, noticing the blonde streaks the sun had painted in his hair, the healthiness of his coffee tan, his eyes and teeth glinting white. How could Josephine have stood him up like that? Suddenly I wanted to push through the room and hug him and assure him she didn't deserve him, someone much more worthy would come along one day.

"Expecting her Lord Krishna to arrive and save her, Rukmini glanced across and saw Lord Krishna amongst the other kings. And then, at the very last moment," Ricky emphasised every word, *"he stole her away from her evil husband, took her in his arms and carried her to his chariot and shot away like lightning leaving the whole procession in uproar!"* And Ricky fixed his stare on me, his voice light but his eyes emphatic as if he was trying to make a declaration. *"And as they flew away, the jealous Jarasandha, incensed that he should have been made such an idiot, sent his entire army chasing after them. Rukmini looked back in terror but Lord Krishna said smilingly to her that he would destroy the enemy, there was no need to be afraid . . ."*

He trailed off weakly. There was silence as if everyone was waiting for more, then a round of clapping and cheers. An encore for Navneet to pick up his saringi again. The little boy Balaji got restless and went from my lap back to his mother. Ricky came to my side and as he kissed my ear he whispered: *"Come upstairs – I've got something to say to you."*

22. Upstairs

Upstairs, my stomach lurched with nerves. *Something has gone horribly wrong*, my intuition whispered, *he's about to tell you something you don't want to hear*. Uh oh uh oh uh oh. The feeling suddenly reminded me of situations I had been in before with men and I had never expected it to happen, not now that I was married, and least of all, not with Ricky. Oh God, I fretted, he's so upset over Josephine and now he's going to rebound back onto me. How had we reached this point? Was it my fault, had I led him on?

"Er, look, I should get back to Henry – he might be going mad with worry. I should never have come, this is so irresponsible –"

"Yes, but just, I just – I just want you to see my room."

"Yes, it's lovely," I said.

"I'm glad you like it. I was so touched when these guys offered to let me stay. It's much more fun than being at the hotel. This way I'm getting to see the *real* India."

"Yes, how lovely."

Our tone was too light, words loaded with the unsaid.

There were beautifully woven rugs, ochre melting into scarlet and orange like a sunset, lying on bare brown boards. His guitar lay on the bed, and strangely enough, a womansize Indian doll, made from cloth and stuffing, two fat black plaits resting over her silky sari. He introduced her to me as Olivia, named after me, and I wasn't sure whether to take that as a compliment, but I shook her cloth hand obligingly in any case.

I stood by the window, chewing still on a piece of cardamom that had lodged between my teeth. I gazed at the back of his tanned neck and waited for him to turn to me and tell me he was falling in love with me.

He turned, pulled a thread out of the blanket, and said, "Look – look – I know you're in love with me."

"Me – in love with you?" I spluttered.

"Ah." Suddenly he changed the subject. "D'you know that song, *Everything I Do*? You know, the one by Byran Adams?"

"What?" I shook my head. Me in love with Ricky! The arrogance of it – the cheek of it!

"D'you know it?"

"No, I don't –"

"It goes like this –" he tried to sing a few bars, but they were very tuneless. He cleared his throat, redness creeping over his brown face. "Oh Christ, that sounds corny. No. That's no good. Forget that." He ran his hands through his fringe and then came towards me and I backed away nervously. "No, don't do that, don't run away, I'm not going to attack you. Look." He put his clammy palms on my shoulders and positioned me in front of him as though he was positioning me for a photograph. "Stand there, and we'll start again. Right."

"Ricky, I am not in love –"

"No, just hear me out. Look, I thought of a lot of ways to say this to you – I even wrote a song myself." He held his head in his hands, squeezed his eyes shut. "Okay, let's just do this the straight and honest way. Basically, look, I know this is a complete mess, and I know you're married, Olivia, but I love you, and I always have, ever since I first moved into that house in Sutton."

"What!" I cried.

"Er, since I saw you standing there in your nightie –"

"Ricky, don't give me this crap!" I was angry now.

"Well, yes, okay, that's not entirely true, I thought you were a bit neurotic and zany and Josephine was a lot better looking, but I really did grow to love you. You were so sweet, you are still – I . . ."

Neurotic and zany!

"You never liked me!" I exploded. "To begin with, you got off with my best friend."

"But that's only because you rejected me for Elvis."

"Me? Rejected you?" I gasped.

"Yeah, I mean, you kept coming on to me and I was all revved up to make a move on you all the way up till the party, then we played Spin The Bottle and you snogged Elvis and then before I could kiss you, you ran away from me and went driving off –"

"Ricky, it was an emergency. My mother was pregnant."

"Yeah, but you still made enough time for Elvis, and you so obviously fancied him that I thought I would try to make you jealous by getting off with Leila."

"What! Are you trying to say you never fancied Leila? Look, Ricky, look," I edged over to the bed, then paused nervously; I wanted to hug him but daren't encourage him, so I gently rubbed the shoulder of his rag doll instead. "Look, you're feeling really delicate at the moment and I know it might seem like you like me, but, you know, this country does weird things to your mind, I mean only just now I was conjuring up coconut – when we get back to England maybe you can sit down with Josephine and draw up some points together."

"Points?" Ricky asked, his lip curling with disgust.

"Yes, you know, points on how to improve your relationship," I said, vaguely remembering such recommended advice from *Cosmo*. "Come on, Ricky, you and Josephine suit each other so well."

"No, we don't. We're totally incompatible. She's much too good-looking."

"Oh what, d'you only go for dogs?" I laughed, feeling mildly insulted.

"No, I just think she's had it too easy. She can have anyone she wants and she knows it. I think what she needs is a real bastard to break her heart and soften it up a bit."

"Ricky, that's not very nice. I mean, Josephine can be really sweet sometimes –"

"Look," he picked up the guitar, twanged a few impatient chords, then threw it down on the bed. "This has nothing to do with Josephine."

"You were going to marry her last week," I pointed out gently.

"But in many ways I'm glad I didn't."

242

I gazed up at him in confusion.

"Well . . . well . . . look, I don't want you to think I'm a total old bastard but, well, I mean, I think I was just so mad with you for marrying Dad. And I think she only wanted to get married to me because she wanted to get back at you."

"Get back at me! Why would Josephine want to get back at me, what have I done?"

"I don't know – to be honest, I think she was jealous, that you and Dad were so happy together, that you had something she couldn't have. I guess I was madly jealous too. I think that's why I wouldn't speak to you – it wasn't just my mother, it was just knowing you should be with me."

Oh heavens, this was heavy stuff. I had had men buy me chocolates and flowers and doggie chocs for Roberta but never telling me they loved me a week after ditching their fiancée. Maybe he really did think he loved me despite me being so *zany* and *neurotic*. He really did look very upset. I didn't believe he loved me but I did feel sorry for him.

"And what about me?" I asked tentatively. "I'm married to your dad, Ricky. How d'you think he would feel if he knew we were having this conversation?"

Ricky fell silent and chewed his lip awkwardly. He turned and went over to open the window, breathing in the clotted air. A huge moth flew in and bounced against the light, sizzling to the floor.

"Did you know?" Ricky turned back to me with a sad, defeated smile. "They have this ceremony in India where they celebrate by throwing buckets of coloured water over each other. Isn't that mad! Imagine that! Just walking up to someone you don't know and chucking blue stuff all over them. Where else in the world could you do that?"

I smiled and edged backwards towards the door.

"Wait," Ricky stopped me, "you won't tell Dad, will you . . . ? I mean, you're right, this is totally out of order, I really don't want to mess up your honeymoon, I should never have said anything, but it was just driving me mad. I had to say something. And if we can go back to normal now – well, I'll still love you . . . but that's okay. My dad's a very lucky guy."

He paused, bit his lip and started to shuffle up the edge of one of the rugs with his shoe. "But at the same time, I was kinda hoping . . . No. Forget that. Stupid idea, stupid, stupid me. Oh God, I can't believe I'm actually saying this to you."

"Neither can I," I said, more abruptly. "I think I had better go."

"Wait," his voice stopped me halfway on my escape towards the door. "Look, there's just one last thing I need to know, and this doesn't have to mean anything, you don't have to feel any obligation, this doesn't mean I'm expecting you to leap into bed with me – or anything. Just – do you love me? That's all I wanted to know."

Pause. How could I answer that?

"I do love you Ricky, yes, I do, but just as a friend."

"That's all?"

"That's all."

Pause.

"I don't believe you." Ricky started walking towards me and I backed away. Then he darted in front of me, slamming his back against the door, barring the way. I tried to push him aside and push down the handle but he shook his head obstinately, refusing to budge.

We paused, neither moving, both calculating our next words of defense and attack. Deadlock.

Ricky drew in a deep breath.

"Say," he said slowly, hesitantly, "say – say – we're in a parallel universe. No, don't look at me like that, you're a writer, you've got a good imagination. Pretend you're in a parallel universe and at that party your mother was okay and you kissed me and we got married, would you love me then?"

"Ricky!" I burst out laughing. "This is absurd, let me out!" I dived for the handle again. "Come on, you can't do this to your dad."

"I can't believe I would ever say this, but I want you so much I just don't give a toss – no, no, don't do that, wait – say, we were on a desert island, your husband would never know that we were together, *nobody* would ever ever know . . . I mean, just one night with you might just keep me going for the rest of my life even though I'd spend ever after wanting it to happen again –"

"I believe," I informed him, "that there are no desert islands left because, you see, it's a scientific fact that there are no lands left unexplored." I had no idea if this was true but it threw him for a moment.

"But what if there was . . ." he took a step forwards, "and nobody would ever know . . ." he put his arms around my waist and I drew in a quick breath as he gazed down at me with tears in his eyes. ". . . and it was just you and me, like we are now." He bent his head down and I lifted my head yearningly as he brushed his lips against mine –

Olivia, what the hell are you doing?

I pushed him away, wiping away his kiss with the back of my hand.

"Look, Ricky, you just can't do this to me!" I was so mad I wanted to hit him. "You can't be so selfish, you can't just walk into my life and mess it up like this, I – I – I – just can't believe your nerve."

"I'm really sorry." He looked confounded. "It's just –" his voice cracked, "I love you Olivia."

"Let me out, Ricky." I shut my eyes, shut him out.

"I do love you and no matter what you say I'm always going to love you."

"Please let me out Ricky," I said in a detached voice.

"Not until you say you forgive me. I don't want you to be mad at me. I just had to tell you. I love you."

"No more, please, I forgive you, okay, I forgive you!" I moaned, putting my hands over my face.

When I removed them, he had stepped away and the door was open for me. And then I couldn't move. Why did I feel so disappointed?

"Well, I've said it now. And I'm really sorry and I just want you to know if – if you ever want me, I'm here, and if not, that's fine. I just want you to be happy, Olivia . . . Let's talk more about this. Look, I should walk you home, you shouldn't be out alone at this time of night –"

"No, really, I'm fine," I insisted. "The hotel's only a few streets away."

As I hurried down the stairs my heart was crying, go

back, go back, and my mind was yelling, *shut up and let's get out of here.*

As I walked out into the streets, lanterns forming halos of light in the darkness, I looked up and saw Ricky standing at the window, looking down at me, his eyes flicking quickly to hide his tears. He gave a little wave. *I can't bear it, why did he have to do this?* My heart twisted. I hurried away without looking back.

Back at the hotel, Henry awoke as I came into the room. The room smelt of sickness, unsavoury after the sweet sandalwood that had lingered in Ricky's room. I went to my husband's side and touched his face and asked softly how he was feeling.

"Awful," he groaned, "where've you been? I called out for you and you weren't here."

"I've been here," I hated myself for lying, "you must have been dreaming, I've been here by your side."

"Have you . . . ?" he moaned in bewilderment.

"I'm sorry. Here." I threw the remains of his water out of the window and refilled his glass with Evian. "I – look, I know you're ill, but I was wondering if we could go. I hate it here, I just want to go home."

I pleated the sheet between my fingers, waiting for him to object with his typical bullish obstinacy and say he had paid a thousand pounds and he was determined to get his every penny's worth. But he merely handed back his glass with a shaky hand.

"Oh God, let's just get out of here," he muttered. "I'm so sorry, darling, I'm so sorry it's been such a disappointment for you!" He wiped his cracked lips.

"Oh, Henry, it hasn't!" I cried. "And it's not your fault."

I leaned down and kissed him, not caring about the rotting taste of his sickness, not caring if I got ill – it would almost be preferable to be locked in bed sweating together, safe away from Ricky and the dusty streets and temples . . .

23. Normal Married Life

It was such a relief to be back in England again.

Compared to the technicolour sensuality of India, everything was grey: the people, pavements, sky, weather. Beautifully, traditionally, Englishly grey. Cold churches and austere commuters with umbrellas and newspapers.

The doctor told Henry to take plenty of rest. I brought him water and read to him and yet all the time there was an awkward, niggling, irritated feeling, like sand in your sandals at the beach, only I couldn't wash the grit away.

A week went by and I heard nothing from Ricky. I didn't know whether to be happy or frightened. What if, I couldn't help wondering, he really has gone and – you know – taken a bottle of paracetamols? I mean, Ricky was so in love with life it was hard to imagine, but then again you never ever really knew what was going on deep in a person's mind. Perhaps I was being a cruel-hearted bitch, perhaps it would be all my fault, perhaps in his suicide note he would blame me . . .

Oh shit.

I phoned Josephine.

"He's gone! Just like that! We were due to go and

see a relationship counsellor. We were all booked in and I was made up to go and he came downstairs with a bloody rucksack and said he wanted to go off travelling. Said he needed some *space*. I give up on him, Olivia, I really do. If he's not careful by the time he gets back I'll have found someone else."

"But – but where's he gone?"

"Oh, Australia or something. I just hope he goes bungie-jumping and his eyes pop out and the rope breaks."

"Josephine!" I yelped.

"Well, after the way he treated me."

"So, so, how long for?"

"Six months – who knows? Forever, I hope. Anyway, let's not talk about Ricky. I don't want to talk about Ricky. Tell me about you and Henry and India, let's hear something positive for a change . . ."

So that, I thought, as I put down the phone, was that. All of a sudden, I felt really funny, sort of empty and colourless.

Still, now at least I could forget him and Henry and I could get on with having a normal marriage . . .

As the memories of Ricky faded into the background, the first three months of our marriage were indeed very blissful. Stuck in the dead of the countryside, a mile from the nearest rambling little station, I hardly ever got to see Leila or Josephine and that clubbing pubbing existence seemed lifetimes ago. Henry introduced me to a completely new way of life: theatre, opera, classical music and expensive dinners in London where he seemed delighted in having me taste octopus, escargot, caviar . . . I tried to protest that I was a veggie but he asserted, "Come on, Olivia, you're much too thin, it's most unhealthy." I tried to give him a lecture on factory farming but he wasn't having any of it. And so I started eating meat and it became a running joke between us that he was trying to fatten me up.

Often, despite Henry's paranoia of the press, we were snapped by reporters and though Henry moaned about the invasion of privacy, I think he was secretly rather pleased. I cut out the photographs from *Hello* magazine and pasted them into my diary. I liked to keep looking over them, more for Henry than me: I always looked so dreadful, caught at the wrong angle, mascara running, hair frizzing. But Henry always looked great: dark, menacing, exuding strength and power.

He was even more magnetic on television. Every Sunday, as the BBC Merc came to pick him up to drive him down to the Shepherd's Bush studios, I would sit up, hugging a cushion to my chest, flooded with adoring pride. It did make me laugh, though, to see how charmingly two-faced he could be.

For example – at breakfast, he would complain about an author, writing him off as, "Can't write for toffee. Total crap, and he stole one of my endings." Then, later that evening, he'd interview the same author, oozing with charm and saying, "Your novels have sold astoundingly well in over twenty countries . . ."

"Never shit on anyone important is my motto," Henry explained to me. "You never know when they might be useful to you."

After his shows, he was always at his most virile, as

though his ego was singing with happiness, teasing and touching me for hours on end until I was begging for him, gasping that I loved him, swearing I would never love another, until he plunged into me vehemently.

In June his series ended and he started on the final draft of his latest book, a commercial thriller, sweating away to meet a Macmillan deadline, often disappearing into his study straight after breakfast and not waking me till the dead of the night. But I didn't mind; I was happy taking Roberta for walks and getting a sexy tan. It was better always to be outdoors in the sun because the thick stone walls of Rochester made the place feel like a freezer even in the height of summer. Though Henry, as ever, was tight and frugal, refusing to let me put on the central heating.

I never understood why he worried so much about money. He had so much of it, but tax returns and gas bills and Agatha's constant demands always sent him into vile moods.

We went less and less to London and had Henry's friends over to dinner more often. It was great fun playing the hostess, dressing up and pretending to have cooked Denise's food, but Henry's friends just weren't my type. They were all young – "So he can have groupies to look up to him" – Josephine noted, and they tended to be very literary, arguing vehemently over different versions of *The Prelude* or Wilde's plays or Aristotle's *Poetics*.

I never knew what to say so I would smile and chop my dinner up and eat it slowly; I felt even worse when Henry complained that I didn't say enough; then, when I did try, one young chap got so keen that Henry accused me of flirting. He had a very jealous Scorpio streak; the slightest compliment from another man and I would feel his hand bristling on my knee and once he came into the stables and pushed Phil our stable boy up against the wall. I'd only been lighting his cigarette and Henry had seen it all wrong but Phil was sacked the next day. Shaken, I confided in Josephine, who told me off and said I was being cramped. After that, I didn't like to confide our problems anymore. They're just jealous because I've found the most wonderful man in the world, I thought defensively. I felt as though our love was a candle I wanted to put two hands around, to protect the flame from everyone.

But if Henry seemed to be sharp-tongued and cynical on the outside, he had a warm, generous streak that other people failed to glimpse. One evening, we were playing a game of chess, he giving me so much grandmasterly advice that I had to pretend to lose so as not to hurt his ego, when he casually dropped his best bombshell.

"I've arranged for us to have lunch tomorrow with a publisher called Clare Yates, regarding the publication of your erotic historical romance."

"I've only written a few chapters," I exaggerated wildly as we sat in the back of his Merc, being driven to the Ritz.

"Don't worry," Henry squeezed my hand, "everything's under control."

I squeezed his hand back and then kissed him, smiling up at him in adoration. I was fizzing like a shaken bottle of Krug – twenty-five years of failure and now at last, as well as having a delicious husband, I was about to get published! I could hardly believe my luck; it was as though I'd married a god or a genie.

Clare Yates turned out to be a very thin lady with large purple glasses and a shock of red fizzy hair. She talked a lot and very fast.

"Well, Olivia," she said finally as we reached the desserts, "I have a lady called Isabella Johnson who would be very happy to write *Racing Pulse* for you . . ." Seeing my face, she added quickly, "Don't worry – her credentials are good, she's written for a variety of female mags, including *Vogue* and *The Tatler* . . ."

"Oh," I said, "right." I looked at her and then at Henry, who were both looking at me expectantly. I twisted my napkin uneasily – what had I missed? "Erm, so, like, how do we . . . I mean is it some kind of telepathy thing . . . ?"

Clare's eyes widened, then she giggled and Henry shook his head and patted my knee.

"Olivia, my darling, Isabella is going to be a ghost writer for you."

"You're obviously very marketable," Clare went on eagerly. "Young writers are very fashionable, and you're very attractive, Olivia, but this new range is being published according to a set format, style and length . . ."

"Is this okay?" Henry asked on the way home, as though I hadn't been quite as pleased as he had expected. "After all, I couldn't really see you working nine to nine reaching a deadline – you've got far too much sunbathing and shopping to do."

Which was completely true, and yet his comment irked me in a way I couldn't quite define. But I just smiled and shrugged and said of course.

Perhaps, I reflected, it was because it would have been nice to have something to do. I was starting to get bored, with nobody to talk to except cows and sheep, and nothing to do except re-read Jilly Cooper or *More* problem pages and stuff myself on chocolate Hob Nobs.

I started to fret that perhaps Henry was trying to make a point. Perhaps I wasn't as clever as he wanted me to be. *But in that case, why did he marry me?* I argued back weakly.

Perhaps I ought to write something seriously intellectual. Something worthy of the Booker Prize. The sort of thing sixth formers were forced to read in schools and hated vehemently. The sort of thing that the BBC would make grim three-hour adaptations of.

It was then that *Aristole Revisited* was conceived.

I was so fired up and inspired I decided to pay Henry a visit. Ignoring the *Do Not Disturb* sign on his study door, I found him staring at his Toshiba. He continued tapping away as I tip-toed up behind him.

I went round to his side and slipped myself onto his lap.

"I'm trying to write," he protested faintly, circling his arms around my waist and tapping a few more words in.

"Oh, Henry, I've had this great idea for a novel. It's all going to be about a six-year-old girl in the Amazon rainforest who has past life regression and finds out she was once Aristotle," I explained excitedly. "It's going to be eight hundred pages long at least."

"Sounds like a real epic," said Henry and I caught a note of teasing in his voice.

Just you wait, I thought petulantly, just you wait till I beat you to the Whitbread, or whatever it was he'd just been nominated for. I sat on his lap for a while longer, feeling heavy and unwanted, until he tipped me off irritably.

"Olivia, I'm writing," he repeated in a cross voice.

"Well, can I just sit here and do some writing too?" I asked.

He looked really moody, as though I'd just said I wanted to turn on the TV full blast and practise cymbal-crashing. But I sat down at the table alongside him and chewed on the end of my pencil. Now, Aristotle . . . Aristotle . . . I couldn't concentrate, I couldn't help watching him in fascination. For about ten minutes, his fountain-pen scratched away non-stop. Then, for another ten minutes, he just sat there, unmoving, staring at an oak tree outside the window, unblinking, like one of those desert lizards spotting prey.

"What the fuck are you looking at?" he suddenly turned on me, and I quickly turned a page of my work.

I lifted my A4 up to cover my face and sat there nervously, pretending to check intently for spelling mistakes. Goodness, he was in a bad mood.

Finally, I dared to lower my book an inch and saw that he was now writing frantically hard, thank goodness.

I was dying to go to the loo, so I squeezed my thighs

together bravely and pretended to carry on scribbling. My stomach rumbled loudly. I'd been snacking all day but hadn't bothered to cook lunch.

Very slowly, I edged my hand down towards the drawer. His shoulders remained hunched, he kept scribbling. I slid it open and looked inside for the faint possibility of a chocolate bar – or at the worst, one of his Extra Strong Mints. Oh, mmm, there was a yummy bar of Galaxy.

I tore off the wrapper. His pencil hovered. I froze.

"Can't you please keep quiet for more than five minutes!" he howled.

I froze and nodded my head an inch. He went back to his work, shuffling his papers together and letting out a long tired sigh. Perhaps, I thought unhappily, I would be famous like Coleridge's Lady from Porlock, the interrupting wife who ruined the great Sir Henry Caldwell's epic masterpiece . . .

My bladder was going to burst, I just couldn't take anymore.

I jumped up.

"I'm going, I'm go –"

He picked up a blue and white patterned vase and threw it across the room at me. I felt the whizz of air past my ear. The vase hit the wall. China lay across the carpet.

"*Can't you – just – leave me – in – peace –*" he was so angry he could hardly get the words out, his hands on his temples.

"I'm going," I whimpered, dashing out.

In the corridor, Denise was dusting and gazed at me with wide, frightened eyes.

"Did something crash?" she asked.

"Erm, did it?" I asked. "Erm, yes, oh that, it was just a vase, one of the cheap vases, thank goodness," I lied.

I then did an Irish jig of nerves from one foot to the other as she insisted on going downstairs and bringing back up a dustpan and brush. She passed it over and paused, waiting for me to go back in.

At last, I opened the door an inch, threw the brush and pan in, slammed the door, cried to Denise, "Just going for a breath of fresh air, won't be long, byeeee", and ran off.

I ran and ran and ran, all the way down the gravel driveway, along the grassy roadside, half expecting to turn and see Henry coming after me with an axe. Diving into a nearby little café, I hurried to the loo, then sat down by the window and ordered some tea. There was some spilt sugar on the table and I kept pushing it about, making patterns: a rainbow, a heart, a bow, a jagged broken heart.

My mind snaked back and forth, like two lawyers prosecuting and defending Sir C.

"But," appealed the defense, "Sir Caldwell is a writer. He is an artist, a profession few people in our society understand."

Promptly, the lawyer for the prosecution jumped up and said,

"Objection – no piece of art, no matter how important merits such an act of physical violence when all my client did was unpeel a chocolate bar."

What's going on? I thought miserably, What kind of psycho have I married? I had read about cases like this in *Cosmo* – men who seemed charming princes when you first met them, showering you with flowers and chocolates but later blows and punches. I had never understood why the victims didn't just tell their batterers to go and bugger off but now I understood completely.

Or maybe it was just me. Perhaps I was behaving just as dreadfully as Agatha always had, instead of his first wife Mary, who had always been wonderfully loving and supportive. Perhaps he was starting to wish he had never married me.

As my brain snapped, crackled and popped with what ifs and yes buts, my eyes strayed to the paintings lining the cafe walls like feathers in a nest.

They were all very twee: dogs loping in the countryside, little cottages like snug nests in the countryside, etc. etc. I found myself buying a small one of some little ducks in a countryside lake for fifteen pounds then my legs seemed to carry me back home.

By the time I got back it was nearly completely dark. I almost fell back down the steps when Henry opened the door. At first we just looked at each other. Then I shoved the picture in his hands.

"I, er, bought this for you."

Instinctively, I ducked, as though he was going to throw it at me, and he suddenly touched my cheek, looking hurt. "Don't do that. Don't. I won't hurt you. I'm sorry, I didn't mean to scare –"

"Oh there you are, dear," Denise appeared, "where did you go? Henry was worried, he was nearly calling the police but I told him you'd gone for a walk."

"Yes," I swallowed, "I went for a walk."

She offered me some tea but I had spent all afternoon drinking enough tea to last a lifetime, and Henry
soon bore me off upstairs.

As soon as we were inside the bedroom he started
shouting again – "Where the hell were you?" and, "I
was worried sick!" My heart quailed and I started to
edge towards the bedroom door, then I saw the fear
flashing in his eyes and realised he really had been
worried. I suddenly jumped up and cut off "I was
nearly calling the police –" with an apologetic kiss.

He looked startled, even more so when I unbuttoned his shirt and started to cover his chest with
nervous little butterfly kisses.

He raised his hand to touch my hair and I flinched
again and he cried, "Olivia, I'm so sorry, I'm not going
to hurt you." He flung his arms around me and held
me tight against him so that I could hardly breathe,
stroking my hair and kissing my head all over,
murmuring, "I'm so sorry, I'm so sorry, it won't ever
happen again . . ."

We lay in each others' arms in the darkness, listening
to each others' heartbeats and the faint hoot of an owl.

"Anyway," Henry said, slowly drawing back a curl
from my face with a tenderness that melted my heart
to mush and made me reach up and interrupt him with
a kiss. "Anyway," he said smilingly, "I've been thinking
about you being bored, and I know you need something to keep you busy and happy. So while you ran
away, I arranged a job for you on a womens' magazine."

"Oh Henry!"

"Nothing big – just something easy you can manage, nothing too demanding. Just a few days a week, and you'll have to commute to London . . ."

"I can do that, I can!" I cried, spilling over with gratitude.

"I spoke to the editor and she seemed very happy. She's a good friend of mine, I twisted her arm a few years back to get Ricky onto Features. And you won't be too lonely because Ricky's due back from Australia soon. He'll be there to show you round and look after you."

"Ricky!" my heart thudded. "Oh. Oh, right. Well."

"Is that okay?" Henry gave me a funny look.

Well, what could I say? 'Henry, your son tried to break our marriage up and made a move on me during our honeymoon and so I was hoping to avoid him if I possibly could?'

"Oh, yes," I said faintly, curling my arms tight around his chest. Sod Ricky, I loved my husband so much I wasn't going to let anything come between us. "Thank you, thank you, I love you, thank you . . ."

He lifted his arm so that I could nestle my head against his shoulder. He stroked my hair and kissed my head and told me that he loved me too.

I told him, "I love you" all the time – at dinner, in an exuberant burst of bliss when we were out walking in the beauty of the countryside, when he bought me a new dress.

He only ever said "I love you" in the darkness, when I couldn't see his face, in a quiet, almost shy voice.

24. Vixen

Entering the *Vixen* offices a fortnight later, I was determined to appear as thick, ill-presented and unemployable as possible. There was just *no way* I wanted to work with Ricky. And yet that morning I found myself ironing away at my lavender suit, packing a pair of tights into my bag in fear of inevitable ladders.

Henry had said it would just be a little chat to sort out hours, but even so, I was ready for every question they might ask. I'd been up till three reading thirty issues of *Cosmo*. I'd written a sample column on underwater deliveries. Every pore of my brain was saturated with facts and figures on every female topic from nappy rash to thrush to leg waxing. My head felt so full that I couldn't even remember my date of birth, but I could tell you precisely how many times an hour a man thinks of sex: seven.

Or was that every minute? Argh! Shit, Olivia, think, think, I panicked, as I strolled along the grey-carpeted hallways of the EMAP Elan complex. I got into the lift, checked my lipstick in the mirror and then banged my head against the glass.

"How many times, how many times a minute does a man think of sex?"

Just at that moment a middle-aged man in a suit walked in. He gave me a most curious glance. I smiled, mumbled something about "Market Research," and spent the rest of the ride with a tomato-red face, my eyes fixed desperately on the lift barometer zinging up past floors 1 . . . 2 . . . 3.

As he got out on floor 3, he turned with a slightly sheepish smile and shrug, and said, "Six times, I'd say."

He blushed and hurried off. As the lift doors closed, I collapsed into laughter. How embarrassing! Oh goodness, I suddenly thought, I hope by some horrible twist of fate he's not the one interviewing me. Argh!

The lift doors opened at level 5.

I pulled down the hem of my short lavender skirt and took in a deep breath.

"Hi, I'm Olivia Caldwell. I'm here to start work with *Vixen* on, erm, Top Tips," I introduced myself to a beautiful, sulky receptionist, who pointed the way.

I strolled into a big, big office crammed from wall to wall with desks.

The first thing that hit me was the noise. It was like walking into a party. Capital Radio blaring at one end fought with Classic FM from the other. Computers buzzed; keys clicked; someone screamed, "Who's nicked my rubber?"; a paper aeroplane, made from a pin-up of Cindy Crawford sailed through the air. Everywhere were beautiful shiny Career Girls, adorned in Miss Selfridges suits, flicking back streaked, layered Jennifer Anniston hair. "What d'you mean you can't give me his number?" one blonde yelled into the phone, "Me and Leonardo are like this," she crossed two fingers.

I couldn't help looking for Ricky but he was nowhere to be seen.

I held my head high and tried not to teeter in my high heels. Outside the office I paused uncertainly. Should I wait? Knock? A desk away, a beautiful girl with chestnut ringlets was sitting giving me an appraising, unhelpful glance.

"Are you Olivia?"

I nodded, rubbing my sweaty palms together.

"Get me a cup of tea, would you, darling?" she asked in a silky but nevertheless no-nonsense tone.

So this was Jenny. Henry had warned me that she might be 'a bit abrupt'. Now I saw what he meant. I looked around wildly for a tea trolley. She clicked her fingers and I was surprised to see the mug and kettle right by her feet. She yawned lazily as I knelt down beside her, plugging in the kettle. As I spooned out sugar, I felt her fingers brush the crown of my head and I jumped back.

"Dandruff." She blew the tips of her manicured nails and gave me a blithe smile. "Ever tried 'Head and Shoulders'?" she imitated the advert. Then, when I handed her the tea she winced and said, "How many sugars? I don't take sugar."

I hung my head and mumbled sorry, silently seething. What a bitch. Could I survive working for her much longer than five minutes? But if I walked out now, Henry would be so disappointed in me.

"Hi there," an unexpected male voice floated behind me. I jumped, instantly thinking it must be Ricky. But I turned to see a tall man with spiky dark hair and a foxy face.

"I'm Ferras," he said, taking my hand and kissing it, looking up at me from under dark lashes with a very wicked stare. I grinned, taking an instant liking to him; I could tell his type at once: the flirty, gossipy brand who couldn't pick up a stapler without phallic innuendo or see you say three words to a bloke without a nudge, nudge, wink, wink, hope you used protection, darling.

"Oh stop that, Ferras!" the boss snarled in withering disgust, "I've got another letter for you." She flung a pad at him and he caught it deftly. "He tries it on with everyone here," she added to me dismissively. Then she patted the chair beside her and handed me a pencil and jotter. "I want to dictate a reply to this most banal letter. Listen to this," she snapped, imitating a high-pitched voice of stricken desperation, *"I'm writing to you because I don't know who to turn to. Basically, my problem is this: I have married the perfect man and we've been together for four months now. At first everything was so perfect. But over the last two months I've really started to suffer from boredom . . ."* I mean, what a stupid cow! What a complete doormat! All she cares about is being happy to fit with her husband's needs. God, I might as well suggest she just take a bottle of paracetamols and be done with it."

"Olivia, this is Emily," said Ferras, with a wry smile. "Queen of Agony Aunts. Solves the problems of the nation with her maternal and tender loving care."

I couldn't stop staring at her with a crimson face. So she was Emily. Not Jenny. And here I was making her tea and behaving like a complete doormat.

"So what are you going to be doing for us, Olivia?"

Ferras raised an eyebrow as if expecting me to reply: "Sexual Positions" or "Ten Ways to Make Your Man Happy In Bed."

"Oh, just Top Tips," I confessed sulkily, seeing Emily hide a derogatory smile.

"Oh God, why are you doing that, you mad girl? That's the bum job nobody wants. Still, it's great to have another beautiful lady in the office," he said, giving me another wicked smile. Then the smile vanished as he nudged and pointed frantically. Emily too put down her tea with a sploshed bang and started typing quickly.

I turned to see a short Japanese girl, about five feet tall, wearing jeans, her dark hair flipped into a scrappy ponytail.

She put her hands on her hips and glared at me. "Here for the interview?"

I nodded mutely. It was amazing how someone who was half a foot shorter than me could make me feel so small.

Her office was sparse and neat compared to the overflowing chaos of the main office. The furniture was minimalist and there were just a few scraps of paper on her desk. The odd thin green pot plant was the only colour in the cool greyness.

Another girl was sitting on a chair. She was wearing a turquoise flowery skirt which just covered her suspenders, her red-brown hair trussed up in an enormous ebony paperclip. She was chewing gum and said, "Hiya" in a bolshy Essex accent as I came in.

"This is Chrysanthemum Peters," Jenny introduced her abruptly.

Chrysanthemum gave me the thumbs up. I sat down on the edge of the chair, and gave a nervous smile.

Jenny sat down and rubbed her knuckles. She took some Aloe Vera gel and slapped some onto her hands.

"I get rashes during the summer," she said to me, as if she was trying to be chatty and put me at ease but I only felt more uptight.

"So," she asked, back to brisk business mode, "have you had a lot of experience in female mags?"

I was slightly taken aback. What about the little cosy chat over a cup of tea which Henry had promised? Surely Henry had told her my only qualification was that I was married to him? Was he expecting me to bluff?

"Well, I, er, love reading, er, *Cosmo*," I said at last.

"*Cosmo*, what's that?"

"I meant, *Cosmopolitan*," I blushed.

"Olivia," Chrysanthemum corrected me brightly, "*Cosmo* is a swearword in this office." She shook her head and tut-tutted with pouty lips.

Oh dear God, only one question and already I was sliding backwards.

We were interrupted by a knock at the door. Jenny automatically snapped "Get out!" but a horribly familiar face popped around the door, his blonde fringe falling over his sunglasses. Ricky.

"Ricky, we're interviewing!" Jenny snapped, but I noticed a distinct softening in her voice. She didn't even object when he came and sat down next to me, unlacing his brown boots, propping his feet (encased in Wallace & Grommit socks) up on her desk, then rustling out a packet of Rolos, dropping them all over the carpet. Chrysanthemum also took a glance at herself in the window reflection and crossed her legs so that her skirt rucked up a few inches.

"So, Olivia?" Ricky picked up a ruler and pretended to use it as a microphone. He put on his best cheesy American chatshow voice, "What do you think you can contribute to Top Tips?"

I could hardly believe his nerve. Two months ago he had been declaring undying love and now, without the slightest shred of embarrassment, he was thrusting a Helix in my face and pretending to be Oprah Winfrey. I turned to Jenny but she pinned her black-currant eyes on me and nodded her head. I swallowed.

"Well, I have a degree in English and during my university years I wrote a lot of articles for student papers (well, I once wrote a review on *Four Weddings* which ended up being edited out, but still), and I, er, I've done a lot of research and I know you need to put lemon juice on avocados and that men think of sex six times a minute," I burst out in a rushed gabble.

I could hear bloody Ricky repressing a guffaw. Jenny gave me an incredulous glance. Chrysanthemum grinned, her panda-lined eyes widening, and said excitedly, "Sixty times a minute, more like."

"Olivia," Jenny put her hands in a steeple and said with forced gentleness, "our readers write in asking how to remove a stain from a table, not what sexual position to do with the table."

Silence. I could feel Ricky's eyes on me and I stared at my nails. Hard. Great, thanks so much, I shouted at him silently, you ruined my honeymoon and now my job interview too.

"Oh, why the fuck are you bothering with these questions anyway?" Ricky broke the silence. "Olivia's obviously going to be great – she's smart, she's funny, she's really pretty, and she's married to my dad who's surely the most demanding man to live with – she has to run around all the time looking after him."

Jenny stopped banging her ruler against her In-Tray and sat up, looking more impressed.

"What's it like being married to him?" Chrysanthemum blurted out. "I mean, he just looks so sexy on TV."

Jenny gave her a shut-up look and Chrysanthemum muffled a squealish giggle behind her hand.

"Very lovely, thanks," I said, blushing proudly and giving Ricky a pointed glance.

After that, the rest of the interview went swimmingly. The mention of Henry, lurking in the background with almost Godfatherly presence, reminded Jenny that I could be a very useful contact. And before I knew it, she was shaking my hand and saying she would be delighted to work with me.

Shit! I'd got the job! Nine to five! Just like that. A tremor of fear and excitement shivered through me. I could hardly wait to tell Henry! *Whopppeeeeee!*

"So you're going to join the force," Ricky said exuberantly as he escorted me into the lift. "Can't wait!"

"Yeah, well, don't get any funny ideas," I snapped.

"Don't worry, I won't," he snapped back, looking hurt and fed-up.

As the lift jolted downwards, we stood in hot silence. Then as it pinged to the first floor I walked out without saying goodbye.

*   *   *

For my first month at *Vixen,* I never worked so hard in all my life. Jenny's secretary had just walked out and besides doing Top Tips I soon found myself coming in extra days to cover all the extra typing and faxing and photocopying Jenny lumbered on me. Every time anybody needed a job done, Jenny just waved her hand and said, "Give it to Olivia." As Ferras summed up perfectly, "You've been branded general dogs-body."

"You should just tell her where to go," Ricky asserted, complaining that he couldn't pull faces across the room at me because my In-Tray was worse than the Leaning Tower of Pisa. But I daren't say a word; somehow I had a feeling I was being stretched, tested. Henry had told me to give the job my all and make me proud of him.

The biggest challenge was getting used to the girls. They were slow and begrudging in accepting me, especially when Ricky was always paying me so much attention. It seemed as though everyone in the office was in love with him except for me. Ferras was even running an underground betting shop on which of the girls would be most likely to get him first – the top contenders being Emily (keen but sharp-tongued and Ricky liked a soft touch), Chrysanthemum (equally keen but loose and liable to change her mind) and even Jenny (but such a workaholic she'd barely have the time to even consider it). He flirted so wildly with all of them, any one seemed possible at any moment.

At first I was cold and abrupt to Ricky, but he just ignored me; so then I tried my best to ignore him, but it was very hard when he was chucking aeroplanes at me or ringing my extension putting on silly accents or interrupting me with ICQ messages:

So, Ms Bliss, how are you this morning? Today I got myself a brand new willy, twelve inches long.

As you do.

All the girls at work are going mad over it. I have to glue it on every morning, at night I keep it in a preserving glass.

You'd better not muddle it up with your false teeth.

Ricky put down his HP sauce sandwich and stood on his chair, shaking his head at me and crying exuberantly, "Olivia, you're disgusting!"

In case you missed me yesterday, I was out interviewing divorced women. Some of them were really woof-woof and when they got upset I did my best to comfort them.

I'm sure you did, I typed back. *Now bugger off. I've just had my knuckles rapped by Jenny for being late again and she's given me a ton of extra work and I have to find out the best way to get biro stains out of cotton sheets.*

Tell her to chuck them away. And don't worry about Jenny, her miaow is worse than her bite.

Easy for you to say. She doesn't fancy me.

Oh I wish I wish! I wish she would give me a bollocking, she looks so sexy when she's angry. I tried to rile her this morning by suggesting a new idea for the front cover: Denise Van Outen, naked, covered with sugar paper. And then you have to eat / lick it off.

271

Ricky, that is disgusting!

Just what Jenny said. She hit me over the head with her ruler. But seriously, Princess of the Fairies, will you come for a drink with me this afternoon? I've got something really important to talk to you about.

I can't, I retreated at last to our Northern banter, *I've got loads to do and then I've got to go home to feed my husband and five kids when they come back from t'pit.*

Oh come on, Olivia, pllleeeeeeeeeeeeeeeease ... It's really important.

Oh, okay, I gave in at last, very reluctantly.

By three o'clock I started to feel uneasy again. Alright, so Ricky hadn't made any more moves; in fact, it was as though India had never happened, but still . . . perhaps I should have called up Leila and Josephine and invited them along too.

But on the tube Ricky was as relaxed and flamboyant as ever, offering me a seat and hanging onto a pole, munching into a banana and reading out the 'Poems on the Tube' in a sarcastic voice and sending a pack of French school tourists into giggles.

"Bugger, why don't they ever have bins on platforms, it's so annoying," he complained as we got off at Leicester Square. Then I pushed him in horror as he deposited his banana skin in a busker's tweed cap and ran off laughing. The busker curled his fist.

"Sorry," I apologised, opening my purse and, for lack of change, giving him a fiver.

In the pub Ricky offered to buy me a drink but then, typically, found he had run out of money and no credit cards were accepted, so I had to get my purse out. Feeling nervous again, I kept joking around, squabbling with him on how many drinks he owed me.

"You should buy me one for my incredibly scintillating company," Ricky declared.

"You owe me one for dragging me out from my desk," I fought back.

"You're lucky you get dragged away. Top Tips is such a poo job. Still, yesterday I got sent out onto the streets asking young girls what their ideal date would be and who they preferred out of Leo Caprio, Keanu Reeves and Ewan MacGregor. It was so embarrassing."

"I bet you loved it," I retorted, reaching over and examining his clipboard, intrigued to see the responses. "How extraordinary! Most girls' ideal male happened to be 'blonde, brown-eyed, tall and slim'. What a coincidence."

"That's me," Ricky glowed proudly, "the perfect male."

"Yeah, right."

He pulled a hurt expression, so I tugged his fringe gently and he managed a smile.

"D'you think I could ask you a question?" he suddenly got all serious on me.

I paused uneasily and took a big gulp of Baileys. This sounded dangerous.

Then, when he pulled a small blue velvet jewel box out of his 501s, I spat out a mouthful of Baileys all over his jacket.

"Oh God, I'm so sorry," I cringed, smearing him desperately with a napkin.

"It's okay, it's okay." Ricky put his cool hand over

mine and I yanked mine away quickly, mopping up the table with the sludgy remains of the tissue.

"It's for Josephine," he said pointedly.

"Oh, oh, oh," I tried to laugh and then slapped the table and nodded emphatically, as if I'd known that all along. But as I gushed compliments about how good they would be together, I could see the amused quirkiness in his eyes, knowing my mistake. Bastard.

"D'you think she'll say yes?" Ricky worried.

I bit my lip and thought: seeing the size of that emerald alone will be enough to convince her. Whether she'll make it to saying 'I do' is another matter.

"I mean, I just don't even know how to say it," Ricky worried. "I keep asking Leila for advice and she keeps nagging me to just do it, but I feel like I'm way over my head. I mean, I've never done this before, I feel like a thirteen-year-old again trying to cook up some chat-up line that beats "D'you come here often?" The more I put it off the worse it gets, like taking an exam or going to the dentist."

"Well, how did you say it last time?" I asked, quite touched to see the normally extrovert Ricky so shy for once.

"Last time? Last time it was her who asked. Well, 'ask' is the ambiguous word. It wasn't so much a case of, 'Shall we get married?' as 'We will get married'."

"That's our Joey," I said, and we both laughed fondly.

In the end, after playing back and forth a variety of approaches: from mentioning it casually during *Blind Date* or before, during or after sex or going really wild and setting off a firework display that would sing '*Will You Marry Me?*' across the sky, we finally agreed on something traditional: candlelit dinner for two, ring, flowers, wine . . .

We managed to get a bouquet of freesias from the florists just before they closed, plus Josephine's favourite Lambrusco Light from Oddbins. Now all that was needed was the meal. I saw Ricky give me a hopeful look and immediately started to protest.

"Henry's home, he'll be waiting for me," I cried.

"Olivia, please," Ricky begged me, going down on one knee. "Please, please, if I don't produce something worthy of *Masterchef,* Josephine'll have me hung, drawn and quartered and served up as Ricky-stew. She's trying to train me up to be the perfect nineties man. You don't know how mad she got last week when I was on the 'Cooking' rota and all I did was melted Mars Bar on toast . . ."

25. Proposal

"Olivia, Olivia, you have to help me, it's a major disaster!" Ricky hissed.

Leila and I looked up from laying out fancy cutlery on the little table, breaking off in mid-gossip.

I left Leila with the cutlery and went into the kitchen. There, I gazed around at the chaos in amazement. Flour powdered the floor and surfaces, half-whisked egg yolks smattered with shell congealed in bowls, and one of Josephine's best pans was filled with an ugly green mess which smelt revolting and looked as though it would be impossible to scrape off even with a gallon of Fairy Liquid. How could he have made so much mess in ten minutes? He was simply a force of Nature.

"I thought we were just doing spaghetti with a pesto sauce," I said in confusion.

"I know, I know," Ricky ran his hands through his hair, "but I thought that was too boring, I really wanted to impress her, so I figured duck a l'orange sounded really sexy."

"But we don't even have half the ingredients," I pointed out, squinting at the cookbook.

"Does it matter?" Ricky asked in surprise. "I mean, I

put in some substitutes, I was going to use flour instead of baking powder and mix up mayonnaise with ketchup instead of soy sauce."

I shook my head in exasperation and he put on an innocent face. I sighed and said,

"Well, okay, let's start again."

"Thank you, thank you!" Ricky engulfed me in a hug and told me I was a total lifesaver, then jumped away nervously, hearing voices at the door. Josephine was home.

"Sssh!" he said guiltily. "If they come in, you hide, okay!"

We stood frozen for a moment, then exhaled with relief as, as planned, Leila bore Josephine off for a quick drink at The Moon On the Hill and Josephine went with minimal fuss.

Ricky let out his breath. "Okay, let's hurry, they'll probably only be gone half an hour."

I went to the shelf and pulled down a cookbook.

"When in doubt, use Delia Smith," I instructed.

"I'm highly suspicious of Delia," said Ricky, losing my page as he flicked over to her face on the cover. "She's definitely going to be the next Hitler of our generation. Just look what happened when she said use cranberries – the supermarkets were overflowing with them. And look at that picture – despite the smile on her face, there's a dangerous steely look in those blue eyes, like Thatcher. She's aiming for world takeover, don't laugh, just you wait and see!"

As you can imagine, it was impossible to concentrate on finding a recipe with Ricky chattering away and asking if we could do pancakes so we could throw them up and see if they stuck to the ceiling. So much for his earlier panicking – I swear it was all an act to get me to do the cooking!

"Why don't we just begin with dessert?" I said at last. "How about whipping up a quick chocolate mousse, I can make that blindfold."

"You are a chocoholic, aren't you?" said Ricky. "I'm growing more and more convinced that the way to a woman's heart is through chocolate. Maybe I should get Josephine one of those massive Thorntons' selections."

We decided to go back to spaghetti for the main course which should have been simple, but Ricky kept messing about and doing impressions of Lloyd Grossman, using a spoon for a microphone.

Then he hoisted himself up on the surface, munching away at the Green & Black's, which was supposed to be for dessert.

"Okay, that's enough," I yanked the chocolate back off him, so then he stole the squirty cream instead.

He squeezed some onto his fingers, just to "test" that it was okay.

"Hmm, yummy," he said, and then squirted some more for me to taste. His fingers were a nice salty contrast to the sweet cream.

I went to the sink and started to fill up the pan.

"So," I cleared my throat, "have you worked out what moment you're going to –"

I cried out and turned, feeling something cold slither down the back of my neck. It was Ricky, messing around with the cream.

"You bastard!" I yelped. I grabbed a cloth and flicked

water at him and he grabbed me and pushed me back against the sink, holding the can threateningly above my head. I was laughing so much, I couldn't fight him.

"Leave me alone, you big bully, I can do Judo," I lied. For a few minutes we jostled as I tried, totally ineffectually, to trip him up.

"Try a bit harder. Wow, I can see you really were a black belt," he kept taking the piss, then he nimbly slipped his Nike around the back of my leg and tripped me onto the floor on my back.

He had my waist between his knees. With one hand, he grabbed my wrists and pinned them behind my head. With the other, he gripped onto the can, his eyes gleaming.

"Let me go!" I squealed, trying to struggle out of his iron grip.

Ricky laughed his head off and shook the can very slowly.

"Now, what shall I spray first?" He shook his blonde hair off his forehead and cocked his head to one side, surveying me up and down. "How about some cream in your ear?"

"I'll get you for this," I cried, "just you wait. You're so mean, I came down here to help you with your cooking and now you assault me and cover me with cream. Just you wait! I shall tell Josephine and she'll divorce you!"

"Oh, I'm really scared," Ricky drawled, and sprayed a little blob on my nose.

I fought my hands away and very nearly escaped but he threw himself down on me, pinning me to the floor.

My cheeks burned. I stopped struggling. He was so heavy on top of me, I could feel the hard muscular length of his thighs on mine and something even harder pressing against my stomach.

Slowly, his hand shaking the can came to a halt and he loosened his grip. I tried to quieten my fluttering breath. His brown eyes were glued to mine with shocked intensity. He drew back a curl from my face and suddenly he was leaning down in a blur and I found myself lifting my head automatically, an ache thick in the back of my throat –

"Um. Ah," Ricky pulled back abruptly and stood up. "Yeah, well . . . so. Anyway."

I sat up, smoothing down my hair, a blush over my face like a rash. He reached out to help me up, then, as I felt the tingle of our fingers, he suddenly let go so I fell back against the table.

"Are you okay?" Ricky asked in alarm.

"Fine, fine," I said, rubbing my bruised back.

The click of the front door opening. Josephine. And Leila.

For a moment Ricky and I gazed at each other in panic. The next minute, Josephine had come into the kitchen.

"Oh wow, Olivia, haven't seen you for ages!" she engulfed me in an enthusiastic hug.

"Er, Olivia was just popping by to see if we all fancied going out for a meal," Ricky gabbled.

"Well," said Josephine laughingly, looking round at the chaos of the kitchen, "looks like a good idea. Oh how lovely," she tucked my arm through mine, "let's make a real night of it, it feels just like the old days again!"

*   *   *

We went to Sutton UCI to see a movie first. Josephine picked out *Wings of A Dove*. I could see at once from Ricky's face that he was disappointed – it wasn't the type of *Indiana Jones* action-packed movie he normally went for, but for once he shut up.

We loaded up with Cokes and popcorn and Ben and Jerrys. In the cinema, I tried to jiggle backwards so Josephine would end up next to Ricky but she pushed me forward so the order ended up all wrong – Josephine, then Leila, then me, then Ricky.

Ricky kept playing with the ring from palm to palm; he seemed restless, whether from nerves or boredom I couldn't tell. I realised I'd only seen the film the previous week with Henry but I could hardly focus anyway, still shocked by what had happened in the kitchen. It's alright, I kept trying to reassure myself, it's okay to fancy other people from time to time. After all, that usherette was pretty horny. The guy in the film was damn sexy. But not as sexy as Ricky, I found myself thinking. Then, as our hands brushed in the popcorn, I found myself showering it all over the floor.

"Shit!" said Ricky.

"Sorry," I said, glad of the darkness to hide my red face.

"No! Shit-as-in-I've-just-dropped-the-ring-in-the-popcorn," Ricky whispered through clenched teeth into my ear.

We spent the next ten minutes surreptitiously dipping our fingers into it, but it was no use.

"Fuck," I said.

"Bloody buggery hell," said Ricky, promptly up-turning it over the floor.

"Ricky, now you'll lose it!" I hissed.

The couple in front turned to give us the most filthy looks. Josephine scowled across as Ricky and I slid off our seats and searched around the floor.

"Can I borrow your searchlight?" Ricky asked the usherette at last. Then, "Oh man, it's under the seat." Reaching out, he retrieved it, but not without disturbing the blonde bimbo who looked back, no doubt thinking she was being groped.

"Are you trying it on with my bird?" hissed her skin-head boyfriend.

"You caused a rumpus throughout the entire film!" Josephine complained to Ricky as we sat in the local Indian afterwards, waiting for our food. "You're always so immature."

"It was Olivia too," Ricky moaned, then yelped as I kicked him under the table. "Anyway, it was a bloody boring film. I'll probably have to review it for *Vixen*. 'The only plot existing in the film was a succession of pained angst expressions from Ms Bonham Carter.'" He did an impression of her tragic glance that had me and Leila in fits of giggles. When I'd seen the film with Henry, we'd spent hours afterwards dissecting it; Henry, being a great fan of Henry James, drawing compar-isons with the original and declaring it was a travesty that Bonham Carter hadn't got an Oscar, and I'd pretended to agree.

As the main course was served, however, Josephine softened up and by the end she and Ricky were even sharing their biriani and almond naan breads.

"Let's go to the loo, Olivia," Leila said loudly, giving me a pointed look.

"I wonder if he'll pluck up the guts," I said, inside the ladies', fingering a bowl of pot pouri. "Funny how they argue all the time, makes one wonder if they really suit each other."

"Well," said Leila, rinsing her hands in the sink, "opposites attract. Look at you and Henry, he's so hard, and you're so soft. Strange, isn't it," she added in a soft voice, "to think we all liked him to begin with? But I think Josephine suits him best, somehow."

I turned and hastily wiped my hands on a green paper towel. Christ, was it that obvious how much I liked him?

When we went back into the restaurant, they were holding hands and looking very romantic.

"Well?" Leila asked brightly as we sat down.

"Well what?" Josephine tossed back her blonde hair. She narrowed her eyes at us. "You two are up to something – what? You've got a conspiratorial air."

"Oh no," we adopted innocent faces. As Josephine waved for the bill, Leila glared at Ricky and he gnawed his lip.

Oh well, I thought hopefully, maybe he's changing his mind, maybe he'll never pluck up the guts. But as we were eating the mints at the end, he went to the mens' and then came striding back purposefully. Picking up Josephine's fork, he tapped it against the glass until the whole room was silent. Even a group of rowdy lads singing Everton songs shut up and looked over. A waiter, carrying a tray of tall white *lassis,* stopped in the middle of the room.

"I want everyone to bear witness to what I'm about to say to the girl I love most in the world," said Ricky with trembling bravery. Falling to his knees, he held out the ring, still dusty from the popcorn. "Josephine, please, please will you say yes?"

I was so moved, so sucked in by his speech, as though he was somehow addressing me, that I felt tears prick my eyes. Then I blinked as I saw Josephine look around nervously. Ricky, still kneeling, pawed her nervously like a Labrador wanting to climb onto her lap.

"I'm sorry," said Josephine at last, bowing her head, gently pushing him away.

Silence.

"Aw, go on love," shouted one of the rugby lads.

"Nah! She's way too sexy for that bastard, come over here, love, I'll show you a good time," offered another. Ricky swung around and looked as though he was about to punch him. When he turned back, there was such a hurt, gutted look on his face that I wanted to hold him, so tightly that I'd hug all his pain out of him.

We all jumped when Ricky's mobile rang. It was Henry, wanting to know when I was coming home.

"We were supposed to be dining with Gus and Fanny," he reminded me curtly.

Oh shit! I'd forgotten all about that!

I was glad to escape. Thank goodness I had three trains to catch – I needed serious time to think.

By the end of my journey, I had worked the whole situation out. I didn't really really fancy Ricky. I realised that I just liked the *idea of him*. Just like when you go on a first date with someone and it's perfect because you don't really know them so you can create some fantasy as though you're picking attributes for a genetically engineered baby, like *His hands look big, isn't it a rule that other parts of his body should correspond?*, or, *That watch is expensive, I'm just certain he's loaded and we'll end up living together in his castle*. Etc.

In reality, Ricky and I would be all wrong. He was too loud and mad. And we were both so crap with money, if we ever had lived together our house would end up being repossessed. Leila was right – he needed an opposite like Josephine to keep him in line, just like I needed Henry to help keep my feet on the ground . . .

As the train pulled into the station, however, I didn't want to get off. Henry had been making mutterings recently about how much time I was spending away from him. He'd sounded pretty mad on the phone.

When I got back, Henry was already waiting by the front door. He was dressed in black tie and had an equally black look on his face. When I went up to kiss him, his face was taut, as if the skin was tightly stretched over the bone.

"D'you want to come into my study for a chat?" he asked.

I felt as though I was being summoned for the cane.

I followed him in, chattering nervously, then shut up when I saw Ms French slowly packing up her briefcase. She gave me a tight, brisk hello. *I swear she's taken up the hem on that tweed skirt*, I noted, unable to prevent my bitchiness, and she certainly was too old to have the legs for it.

"I presume you had a ton of extra work?" he suddenly feigned such a soft sympathetic voice that I nodded apologetically.

"Well, I'm sorry, dear, but I think it's time for you to resign."

"What!" What! What, resign and give up the glorious roller-coaster rush of deadlines and telephones endlessly ringing with ever-increasing circles of gossip and drinks after work? Give it all up to go back to drifting uselessly around the house like a lump of drift-wood, going to the fridge every hour to fill up the emptiness, checking 1471 to see if anyone might have called? And never seeing Ricky again, not having him there every day to leave silly screen-savers on my computer and interrupt my work with crazy e-mails?

"I can't," I said in a high voice. "I won't, I can't, I've got a c-contract . . ."

"I can talk to Jenny for you."

"But —"

Henry cut me off, turning to Ms French and asking if she would work late with him on Friday evening.

"Of course." She made a note with her super-sharp HB pencil in her little black diary. I stood, fuming and waiting for her to leave, buying time to think, to hold my calm. I hated the way that he always remained so cool and logical when we argued, while I blew my top and then afterwards thought of all the things I should have said.

But Henry started speaking obliviously:

"You simply can't go on."

For a moment I thought he was going to say some-thing about Ricky. *Had he guessed?*

"I mean, look, we hardly see each other anymore."

"Well, we never saw each other anyway, you were always doing your book."

"The book is finished now and I would like to spend some time with my wife."

I opened my mouth and glared at Ms French, who, I swear, was lingering.

"I am intelligent, you know," I said in a defiant whisper.

"I never said you weren't," said Henry in surprise, though I swear I saw a tiny smile flicker on his thin lips.

"I mean, just because you're in Mensa, you're not the only one with a brain. I can have a good home and a good career – this is the nineties, it's different for women now."

"You sound as though you're regurgitating Josephinespeak," said Henry sardonically and I was sure I caught a guffaw from Ms French.. I immediately gave her an icy glare that snapped: *don't you gang up on me*.

"Excuse me?" I said. "Can you please go? Unless you want to stay here and listen to me telling my husband that I think he's a total chauvinist pig and I don't give a toss what he says, I am not giving up my job!"

Hardly able to believe my daring, I stormed out.

The next morning at breakfast, we met halfway in some kind of Cold War, not arguing, all emotions sewn up tightly under a blanket of very polite, embroidered chit-chat. I was all dressed up, tearing around with kirby grips hanging out of my hair, toast hanging out of my mouth, inwardly shaking and waiting for him to try and stop me. But he didn't say a word.

I had just got up and guiltily kissed the tip of his ear goodbye, when he said in a tone of cool surprise:

"Where are you going? I need the car today."

My jaw dropped. My eyes flicked to the clock. If I didn't leave right now, I would miss the 7:35 train and be late yet again.

"I – okay. Right," I said coolly. Determined to show he was not going to crush me, I dropped the keys in his upturned palm and declared that I would call a taxi.

"Because," Henry's voice stopped me, "we're going shopping. No buts. I called Jenny and told her you needed a day off. I'm taking you out to London to be thoroughly spoilt."

I didn't know whether I wanted to hit him or kiss him. It was the same for the rest of the day. In true *Pretty Woman* fashion, wherever we went, he got the assistants to close the shop. Lounging back in an armchair, sipping white wine, he snapped his fingers like a king commanding a dancing girl as I marched in front of him, picking and matching and giving various verdicts – "too short" – "better with the pink skirt" – "very sexy, my dear" – as I tried on practically everything in the shop.

"A lot better than your Top Shop rubbish," Henry declared, signing a Cootes check and handing over my Spice Girls black flares to the assistant to throw away.

As we walked out, loaded with bags, we passed the *Vixen* offices and I couldn't resist begging Henry if I could just pop in to check everything was okay.

Henry came up with me. As we walked hand in

hand through the aisles of desk, nearly every head turned with admiring and envious glances. Chrysanthemum even came up and asked him for an autograph.

"Delightful name," Henry, never one to resist a beautiful lady, switched on the charm, signing her jotter pad for her.

"For God's sake, he's not that famous," Emily muttered behind me so that only I could hear. I ignored her and sat down to check my e-mails. Watching Henry pop into Jenny's office, my stomach lurched with fear. What if he was arranging for me to resign?

I knew he'd been amazingly generous, but no matter how many nice dresses he bought, it was still so unfair. He had got me the job in the first place. What was I, his puppet or something? I couldn't help thinking that Emily or Chrysanthemum or any of the girls in the office would never end up in this situation.

Beep! my Toshiba chirped, as an IQC message popped up on screen. Ricky! Oh wow, in my Henry worries I'd nearly forgotten . . . I looked up across the room and the expression in his eyes was sad.

Oh poor Ricky, I thought, yet feeling horribly, selfishly confused. I just felt I needed him right now. I didn't want him to get engaged and leave work and be all stable and happy, I wanted him to fancy me and love me and give me advice on what on earth to do about Henry . . .

Then I stared at the screen in shock.

I asked her again!
And:
She said yes!

*   *   *

"I talked to Jenny about the job and we decided to reduce your hours to just one day a week," Henry announced in the car on the way back.

"Oh, you decided, did you?" I retorted sulkily.

Henry raised an eyebrow and there was a cross pause.

"I don't know what's got into you lately," he said roughly, "but ever since you've taken that job, I haven't liked your attitude, Olivia."

I crossed my arms and for a moment we sat in angry silence. Then his mobile rang.

"It's for you," he passed it over.

For a moment I suffered a ridiculous, wild hope that it was Ricky, saying he'd changed his mind. It was Josephine.

"Oh, Olivia, we're getting married, we're getting married. Oh God, I'm so excited! I just picked out the dress – did you see the size of the ring?"

"What made you change your mind?" Seeing Henry gazing over enquiringly, I mouthed, "Josephine and Ricky" and pointed to my wedding ring. Henry let out a groan and looked appalled.

"It was last night that changed my mind," she said dreamily. "We made love for the first time ever."

"What!"

"Well, obviously we've you know – kissed and so on – and slept together, but not slept *slept* together. You see, before, I'd been saving myself for our wedding night – only that never quite happened, so . . . anyway, last night we had the most frightful row and he kept begging me to marry him and I kept saying it would never work but somehow we ended up in bed together, and – God, Olivia, he is just *the* best lover, you cannot imagine. I mean, he's like some incarnation out of *Cosmo*. So rough, yet so sensitive. And you should have seen the size –"

"Oh wow, right," I said hurriedly, feeling rather sick.

"After that, there was no way I was going to say no. Sexual fusion is the key element in any marriage."

After I had given my congratulations, Henry was still sour.

"Well, Josephine's parents can pay for the whole lot," he snapped with typical frugality. "There's no way I'm forking out six thousand only to have Ricky not turn up or Josephine decide she prefers the choirboy."

I was appalled at how much hope his words gave me.

26. Hen Night

Josephine, as if nostalgically clinging to the last shreds of being young, free and single, wanted to go out and have the wildest time possible. She had turned up Cher full volume and was Irish-jigging all over the bed, singing in perfect soprano, "If you wanna know if he loves you so, it's in his dick", until we all collapsed about laughing.

"Come on," Josephine pulled Leila, who was looking slightly morose, up onto the bed, forcing her to dance. "Where shall it be, the Hippo?" Then her eyes lit up. "Hey, I know, I know!"

"Where!" I turned around from rummaging through her wardrobe.

Josephine whistled an impression of a sexy strip-tease song and slowly slid off her dressing-gown, throwing it across the room. Unfortunately, at the same moment, Ricky chose to enter and it went flying across his head. For a few moments he bumbled around like a confused ghost, then he pulled it off, grinning. Josephine quickly covered herself up huffily.

"So girls, where is it to be?" he asked.

"Oh, I've told you, Ricky!" Josephine snapped, turning away and starting to make up her eyebrows with strong, angry sweeps. "It's a Hen night. You can't come."

"Well, you're the one who wouldn't let me have a Stag night," Ricky protested. He pulled one of his sad faces and Leila and I instinctively hurried to his side, cuddling and comforting him.

"Anyway," Josephine softened slightly, "you won't want to join us for where we're going. We're going to see men take off their clothes! Chippendales! Leila's friend from the football team told us all about it. They dress up as policemen and everything."

"Well, he really should come to keep an eye on us and keep us out of trouble," said Leila, shooting Josephine a rather curious, faintly disapproving glance as she watched her select a shimmering silver dress from her wardrobe. She looked as if she was going on the pull, not celebrating the night before her wedding.

"Oh, okay," Josephine ran up to Ricky and hugged him with surprising tenderness, giving him a kiss on the lips. I felt my stomach turn and looked away.

Josephine drove at ninety miles per hour up to London, even embarking on a semi-car-chase with a bunch of Frenchie boys. As she cut in front of them and zoomed away in a cloud of smoke, they gave us angry 'V' signs, and she called back, "*Ton lit ou mon?*" Leila and I exchanged glances, sharing the same thought: *What has got into her tonight?* Josephine was naturally extrovert, but she was normally so polite, with that refined finishing-school air of a natural lady. My stomach lurched uneasily. I hoped she wasn't going to take me aside for a repeat performance of,

"Oh Olivia, I just don't know if I'm ready for such a commitment . . ."

An hour later, as we were wandering down the third dark alleyway that led only to heaps of black bin-bags, tramps and dodgy sex shops, Josephine stopped me to lean on my shoulder, take off her cream high heel and rub her swollen ankle.

"Oh, Olivia!" she said in exasperation, as if the whole thing had been *my* idea. "I thought you said you had the address."

"I could try Mandy again," Leila offered lamely, but she had already tried Mandy twice and she was clearly out partying and having all the fun we should have been enjoying.

"We could ask that man over there." Josephine spotted a dodgy Italian-looking bloke cloaked in a flasher's raincoat who was leaning against a wall giving us lecherous glances. "You should, Ricky, you're supposed to be protecting us!"

Ricky merely pulled a face and we all spent three minutes pushing each other and saying, "No, you do it!" until finally I walked forwards, took a deep breath, and asked him.

"Er, d'you know, perhaps, where, you know, er, Gershwins is?" I tried frantically to wrench some GCSE Italian from my memory but after a third of a bottle of champagne all I could come up with was, "*Er, comme star bene?*"

"Yes, yes!" he replied, his eyes oozing over my legs. "Ah yes. We go – yes – for coffee? A dance, maybe?" He hummed a snatch of tune that sounded suspiciously Michael Bolton.

"Er, no," I tried desperately to regain hold on the conversation. "No, I mean, we're looking for *Gershwins*. Can you *help* us?"

"Uh, Gershwins? Oh – Gershwins! Aha. Ah, a little strip?" He swayed his hips, raising a suggestive eyebrow.

"Yes, yes, a little strip," I repeated, feeling my cheeks ripening with the speed of a genetically engineered tomato as I thought: what the hell are we doing here?

"Hey, follow me, follow me," he beckoned us.

I looked back at the others and beckoned them, smiling with false confidence. They followed behind, leaving me to make lame chit-chat with the Italian and pretend to misunderstand invitations re: his flat, villa in Italy, the alleyway just over there and so on. Finally he pointed to a small side street where a bouncer was standing outside a green door.

"There, there!" he pointed.

"Oh, thank you!" I gasped in relief.

"My pleasure." He gave a slippery smile and planted a wet kiss on my hand.

Then when he was gone, I made sick noises and wiped my hand on Ricky's sleeve and he groaned and we shoved each other playfully.

"Urgh, he was so slimy!" Josephine kept exclaiming as we approached the bouncer. He was a fat bearded man with the token earring in his left ear.

I must say that he gave us a rather bemused once-over. I started to get paranoid: I had a slightly baby face and a few days before I even got turned down in an 18s pub. But all he said was,

"Are you sure you girls want to come in here?" as

though respectable ladies like us would never entertain the thought of watching men undress.

"We're sure," said Josephine boldly, as we proudly handed over our tenners to get in.

We walked down a long, black, windy staircase showered with silver glitter. Seeing the cave-like booths, I felt a shiver of erotic anticipation.

Then, as Josephine stopped dead with her mouth open, I followed her gaze and felt my heart fall like a stone. Beside me, Ricky was cracking up with glee.

Oh shit.

There were no men. Well no – there were men. I mean, the club was filled with men of all ages, shapes and sizes. The trouble was, they were ogling the women. If you see the problem.

Leila and I were ready to run out there and then but Ricky grabbed our wrists teasingly.

"Oh no, you're not getting out of it that easily," he laughed.

We really would have legged it, but Josephine was just as adamant as Ricky, ordering drinks and dragging us down into a corner and sitting us down as though we were rebellious kids.

"We're living in the Nineties," she emphasised. "We're all open now. We're not ashamed of our bodies or our sexuality. Women can look at women," she added, her voice breaking. slightly as she took a huge quivering gulp of Bacardi. Then she nudged a wide-eyed Ricky sharply in the ribs, "Stop staring at them!"

For the first ten minutes, everyone except Ricky stared at the graffiti on the table. But after a while we plucked up courage to watch, and it really wasn't that dramatic.

To be honest, there was truly nothing sexy about the show. It just left one with a slightly nasty taste in the mouth. It wasn't like you see in Hollywood films with gorgeous shiny babes performing incredible dance routines. Most of the women had saggy pear-shaped figures, skin that, despite the clownish make-up, looked tired and jaded, eyes cold and unsparkling.

Soon Leila and I were chatting and watching the women without even seeing them. Ricky and Josephine started to bicker again; Ricky kept licking his lips and saying, "God, will you look at the tits on her!" Really, I thought, he shouldn't wind her up, he should know by now Josephine didn't have any sense of humour when it came to anything vaguely sexist.

Getting up, she stormed over to the bar. A few minutes later, however, it became clear that her motive was not really anger. She had spotted a group of rather yummy accountants, all black macs and briefcases and glasses and fat cheque-books. Soon they were surrounding her like jackals and between their ebony heads, I caught a glimpse of her tossing back her blonde hair with laughter, her pale pink wrist flashing as she fingered her earring. Ricky looked punished and walked off, saying he needed a pee.

"Will you look at her!" Leila said with uncharacteristic disgust. "I don't know what she's playing at but it's so out of order."

Sensing that Leila still had rather a soft spot for Ricky, I smiled awkwardly and took a sip of my drink.

"Do something, Olivia," Leila said as Ricky strolled back. "I can't stand her."

So I offered to buy a round of drinks and went over to the bar to deliver a tactful little chat, but Josephine, with skilful timing, drew away to a distant table around the other side of the club. She was out of Ricky's sight, which was just as well because she was nearly sitting on someone's lap. I sighed and tapped the counter, wishing that the bitchy-looking barmaid would stop pretending to ignore me.

I tapped my change on the counter, but she still ignored me, lounging against the bar, chewing her gum like a bored cow munching grass.

I *ahemed* loudly but she merely looked at her nails.

Then I felt a tap on the shoulder. It was Ricky. He grinned and jerked his finger over at the table.

"Leila's being swamped by a group of Harrow schoolboys. Well, I didn't want to cramp her style."

I forced my laughter with a beating heart. If he just looks up and swivels his head just a few inches to the right, I worried, he will see Josephine spreading out the napkin on the table and getting the accountant to draw a picture for psychological analysis: one of her prime pulling tactics. I didn't trust Ricky not to get all macho and walk up and punch him.

I tried to steer him back to the table, but he was determined to buy his drinks. In despair, I blurted out improvisationally, "D'you want to dance?"

"What? Here?" Ricky looked around the haze of smoke, the seedy thump of Annie Lennox.

"Well, I know it's not exactly a moonlit terrace in Venice . . ." I mumbled.

"Well, sure," he smiled.

I drew him away from the bar to the distant edge of the room where the black walls were covered with dirty silver scratches. The boom-boom of the dance beat vibrated off the walls like tin balls. He put his palms gently on my hip bones and I swallowed and kept my eyes fixed on the Nike logo on his green and white sweater.

Annie Lennox was replaced by the slow, throaty croon of a female blues singer. A stripper appeared dressed as a white swan, arching back onto the floor with the unexpected grace of a ballerina. Ricky took a step closer to me and I took a nimble, nervous step back. We swayed for another few minutes. I could feel the blood beating in my cheeks and pulsating along the edges of my hairline, a thick lump in my throat which somehow I couldn't swallow away. I was about to ask if we should go back to Leila, but I couldn't even see where our initial table was; the smoke from cigars and the dry-ice machine was so thick it was as though we were suspended in a cloud. Then he took a step forwards and put his arms around me.

His brown eyes fixed on me with rather alarming intensity. I looked up into those eyes and I felt a sudden wave of lust unroll through my stomach like a red carpet of invitation. Oh gosh, oh mmm. Then I felt his hands creeping up my back and pulling me harder against him, the warmth of his excited, sighing breath in my ear. My mind was full of worries like buzzing flies: what if Josephine sees, what if Leila sees, no, Olivia, you can't start this all over again, if you give in once you'll fall like a row of dominoes, this will never stop, it's stupid, it can't happen, mustn't happen.

And yet I found myself falling against him as though I could have rested in his arms all night. I closed my eyes and put my head against his chest. He smelt clean, like Johnson's Baby Shampoo. He put a hand on my head and started to stroke my hair gently.

The music changed to *Great Balls of Fire*. A new act was just starting, of a rather gymnastic flavour, which involved back-flipping-cartwheeling from one end of the room to the other.

I pulled back from Ricky. For a moment we stared at each other breathlessly, the mist swirling up and around like a London smog.

"I —"

He took my hand and started to pull me away.

"I —" but before I could say another word he was clattering up the winding fire-escape steps. At the door, I stopped him, breaking away my hand.

"What the hell are you doing? Where are we going?"

"We have to get out of here! We've got to talk."

I looked up at his brown eyes. And all the little 'No, you can'ts' zinging through my mind like annoying flies were suddenly dissolved in one big puff of killer spray that said, "*Yes!*"

I took his hand and we pushed open the door and ran out into the night.

27. The Morning After

When I woke up, for a moment I thought I had put my SleepEasy blindfold on too tight, there was such a heavy pressure behind my eyes and forehead. Then I licked my pasty lips, tasting a gunky morning residue of beer and old cheese. I shivered and pulled the duvet over, reaching out for Henry's warmth. Then I caught a whiff of a new scent, something foreign and suspiciously Johnsons' Baby Shampoo-ish. And hang on, wasn't this mattress much too springy, and surely our ceiling wasn't pink? I blinked, my heart freezing. I was lying in bed next to a total stranger. Shit! I sat up, the duvet falling from my – naked? – naked! body. My eyes whizzed from my clothes, neatly folded and piled on the chair – to the window, the curtains half drawn, the sharp London silhouette against the drizzly dawn – to the blonde Adonis lying on my pillow.

Then I did a double take. Argh! I was lying in bed with Ricky!

For some time, I stared and gulped, stared and gulped. I tried to yank at my memory, some comforting, reassuring thing, like me having an accident and Ricky wanting me to rest and lie down, or – or – something, but my brain felt as though it had been through a cement mixer. It was the worst hangover I'd ever had. The only answer was just to get out of there fast before I did remember something I really didn't want to recall.

I gently eased out of the covers, every creak and squeak like a bomb going off. I tip-toed over to the chair, gathered up my sticky clothes, slunk into the bathroom. Suddenly bile retched up in the back of my throat, and I leant on the sink, but only spit came out.

As I pulled up my tights, I heard a creak, and pissing myself that I had woken him up, I froze, wrenching a big snaky ladder up the tights. Then there was nothing but silence and the drip-splash of the tap. I hurried now, flicking up half the buttons on my blouse, yanking on my skirt, short and red and swirly, etched with black flowers.

As I sat on the edge of the bath, doing up my laces, I suddenly remembered buying that skirt. Josephine and I had gone into New Look and, as ever, I had spotted it first and, as ever, she had cried, "How gorgeous!" and pretended she had spotted it all along. Luckily, there had been two left on the rack so we both bought them, Josephine declaring it looked much better on me with all the complacency of knowing it looked much better on her. Now I thought of her terrible ways with a tight fondness, suddenly drenched in self-loathing. Josephine might bully me or say my hair looked crap or I had no taste in men, but never, never, no way would she ever sleep with my bloke the night before we were due to marry. No matter how much she fancied him, even Josephine would have pushed him away. I looked at myself in the mirror and hated my reflection and decided to get out of there fast.

In the bedroom, I set the alarm on Ricky's digital so that he would wake up for nine, leaving him two hours to get back and ready and into church. Seeing his fair hair sprayed out on the pillow, I had to stuff my fists in my pockets to stop myself from reaching out and stroking it. Leaving him was like a plaster being ripped from a wound. Hurrying away, I closed the door gently, and then tripped and stumbled out into the first rays of a London dawn.

28. Wedding No 2

Josephine, with her love for psychology, had once told me about a state of shock so great that a man can murder his wife and then go whistling back to the gardening in complete innocence, his brain so unable to cope with what he has done that the memory just blots it out, erases it like an old video. All the way on the tube I sat trembling in my hangover, trying to remember the Night Before, and yet almost relieved to find I could remember almost nothing. I was in a complete state; I slotted my underground ticket into the machine upside down; then, on the bus, I looked down and saw that I had put on Ricky's black Hush Puppy shoes!

I flew to the doors and pinged the bell, ignoring the gruff growl from the driver that it wasn't a request stop. Nearly flying off the bus, I stood in the middle of the pavement, ripping the shoes off my feet, looking about wildly. I had got off at Carshalton Ponds and I was ready to watch the Hush Puppies sink into the murky depths, when I saw a police car veer by. I jumped nervously, feeling like a criminal about to destroy the evidence. Oh God, how could I have been so stupid?

"You alright, love?" a policeman leaned out of the car.

"I'm, I'm fine," I murmured, quickly putting the shoes back on.

They very kindly offered me a lift home, and when I saw my reflection in the front mirror I saw why: I looked like a rape victim, my clothes all dishevelled, buttons falling undone, my hair like Tina Turner, my freckles standing out like chocolate drops.

Dropping me off, the policeman came right up to the door and I stood there, surreptitiously bending down to undo the laces of my shoes, peel them off and –

"Oh!" the policeman jumped as he heard the clang of the shoes hitting the dustbin. I smiled up at him cheerfully.

Josephine flung open the door, clearly halfway through being made-up, her face painted like a beautiful harlequin, silky and white in her under-gown shift.

"Oh, there you are!" she screeched, dragging me in. "Oh, Olivia, we were worried sick! Oh, thank you, officer," she beamed at him, as though I was her naughty child who had gone running off again. "Would you like some tea?"

"Oh, no thanks," he blushed and twisted his hat happily. "Better be getting off, thanks."

I was quickly interrogated and yanked upstairs and undressed and pushed into the shower, then yanked out, towel thrown at me, and sat down on a dressing-stool in front of Sharon the local hairdresser. As she blew-dry my curls the hot air felt like a desert heat descending on my poor muddled brain. Even worse, she started giving us a run through of all twenty-nine weddings or so she'd been to, tactlessly oblivious to Josephine's ever-increasing panic.

"Well, she'd just walked up the aisle," Sharon started to yank my curls into a plait, and with every twist I thought my brain would be torn apart, "and they were just about to say 'I Do' when a lot of men from the council came in and said, 'Sorry, love, but we're going to have to close the church up – we've looked at the residents' complaints and decided against planning permission.'"

"Oh God, what happened?" I asked.

"Oh, she went Buddhist after that and got –"

"He's not going to turn up, is he?" Josephine suddenly cut in, as if she hadn't heard a word. "Olivia, are you sure you didn't see him go off with anyone last night?"

"I swear," I said, reiterating my story very slowly so as not to slip on a single detail. "We both split a taxi and then I went off to my mum's and he didn't say where he was going. Honestly, we just left on this wild impulse, it was all his idea." Oh God, I was such a coward. "He just buggered off and I remember him saying something like, 'The night is still young'."

"Oh no!" Josephine's voice was like fingernails on a blackboard. "Oh great. He's probably just waking up now in some hooker's bedroom, tied up to a bed – well, I hope he bloody chokes on her suspenders."

And with that she burst into tears. I broke away from Sharon, and called Leila in desperately and we patted and comforted her and said not to worry, everything would be alright.

Josephine, who was determined not to spend the afternoon careering around the block in a taxi, was waiting outside the church like a hawk. When Ricky actually turned up on time, getting out of a mini cab, she was so prepared for tragedy that for a moment she blinked at him in amazement, as though he'd just descended from another planet. Then she looked at his pale face and greasy hair and dishevelled suit and started to smooth her hands over him as though they were irons.

"Oh, Ricky, I told you you should have left it with me to iron," she moaned. "Couldn't you at least have made an effort on our wedding day?"

"You're not supposed to be seeing me now, it's bad luck," said Ricky blandly, gazing over at me as I scuffed my white slipper in the gravel. I turned away quickly, jolted like a druggie with a flashback: Ricky and I sitting cuddled up in the bar booth, drinking and drinking and then scraping together our loose change to buy another drink to share between us. Him ordering me to draw my feet in as he carried me clumsily up the stairs, me hardly able to see as I reached up affectionately to plait his long fringe –

"Ricky, oh God, I can't believe it!" Josephine half-cried, half-choked in disgust.

She pointed to his feet. He was wearing his Nikes.

As Josephine sent Leila scouring the congregation to borrow new shoes, Ricky looked as though he was simply too weary to stand anymore. Sitting on the church steps, he lit up a cigarette, staring into space, ignoring Josephine's complaints that the smoke was polluting her dress. Finally, he sighed, got up and came over to my side.

"Can I have a word with you?" he asked me out of the edge of his mouth.

Out of the corner of my eye I could see Josephine watching us uneasily. It was as though she was so terrified of him calling it off, she wanted to provoke him into doing it, just to feel safe in her misery.

"Nice day, isn't it?" I said loudly.

"Please," Ricky pleaded slightly louder.

I couldn't bear it. I could see from the look in his eyes that he was about to start one of his "I'm-so-much-better-for-you-than-Henry" arguments.

"No," I said firmly, turning away from him and going to Josephine's side to pick up her train.

Ricky threw down his cigarette, snorted smoke out of his nose like an angry bull, and stormed off into church. His borrowed shoes were slightly too big for him and he slid slightly on the polished floor. I had a sudden vision of lying on the bed and blurrily watching him walk to the bathroom, the curve of his naked back, his buttocks . . .

Like an inverted Sod's Law, where everyone was so convinced it was going to go wrong it could only go right, the ceremony could not have gone more smoothly. Josephine glided up the church; Ricky looked handsome and said the right words; nobody had any objections. The priest, who was the same thin goatee-bearded man from before, began to relax and speak with more confidence. Beneath the white rim of his vicar's gown I saw the conspicuous green laces of a Nike peeking out.

Rings were exchanged; vows were exchanged; Ricky kissed the bride and they were married.

I watched with my surface mind on the present, my

subconscious lingering on the past, supplying fantasies where memory failed me; visions of Ricky's hands curving over the roundness of my shoulders, the warmth of his body writhing against mine. I watched the man I loved kissing my best friend and declaring to spend the rest of his life loving her through the good and the bad, and felt bile rising up in my throat and turned and ran down the aisle. I only just made it outside in time, puking up over a patch of clean earth, only to hear Baby Bridesmaid's dismayed cry:

"Oh no, that's the bit where the Brownies planted their seedlings!"

I licked my cracked lips, seeing a few old ladies in flowered hats peering out and gazing at me curiously. Henry barged past them, clicked his fingers, sent them fluttering back into church, and came to my side, putting a weighty, soothing hand on my shoulder.

"You okay?"

I nodded, my gaze on the red carnation in his pocket, unable to meet his gaze.

"Some fresh air is what you need."

We looped arms and walked slowly around the graveyard. Henry paused now and again to examine the stones, pointing out a lady aged one hundred and two, a girl aged thirteen. Fragments of last night's chat, whispered in the dead of the night, were flying through my mind like the autumn leaves, echoing through my mind like the church bells . . .

"D'you believe in life after death?"

"I think so. My father always had this view of heaven and hell. You know, my father was so obsessed with not going to hell, he seemed far more interested in the devil

309

than God." I pleated the edge of the sheet shyly and added I knew it sounded silly, but I was afraid sometimes of Ricky or someone I really loved dying, even though we had so many years ahead of us. Ricky hugged me fiercely and said he was not frightened of death.

"If I die before you, I shall come back to haunt you," I warned him, smiling reproachfully.

He rubbed his nose against mine in an Eskimo kiss, moving his face so close to mine that our noses squashed, our pupils nearly meeting, so that all I could see was the round circle of his pupil, the red veins of his eye white.

"When we die," he whispered against my cheek, "we have to die together. We have to be buried together, we have to be burnt together, and we'll float up out of our bodies and sit on the clouds, laughing down at everyone and casting spells and throwing Cupid arrows. We'll be the most mischievous angels in heaven."

"D'you believe in angels?" I asked.

"You're an angel," Ricky kissed me.

"How would you like to die?"

"Easily, in my sleep. How would you?"

"Death by chocolate," I laughed, and we giggled against each other.

But then he had looked straight into my eyes and said more earnestly, "But wouldn't it be awful to die knowing you'd never done what you really wanted because you'd been held back by fear, that you'd only half lived your life . . . ?"

"Olivia! Olivia!" Henry suddenly brought me back

down to earth. I blinked and turned back to face him. His square face suddenly looked puggish and brutal compared to the sensitive lines of Ricky's.

"Are you okay?"

I saw Ricky and Josephine emerging from the church, posing for the photographers. *"Come on, Olivia,"* Ricky had gripped my shoulders, *"the only thing holding you back is fear! We have to do this! D'you want to waste the rest of your life, knowing you're married to the wrong man? Once I marry her, it will be too complicated, too late. D'you understand?"* He was nearly shaking me like a ragdoll. *"Too late!"*

"Are you alright, Olivia?" Henry repeated.

"I think I'm going to be sick again," I whimpered.

I spent the wedding party clinging to Henry's arm, sensing Ricky's prowling presence near me all the time like a shadow. As we sat down for the wedding speeches, Henry removed the prawns from my plate and refused to let me eat anything expect light salad. He didn't even allow me the comfort of the Sarah Lee gateau that I was dying to glut my misery on.

As Ricky stood up to make his speech, I poked my cucumber miserably. Was it just me, had the speeches gone like this at our wedding? I didn't think I could take much more.

Ricky's speech was hilarious. Picking up a book entitled, *How to Make A Wedding Speech*, he quoted it all the way through like a robot, "And now it gives instructions that I must thank the bride's parents, so, Mr and Mrs Wilkinson," he nodded at them gravely, "I do thank you very much . . ."

Then he concluded:

"I just also wanted to add . . . last night I found myself going to bed with Olivia."

There was a ruffled ripple throughout the hall, the wind lifting the flaps of the tent like shocked open mouths. Besides me, Henry chuckled incredulously, waiting for the punch-line.

I could hear the drum-beat of my heart in my ears. He was going to say it, here now, in front of everyone. I felt horrified and ecstatic all at once.

"But," said Ricky, "by that I mean lying side by side, completely pissed out of heads after a rather wild Stag / Hen night that concluded in Soho. Olivia I should thank, for keeping me on the straight and narrow."

There was a general feeling of uncertain relief. Josephine was gazing across at me with a faint frown, and I beamed at her like something out of toothpaste ad.

"Because from now on," Ricky cleared his throat, "I just want to declare to everyone, really, there's going to be no more drunken nights, no more messing around. I love my wife," he raised his glass to Josephine, "and I intend to be the best possible husband ever. I'm going to be a complete icon of the Nineties man – I'll do your dishes, washing, whatever. I just want you to know I'm going to be completely devoted to you."

There was a collective sigh of relief and Josephine smiled tremblingly and leaned over to kiss him. Henry looked rather taken aback and muttered very quietly, "Nineties man? What's she done to my son?"

As the dancing and romancing began, I retreated to

the toilets. I was just attempting to smudge on some more plum lipstick, when Ricky barged in after me. I jumped, seeing him gazing at me gazing at him in the mirror.

"Congratulations," I blurted out, offering my hand to the mirror, then turning, offering my hand to him, then, realising it was still wet, hastily wiping it on a towel and binding both hands behind my back.

"Olivia, about last night –" He stopped me going by placing two hands on my shoulders.

"What?" I gazed up into his earnest brown eyes. Seeing the love in those eyes, feeling the love in his touch, I nearly wilted into his arms. "I don't remember anything. What actually happened?"

"Nothing – nothing happened."

"What?"

"We didn't –" he cocked his head. "You know."

"Oh. Oh. But . . . how did my clothes . . ."

"We just – we were drunk – look, I did take you up to the hotel bedroom, because you were so pissed you could hardly walk and I did well, undress you, because of that mad guy in the bar who sprayed champagne about when we were all doing the Conga, remember?"

"Vaguely, well, but did we . . ."

"You were drenched. I had to take them off. Didn't want you getting hypothermia, or something," he trailed off in sheepish embarrassment.

"Oh, I see."

"Well, okay, okay, look, I did kiss you and try it on, but you kept pushing me away. I mean, I tried every-thing, God, we talked for hours, don't you remember?"

"Bits of it."

"Well, it went back and forth like a bloody Wimbledon match. And so I kind of figured that if you resisted that much, you must really love Henry."

A hesitant, questioning pause.

"Yes," I said at last, automatically. "Yes, I do."

"Well," Ricky lifted his hands from my shoulders. "The best man has won."

Yes, my inner voice cried, but I love you so much more.

"What about Josephine?"

"I – I – we'll be alright. It's for the best, we'll make the best of it."

Pause.

"Yes," I said.

"Yes," he said.

Ricky leaned forwards and kissed my temple. Then he bent down and whispered in my ear,

"I love you so much." And walked out.

I turned away in a blur, nearly ready to run after him and fall at his feet in front of three hundred-odd wedding guests, when Josephine and Leila and Melanie came dancing in, a blast of Irish folk song shaking me back to reality as the door swung open.

"Oh, Olivia, Olivia," Josephine grabbed my hands and danced me round and round until I was dizzy. "I'm so happy, I'm so happy, it's the happiest day of my life!"

We stood beneath the arch of the church, showering confetti over the happy bride and groom as they bundled into the taxi. Seeing Josephine get out again, my heart lifted with false hope, only to see her cry, "I forgot!" She tossed her rose bouquet high, high into the air, slipping back into the taxi, kissing and patting Ricky.

I caught the bouquet almost without thinking. I felt the thorns prick my palms, vaguely aware of Melanie nudging me with joking jealously and saying you're already sorted, what about us single girls? I started to cry as I watched the taxi drive away, and more so, when I saw Henry on the verge of proud tears too. *Run after them, run after them*, the voice died away, giving up hope. *Tomorrow is the start of the rest of our lives*, Ricky had said. *We either live our lives as though we're dead, going through the motions, or we can be together*. But it was too late now. Too late. I felt as though my heart had turned to dust. I watched the taxi turn the corner, the garlands and balloons flying out joyously, and then it had gone and it was over.

29. Back

The day Ricky was due to come back from his honeymoon, you could feel the excitement rippling through the office. Chrysanthemum had bought herself a brand new hairclip with a large, silk fuchsia that spurted petals like a firework; Emily had impulsively dyed her hair to much the same pale blonde shade as Josephine's; even Jenny was far more chatty than usual, popping out of her office to gossip with everyone, her eyes wandering towards the door.

"Odds: ten to one he comes back divorced," Ferras announced, re-opening his betting shop.

"You old cynic," I reprimanded him but I had to admit that my heart was jumping like a frog on speed. If he tries it on, I thought, no matter how tempting he is, I shall refuse him.

I went out for my lunch-break at twelve and when I returned a crowd had gathered around Ricky's desk. As I edged up, Chrysanthemum jumped at me and then put a hand on her breast.

"Oh God, I thought you were Jenny," she cried dramatically. Curling her hair around my ear, she whispered loudly, "He's completely smashed!"

Standing on tip-toe I saw him. He had never looked

smarter, dressed in an unusually trim grey suit with a starched white shirt, and at the same time, never in such a state, cigarette spilling ash from his hand, his blonde fringe falling into his eyes, his hand groping to pull Emily onto his lap, while she cooed and pushed him away in delight. Raising his head, he looked right at me with squiffy unseeing eyes and croaked, "I think I'm going to puke!"

Chrysanthemum, fighting with Emily to play the role of mother, smoothed down his collar, removed his cigarette and asked him how many he'd had.

Ricky counted on wobbly fingers:

"Well, I started since we flew in this morning at breakfast so that makes half a bottle of whiskey from the duty free and then I had the rest of some old gin at home and then I ended up at a pub with this old bloke who kept buying me beer, he'd had six wives, six bloody wives can you believe it, the first one he said was crap in bed, the second messed up his allotment by planting beans where the cabbages had been, the third was a lesbian, or was that the fourth . . . ?" Ricky frowned and wrenched the petals of the flower off Chrysanthemum's paper clip, mumbling "She loves me, she loves me not, she loves me . . ."

"Do I take it," Chrysanthemum asked hopefully, "the honeymoon didn't go too well?"

There was a flurry of panic as Ferras hissed warningly, "Jenny!" Everyone scattered like pigeons, except for Emily and Chrysanthemum, who stood loyally by his side.

Jenny walked up to him with an uncharacteristic smile.

"Ricky my boy, how are you?"

Ricky looked up at her weakly, keeping his mouth clamped shut, his head lolling as he attempted a nod.

"Come into my office," Jenny invited him.

Ricky stood up and ricocheted off the filing cabinet, crumpling to the floor. Jenny's face tightened as she bent over him, waving away the drink fumes. With her help, he managed to rise and lean uncertainly against the desk, like a single book swaying on a shelf.

"Just what the hell are you on?" Jenny snapped.

"Oh, you're so sexy when you're angry," Ricky said, and then grabbed her and kissed her smuttily. Jenny pulled back and slapped him. He recoiled with dazed surprise.

"You two," Jenny glared at Chrysanthemum and Emily, "take him away to the loos and sober him up and bring him straight back to my office." Then she huffed off, slamming her door with a thunderous bang.

As Ricky was led back to her office, his hair damp from the water splashed over him, supported by Emily and Chrysanthemum like two crutches on either side, a silence descended over the office. You could hear nothing but the click-clack of nails on keys as everyone strained to catch the dreaded words 'fired' or 'P45'. Several of the girls had coats on, as if they were ready to walk out with him. It was as if Ricky was the prow on a ship, and if he went, everyone would lose their faith.

Finally Ricky emerged unsteadily, looking much more on planet earth. Girls flocked around him, offering him tea or chocolate, but Jenny stuck her head out of the office and barked, "Leave him alone! He's got an article to write by tomorrow. Let him concentrate!"

As soon as Jenny was safely away, however, the girls poured back over him. As I pretended to focus hard on browsing the web, I managed to deduce that he had only been given a rap over the knuckles, and, as though he was a naughty boy being given lines, a 2500 word article on marriage in the 90s.

I waited until they had finally filtered back to their desks before sending him an ICQ mail. I fiddled with several drafts but in the end just decided to play it casual.

Hiya, I wrote, *how's it going? Hope you had a lovely honeymoon, O.*

No reply. I knew he was on the net because I had just heard the beep and fuzz of his modem, so I tried again:

I was wondering if I could have some advice on Top Tips since you're now a domesticated husband . . . ?

No reply. I gazed over at his blonde head, willing him to look up, but it was as if I wasn't even in the office, as if the fatal night had never happened, as if we were just people who vaguely knew each other and worked together. I felt a feeling of unease tug over me, but I just assumed that he was engrossed in his article, and, knowing he didn't like to be disturbed, went back to mine.

"Hey, listen to this!" Ricky clicked his fingers, and I automatically lifted my head, only to see he was beckoning Emily over. She leaned against his desk so that her short skirt could ruck up and listened intently as he read flamboyantly aloud, *"Marriage is a contagious*

319

disease that most people acquire at around the age of twenty-seven. It appears to be more predominant amongst the female species rather than the male, who maybe suffer early symptoms which do not turn into full-blown illness until even as late as the mid-forties. Suddenly, the sufferer wakes up in bed one morning and decides their cat or dog is no longer a satisfactory sleeping partner. Suddenly they find themselves being invited to the weddings of all their friends who swore they would never marry. Even at the wedding, they cast their eye desperately around, from the vicar to the choirboy, thinking, could he be the one, oh sod, he'll do . . .

"Marriage has nothing to do with love. It rests on the foundation of fear. There are two types of people in life: those who do what they want, those who do what they are told. The ones in the first category always get divorced, and those in the second never have the guts to. So they learn to tolerate each other. They pretend, they live a life, they sit at breakfast and discuss work and dropping in at Marks & Spencers on the way home to buy some dinky little sausage rolls or something equally banal.

"Marriage is a bore. A full-stop. A dead end. You only have to look at literature. Every romance describes courtship. As soon as the couple are wedded the curtains drop, we lose interest, we reach the final page . . ."

By now nearly the whole office was listening and everyone was laughing uneasily as Ricky 's voice rose with flair and anger.

"They should make marriage illegal. Ban it! To think

two young people are allowed to go into a church anywhere and get married, and yet it's still against the law to smoke cannabis! Society's values are just all upside down. Whadaya think, hey? Cool. Huh?" He looked over at Chrysanthemum, as if, I swear, to deliberately wind up Emily.

"Brill!" Chrysanthemum sharpened her pencil. "All that in only half an hour! I can't believe how fast you write!"

Ricky looked smug and returned to his PC. I swallowed and went back to my computer. I was about to try one more ICQ, but stopped myself. Don't bug him, I thought – whatever went wrong on the honeymoon, he's obviously feeling completely crap – he's keeping his distance because he doesn't want to lash out and hurt you.

But as I gazed at his profile, the smooth slope of his nose, the sculptured lips, I could still taste his kisses, feel the echo of his touch. I couldn't resist.

Hey, Ricky, great article. But marriage really isn't that bad, is it?

I could see letters forming on the screen, sensed his attention in my direction. He was replying! Oh, thank God for that!

Fuck off and leave me alone. I don't want you to write to me anymore, okay? Just leave me alone. R.

I sat back in my chair. I felt as though I had been punched in the stomach. I looked over but he was deliberately avoiding my gaze, running his pencil over his calendar, pretending to check a date.

"Ricky!" Josephine wove her way through the desks,

oblivious to the stares that shot at her from all directions like lasers. She was looking absolutely fantastic, her blonde hair bleached nearly white, pinned up in a wispy bun, her long tanned legs flaring out of her checked sarong. Pausing by my table, she started and then leaned down to give me a hug. Of course, singling me out as her friend automatically put me in the office enemy camp.

"Hi, how's it going? How was your holiday, erm, honeymoon?"

"Oh, super," Josephine enthused. "We had a great time, didn't we, dear?" She went to Ricky's side and kissed the back of his neck. He flinched and carried on typing intently.

"Come on," she purred in his ear, "I don't want to eat late, you can do it tomorrow."

"I want to do it now," Ricky snapped.

For a moment they bickered quietly while everyone else pretended not to listen and Chrysanthemum misfiled a bundle of articles in her glee. Finally Ricky stood up, switched off his computer and walked out. As he strolled past my desk, he gave me such a venomous look that I felt my heart quail. Josephine blew me a kiss goodbye and hurried after him.

For the first time in my life, I felt I actually hated someone.

I couldn't believe how horrible he was being. Like a scab you can't help picking at even though you know it bleeds, I kept returning to the computer, reading his lines with increasing anger. What right did he have to take it out on me! What else did he expect me to do!? He was the one who had chased me, I had never asked him to have an affair. If he had only asked me to marry him right from the start none of this mess would have happened.

Bastard.

The following week was our staff meeting.

Jenny had recently introduced a kind of democratic free-for-all where once a month we all leafed through the pages of last month's issue which was supposed to inspire us to make constructive criticism about each other's work but largely turned into a lecture on how Jenny wanted things done.

These meetings were normally regarded as cringeful bores and the only thing that kept everyone from falling asleep was the bitching between Chrysanthemum and Emily as they slagged each other's pieces off, and Ricky's continual stream of quips and trivial demands, such as a Haagen Dazs ice-cream freezer in the canteen, or could he take off on a trip to Bermuda for a month and claim it on business expenses so he could write a piece on the Caribbean?

Today, however, Ricky turned up on time instead of coming in halfway through and then disruptively passing chewing-gum around. I noticed that he was wearing his suit again and kept checking his watch almost nervously. Well, who would have thought Ricky would have turned into a henpecked husband?

"Any points anyone would like to express to begin with?" Jenny rolled up her sleeves.

"Yes!" Ricky sat up. "I have a complaint to make about Olivia's 'Top Tips' page."

Everyone else tittered, waiting for some silly joke

about washing powders. But he spread the offending page open on his lap and jabbed it angrily, his new Rolex slipping up and down his wrist.

"For a start, since Olivia has been working on the page, it's been considerably reduced. Second, this tip concerning avocados was used only three months back, and third, it was inaccurate that time too."

There was an awkward pause. I saw Chrysanthemum nodding her head in catty agreement. Suddenly I looked around at them all and felt my tide of popularity turning against me. Not one person here, I realised, is a real friend. They've only liked me, begrudgingly, because I was once Ricky's favourite. Now his hate for me would infect them all like a cancer.

"Right, well," said Jenny, with gentle sharpness, "watch out for repetitions, Olivia, and maybe you can, say, increase from four to five tips."

"I wouldn't." Ricky feigned a yawn and said, "They're boring enough as it is."

Emily tittered and cried, "Bully!", poking him with a pencil. Ricky didn't even look at me. It was as though I wasn't even in the room.

I put down my pad and swallowed and said, "Jenny, I'm resigning."

I saw Ricky start but still he didn't look over. Everyone rustled uncomfortably.

"Now come on, Olivia," said Jenny, "don't be too sensitive. Ricky was just making a point and that was fair enough –"

"No," I said vehemently, shaking my head, slowly turning scarlet, "I want to resign. Really. I've been thinking it over for a while, and I want to spend more time with my husband."

I heard a faint snort from Ricky.

"Well," said Jenny, "why don't we have a little chat about it at the end?" And she continued with her points, Chrysanthemum scratching down big loopy lazy minutes.

At the end, Jenny walked up to me, and shook my hand and wished me good luck and best wishes. Ferras patted me on the back and said he would miss me.

"Oh, isn't it a shame?" Emily looked at me with her head cocked to one side, then looking at Ricky as if trying to prove how caring and sympathetic she could be. Ricky merely shrugged and leaned forwards, crumpling up his Coke can.

"I'll be glad to see the back of her," he muttered.

It took all my strength to stop myself from hitting him before I stormed out.

I had been asked a hundred times if I wanted an office party for leaving *Vixen* and a hundred times, I had said 'no'. But everyone was determined that I should have one.

I spent the day finishing off a few tips, cleaning out my desk. Every time someone approached me, I pretended to be too busy to have time to chat. At four I had finished and there was nothing to do. I sat there, gazing around at everyone gossiping and chattering, and I felt like a stranger in an alien world. I didn't know what to say to anyone anymore.

Seeing Ricky enter the room, I suddenly got up and hurried out. I went for a long walk in Regents Park.

By the time I returned, the party had already started. The desks had been pushed back, the lights dimmed, paper chains trailing over the walls, paper cups filled with punch spilling over the carpet, despite Jenny's hawkish eye. But as I walked in, everyone chorused, "*Olivia!*" and showered me with presents. Jenny handed me a huge card and Ferras sat me down on a chair so that I could read through all their lovely messages. I was so touched that even when Emily gave me back the brush set I had given her for her birthday only a fortnight ago, I nearly burst into tears.

Emily smiled and swished her skirt and then returned to Ricky. He was leaning against the wall with a drink in his hand, watching everyone with a hard glittering look in his eyes, a slightly derogatory smile curling at his lips. She wound her feather boa around his neck and whispered something in his ear and put down his drink and led him outside.

I blinked and buried myself back into the card. I found my eyes scanning wildly for Ricky's signature but it wasn't there. He was the only one who hadn't bothered.

Suddenly the thought of him with Emily was like a hand reaching into my heart and twisting it into a hot, tight ball. I felt like a complete slut. I wanted to go home and sink into a warm bath and wash his memory away from me, forget that I'd ever been so stupid as to fall for "I love you" and become another notch on his plank.

Towards eight o'clock, the party grew wilder as someone put on *Come on, Eileen* and we all danced around in a circle, kicking up our legs and singing along. I kept throwing back my head, tossing my curls out of my eyes, my arms aching as Jenny's fingers clawed into my shoulder blade. Then I felt a tap on my shoulder and Ferras yelling, "Phone!"

I hurried to the desk, trying to ignore Ferras blowing a party-popper in my ear.

At first he was gabbling so fast, in a mixture of Italian and English, that I couldn't work out what he was on about. Then I realised it was Calvin, and my mother had gone into labour.

"Kingston Hospital!" he cried. "Come quick!"

"I'll be right there!"

I ran halfway out, then back in to call Henry, but there was no reply.

I was bursting for the loo, so I dodged into the toilets, only to run slap-bang into Emily. Her face was streaked with mascara streams, her buxom chest heaving out of her tight black velvet top.

"Oh, Olivia," she sobbed. "He doesn't love me, nobody loves me, I'm ugly and fat and nobody is ever going to want to go out with me."

"Emily, come on!" I hugged her, quite shocked to see her so vulnerable, so different from her usual curl-tossing, pouting, swanky-hips-walking self. "You're beautiful, and loads of people fancy you, don't you know?"

"But not Ricky!" she wailed. "Oh God, he says he's in love with someone else! Not Josephine, but someone else else! Who is it! You must know, Olivia, come on, tell me, so I can go to her house and kill her! Tell me, come on, you're his confidante, he says he tells you everything."

"Well, he honestly hasn't said a word to me," I said in amazement, "honestly, I really don't know, but look, I'm so sorry, I really must go, my mum's having a baby."

I tried to hug her but she pushed me away and said, "Oh, go on, then, desert me."

I opened my mouth but she turned her back on me. I shook my head; I didn't have time for this. I ran out of the door and down the steps and then collided with Ricky who was sitting on the edge of a step, smoking a cigarette with an ashen face. Seeing me, his narrowed eyes travelled up and over me, suspicious, mistrusting.

"Oh, Ricky," I begged him, "my mother's having the baby. I need to get to the hospital right now. Could I borrow your car? I'd bring it right back, okay?"

"*Bertha* is a very special car," he blew his smoke tauntingly into my face, "and you're not insured."

"Please, Ricky, maybe you could drive me."

Ricky gave an exhausted sigh and rubbed his bleary eyes with one hand. As the swing doors banged open, he looked up and beckoned to Ferras.

"Hey, gotta car? Olivia's in a tizz."

"Sorry, came on my bike," said Ferras, but he raised a flirty eyebrow. "You can always sit on the back."

"Look," I wrung my hands, trying not to sound hysterical, "my mother's in labour. I need a lift. Please, can one of you just help me?"

Ferras, realising the seriousness of the situation, put his paper cup down on the floor and went zooming back into the party, assuring me he'd find somebody.

I waited by the stairs, gazing out of the window across the silhouettes of city spires, winding my handbag strap around my trembling hand. I found myself praying to Krishna that she would be alright, then I shook myself: Krishna was Ricky's God, not mine.

"Come on then."

"What?" I jumped.

Ricky stubbed his cigarette out wearily, jangling his car keys.

"Just this once," he said, as though he was doing me the favour of a lifetime.

30. Emergency

"We're not going to make it," I snapped at Ricky as the car ground to a halt in the middle of honking caterpillars of London traffic. "Maybe I should just get out and take the tube."

At the next traffic-lights, I jumped out quickly at a local newsagents, buying a Snickers (crucial chocolate bar for emergencies, full of peanuts and toffee and other stamina-building blocks) and a bag of yellow-coated bonbons, my mum's favourite.

"Oh, Ricky," I wailed, as the lights went red again.

"Shut up and stop moaning," said Ricky.

Twenty minutes later, we arrived at the hospital ward. My mum was sitting up in bed, panting, red-faced, one hand clutching her stomach, the other her back.

"Olivia!" she cried.

I ran to her side and clutched her hand. At the foot of the bed stood Jed and Calvin, both convinced they were the father, both looking at each other as though they were about to beat each other up. They started when my mum suddenly suffered a contraction.

"Oh, Olivia," she wailed, "never have a baby."

"How long before it comes out?" I asked the nurse in distress.

"Well, she's been having contractions for five hours, but it could be hours still."

"Hours! Can't you see how much pain she's in? Can't you get it out sooner?" I demanded.

Ricky, eager to avoid becoming entangled in the family mesh, backed out hastily. I called a quick thanks after him but he made such a rapid exit, I don't think he even heard. Jed and Calvin gave me amused glances. I glared at them, and turned to Mum, relieved to see the pain had temporarily suspended.

I sat there, clutching the sweaty bag of bonbons in one hand (wondering why on earth I'd bought them – she could hardly chew at them while giving birth) and trying not to wince as she dug her nails in my other hand. Sometimes Mum seemed relaxed and bossy, snapping at Calvin and Jed to stop arguing over what colour the nursery should be painted, recalling with pride how Scott, my older brother, had taken fourteen hours to come out. At other times she was girlish, whimpering at me not to leave her, and murmuring incomprehensible nonsense about my father not being there for her.

On and on the contractions came and went. Despite being brought cups of coffee by a grinning Calvin, whom I sensed, like so many of mum's boyfriends, was someone trying to win me over, I felt my eyelids becoming heavy. I must stay awake, I willed myself, I must muster up my energy for the bit where we all have to shout "*Push!*" I knew that had to happen at some point.

I looked up and saw Calvin asleep and Jed chatting up a pretty blonde nurse. The air in the room felt thick like cotton wool, the walls seemed to be coming in on me. I was wheezing for oxygen as though I was in outer space. I was craving for the sweet heaviness of chocolate in my stomach, the zing of a caffeine high.

"I'll be right back," I squeezed Mum's hand.

In the canteen, the air seemed cool and sweet as apples. I went to call Henry but I still couldn't get through. I ached for him to be there by my side. In my hazy lack of sleep, I was convinced he was not answering on purpose, to punish me.

I jumped as I suddenly spotted Ricky sitting at a grotty table at the end, his tea turning cold, his fingers tracing a graffiti carving. What the hell was he still doing there? I was about to run out before he noticed me, but I was utterly gagging for chocolate by now. I was just collecting my Snickers when his voice caught me. I went and sat down on the orange plastic chair opposite him, nibbling nervously at the edge of my Snickers.

"Want some?" I found myself offering him.

He looked at it sullenly as though it was polluted from my saliva, then grabbed it ungraciously.

"Don't eat it all," I snapped, seeing him wolf half the bar in one bite.

Ricky flung it back across the table. My eyes fell on the print of his teeth in the chocolate and I shuddered with unexpected desire. For a moment we sat in bristling silence, trying to ignore the cackles of nurses at the next table.

"Why are you so mad at me?" I burst out at last. "Why have you been so mean?"

Ricky shook his head in shock, then pulled an incredulous face as though it couldn't be more obvious. "You're unbelievable. Why the hell d'you think?"

"I don't know, I don't know what goes on in your head, I mean, one minute you were begging me to marry you and then you married her and now all of a sudden you hate me."

"Well, you're the one who walked out of the hotel and ignored me through the wedding and then had a fucking affair with some other guy."

"I'm sorry?" My hands went limp with confusion. Ricky grabbed the Snickers bar back and took a huge shaky bite, turning away shiftily. He looked down, fiddling with the wrapper. "Josephine told me all about it on our honeymoon."

"Who?" Was this another one of Henry's paranoias?

"Oh, don't make out all Little Miss Innocent with me," Ricky fluttered his lashes sarcastically. "Josephine said you told her. You and Phil."

"Phil? *Who?*" What on earth was he talking about?

"Phil, that bloke in the stables, and Henry got really pissed off and had him up against the wall, right?"

"Oh, that, *that*!" I cried.

"Oh that!" Ricky echoed in disgust. "Just a little bit on the side, so easy to forget."

"As a matter of fact," I spluttered, "nothing happened! *Nothing!* Henry knew it was all a misunderstanding. I mean, it happened ages ago. What – last June, I think. Josephine was just exaggerating, I don't know why she said that. Henry came in – he thought he saw something but he got it all wrong, you know how jealous he gets. I was just lighting his cigarette."

"Never heard it called that before."

"Well, I'm not going to bother to explain because you won't listen, you –" I grabbed back the tiny remains of my Snickers, "have just eaten all my bloody chocolate and my mum is in labour and needs me and I can't be doing this."

But I was too late. Mum had been rushed off to the labour room, and Kirsty Louise Marcia Loretta Bliss was already emerging . . .

We ran clattering up the stairs, hand in hand, passing Jed by the coffee machine. Instead of sporting a green face-mask and clutching Mum's hand, he was exchanging telephone numbers with the blonde nurse. Up in the labour room, two nurses were dragging out the body of Calvin, who had fainted with shock. Ricky and I heard Mum moaning and groaning like a banshee and looked at each nervously.

"I'm going to go get another cup of tea from the canteen," said Ricky, buggering off.

I took a deep breath and went into the room.

Later, after all the blood, sweat and tears, after little Kirsty had been weighed and prodded and wrapped up in a blanket, Mum sat up in bed, clutching her, looking utterly euphoric.

"Oh, isn't she just the most beautiful thing you've ever seen?" she said to me, tears glistening in her eyes.

She didn't look beautiful at all to me – she looked very ugly, all puckered pinkie skin and white fluffy stuff sticking to her. But I was unspeakably moved by the love my mum was giving her, you could almost feel it radiating off her.

"Oh Mummy," I said, leaning over to hug her gently and for several minutes I remained clasped in an embrace with my mum and new baby sister.

New baby sister! I was still just getting used to the idea. I sat on the edge of the bed and I touched her hand gently. Her fingers were so tiny. Her skin as soft as blossom. She had eyes that were unmistakably Calvin's. They stared up at me and I smiled down at her. She gurgled and then burst into tears.

The wails of the baby brought Calvin to the bedside.

"Ah, my darling, my little angel," he crooned, taking her in his arms, and amazingly enough, she stopped crying at once. "Ah, we must call her Loretta."

"No way," Jed drawled, entering, "I was planning on Marcia."

He held out his arms for her but Calvin backed away, with a guarded look in his dark eyes, like a bull being cornered by a matador. My mum and I watched the baby uneasily; it seemed like a precious fragile ornament that might be dropped at any moment.

"I think it's time Olivia's mum had some sleep," Ricky intervened. I jumped and saw him standing in the doorway, hands in pockets. "You can discuss names tomorrow morning, but for now I'm sure we're all very tired."

Ricky was wonderfully bossy. Calvin gave the baby back to my mum, who gave her one last fond cuddle and kiss goodnight before the nurse put her in the cot by her bed. Calvin and Jed left reluctantly and I stayed by my mother's side.

"Loretta and Marcia indeed!" she muttered indignantly, yawning. "I shall call her Kirsty."

Not long afterwards, she fell asleep. Despite the tired lines on her face and the greasy hair flopping over her forehead, there was a new angelic softness to her features. I started to feel tearful again.

Ricky interrupted my prayers for her by coming up behind me and gently pressing a new Snickers bar into my hands. I looked up quickly to see him gazing down with an apology in his eyes, his hand patting my shoulder gently.

"Maybe you'd better come home," he said. "It's nearly eleven-thirty and you look knackered. Come on, I'll give you a lift."

"Even though I'm supposedly a terrible adulteress?" I couldn't resist, as he helped me on with my coat. I still couldn't believe he'd been so vile to me, all over the tiniest misunderstanding. Though such a strong reaction was, on the other hand, very flattering . . .

"Yeah, well, erm . . ." he did up the buttons of my coat, looking most sheepish.

As we walked slowly down the steps, Ricky said, "Shall we, erm, go somewhere? Talk things through? If you're not too tired?"

"Oh, no, that would be lovely. Thanks for giving me the lift, it's really sweet of you."

"Oh, not at all, it's the least I could do."

"Well, thanks."

*　　*　　*

To my relief, the hotel bar was very twee and touristy. There were only a few rich couples sitting on the leather sofas, having a late-night supper. Ricky sat me down and went to order some drinks. I stared at the oil paintings on the walls, stags leaping through forests, countryside cottages. A real log fire burned in the grate. Mozart hummed soothingly in the background.

We drank tea and ate chips.

"Chips! My God!" Ricky cried lustfully. "Oh wow! Olivia, you don't know what it's like living with Josephine and being forced to eat nothing but those little cardboard crackers with a lump of Philadelphia and a rind of cucumber – if I'm lucky."

"You're not fat," I said in bewilderment.

"No, but it's called 'Diet Sympathy' – i.e. if she's slimming and I'm stuffing myself with burgers, it makes her feel left out."

"Oh well, I'm sure it's very healthy for you," I defended her self-consciously.

Somehow it was as though we had gone right back to square one, to those days when he had first moved into Josephine's house, the conversation chatty and easy. We recalled the delivery with awe and Ricky asked if I was planning on having kids and I said I wasn't sure, Henry wasn't very keen on any more, but I wouldn't mind. Ricky said that Josephine didn't like kids and since Jamie had moved in, he was driving her mad with all the mess and noise and Children's ITV. Ricky tried to make a joke of it but I could see how hurt he was inside.

"The trouble is, Jamie knows when he's not wanted.

And then he starts to try and get attention and plays up. The other day he filled her mascara bottle with Marmite."

"Oh, my God!" I shrieked. "Oh poor Josephine!"

Ricky, with his typical Incredible Hulk appetite, finished his chips and then, seeing I hadn't eaten much, chided me and said I needed fattening up, and started on mine. I fought him off, and we battled each other with our forks, giggling.

"I know what you need," said Ricky, getting up and hailing a waitress.

He returned with more drinks from the bar, and a few minutes later, I was surprised by a smiling waitress bringing a bowl of tiramisu.

"I ordered it for Ms Chocoholic," Ricky grinned.

"Oh, you shouldn't have," I protested weakly, my eyes gleaming at the sheen of ice cream. For a few moments he watched me tuck in with a funny, affectionate smile, then he cleared his throat and confessed:

"Actually, Josephine and I have agreed on an Open Relationship."

"You what?" I put the bowl down in amazement. "But you're married."

"Yeah, well, it was her idea! I mean, it was the first night of our honeymoon in Majorca and every night all she wanted to do was go clubbing and there were blokes all over her. And she just started going on about her repressed upbringing and how she'd always been such a good girl and she felt marriage shouldn't be the end of fun and since neither of us were good at commitment, it did seem a good idea. Only, it sounded cool in theory, but in practice . . ." he lowered his voice, looking shifty, as though wondering whether he should really be telling me this, "I mean, a week into our honeymoon and she went off with some other guy, this hairdresser from some Greek island, all chest hair and medallions!"

"You're kidding!"

"Yeah." Ricky stared down at his fork. "I ended up with some Essex girl called Sharon."

"You what!" I hissed, torn inside out with jealousy.

"Don't worry, I didn't sleep with her," he said hastily. "And Josephine, it turned out, never slept with hers. She came back in the dead of night complaining he'd got a penis the size of her little finger. 'I had to pretend to have a sudden period attack,' she confessed to me. 'The poor guy,' I said. She was really disappointed in me for not sleeping with Sharon but at the same time, if I had, I think she would have been mad with jealousy too. It was awful, Olivia," he added, pleadingly. "I just don't get her, she always has to complicate everything into one big psychological game. And then she was going on about how you and Henry are never loyal to each other, because Henry still sees Agatha and you had some fling with the stable boy."

"No, no!" I protested hotly. "I swear –" I paused as he gently dabbed away some chocolate with the edge of his napkin. "– it was nothing, Ricky, I wouldn't do that to Henry."

We sat in silence for a moment. I was still so shocked. I thought Henry and I had problems, but they were nothing compared to this . . .

"So there was really nothing with you and Phil?" Ricky asked.

"No!" I said, and then looked at him. "And you and Sharon?"

"The most I did was get her a drink, honest."

"Oh, right. Well, good."

Ricky smiled awkwardly, picked up my bowl and scooped up a big brown chunk with a spoon, pushing it towards my mouth. I shied away, and then opened my mouth, feeling the taste of the chocolate dust fizz and dissolve on my tongue. He started to feed me, gently tipping the ice cream into my mouth, his fingers brushing away smears on my lips, the palm of his hand caressing the back of mine, reaching up and pushing away a curl from my face, slipping back down over my knee and the inside of my thigh, pushing more ice cream into my mouth, his brown eyes fixed on me like scorching ice until I was nearly dizzy with longing and it was as if there was nobody else in the room, just me and him touching and gazing at each other.

The spoon clattered back into the bowl. All gone. I watched him put the bowl down on the table and shook myself out of the trance.

"Ricky, we have to get back. Henry will be wondering where I am. Maybe you should give Josephine a call."

"Olivia, come on –" He curled his palm around the back of my head and I pushed him away.

"Ricky, stop it!"

He leaned over me, his brown eyes holding mine.

"If you don't stop –"

He leaned over and silenced me with a kiss. I burst into tears.

"Olivia!"

I pushed him away, shaking my head, swivelling away from him.

"Olivia, I'm really sorry, I didn't mean – I just thought you –" he let out a sigh of exasperation, pushed back his hair with his hands.

I turned my head away, brushing my curls over my face, sniffing, giving a little shake of my head.

"Look, I'm really sorry, can I, er, get you anything?" he offered. He pushed the drink into my hands. My mouth felt like jelly against the glass.

"D'you want some crisps?" he offered desperately.

I shook my head.

"Chocolate! I still owe you another one!"

I patted the bulge in my pocket. He blew out his breath.

"Shall I go and leave you alone?"

I nodded vehemently. He paused petulantly.

"Is it okay if I just sit here with you?"

I managed a little shrug.

In his desperation, he started to make silly, almost surreal jokes about everything.

"That dog's looking a bit dead, isn't it?" he pointed to a bare skin lying in front of the fire. A tiny smile pulled at my lips. "Ah, now, look, you're smiling!" Ricky teased me triumphantly. Then a pair of elderly men came down and Ricky started to seriously take the piss in a low voice, doing a surreal fake Northern accent and pretending that they were describing their vegetables. "Eh, my crops were huge this year, my turnip was the size of a watermelon!"

I started to laugh hysterically, then cry. One of the old men put down his cap and looked over at me. Ricky put his hand on my shoulder and I clenched my tissue.

"Ricky, shut up," I said.

"Eh, by gum –"

"*Will you just shut up!*" I burst out.

Ricky started, his mouth hanging open. Suddenly I grabbed up the lapels of his jacket and yanked him over to me, kissing him with all my might. He put his arms around me and looked as though he might weep for joy.

"Oh, I love you," I broke down, kissing the top of his head, "I love you so much!"

Ricky looked up and suddenly it was unbearable, all the pulls and guilts and fears and no's clashing through my mind like opposing hurricanes and thundering into my nails clawing his hair. He tried to kiss me again and I slapped him hard across the face, so that you could hear the bone crack. "I – I – I love you, I hate you, oh God, why did you have to do this to me!" All of a sudden, I found myself hitting him, curling my fists, punching against his chest. "I can't stand this! I can't do this!" He pulled away and laughed, catching my wrists. "It's not funny!" I screamed, and I slapped him *wham*! across the cheek. The sound of the thwack, the shock of seeing the gash in his cheek from my wedding ring, froze me with horror. Equally shocked, he touched his cheek, frowning incredulously at the blood on his fingers.

The room had fallen silent. All that you could hear

was the merry tinkle of Mozart and my own hysterical sobbing.

Ricky quickly pulled me to my feet. As he hurried me out to the reception, I heard one of the rich American couples saying we could do with the miracles of their marriage guidance counsellor.

The startled hotel man, no doubt thinking I was a total drunk, handed over the key with reluctance, looking slightly alarmed. Then somehow through the blur of tears I saw the stairs and felt Ricky's strong arms lifting me up, across the patterned swirl of a carpet and into a bedroom, setting me down on the bed. I kept trying to say sorry, but he shushed me and went to get some water.

"I'm so sorry, oh, I'm so sorry," I pressed my fingers against the bridge of my nose. Had I done that to him, was that really me? "I'm so sorry." I collapsed onto the bed, crying again, burying my face in the covers, shaking with big wracking raw sobs that cracked my ribs and left my throat dry. Ricky came to my side and gently stroked my hair and face, shushing me, tenderly muttering little sayings, "Come on, now, Olivia, that's right, cry, my dear, get it all out, it's going to be alright, I love you, it's going to be alright."

He hurried to get me water, but I couldn't drink. I couldn't move, I could only lie there, crying, feeling as though my forehead was going to split open with grief. Gradually, the tears softened into quiet sobs. Still I lay with my back to him, clutching the bedspread up against my chest, closing my eyes, feeling his fingers light on my cheek. My breath quietened; my brain was muzzy, full of cotton wool. I tried to lift my head but it was too heavy. I just wanted to lie in the darkness. Dark and quiet, a soft voice, a hand on my hair. I eventually fell into an exhausted sleep.

31. Surrender

When I woke up, it was dark. Through a crusty veil of yellow sleepydust, a flowered wallpaper pattern emerged. I blinked, sitting up. A man was sitting on a wicker chair by the window watching me. *Where am I who am I what happened?* Panic whistled through me.

"Ricky!" I burst out. I checked my watch. Shit, it was three in the morning.

He was looking utterly dejected. The ash-tray beside him was brimming with butts.

"Olivia." Through the tangle of his blonde fringe, his eyes were filled with remorse. "I'm really sorry, I've been so out of order. If Henry was here now he'd bloody sock me one, and I'd deserve it."

"No, no." Still lost in the hazy dreamlike state between waking and sleeping, as though acting from my subconscious, I slid off the bed and went to him, kneeling by his feet, stroking his hands and saying that it wasn't his fault, it was nobody's fault.

Ricky gazed down at me and for a moment our gazes locked. His eyes flitted to my lips, then he stood up abruptly, nearly knocking me over, pulling on his jacket, striding to the door.

I rose shakily to my feet and stared at him in disbelief.

"Well?" he asked, "Don't you think we should be getting home?"

Outside in the corridor, I was so mad I couldn't, wouldn't walk beside him. Instead I trailed some way behind, arms crossed. I just felt so horribly humiliated, as though I'd been the one immorally seducing him and not the other way round.

"Maybe I should just call Henry and get him to pick me up," I said, unable to bear the thought of the journey back.

Ricky paused and chewed his lip. Then, as a bellboy came trundling a huge load of cases down the corridor, a late night guest following him behind, Ricky gently pushed me aside to make way. Our bodies brushed, I felt him pressed up against me. My heart and legs were beating. Everything was muzzy, without thought or reason. His lips brushed mine. The cases trundled past. Then he lowered his mouth to mine and kissed me forcefully, clasping his arms around me.

"Oh, Ricky." I sank into the warm cave of his chest and arms and in one split second I surrendered.

He took my hand and led me quickly back to our room, rattling the door handle in exasperation. In the end he had to call the bellboy to open it, pretending I'd left my handbag inside. I went in and sat on the bed, took off my shoes. Ricky leant against the door, looking doubtful and sheepish again.

"So this is just a one-night stand?" he asked across the room.

I searched for the expression on his face but it was too dark.

"I guess, yes."

"I mean, I guess we should just, ah, get this out of our system. Just one night together, and we both swear not to tell Josephine or Henry."

"Well, I thought that you and Josephine had an open relationship," I blurted out.

"I mean this, Olivia, if Dad found out . . ."

"Sorry, I swear," I swallowed as though I was taking an oath in court.

He came forwards, then edged away, taking off his jacket, fiddling around, and then slinging it over the back of the chair. He sat on the edge of the bed, looking worried.

I didn't want him to look worried. I wanted him to be all manly and forceful again as he had been a few moments ago.

"I don't have any condoms," he confessed.

"Well, that's okay, I just had my period, it only finished yesterday. That means it's safe, I mean me and Henry often take advantage of . . ." I trailed off awkwardly.

There was a silence.

"Are you sure we should be doing this? Maybe you're right —"

"No, don't stop, just bloody kiss me before I lose my nerve and bloody run," I cried.

We looked at each other nervously, then burst into laughter. The tension slackened with relief. He lay down beside me, taking my face in his hands, and kissed me sweetly, so softly. I could feel my heart running warm and fluid with bliss and I couldn't help but giggle. Our lips shook with laughter against each other. Ricky broke off and laughed at the ceiling and then reached out for me again and exclaimed, "Olivia, I do love you so much!"

He looked at me with eyes fluid with love. I felt my insides turn to mush.

"Okay, let's just, let's just do this," he said breathlessly. "Let's just forget everything and everyone. I love you so much, this can't be wrong."

He pulled me against him and we started to kiss again – small butterfly kisses. Our eyes were pinned on each other, our hands wandering uncertainly over the new glorious territory of each other's faces and hair and backs, uncertain when or where to break the boundaries into erogenous zones, self-conscious and awkward like schoolchildren sharing their first kiss.

Then, as his breathing started to quicken, and he pulled me hard against him so I could feel how excited he was, I felt a thrill of desire leap up my spine like a cobra. *Olivia, I love you so much!* kept ringing excitedly in my mind. I kissed him with all my might and joy, and he parted my lips with his tongue, until our lips were so hard against each other we were eat-kissing. Our hands knocked as they flew to fumble at buttons; we laughed and I swallowed nervously as he unzipped my crop top, leaning down to kiss my breasts. I pushed his head back and smiled at him and buried my lips and teeth in his neck, unbuttoning his shirt, pulling off his Nike T-shirt, hardly able to manage in my excitement, and oh *mmm* how lovely and warm

and soft his skin was, how broad and long his back!
He kissed my stomach as I tried to unbutton his
trousers and I looked at him scorchingly to say *Come
inside me, come inside me now*.

He pulled himself over me and kissed me fiercely.
He made love to me clutching me tightly, his hard
chest squashing against my breasts, his stubbled jaw
sand-papering my cheek. I thought of Henry . . . desire
tidal-waved through my mind, washing away worries
like the tide cleaning sand. I could feel him inside me
and I ran my hands over his back, up up the notches
of his spine, my mind black, filled with pin-pricks of
light that grew bigger and bigger until my head was a
big white balloon expanding with light and my hands
were clawing his hair and I heard myself crying out for
him . . .

For some time afterwards we lay there, he still inside
me, listening to each other's breath ebbing away,
exchanging tender, hazy kisses and caresses. Outside
the sky was deepest indigo and an aeroplane cut a path
of gold through the darkness. I thought of people travelling to foreign lands, escaping, freedom, new faces.
I thought of Henry and how he had never made love
to me like this and a shudder of guilt and desire rippled
through me. Now I knew, I really knew, there was no
going back – the love I felt for Henry was like placing
a candle in front of the sun compared to my love for
Ricky. I stroked his blonde fringe over his forehead to
hide his eyes, digging my teeth so sharply into my lip
to stop the tears that I tasted blood. Oh God, what was
I going to do, what was I going to do, how did I end
up here, how did it all come to this –

Ricky lifted his head and looked down at me with sleepy, satisfied eyes. He pushed my curls back from my face, then his eyes widened in alarm as he felt the wetness of my cheeks.

"What is it? I'm sorry, did I hurt you – did we make a complete fuck-up –"

"No," I shook my head frantically, smiling up at him through the blur of tears. "I'm just so happy," I lied. "I'm just crying because I'm so happy to be with you . . . because I love you."

That wasn't a lie.

"I love you!" he said, hugging me tightly. "I don't want you to cry, I don't want you to worry, don't worry, Olivia, everything's going to be alright. I'm here now, everything's going to be alright."

He pulled away from me and pulled the covers over us so that we were cocooned in white cotton. His caresses and soft words soothed me and I felt myself letting go, letting the fears curl away like dead leaves on the wind. Everything will always be alright. Later on, I never forgot those words.

We lay in silence for some time, warm, as though bound together. Sometimes I closed my eyes and listened to the beat of his heart against the noise of the traffic outside, the chatter of guests in the hallway, two girls who had been out on the pull. Or sometimes I opened my eyes and watched his face, trying to memorise and paste in my memory the square jaw and turned-up nose and his eyelashes, dark, but lightened here and there by the sun, like the gold flecks on a bee's coat. The different shadows forming on his skin as the room grew lighter with the faint traces of dawn.

Or sometimes I opened my eyes and with a delicious jolt found him staring at me. Or sometimes we just lay and stared, loving each other with our eyes, and there was nothing to say, just peace in the silence.

Peace. For some time I felt as though I was simply swimming along, drifting in a tide of easy bliss. Nothing seemed to matter. The world was shut out, time was suspended, I was only aware of him. I didn't want to do anything, or be anywhere else. I started to feel sleepy and I snuggled up against him and he ran his hands over my back. I noticed he had a light mole on his shoulder and I circled the outline with my forefinger. I found myself yawning into his shoulder and falling half-asleep but staying half-awake, aware of the white light in my mind again, and a new feeling inside. A feeling of lightness, abstractness, freedom, that same delicious sensation of surrender as when I had given in to his first kiss. Hazily I recalled Ricky's words, the final lines of Eliot's poem, *shantih shantih shantih* . . . *that peace which passeth all understanding* . . . everything will always be alright . . . my mind rose and fell on gentle waves of love . . . nothing else matters, except I love Ricky, nothing else matters except that I love Ricky . . .

The thought of the Henry waiting up at home for me pin-pricked the bubbles of bliss. I found myself rising up out of sleep.

"What?" Ricky asked, sensitive at once to my fear.

"What time is it?" I asked.

He turned and felt around for his watch which he had thrown on the carpet.

It was five o'clock in the morning. Heavens – we'd

been here hours! How could the night have been so quick and yet so long?

"I'd better be getting back," I said abruptly. "And you had too."

We lay in sadness for some time and then I rose up, looking around the carpet for my clothes.

"Oh, don't go," Ricky whimpered, pulling me back down tight against him. "Don't go."

He held me against him for some time and finally let out a long sigh.

"I guess we should go," he said at last.

"I do love you but we should go," I said, after a while.

"Yes," said Ricky. "I love you."

"I love you."

Neither of us moved.

32. Torn

At around six in the morning, we slipped away from the hotel and Ricky drove me back home to Buckinghamshire. It was deathly, eerily quiet, the world all silent and asleep around us. Grass nodded with wet, dewy heads in the still fields; birds started to trill cautiously in anticipation of dawn; a milk cart droned in the distance.

I had been through so much, I was completely knackered. There was too much to think about, too much to feel. Inside I could feel hot tears welling up at the thought of us parting. My head nodded sleepily, dulling and muzzying the loneliness . . .

"You have to leave him," Ricky suddenly woke me up.

"What?"

"Olivia, you have to! You do want to, don't you, you do?"

"Well – yes – but – I –"

Ricky drew the car to a halt. He took my hands in his and started to gabble.

"Look, come on, Olivia, we can do it, we can, we can do it right now, if Dad's not in we can just go and pack up a case, I mean we don't even have to do that, we can go and just take off and travel and see Europe, we can see France!"

"I hate France," I said, half-crying, half-laughing. "The men all ogle you."

Ricky smiled too, gripping my hands tighter, speaking faster and faster.

"We can go back to India! You can have an Indian birth, we can have an Indian wedding, with fire and hymns, and – and – look, we can survive, I'm not being spacey, I've got it all worked out. I'm going to write this book, I've been thinking about it for ages, it's going to be a kind of backpacker novel in the East, funny but spiritual, I think people like spiritual stuff now more, I think it might really sell and then I'll be rich and I'll treat you so well, I love you so much, you'll be my princess and I'll wait on you and cook for you and do anything, anything you want . . ."

I listened to him, nodding and biting back my smiles, swept away on the wave of his thought, thinking on the surface: *maybe we can, maybe it is really possible, anything is possible . . .*

It's all just words, a deeper part of me, more fixed and adamant, shook a firm, brisk head. *This is mad, it's crazy, it's a silly fantasy . . .*

I tried to draw my hands away from his but he held on too tightly. I turned my head away in exasperation.

"Please, look, Ricky, we both know it just isn't going to happen . . ."

"But why not?" Ricky asked earnestly. "Why not? Give me a reason. Give me twenty good reasons why not! Ten!"

"Ricky!" I folded my arms, shaking my head. "Well,

to begin with, it's just completely mad, that's why we can't!"

"But who cares if it's completely mad? The reason we go so well together is because we're both completely mad!"

I smiled again and picked at the edge of the seat. "Number two, we're – we don't have the means . . ."

"Oh, I see," said Ricky, pulling a grim face, and drawing away. "I see. Money. That's it. So this is what it's all about – money," he said in disgust. "You can't bear not to have your title and your big house – that's the only reason you married him, isn't it?"

"Ricky, we're not talking about me, you don't understand –"

"But I've got money! You know I'm going to write this book. I can get it published, I can, with Henry as my dad I have all the contacts. And I will write it, with you to inspire me I can do anything . . ."

"But, I need a firm guarantee, my mother, you see –" I cried, thinking: he's not listening, he's not listening to me.

"D'you really think I'd let you down, don't you know I'll take care of you? Christ, Olivia, I can give you money! You want my money?" He opened his wallet and threw a flurry of five-pound notes at me. His voice started to rise, "You can have all my money, but it's not going to be enough, is it –"

"You don't understand!" I yelled, and he stopped, breathless and wide-eyed. "Oh, you just won't listen!" I screeched, throwing a handful of notes back at him.

"I'm sorry," he recoiled meekly. "Tell me. Make me understand."

For a moment I sat with my arms crossed, narrowing my watering eyes, fixing on the line of the horizon. I didn't want him to see I was crying. If he tried to comfort me I only wanted to shove him away.

"Look," I said at last, "it's my mum."

"Go on," Ricky gulped.

"Well, you know the story," I let out a long sigh. "Henry has bought her that big house in Kingston and she's so happy, I mean, she's had such a crap life with my dad leaving her. The one thing she wanted was money. You know what Henry's like. People are either his friends or his enemies. If I go, he'll hate me, he'll hate me so much he'll throw her out and what with her baby . . ."

I waited, wanting him to say something wonderful, to come up with another fantastic plan.

"Yeah," Ricky conceded at last. "It's true . . . but."

"Yes?" I snapped in relief.

"Olivia, it's your life. You can't live your mother's life for her. I mean, you can't live the rest of your life trying to maintain some kind of equilibrium where you're pleasing everyone except for you. I mean, I think this is just your trouble –"

A tractor chugged up behind us impatiently and Ricky sighed. The tractor-man leaned out of his window and waved pointedly. Ricky let out his breath, started up the car and pulled it in to the side, allowing him to pass. I sat with my arms folded, my mouth pressed together to stop the insults coming out –

"What d'you mean, that's my problem? What problem?" I burst out as soon as the tractor had passed.

"Look, I'm not saying it's a fault – I mean, it's what's

so sweet about you – you never like to offend anyone
so you just say something to please them. But sometimes you just need to be selfish. Like – like – you
know, the end of *King Lear*."

"I'm sorry?" I was still reeling. This last accusation
had hit very hard and deep.

"The end of *King Lear* where Edmund – or is it
Edward – fuck it, he says, '*Speak what we feel, not what
we ought to say.*'"

I paused, still feeling shocked. He was looking at me
with such earnest sympathy that I wanted to hit him.
What was he trying to be, my counsellor? What right
did he have to analyse me? He didn't even know me!

I searched my mind for some clever quote, some
Shakespeare snippet but could think of nothing.

"I mean, to be honest, I think you've got worse since
you married Dad. He's so bossy, and you're . . . not."

"So now you're saying I'm a doormat," I cried, stung;
he sounded just like Emily. "Well, well, it's better than
you and Josephine, always bickering, at least Henry
and I have a happy marriage which is more than you
have . . ." I trailed off when I saw his face.

"No – but – look, look, I'm not saying you're a
doormat at all, I'm just saying you're really kind and if
anything Henry takes advantage, I'm saying – what I'm
saying is – oh forget it. You know what I mean – urgh!"
Throwing up his hands in exasperation, he turned
away, banged his forehead against the steering wheel.
I winced and instinctively reached out, stroking his
head, smoothing his fringe, nudging the back of my
knuckles against his cheek-bone. He nuzzled it back
sadly.

What have I done? I gazed down at the top of his fair head. I knew this would happen, I knew it could never be one night, you couldn't just turn on and off feelings like a tap.

Ricky suddenly sat up and smashed his fist into the steering wheel.

"Don't –" I said.

"Why can't you leave him?" he suddenly begged, with the desperation of a small boy. "Why? Why? Why?"

"Because I just can't!"

"What is it, is it fear? Are you worried what people might think?"

"Ricky, I've told you, I've told you – I just can't – I don't – I can't, I mean, what am I going to say to him, Ricky? How would I ever say it?" I broke down.

Ricky took my hands in his and it was as though we had come right back in a circle to Square One.

"I'll do all the talking," he said in a rush. "I mean, can you imagine how terrified I feel, telling my dad I want his wife? But look, okay, when I found out that I'd got some girl I hardly knew pregnant with my boy Jamie, I dreaded telling Dad. I thought he'd go mad, and he bloody well did. But when he'd cooled down and I'd explained it was an accident, he understood. We've just got to be honest, it's so much better than going behind his back – that I can't stand. But if we just say how much we love each other, he has to understand, he has to!" He swung away and thrust his keys into the ignition.

"Ricky what are you doing?"

Ricky pushed into first, steam-rolling over a bank of

elderflower as he drove off the bank and back onto the road.

"We're going to tell him," Ricky stated, putting his foot down on the accelerator.

"Ricky, we can't! Stop! Stop!" I cried weakly, ineffectually. His jaw remained set and he charged into third gear.

"Ricky! I'll jump out, I mean it, I will!" I reached for the door but he slammed the child-lock on just in time.

"Ricky!" Panic flooded over me. The thought of Henry's face. He'd *kill* him. He'd kill *me*. Seriously. When Henry lost his temper, he lost it, he was just mad – like the time he'd been paranoid about Phil the stable boy, yanked him by the collar and smashed him up against the wall. Didn't Ricky have any idea? Didn't he realise? Surely he knew his dad, surely he'd realise? What, did he think just because he was Henry's son that would make any difference? That Henry would sit down with us with his cheque book in his lap, smile over his spectacles and say "How shall we arrange a standing order?" like something out of a bank advert, leaving us to live happily ever after? He was crazy.

"Ricky, Ricky, please," I begged, jabbering, "come on, let's just give it a few weeks, come on, we need time to think and plan and draw up a list, we need to sort out clothes and a joint bank account because I'm with Barclays and you're with Lloyds, Ricky, please, just a few days!"

"Then it will never happen," said Ricky. "It's now or never."

"*No!*" In my desperation, I reached over and half-collided, half-fell against him, punching his legs, turning the wheel. The car swerved and trees spun across the sky. The gear-stick punched into my stomach. The wheels skidded, the engine grated. The car groaned to a halt halfway across the road.

Ricky pulled me up and tried to kiss me and I shoved him away, unclipping my seat belt with shaking hands.

He buried his head in his hands. He started to cry. Oh God.

"Ricky," I begged, reaching back over, trying to kiss his tears away, but he turned his face in angry embarrassment, brushing them away with his cuffs.

I reached into his pocket and lit a cigarette for him, feeding him a quick suck. He breathed out, coughed, dropped it accidentally onto the floor. For a moment we sat in silence, watching the red ambers burn dead.

He was gnawing his lip so hard there was blood. I couldn't resist, I felt for him so badly. I licked the blood from his lips, swallowing the salty taste. His lips curved against mine in a wobbly smile. For a moment we kissed desperately. Then I broke away.

"I really love you," he whispered. "Please stay," he pleaded one last time, but his voice was defeated, knowing the answer was no.

"We had our night together and that was that," I said unsteadily, turning away before I could register the incredulity on his face. I said sorry and clicked up the lock and even as my legs landed rubbery on the grassy bank, my brain was yelling, *Stay, Olivia, you know it's what you want: Stay.*

"If you don't come with me now," said Ricky in a quiet trembling voice, "this is it. It's over. I can't have an affair, I can't keep creeping behind his back. You're the one who talked about *responsibility*. What… d'you think it's responsible to lie like this?"

Stay stay stay.

I didn't even look back at him, but I could hear him blowing out a breath of disbelief.

"You don't even love me," he started, "it was just sex for you, wasn't it, just a good *fuck!* Well, I hope you're *satisfied*. I'm going to call him and say what we've done –"

I couldn't stand any more. I slammed the door on him and started to hurry away, my feet slippery on the bank. He opened the door and called sorry's after me, begging me to come back. Terrified he was going to come after me, I started to run and run, leaping onto the road, my feet pounding in my ears.

I came to a panting halt outside a phone box and dialled up Henry, begging him to be in. It rang twenty times and I was about to drop it in despair when he answered.

"Oh Henry," I gasped, "my mother's had her baby and I'm stranded halfway between Leighton Buzzard and home and I'm really scared –"

"What the hell? What the hell are you doing there? You were supposed to meet me in London for the Peacocks' dinner party and –"

"But Mum had her baby and I couldn't get through to you –"

"No, I've been up all night writing, "I switched the ringer off earlier when I was writing, I didn't realise it was still off."

"And I got a lift with this horrible nutter, and –"

"You did what?" Henry barked.

"And, and," I sobbed, "he tried it on with me and I had to run away and now I'm stranded."

"Stay there," said Henry in a dangerously calm voice. "I'll be right over."

I had never been so glad to see my husband. He took me in his arms and held me tightly and I sobbed and sobbed into his jumper. I couldn't distinguish anymore between what were tears of joy for the baby or tears of grief for Ricky or just tears of exhaustion, I just had to cry and cry, with the unfortunate result that Henry was convinced the nutter had tried to rape me and wanted to drag me down to the police station there and then.

"What did I tell you?" he said with furious protectiveness as we zoomed back home. "I told you to resign, and now look what a mess you're in."

I fell into a deep troubled sleep and awoke at around three in the afternoon to find Henry watching over me. Now that I had resigned he was all over me again, as sweet and doting as he had been on our honeymoon. He brought me up some soup and hot chocolate and listened delightedly as, in between sips, I told him all about the new darling baby. He even let Roberta come and bound up on the bed instead of shutting her out as usual. Somehow his kindness was excruciating; I almost longed for him to be moody and shout at me – then somehow I might not feel so guilty, so hot with shame every time he looked me in the eye that I had to quickly look away.

"D'you feel well enough to visit?" he asked.

"Oh, yes, I'd love to," I cried; anything to get out of

the house and run away from myself.

"Actually," he checked his watch. "Maybe a bit later. I just spoke to Ricky on the phone – he's coming over."

Argh! Shit! My hand gripped Roberta's coat so tightly she yelped. *Henry on the phone to Ricky!* Ricky's parting threat echoed in my mind: *I'm going to phone him, Olivia, and tell him about us!*

"He and Josephine are at each other like dogs again. Anyway, she's thrown him out and poor Jamie's been sent to live with his grandmother which is probably best but I said Ricky could come over and stay here for a few weeks. You don't mind, do you darling –"

"Well, yes!" I exploded. Then, seeing his surprise at my reaction, I tried to say more steadily. "Well, well, it's just nice, now that I've, erm, resigned, to have the house to ourselves."

"But we're got sixty rooms," Henry pointed out, frowning. "Anyway, I've said yes now. Come on, don't be difficult, he'll be at the other end of the house, you'll hardly know he's there . . ."

PART FOUR: THE FINAL AFFAIR
33. To Say Or Not To Say

The day my father had announced that he was having an affair, Mum had burnt the tea as usual, and my brother Scott and I had been arguing over the remote control and *Heartbreak High* on BBC2 and *Happy Days* on Channel 4. Mum had yelled at us to shut up just as Dad walked in and afterwards I fretted for months that it was all my fault, that if I'd been sitting at the table quietly doing my homework, Mum wouldn't have been so distracted and there wouldn't have been smoke billowing out of the oven setting off the smoke alarm and Dad wouldn't have rolled his eyes and said coldly and quietly,

"I'm afraid I'm leaving you, for good."

I had lifted the net curtains at our bay window and seen the girl my father was going off with. She was young and blonde and cherub-like. She'd been leader of the Girl Guide pack and I'd innocently collected conkers and sewn on badges with her without ever knowing that she was silently screwing my father behind the altar or wherever. "I do want us to be friends," she kept begging me afterwards and I had spat at her in disgust and written, '*Marie is a slag!*

across the girls' toilets and then got suspended for a day. How ironic to think here I was now, in exactly the same sick situation.

Would the whole thing repeat itself to the awful end? I wondered morosely that evening as I stood in the kitchen, attempting to cook dinner. Would I end up as Mum had before I'd married Henry and he's saved us both? Stuck in a Croydon bed-sit, caught in some crap office job, endlessly cutting coupons out of magazines to save money and splurging every last penny on lottery instants?

No.

"No," I said out loud, stirring the baked beans forcefully with a fork. *"No no no!"*

The day I'd married Henry, I'd been so proud, almost smug, that I was different from my family, somehow better than them, for marrying such a famous rich man and making a success of my life. I'd been so sure it would be for life, I'd pictured Henry and me being old together, with grandchildren, doing graceful things for charity.

How could I have gone off him so quickly, just like I'd gone off all my boyfriends so quickly before him? My mum had always accused me of being fickle, like when I'd secretly got engaged to Pete the local car mechanic, convinced he was my soul mate, and then accidentally, um, drunkenly, got off with his much more gorgeous best friend at his eighteenth. It was just the same situation repeating itself, only before it had been a minor embarrassment and now it was an earthquake of mega proportions simply because I was a few years older.

The glitter always has to fade, I considered; if I did run off with Ricky, the same thing might happen with him.

But I couldn't imagine it, I argued back weakly, he's so sexy and yummy and fun to be with –

"But when you first met Henry you thought he was perfect," I argued back loudly, into the baked beans, putting down the fork and picking up the shakers. "He seemed so old and mature and knew everything about life, you practically thought he was God."

I had to stay with Henry. It was so much more sensible and secure.

Hearing Ricky's voice outside in the corridor, foot-steps up and down the stairs as he and Henry carried up his stuff from the Beatle to his guest bedroom, the fork started to shake. Still, I reasoned, he and Josephine were more turn-off-and-on-able than British Gas, they were bound be back together within a week. If I could just hold out that long and try and avoid Ricky as much as possible – and anyway, surely Ricky wouldn't have the nerve to try anything with Henry around –

I gasped as Ricky walked into the room. He came right up me, sniffing the pans.

"Mmm, smells delicious," he said, then, as I turned away, blushing madly, he said, "My dear, you're putting salt in the rice pudding and sugar in the baked beans."

I was about to tell him where to go, when he took the shakers out of my hands.

"What are you doing-" I began, then shut up when he put his hand on the back of my neck, pulled me forwards and kissed me.

Instantly, I found my knees going weak and my arms curling up around his neck despite myself, sinking in relief against him, breathing in that gorgeous Ricky smell. How could I possibly choose Henry over him? God, I hadn't even realised how much I missed him, like not knowing you were hungry till you smelt and tasted food. Now at last I felt whole again.

"I'm so sorry I was such a bastard," Ricky murmured in my hair. "I never thought you thought it was just a zipless fuck. I didn't want to let you go."

Realising the pans were burning, we pulled apart. Turning my back to him, the steam made my cheeks go even hotter. Suddenly I felt wildly, recklessly happy, all the tension and tiredness I'd suffered in the last day or so vaporising. Who cared about stability and money?

"Alright," I said breathlessly, "okay. I'll tell Henry. I'll tell him it's over."

"Tell me what?"

My fork fell into the pan as Henry walked in, rubbing his rumbling tummy.

"Erm, the food – it's a bit burnt," I spluttered, reaching for the fork, then yelping as I burnt myself.

"Sorry, my wife's not the best cook," Henry apologised, rolling his eyes at Ricky and extracting the fork with a sieve.

"I'm sure it will be lovely," Ricky defended me valiantly.

From then on, every moment we managed to sneak an illicit kiss or take a quick walk in the nearby wood, Ricky and I discussed the Situation.

"*I'm* going to tell him," I'd insisted, "it's got to come from me."

It was easier said than done.

I very nearly said it when we went out shopping at Waitrose the following week, but just as I'd swallowed and opened my mouth, Henry realised we'd forgotten the washing powder and hurried off to another aisle. Tuesday, he was in all day, but, reading my Libra stars in *The Daily Mail* that morning, I discovered it was a troubled time for conflict and 'confrontation was best avoided' so that put Tuesday out. On Wednesday, I found myself walking up and down outside his study, my hands sweating, heart beating, nearly, ever so nearly walking in and saying it . . . but not quite.

Christ, I'm becoming worse than Hamlet, I thought miserably, then tried to reassure myself that it just wasn't the right time, the destined moment would come and all would fall into place.

"The question is, whether it's going to be before the end of the century," Ricky said sulkily when I explained this to him.

Another problem which only tangled the messy knots of confusion even tighter was my sudden concern that Henry was having an affair too. I had no evidence. I'd searched the beds for stray hairs but found only his wiry black curls, sniffed his jackets for perfume but only smelt dry-cleaning fluid. This is all in your mind, I said firmly, you don't trust him anymore because you know he can't trust you.

But still, I knew that something was up – it was just a shifty air about him, the way he kept cutting off calls abruptly whenever I came into his study. I kept dialling

1471 and detected a few strange numbers, but when I once dared to press call-back I got "Hello, Wyndham's Theatre reservations?" and promptly put the phone down.

Then, one morning I woke up to find Henry was out jogging. I lay in bed for about twenty minutes, worrying, when the phone rang again. At the same time, Henry picked it up in his study extension downstairs.

"Hello, hello?" a vaguely familiar female voice asked.

"Yes, this one's for me," said Henry.

I put the phone down, then rounded on myself. Now hang on a minute! Who would be calling him at nine on a Saturday morning, if not to arrange a secret rendezvous in a hotel that evening?

Tip-toeing back across the carpet, I picked the receiver up oh-so-gently and listened holding my breath.

"Well, look, you really had better make sure Olivia doesn't find out," she was laughing.

"Oh, don't worry, she's much too dizzy, she won't notice a thing," Henry said in reply.

Ever-so-gently, I replaced the receiver on the hook. I would know that voice anywhere: Josephine. Josephine! Not his secretary Ms French. Not that publisher Clare Yates. Not even Denise, which had been one of my wilder guesses. But Josephine. My very own best friend. Having an affair with my husband. Her father-in-law!

My first thought was: *how dare she*! It was so typical of her! She'd always wanted to marry a man with an American Express and she'd never recovered from me beating her to it.

This explains everything, I thought feverishly: why I kept pressing her 1471 and finding her number and then calling her up to find she'd called about the most trivial little thing, like what I wanted for Christmas, or she'd seen a great skirt in a Top Shop sale.

Dressing hurriedly, unable to bear seeing Henry, I went out and took consolation in the little chapel that nestled on the edge of our grounds. I knelt down before the grim grey archangel statue and tried not to picture Henry taking her in his arms and kissing her lasciviously and saying all those sexy husky things he'd say to me . . .

"Oh God, I'm such a hypocrite," I caught myself. "This is crazy. I don't even love him anymore, why do I feel so jealous?"

As the church door swung up, I jumped to my feet, feeling silly. It was Ricky, wearing jogging bottoms and Nikes, red-faced and huffy from a run.

"Hiya," he said casually, "how's it going?"

"Okay," I mumbled unhappily.

He sat on a pew, stretching out his long legs, and then picked up a hymn book and did an impression of the vicar singing 'We plough the fields . . . ', capturing his thin reedy voice wonderfully so that I found myself laughing despite myself. Then, closing the book and putting it on his knee, he cocked his head to one side.

"So . . . ?"

"So . . . ?"

"Soooo?" Ricky looked at me meaningfully. "Have you . . . ?"

"Yes."

"Yes?" Ricky leapt forward eagerly.

"Well, yes in the sense of yes in the future, if you know what I mean, like that Eliot poem, where, erm, time future is contained in time present, if you know what I mean."

"No," said Ricky pointedly.

"Well, look," I cried, "I've just got to do it at the right time, you know. Like – like that passage in the Bible. You know – there's a time to dance, a time to sing." Avoiding his stare, I picked up a Bible and quickly started to flick through. "I know where it is . . . it's here somewhere . . ." My father had read it to me enough times when I was a kid, I ought to know where it was.

Ricky stood up and gently eased the book out of my hands.

"Somehow I don't think you're going to find a page saying there's a good time to tell your husband you happen to being having an affair with his son, Olivia. I think you have to choose that time yourself."

"Well, it's not my fault!" I cried in despair. "I mean I was all set to and then I go and find out – find out he's having an affair with Josephine!" Seeing Ricky shaking his head in astonishment, I quickly gabbled out all the evidence.

"No, you've got it all wrong," he cut in. "Olivia, he and Josephine are planning a surprise party for your twenty-sixth. It's going to be massive – two hundred-odd people, champagne, disco, everything. I'm not supposed to tell you, really."

"Really?" I asked wonderously. Of course, I was going to be twenty-six in three weeks time. The ninth of September. And to think I'd been so blinkered by my worries, I'd forgotten. "But that's awful!" I burst out. "I mean that's no good, now I can't say it, not with him throwing me this party and everything!"

"That's just why you have to do it now," Ricky said sharply. "If you wait till after it will be much much worse. He's putting in the order for Krug tomorrow – you have to do it by then."

"Well, if you stopped pressurising me it would be okay!" I shot back, so upset I pushed past him and ran out of the church, crunching furiously across the gravel, ignoring his call after me. It was all okay for him to try and rush me into breaking up my marriage when his was already in tatters – the way he was bullying me was worse than Henry –

"Excuse me – Lady Olivia Caldwell?" A girlish-looking man in a very smart pin-striped suit was waiting in the hallway with a large briefcase.

"Ah, Harry," Henry intercepted, coming forwards to shake his hand. "Do come into the sitting-room." He took my hand and pulled me in too. "Harry's come to measure me up for a few new suits, and a dress for you." He turned back to Harry.

"What's it for?" I couldn't resist asking as Harry positioned me in the centre of the room and Henry slumped on the couch. "Are we, erm, going to be doing something special soon?"

"No," said Henry briskly. "I was just thinking you might like a new dress."

"Oh really?" Seeing him narrow his eyes at me, I fixed mine on the wall, biting back a smile of excitement.

"Oli-vi-a," said Henry in exasperation. "Who told you, come on now! Was it Ricky?"

"No, I just found out. Oh Henry, thank you so much, it's so sweet of you!" I couldn't resist breaking away and going to give him a hug. Henry shook his head affectionately and pushed me back.

"Well, I'm determined that you shall be the belle of your ball. I want to see her in navy, it brings out the colour of her eyes. Something traditional, a full skirt, puff sleeves."

As the dressmaker pushed my arms up gently to measure my waist, Henry watched us with deliberate, flickering dark eyes. Harry the dressmaker started to whistle nervously through his buck teeth.

"Make sure you get the waist properly. I want it tight around the waist. She has a beautiful tapering waist, don't you agree?" There was a ghost of a smile on Henry's thin lips.

"Yes, yes," Harry muttered, turning pink. I held my head high, feeling the tape measure brushing my hips, feeling Henry's eyes on us, loving and hating it, turning it all into one of his games.

"He wanted you," Henry strode back in and confronted me, when Harry had gone.

"No, I don't think so," I murmured uneasily, reaching down to pick a thread from a cushion. When he got in these moods, I never knew how to react, it was like playing emotional chess, not knowing where the next attack was coming from, where to retaliate.

He stepped forwards menacingly and I stumbled

back onto the couch. I gasped as he pinned himself down on top of me, pushing me into the cushions, kissing me passionately.

"I like to see other men wanting you," he murmured thickly. "It makes me know how much I want to keep you." He pushed up the fabric of my skirt brutally.

"Henry, we can't." I squirmed uneasily, feeling him push his hardness up against me, my stomach clenching with unexpected desire. "Ricky will be here in a mom —"

"I don't care."

He silenced me by pushing his thumb into my mouth, his other hand circling my thighs. His eyes blazed with victorious desire when he heard me whimper with pleasure, knowing I was putty in his hands.

Over the past week, I had found myself flinching every time Henry tried to touch me, as though his hands were soiled; I'd found myself jumping away, making excuses, jumping into bed and feigning sleep at night.

Now, it was suddenly all so spontaneously erotic, like the first time we had ever made love over the desk in his office, and afterwards we lay trembling and kissing each other.

"Henry," I whispered miserably, "I . . ."

"My dear?" he turned to me, drawing in his breath hoarsely.

"I . . ." I faltered, seeing the unexpected tenderness in his eyes. I felt a sudden cringe of doubt.

"I . . . I love you," I said at last, my voice breaking with guilt. Then I gasped as Ricky walked in and stopped, staring at us in shock. Henry grinned mockingly and ineffectually covered me with a cushion.

"Erm, I – I –" Ricky stuttered.

Oh no! No! Don't say it, Ricky, now really is definitely not the time to say it!

"I was just looking for *The Radio Times*," his voice broke. Strolling over to the coffee table, he picked the paper up and twisted it into a roll. "Great. Well. See you two guys later. Have fun." He walked out looking absolutely crucified.

34. Happy Birthday

For the next few days, Henry was frantically busy with birthday preparations. Anxious for something to do, I kept asking to help but Henry refused to let me even prong a pineapple onto a stick.

"I want this to be the best birthday you've ever had," he kept insisting. So I spent most of my time in the kitchen, watching Denise toss salads and cream truffles and mix up a fruit cake, picking at the food despite her exasperated slaps.

Ricky, meanwhile, was roped into moving tables into the grand hallway and Henry, being a slave-driver and eager to economise, sent him off to mow the huge lawns. In another hushed reunion in the downstairs cupboard, Ricky, my darling, had kissed me and bravely promised he would now take on The Task of Telling Henry. So every time I saw Ricky and Henry alone together, going for walks or having a game of golf on the course that sloped into our grounds, I was feverish with nerves. I even took to using Henry's bird-watching binoculars to try and lip-read.

Still, Ricky didn't say. Not wanting to be a hypocrite, I didn't like to nag. But as the days flew by – 6th – 7th – 8th – I grew jittery. Could it be that he was changing his mind, that he felt too guilty? He and Henry always looked so close, so chummy, as though they shared a special male bond I could never quite share . . .

I spent the whole of my birthday avoiding both Ricky and Henry, declaring I needed ten hours to get ready. Still, Henry didn't seem to be suspicious; it was amazing, I considered, how if you didn't want to know the truth, you didn't see it. Then again, he was engrossed in preps; I could hear him barking instructions like a sergeant major right from my bedroom.

Finally, at ten to eight he popped in to get a tux for Ricky; then, fifteen minutes later, they both came for me.

"Oh, wow, you look sensational," Ricky cried, gazing at the flowing blue silk in unconcealed amazement.

"Doesn't she?" said Henry, looping his arm through mine and gazing down at me fondly. "Madam, will you accompany me to the ball?"

As we swished along the balcony, I saw hundreds of heads swing up. Then there was a volley of clapping; the piano started up and there was a rich chorus of 'Happy Birthday'. We hovered at the top of the stairs. I gazed down at all the smiling faces, all my family and friends looking so beautiful, the long tables set with exquisite food, the net hung from the four corners of the balcony holding hundreds of balloons. God, he must have taken so much time, so much trouble, I just didn't deserve him. I felt so moved I reached out and squeezed his hand and he massaged it gently. Then I turned and realised with a jolt that I'd just held hands with Ricky.

"Oh, thank you, thank you," I broke away abruptly and turned to Henry, flinging my arms around him.

For the next few hours, I was lost in a swirl of people and presents. I felt like a robot programmed to shake a hundred hands, say a hundred' hello how are you's, a hundred smiles until my cheeks were aching, I was dying to sit down and my tummy was rumbling; I was the only one who hadn't eaten. All the time, I was aware of Ricky just a few feet away, leaning against a pillar, nibbling despondently from a handful of peanuts and pointedly ignoring Josephine, who had turned up looking sensational declaring she'd very nearly not come because of him, but had overcome the pain at the last minute. Now she was surrounded by a circle of admiring men in tuxedos; she didn't look as though she was struggling with a great deal of pain, I thought sardonically.

After eating, Henry made a lovely speech to everyone about how much he loved me. By the end, I felt close to tears, especially when Henry beckoned me over and gave me a long kiss and everyone said, "*Aaah . . .*"

"Make a wish," said Henry fondly, handing me the knife.

I closed my eyes and blew. All I could think of was: *Oh God, please give me Ricky somehow without hurting Henry. Please, can this finally be resolved?*

"What did you wish for?" Henry whispered in my ear as I plunged the knife into the rich fruit cake.

"Oh, I can't say, else it won't come true," I laughed,

but my eyes flitted to Ricky, who was watching me intensely as though he had read my thoughts. After that my hands were shaking so much I cut the cake all jagged, cracking up all the icing; Henry tutted and called Denise to take over.

At eleven o'clock Henry called everyone outside again for a mammoth firework display. The lawns were filled with *oohs* and *aahs* as everyone gaped at the green and red and blue explosions. As I goose-pimpled in the cold, Henry took his jacket off and put it around my shoulders and the finale, "*Happy Birthday Olivia*" came up in glittering gold across the stars.

"Oh wow," I whispered, as he looked down at me. "Thank you, thank you so much. I – I just don't know what to say."

"I love you," he whispered, hugging me back. "So much."

I tried, tried to force the words but they wouldn't come. I felt too choked with guilt.

At twelve o'clock, everyone was very drunk and many were ignoring the 'No Smoking' signs. Alicia was going around popping balloons; my younger cousin Melanie was caught lying beneath the piano entwined with the vicar's son and was promptly dragged off by my furiously apologetic aunt. The DJ, taking a break, left the same Boyzone slow song playing over and over. Poppers and smeary paper plates and cocktail umbrellas littered the floor. This is going to take an eternity to clear up, I thought wearily, when tomorrow morning comes.

I escaped to the loo. Looking in the mirror, I saw

that I looked horrendous. Even my curls seemed to be wilting; I flicked water onto the ends and scrunched them up. Inside I felt as though I was seventy-five, not twenty-five.

I sat hunched on the toilet seat for a bit, wanting to be alone. I couldn't work out why, why, when it was supposed to be my best birthday ever, and Henry had spend so many thousands, and everyone was having such a ball, I was having such a miserable time. I couldn't help thinking how much better last year's birthday had been, when we'd gone for a girlie dinner at Pizza Hut. Josephine had bought me a wild book called *Men In Love* which was supposed to be a psychological analysis of male fantasies but was basically pornography and everyone had passed it round and read the juiciest bits out, causing several families to walk out of the restaurant. After several jugs of Martini, we were chucking olives across the room and having ice-cube fights under the table and flirting with the waiters till the manager turned up and chucked the lot of us out.

Last year, if I'd known I would end up marrying a famous rich author, I would have gone wild with joy. Now I longed for that easy single pre-marital existence, where everything was so uncomplicated. The irony was awful; would my mid-life crisis never end? Or was it all just in my head?

Outside in the back corridor, Mel, Josephine and a few others were blasting party-poppers at each other.

"Here!" Mel pushed a pile into my hands, then ducked away screaming as Jack came after her. I grinned, mildly cheered, then dived into a corridor as

Josephine blasted one my way. I backed down the corridor, ready to charge out and surprise her, when there was a sudden explosion behind me. I jumped and turned.

"Ricky! Oh my God!" I put a hand on my racing heart. "You scared the shit out of me! Haven't you read the instructions: do *not* point at people."

Ricky giggled and I found myself smiling despite myself.

"Well, it was the only way to get your attention," he said with an edge to his voice. "Since you've been ignoring me all the time."

"Stop, someone might see!" I gulped, a pulse beating between my legs as I felt him against me.

He looked from left to right to left, then pulled me into the bedroom doubling up as a cloakroom, which was now drenched in coats and scarves and hats and bags. He put his arms around my waist and I lifted my head, then drew back as we heard shrieking in the corridor.

"Here!" Ricky pulled me into the wardrobe, pulling it shut just in time as Melanie popped her head around the door. Hearing her shut the door again, we let out a sigh of relief.

Ricky pushed aside a fur and whispered, "It's just like Narnia in here."

But as he reached for me again, I shook my head and backed up, then yelped as my head banged a coat-hanger.

"Oops," Ricky straightened it up. Then his hand fell to my head, lightly stroking the curls.

"Ricky, don't," I pleaded. "Look, I think I have an idea for plan C."

"I thought we were only on B," he frowned.

"It's not funny," I said. "I think we should both just end this affair. It's over, Ricky. I just can't do this anymore, I can't cope with the stress. I can't sleep at night, I'm permanently jumpy, Henry is starting to suspect, and it – it just – I can't –" Then we both froze as we suddenly heard Henry's voice echoing in the corridor outside.

"Have you seen Olivia anywhere?"

"Shit!" I whispered, straightening my dress, hearing Mel giggle and cry that she thought I was in the loo.

As the bedroom door swung open, we both drew in our breaths, gazing at each other, the glint of eye-whites in the darkness. Then Ricky exhaled in relief as the door closed again.

For an eternity, we stood very still, listening to the crash of each other's hearts. Ricky held me, kissed me and whispered, "Okay, let's meet again tonight, it's too risky to talk now. You go first, I'll come out in five minutes."

I took a deep breath, left the cupboard, and slipped out of the room. I walked up the corridor, out onto the upstairs gallery. Then I jumped as Henry suddenly came out of the corridor I'd just been in.

36. Divorce & Dover

"What were you doing in there in the back corridor? Who were you with?" he asked in my ear.

"Nobody, I was just sorting the coats out. Let's go down. Oh listen!" I cried, as the music changed to *The Dancing Queen*. "My favourite! Let's go and dance!"

I turned and smiled and he gazed at me with narrowed eyes. Suddenly he lunged forwards; I stumbled backwards against a pillar, terrified he was going to hit me, but instead he buried his face in my hair, sniffing suspiciously. Then as Mrs Appleton, the vicar's wife, came up, he curled his arm around my waist, feigning an embrace.

"I simply can't find my coat," she said apologetically.

"In the guest bedroom. Down the corridor, first bedroom on right," Henry jerked his head and just about managed a charming smile.

As she pottered on uncertainly, looking back, Henry smiled and signalled. Then she started as Ricky came barging onto the gallery.

"Come on," I tugged at Henry's hand desperately.

"Wait a minute." Henry looked from me to Ricky to me. I dropped Henry's hand and started to walk very quickly to our bedroom. Feeling Henry descending after me like a hawk, I turned and looked back at him in terror.

Keep calm, I instructed myself firmly, as Henry kicked the door shut and leant back against it. *If you act nervous, it will look as though you have something to hide*.

But as Henry came across the room, I found myself backing up into the velvet curtains. He put his hands on my shoulders, his square nails indenting my skin.

"I want to know what's going on," he said in a cool, flat voice.

"Nothing," I stared hard at the red carnation in his button-hole, then he flipped my chin up. I felt my legs trembling against the pressure of his.

"I want to know what's going on," he said more firmly, his thumb pressing into my chin.

I couldn't speak. He hit me across the face.

"You're having an affair, aren't you? You and my son? After all I've done for you!"

"No, no, it's just – I –" I screamed as he hit me across the other cheek. His palms circled my neck, thumbs pressing against my throat. "Don't lie to me," he slammed me up against the wall, pain shooting up my back. "I want to know what's going on."

He's going to kill me, I thought hysterically, as he shook me like a ragdoll. *Oh Krishna, please protect me*.

My racing brain squeezed out very precise, clear thoughts. I remembered instructions from university self-defence classes; strike in the crotch and then at the top of the nose, where the skin is weak. Break his balls and his nose and then run for it. But as I raised my knee, I found myself slackening, wilting, cringing from hurting him.

"Oh Henry," I sobbed, gasping for air as his thumbs closed in, "I'm really sorry, we didn't mean it, please, please —"

As the door swung open, we both jumped. Ricky stood in the doorway.

"Leave her alone, Dad," he said in a trembling voice. "It wasn't her, it was all my fault. Look, we were seriously going to tell you, we just didn't know what to do, I mean basically we just love each other —"

"You just love each other?" Henry mimicked him savagely, incredulously. As he approached, Ricky started to shake but stood his ground. Then he flinched as Henry suddenly smashed the china flowery lampshade off the bedside table onto the floor. "You're fucking my wife, and you're my son, and you have the nerve to tell me you're in love with this whore?" He took Ricky's collar and pushed him up against the wall.

"Dad, please," Ricky whimpered, trying to gently prise him away, "please let's all sit down and talk this through."

"Like some fucking group therapy session?" Henry's voice started to rise into a shout. "Where we all come out happily accepting that you've been with my wife for the past — how long?" Before Ricky could reply, he punched him in the face. Ricky fought back, and then they were rolling on the floor like two tigers, crunching on the broken china.

"Stop, please, stop," I cried, every crack and punch searing right through me. Grabbing a vase, I tossed the

tulips out and threw the water over Henry and Ricky. It worked. Henry drew away, stood up, smoothing down his clothes with his manicured, shaking hands as though regaining a hold on his temper. He gazed down at Ricky, who was now sitting up, crying, blood pouring from his nose all over his white shirt.

"Just get out," said Henry, in a voice that made my blood turn to ice. "Just get out and don't ever come back. D'you understand? I don't want to see you ever again."

"But —" Ricky grabbed the bedspread and struggled to his feet. I could feel him looking at me pleadingly but I turned away, gazing at the moon in shock. "Please don't hurt her, please Dad, it was all me." I watched his reflection in the window; he took a few steps back, then tried again, "Please, if we could just talk —" I shook my head frantically; no, Ricky, it's no use.

"Get out!" Henry smashed the vase against the wall and Ricky flung open the door, with a blast of happy chatter and pop music; then the door slammed shut. I stood trembling, waiting for Henry to beat me to death. I felt so weak and guilty I almost wanted him to. But he was cool and detached now.

"I want you to wait here," he instructed me. "Wait here, alright?"

I nodded blankly. As he went to the door, he looked back, his hair silver in the moonlight, as though whitened with shock, his dark eyes no longer angry, but full of hurt. I stepped forwards, reached out for him, but the door slammed in my face. I threw myself down on the bed and burst into tears.

The sound of Ricky's voice pulled me out of my grief. I sat up, my heart leaping; *perhaps Henry had gone to talk to him! Or perhaps he'd come back to save me!* Then I realised his voice was distant; it came from the driveway below.

I went to the window to see him with Josephine near the porch.

"What's all this blood?" Josephine was saying as he was caught under the glare of the porch-light.

"I fell off the balcony," he said meekly. "I was pissed."

"Oh, my poor Ricky," She touched his cheek and he nuzzled weakly against her. "I miss you so much. Come back home with me."

They got into the car and zoomed away. I sank down onto the floor, wiping my eyes on the velvet curtain. I was still in such shock I could hardly register it. Roberta came up and whimpered around me, sensing something was wrong, curling up at my feet, rolling her eyes questioningly. "Oh, I'm sorry, my baby Robbie," I stroked her, "but I've been terrible, I've done such awful things."

Outside the music had stopped and the buzz of chatter was dying, the driveway filling up with people pulling on hats and exchanging phone numbers and kisses goodbye.

"Can I say goodbye to my birthday girl?" I heard my mother's voice in the corridor outside. Oh Mum! I was dying to run to her and cry into her lap but Henry's voice loomed:

"She's feeling sick, I think she's asleep. A bit too much champagne and chocolate, and all that excitement . . .

it's better that you don't wake her, I should think." His calm was amazing.

The house slowly fell silent. Henry came back into the room. He sat down on the double bed as though I wasn't there and starting briskly punching numbers into his mobile.

"Hello? First Direct? Yes, I'd like to end a standing order to Mrs Jemima Mullings who receives a payment for Jamie Caldwell, I think it goes monthly into the account . . . Thanks. Super." He cut off and promptly typed in a new number. "Hello? Yes, my Barclaycard number is . . ." he reeled it off. "Sir Caldwell, that's correct. Yes, I have an additional cardholder, Ricky Caldwell – I'd like his card stopped, thank you."

"What are you doing?" I whispered.

"Annie? Sorry, what time is it over there? No . . . fine . . . yes . . . still tomorrow . . . no . . . I'm just hoping you could do me a favour and sort me out a lawyer, maybe the one you used in the McDonald's case? I need someone to change my will, yes, urgently." He switched off and gazed at me with unseeing eyes. "I'm going to America tomorrow, remember? Book tour." He switched his phone on again. "Jenny? Is Ricky still doing Features for you? Yes, I can imagine. I see, oh well, in that case I'm sure you'd be happy to let him go . . ."

Then it sunk in. He was destroying Ricky, everything he had: money, job, his son. All right in front of me, as part of the punishment.

"Henry, stop it," I got up, tugging his sleeve. He put one hand over his mobile and glared at me. "Olivia, get off." He shook me away and I listened, appalled, as, in his most charismatic and reasonable voice, he suggested that he had surprise plans for Ricky with a new magazine and if Jenny could release him it would be a real favour . . .

"Henry, please don't do this!" I lunged forwards and grabbed the phone, accidentally clawing his face. The phone skidded across the bed and fell under the cabinet. Henry sat up, clenching his fists, his eyes psychotic.

"You mustn't," I pleaded –

Suddenly he grabbed me by the hair, throwing me down on the bed, ripping up my dress.

"How many times?" He forced his mouth onto mine. "How many times did you and my son make love on this bed, when I was away, like a stupid idiot –" He kissed my screams away so hard his teeth clashed against mine. He plunged into me like a knife, as though drilling into me: you are my wife, you are my wife. It was very painful.

But I remained blank. Just go through with it. Stay blank. I wanted to close my eyes but he barked at me to keep them open so I stared at the cream plaster, a chip in the ceiling. Oh God, Ricky's gone. He's never going to come back – no, no, I reined in my emotions like wild horses. Stay blank, sexless, soulless. Feeling nothing as Henry's black eyes fixed on me as though trying to force emotion out of me. As though he wanted the satisfaction of seeing me break down.

Afterwards I rolled onto my side, my head throbbing, pain between my legs and behind my eyes. I couldn't sleep. When he turned the light off I willed myself to cry but the shock was still too great. The stress was so engulfing that I couldn't acknowledge it, couldn't feel a thing except lie empty except for the black cloud in my head, whirling like a hurricane.

I fell asleep and woke at eight from a nightmare of Ricky shooting me. I sat up with a sour taste in my mouth, a film of disease, still soiled from the nightmare. I reached out and saw the bed empty and crumpled.

Then Henry came striding in. I sat up in bed.

"I'm off to America. My lawyers will be drawing up some divorce papers as soon as possible, which Ms French will pass on to you shortly."

He walked off before I even had time to protest. I sat frozen for a few minutes, then got up and ran to the balcony, but he was already halfway through the front door. Down below, Denise was picking up all the beer and Coke cans and rubbish from last night and putting them into a big black plastic sack.

For a moment I paused, staring at her with glazed eyes. Then the shock hit me – *divorce papers!*

"You have to give me Henry's number!" I yelled for the fiftieth time at Ms French, whose cold made-up face remained as impassive as ever.

"He's asked me not to give it to anyone, including you, so I have to do as he says," she repeated mechanically.

"But I really really need to speak to him," I was starting to beg now.

"I'm sorry," she said, with a growing edge to her voice, snapping shut her briefcase, "but as I have said, I don't have his permission."

"Well, can't you just bloody ring him and ask him!" I started to yell.

"No, he has already told me."

"Oh no, and it would just be too much fucking trouble to make one simple phone call," I started angrily, then broke off when I saw her face. This wasn't getting me anywhere. "Please," I said more girlishly, "please, it would just be so kind and considerate if you could just tell me what hotel he's staying in."

"Sorry." For a moment her steel eyes swept over me, dishevelled and barefoot in my nightie even though it was now midday. Suddenly, I hated her, all smug and efficient in her smart suit and that bloody spotless briefcase within which was no doubt just the one piece of paper I needed to save our marriage.

"Ricky's on the phone for you," Denise suddenly came in.

I paused, seeing a flicker over French's face. I bet she'd go running right back to Henry and tell him.

"Erm, can you say I'm in the bath?" I forced myself at last.

"Sure."

I had just turned back to French, when Denise came running back,

"He says he's in a call box."

I suddenly had an awful vision of Ricky closeted in the box, tapping his coin against the glass, desperately alone.

"Okay," I picked up the extension in the study and Denise politely backed out, but French lingered. She probably had a tape recorder running in her handbag, I fretted, ready to play out as Evidence in the Divorce

Courts. "Look, Ricky," I began right away, "I'm afraid I can't see you anymore —"

"Olivia, you have to help me," he interrupted moaningly, "Josephine's thrown me out —"

"You *told* Josephine?" I shrieked.

"Well, I had to give some excuse why I'd suddenly mysteriously lost my job and the payment for Jamie had been stopped. Now I'm calling from Emily's house."

"Emily's house?"

"I'm sleeping on her floor. God, Olivia, it's a nightmare, she's either trying to shag me or trying to shag someone else and she won't even let me watch *The Big Breakfast*, she insists on *Anne and Nick...*"

"Oh, poor you," I said with savage sarcasm. "Well, look, Henry has asked for a divorce."

"Oh no!"

"Oh yes. I seriously have to go and sort myself out. I can't speak to you."

"Meet me at the Holborn Pret a Manger at twelve-thirty."

"What? But —" I was cut off by the beeps.

Ms French picked up her case and walked out.

"You won't tell Henry, will you?" I cried after her.

"Tell him what, exactly?" she turned, raising one eyebrow.

"Nothing." I sulkily pulled my nightgown sleeves down over my bitten nails.

"Okay," said Ricky, pushing away his cup of cold tea, "why don't we just toss a coin?"

I smiled sadly and shook my head. We had been

sitting in the café for twenty minutes now, arguing, discussing, going round in the same old dizzying circles, mazes without centres, questions without answers.

"Well, why not?" Ricky asked miserably. "It seems to be the only way you're going to decide. Henry heads, Ricky tails."

"Henry tails," I burst out as the coin flipped up and turned over in the air. Ricky started and the coin fell to the floor. He dived under the table to pick it up. "Heads," he said triumphantly.

"Did we say heads or tails for Henry, I can't remember?" I muttered.

"We said – oh forget it." Ricky picked up his jacket and put the pound coin on the table for his tea. "I'm going."

"No, please don't," I begged, taking his hand, but he pulled it away. "Can't we have a best of three?"

"Look, Olivia, it's either him or me. Now, I'm going to France, and if you want –"

"To France?" I cried. "What's France got to do with it? This is so typical, every time you have problems you run off travelling without facing the situation."

"Don't you talk to me about facing the situation!" Ricky cried, causing several law students to look up from their textbooks in surprise. Then he turned on his heel and left.

For a moment I sat and watched him go in complete turmoil. Then I ran after him.

"I'll come," I said breathlessly. "I'll come to France, I'll come anywhere with you!"

"Oh Liv," he threw his arms around me, "for a moment there, I thought I'd really lost you."

*   *   *

But, as we entered the station, I started to have doubts again. I wanted to go back home and pack a case. I wanted to make long lists of everything to take. I wanted to pick up my lipsticks, I'd just bought a nice red one from The Body Shop, and what about my diary, and what about poor old Roberta was now no doubt panting round the bedroom with her lead in her mouth, wondering what had happened to her daily walk?

"Just call up Denise and ask her to pack a case," Ricky said impatiently.

"Olivia, is that you?" Denise cried in relief when I called up from the noisy London phone box. "Olivia, you have to get back here now. Henry changed his mind. He cancelled his book tour, he didn't even get on the plane!"

"What!"

"He said he just sat at the airport for two hours, thinking of you. He called up wanting to speak to you, so I covered and said you were at the hairdresser's. You've got to get back here now."

"Right, right," I said quickly. "Oh God, okay. Stall him, tell him I'm on my way."

I got out of the phone box.

"Okay, now we can –" Ricky broke off. "What?"

"There's something I need to tell you . . ."

On the train, every face was like a member of the jury, giving us an accusing glare. I huddled up against Ricky, ecstatic with the thought of living in France, with visions of drinking red wine in a huge apartment with a lofty ceiling, sitting in little cafes being arty together. Then, as the old woman opposite us rustled a paper, I felt my heart seize up again, half expecting to see '*Runaways!*' blazing across the front but to my relief there was just another scandal about Peter Mandelson.

"I'm so glad you came with me," Ricky whispered again, nuzzling the top of my head.

Come on, come on, come on, I willed the train from Euston on. I felt as though I was watching a thriller moving, willing the action to move on, the hero to dodge the bullet, escape by the skin of his teeth at the very last minute. Just as long as we got onto the train and out of the country, everything would be alright and I could live with the man I loved forever after. As we arrived in Dover and I caught a glimpse of the sea splashing against the white rocks, I gripped Ricky's hand in anticipation. It was so wonderful and bizarre that, after all these weeks of waiting, we should suddenly at last be together, though in such an unexpected way . . .

But, as we went to buy the ferry tickets, Ricky's credit card was rejected. Ricky kicked up a fuss, declaring, "My wife and I have an urgent meeting to attend to Paris . . ." but they only bristled. Ricky went to call the company, then came back looking seriously depressed.

"I – I –" he sat down, looking sheepish. "I haven't paid my minimum repayments."

"Shit. But what are we going to do? Now we've only got sixty quid. How long is that going to last us?"

"Don't have a go at me," Ricky objected. "Come on, Liv, we've only been together for an hour and already we're arguing about money."

We sat in silence for some time; finally Ricky took my hand and said sheepishly,

"Erm, oh Livy, I'm so sorry, d'you fancy living in Dover?"

37. Brighton

We finally ended up in Brighton, in the cheapest accommodation we could find: a one-bedroomed bed-sit in the crummiest end of town, where all the broke students and druggies and dropouts lived. The room was one of the most frightful I'd ever seen: cracked walls, a coughing radiator which looked as though it should be drawing its pension, and the narrowest of single beds.

"Oh well, at least we can be close at night," said Ricky with a wink, slumping on the bed which gave a ping, the mattress groaning to the floor.

Mrs Williams, a grumpy old bag who showed us round ungraciously as though she was doing us the favour of a lifetime, gave him a frosty look and held out a red-veined hand.

"I'd like a week's rent in advance, if you don't mind."

Ricky reluctantly handed over our last forty pounds, leaving us with a measly two pounds fifty. I turned my back, gazing out through the filmy orange curtains to the alleyway down below where a girl with dyed blonde hair was accepting a dirty brown envelope from a grisly guy in a leather jacket.

"Oh Ricky, what are we going to do?" I fretted when Mrs Williams had gone.

"Buy a lottery ticket?"

For dinner we stole some plums from a back garden, plus the last of a few autumn blackberries. Then we lay in bed wedged up against each other, because that was the only way we could fit, discussing possibilities, feeding each other plums, comforting each other.

"We'll just stay here a few days, a week at the most, then we'll move on. We'll be alright, everything will be alright in the end."

I smiled and stroked his nose; thank goodness for Ricky and his never-ending buoyancy, constantly pulling me out of my black hole of despair.

I finally managed to drop off to sleep, only to be woken at three am by some seriously dodgy noises from the room above: creaks and squeaks of a mattress, accompanied by panting and the noisest and longest female orgasm I've ever heard.

"*Yes, yes, yes, yes* . . ."

"Oh God," Ricky woke up, sighing blearily into my shoulder.

"*Yes, yes . . . oh yes, yes* . . ."

I yawned irritably and rolled onto my other side, wincing as my elbow banged Ricky's ribs.

"*Yes, yes, yes* . . ."

A brief silence. Thank God for that, I thought, rubbing my cramped leg, my knees knocking bits of plaster off the crumbling wall.

"*Yes, yes, yes* . . ."

Ricky checked his digital watch. "She deserves a

place in *The Guinness Book of Records*."

I hunched up my shoulders against him and hummed in my head, trying to block the noise out, trying not to think of our lovely huge four-poster at home. Henry had always got hot easily and I'd always got cold easily so I'd always had three quilts on my side and he just a few sheets on his. Three big snuggly buggly quilts, a bed so huge I could stretch out across it like a star without touching Henry.

"Yes oh yes oh God yes . . ."

"She should be on ads for TSB," said Ricky, "the bank that likes to say . . ."

"*Yes!*" she supplied, right on cue.

I burst into exasperated laughter, then curled my fists in despair as the room next door to us, presumably to cut out her noise, put on Metallica's *Enter Sandman* at top volume. Then there was banging on the stairs and our door was flung open. Mrs Williams stood thunderous in a frilly white nightgown, her grey hair streaming over her shoulders like a Viking warrior.

"If you two don't pack it in, you'll be out tomorrow!" she screeched. Before we had a chance to protest, she was banging next door, yelling for him to turn the music down.

Our door was still swinging open, a blast of freezing air rushing in. Both of us looked at each other, waiting for the other to get up. Ricky pulled one of his boyish faces.

"Okay, I'll get it," I said through gritted teeth. I stomped up, slammed the door and got back in, pulling the covers up around me. Ricky let out a bellow of indignation and yanked them back, stripping me bare. I let out a howl and pulled them back. We lay in cross silence; I closed my eyes in fury. Even now that it was quiet at last, I still couldn't settle, the drip-drip of the drains outside niggling me, pulling me back out of peaceful sleep.

Ricky pulled the pillow over to his side and I screamed and yanked it back in fury, then burst into tears of exasperation.

"Olivia! I'm really sorry." He sat up, putting his arm around me, pushing the pillow back to my side, hurriedly pulling up all the covers back around me. "I'm sorry, this isn't working, is it? Maybe we should just go back."

"No!" I wailed, "I love you, I do love you, it's just so ... so ... *awful.*"

"Look," Ricky wiped my tears away with his thumbs and tilted my head up, gazing down at me with worried, earnest eyes, "we can go, you know. We can go back. Just say if you want to. I love you so much, I hate to see you like this."

I paused, for a moment highly tempted to say 'right now'. Then I looked up into his eyes and remembered how unbearable it had been before, and shook my head.

"I love you. I want to be with you, wherever, whatever . . ." I squeezed his hand unhappily.

"Okay," said Ricky, buoyant as ever, refusing to crack, "Look. Let's just be logical. We need money, we can't do anything without money. Why don't we write a book? We'd only need a few chapters, Henry once confided in me that the whole secret is just getting a good agent. They can get you wild six-figure deals.

That's what we'll do . . . we'll do it, Liv, I know we can . . ."

The next morning, Ricky and I split up and went off to try and open accounts and obtain overdrafts. In Barclays, I shifted uneasily in my chair as the clerk gave my greasy hair and clothes a once-over. The smell of the bed-sit, a cross between dead fish, old cat-hair, and stale smoke, seemed to cling to me like a film.

Without any identification, they politely refused to give me an account. Everything which said I was me – passport, driving licence – was back home.

I rubbed my forehead in despair. It's Henry, I thought wearily. He's still got a power over us, he's making sure we can't go on, the world is in a conspiracy against us, there's no way out.

Come on, now, Olivia, I rallied myself, now you're just getting paranoid. You're just tired. Just keep going. This is a test to see how you can survive. You can't let Henry defeat you. It will get better.

Outside, as I willed my exhausted legs back to the bed-sit, I wondered if Ricky had managed any better. Passing a phone box, I was aching to call mum, but daren't, not wanting to get tracked down, to face what I had done to her. Watching a girl discarding a half-eaten ice lolly onto the beach, I had to put my hand in my pocket to prevent myself from picking it up. My stomach felt positively hollow. I suddenly thought with longing of Denise's apple-pies with dollops of thick double cream.

On a mad impulse, I ran into a newsagents and bought a bar of Dairy Milk with my last fifty pence.

The shop assistant looked taken aback as I tore off the wrapper and devoured the whole thing practically in one gulp. Then I only felt sick and guilty. I should have least saved some for Ricky. I would have to pretend I had dropped the fifty pence in the gutter.

When I got back to the flat, however, I discovered that Ricky, whether through sheer optimism, or his own knack of having Lady Luck always smiling on him, had obtained a job in the local Burger King (only two quid an hour but still) and a computer on hire purchase. He had also miraculously managed to get a loan worth five hundred.

"I got it off Barclays," he said.

"Funny, they didn't like me," I muttered.

"Ah, you just don't have the knack." He pulled me onto his lap and looked at me fiercely. "We're going to do this, okay? Things will get better."

Over the next few days we economised like mad. I made Ricky give up smoking and he made me give up chocolate. And, I managed to get a job too.

It was debatable which of us had the worse job. Mine was pretty appalling: cleaning for a grumpy old man called Mr Craven who owned a pit bull which nearly bit my leg off on my first day. The house was simply disgusting – black all over – white walls smeared with black, the carpet so filthy a faint hint of a pattern was only just discernible, windows like the back of the bus. The only bright and colourful object in the room was the TV, which he slumped in front of and channel-hopped from cricket to game shows.

"It looks as though this place hasn't been cleaned for years," I said at last.

"It hasn't," Mr Craven snapped.

Why the sudden fit of cleanliness? I wondered uneasily. Perhaps the poor old man was lonely. Aware of him looking at my legs, I rinsed out my sponge and tried to smile compassionately. The pit bull growled threateningly.

Ricky and I continued on our bestseller, the book which would end all our problems.

Our first idea was for a Mills & Boon but we couldn't help writing as though we were taking the piss. Our thriller kept turning into *Speed*. Then, just when we were considering an epic Western, Ricky came up with such a fantastic idea that he woke me up in the middle of the night.

"I know! I know I know I know! What is it that everyone is obsessed with?"

"Urgh?" I muttered sleepily.

"No, not urgh! Sex! Relationships! Love! As ever, from *Romeo and Juliet* to *Bridget Jones*, throughout the centuries everyone is obsessed with relationships. Well, how about we do a book together, a kind of Bridget Jones meets Nick Hornby? Wouldn't that be cool? Wouldn't it?"

He was so excited that he got up and switched on the computer, spilling fluorescent green light across the sheets.

"Come on, come on," Ricky clapped his hands, jiggling in his Mr Happy pyjamas which we'd got from the local Oxfam. "Brainstorm! Men and women!

Condoms, threesomes, dates, chat-up lines," he was tapping away, he could hardly keep up. "We need a good opening. A wild opening. Something like, 'I first lost my virginity when I was six years old.'" Ricky paused ponderingly, then, seeing me going back to sleep, slipped back under the covers. "Okay, let's play the Truth Game. That's a good way to generate ideas," he said, with a glint in his eye. "You go first."

"What?" I moaned, rubbing my curls off my forehead, feeling my skin drying up with tiredness. It was three in the morning, I had to get up to clean at nine and Ricky was demanding to play the Truth Game? "Okay, okay," I groaned, "what's your favourite poet?"

"My favourite poet is Yeats, and I like that poem *The Isle of Innisfree*. My dad showed me," he said dreamily, as though momentarily forgetting this was the man I was married to, "that it's a poem not about an island but a state of freedom – i.e. 'in is free'."

"Oh wow, I never thought of that."

"Anyway, this isn't helping the book, the whole point of the Truth Game is an excuse to discuss sex," said Ricky. "What's your sexual fantasy?"

"Oh Ricky!" I smiled, waking up. "Weelllll . . . I like the idea of meeting some random guy on a train and then hardly speaking, just catching eyes and getting off and going to a hotel and making mad love and never seeing him again. But it would never happen, because I'd be way too paranoid that 1) he was a nutter, 2) he had AIDS and 3) we'd just never get on the same train."

"Hmm," said Ricky, "I was hoping for more specific details."

"Well," I murmured in his neck, arching against him,

"I like being kissed, you know, down there. Henry never . . ." I trailed off, feeling my thighs tightening but Ricky seemed preoccupied.

"I want to ask you a serious question. D'you miss Henry? D'you still love him?"

"I can't answer that question," I complained.

"Answer it. We're playing the Truth Game."

"Well, yes, okay, I do still love him. Yes. Not as much as I love you," I added, but he sank back on his pillow, still looking hurt. "That's the trouble with the Truth Game," I said dejectedly, "it depends upon having to lie. Nobody expects you to tell the truth . . ."

"That's such a you thing to say," Ricky accused me. We lay in silence for a while. Then he sighed and reached over, trying to kiss me, but, feeling hurt, I pushed him away. He pulled himself over on top of me, hard and heavy, pushing apart my thighs, increasing the pressure as I clamped them together.

"Kiss me and make up," he demanded.

"You're just saying that because you want to have sex with me."

"True," Ricky giggled as I swiped him. "All this sexy talk has made me feel really randy," he widened his eyes into mine in that wicked way that made me feel wet on the spot. Slowly, he swept his kisses along my neck, over my breasts, down, down, down to my thighs . . .

"I do love you. I want to make you happy, tell me what turns you on," he rubbed his cheek like an adoring pussycat against my tummy. I squealed as he tipped the remains of his Coke can over my bush, then sighed as he started to lick it all off.

"Oh *you* do, oh yes, please, please, carry on, oh Ricky, honestly I love you, I love you so much more . . ."

Thinking about the book filled the yawning days with new hope. During the day, whenever my arms started to ache from hoovering or my hands itch with eczema from the bleach, I would think of The Bestseller. Every time I thought with horrendous guilt of my mother and little Kirsty and how they might be coping, I said a prayer for Krishna to look after them. *We'll be rich soon*, I told myself, *and then I'll be with her again and make it all up and someday she'll understand.*

Every day when he came home from work, I would cook and he would mooch around the kitchen, picking food, moaning about guys spitting on burgers, or angry customers demanding free vegi bean-burgers without realising that was the kids' special offer . . . etc. I would listen and nod, knowing he needed to get it off his chest. Often I would lie him down and give him massages, usually with cheap vegetable oil, but he would sigh and *mmm* with contentment as I stroked his hair and face and hummed *saringi* strains still floating in my memory from my honeymoon in India.

"There's so much love in your touch," he said to me softly.

We would bath together and take it in turn to wash each other's hair. Then, the fun began: writing.

My hands were so sore that Ricky had to do all the typing. Often we spent too long talking, confiding over past loves, laughing over dud chat-up lines and waterbed disasters. Ricky had a lot more stamina than me. When I started to yawn too much, he would tuck me in, kiss my forehead and tell me to sleep. Often I would be woken by a grey dawn to see him still sitting at his desk, hammering away, determined not to be defeated.

We worked so hard that that Saturday we decided to celebrate and have a good time. We'd saved fifty pounds and the new plan now was to get to Ireland, where Ricky had some vague cousins whom we could hang out with.

If there was one good thing about Brighton, it was the nightlife. Pubs and clubs on every other street; the town flooded with girls and boys all looking for love and a place to party.

The floor was throbbing with student bodies. Ricky and I jived on the dancefloor, swinging arms, bumping together, kissing, occasionally doing mock ballroom dancing, me looping under his arm, smiling up at him from under my lashes.

When it got too hot, we went up to a dark shady lovers' corner. Ricky nestled me down onto his lap; as we kissed I could feel his sweat seeping into me and mine into him; it was a nice sensation. Pushing my head back, he gently blew his cool breath over my beading face. I swayed and smiled. Moments like this, I sighed inside, made this whole thing worth surviving – just being with him like this, here, now, with nobody to say it was wrong.

Ricky licked his dry lips. I could feel my tongue furred. But as usual, we were broke again.

"Okay," Ricky took a coin out of his pocket, "heads you go, tails me."

It came down heads. Bugger.

"Well, he looks nice," Ricky pointed out helpfully.

"I know, but what do I say to him?" I moaned; Ricky was so much better at this get-someone-to-buy-me-a-drink-and-then-bugger-off game; in fact, he was a bit too good when last night one girl had bought him a drink and then started unbuttoning his trousers.

"Ask them what underpants they're wearing," said Ricky with a giggle. "I was reading all about this in *The Daily Mail* this morning. If you wear red you're sexy, yellow, you're a bore . . ." He looked down the back of my jeans and I swiped at him as two guys came past, giving us funny looks. "Oo, white," said Ricky. "Uh uh. That means you think cleanliness is next to godliness."

"Well, I am a cleaner now," I muttered. "Hey, maybe them," I suggested, nodding over at two skinheads standing over by the bar who were gazing over at us.

"Er, maybe not," Ricky's arms tensed around me. Sensing at once that something was up, I turned to gaze at him in alarm as his eyes saucered. The skinheads were coming over. Taking two chairs, they sat down opposite us.

"Alright, Mr Caldwell," said the spotty one with the denim cut-offs. As he folded his huge arms his veins knotted and rippled beneath his *whore* tattoo. "You've got three days to pay back the money, right?"

"What money?" I hissed.

"Okay, okay," said Ricky hurriedly, lighting up a cigarette with mock swagger.

The skinhead swiped the cigarette off him, blowing out smoke through his nostrils like a bull as he stood up.

"Three days," he pointed a finger like a bullet, "else my friend here —" the even meatier friend smiled obligingly, "will do you over and you'll be served up as a burger yourself." Kicking over the chair, he walked off.

"Well," said Ricky brightly, "well . . ."

I took his hand and dragged him outside; it was definitely time for A Talk.

Outside on the beach the queues for the club were still winding down the pier. A group of Americans were sitting around a campfire, laughing and swigging beer. *Boom-boom,* shuddered the clubs in the background.

"So who were they?" I demanded, my stomach twisting in fear. Surely Ricky couldn't have . . . surely he wouldn't be so silly as to . . .

"They're friends from work," Ricky avoided my glare. "Okay," he stuffed his hands in his pockets and looked sheepish. "I borrowed the money off them. Not, er, quite Barclays."

"No, Ricky, don't tell me this." I put my hands to my temples.

"Well, I didn't know what else to do," he flung his hands up. "I mean, we needed all this stuff, and I didn't want you to — I mean — there was no other choice. We needed the printer and what about food, for crying out loud, we had to eat, not to mention that hairdryer you wanted —"

"Now don't tell me this is my fault," I protested angrily, kicking an empty green bottle, choking it up with sand. "How much?" I demanded.

"Not much."

"Ricky, just be honest with me," I tried to inject calm into my voice. "Just tell me how much. How can we talk this through and sort it out if you don't tell me how much?"

"Five hundred," he mumbled out of the corner of his mouth.

"Five hundred!"

"Or so. Plus another two fifty for the rent."

"Five hundred and two pounds fifty?"

"No, seven hundred and fifty."

"Seven hundred and fifty!"

"Call it a thousand," Ricky said at last.

"A thousand! A thousand!" I kept repeating hollowly. "How – how can you expect to pay it? They're going to cream you, Ricky! What use will a heater be or a hairdryer tomorrow when we can't possibly pay it back? I mean, here's me saving every measly two pounds fifty and you just throwing it away –"

"I didn't throw it away," his voice was stung with hurt. "I did it for us."

"Without asking me."

"Well, I didn't want you to worry."

"Well, of course, of course I worry!" my voice was so high and sharp a nearby seagull took fright and fluttered away. "Oh Ricky, I can't stand this. I've had enough. I'm going."

We bickered all the way back to the room, where I flung things randomly into carrier bags. Suddenly his face, the soft, sincere apology in his eyes, made me drop the things and walk over and kiss him, all my anger flooding out of me as he clasped me against him, his cheek against mine.

"I'm so sorry," he kept saying. "Don't worry, please, Livy, it's all my problem. Let me sort it all out."

"I just feel we're stuck in a rut." I drew away from him. "Like we're coming up against a brick wall. We were only going to be here a week, then a fortnight, then three weeks. We can't seem to get out of here."

"Well, maybe we should just take off. Hitch a lift. Maybe we should just camp in the forests and live like hermits," he said. "Or maybe go on the run. We can be the next Bonny and Clyde." He looked relieved when I smiled up at him.

This was the joy of being with Ricky: with Henry one argument would be remembered a month later, the acidic grudge never healed. With Ricky it was impossible for us to be angry with each other for long.

We decided to send the book out – our last hope. Only three chapters had been written, and they were full of typos and very ragged, but there was no other choice. The next day we both called in sick and stayed home printing and writing a hard-selling synopsis. Ricky shoplifted a copy of *The Writer's Handbook* and told me to pick out agents. There were simply hundreds of names so in end I simply chose the ones whose names sounded auspicious, had the right vibration: Jonathan Lloyd, Dawn Fozard, Simon Trewin...

"Here," Ricky made me kiss each envelope as he posted them into the box and each time I closed my eyes and said a little prayer to Krishna.

"Just wait," said Ricky excitedly, "if they like you,

they call you up right away. Tomorrow morning, we'll be millionaires!"

The next morning, however, the only people who called in were the debt collectors. They came while we were both at work, turning the bedroom upside down and walking off with the computer and a note saying, *We'll be back*.

"The bastards!" Ricky cried. "Shit, they'd better not steal our ideas."

"I think we have bigger things to worry about," I said, crossing my arms and blinking back tears.

Two nights later, we were just packing everything up, ready to go to a new place in Hove. We had no money to pay for the last week's rent so we were planning to leave in the dead of the night and make a run for it.

Then a police car drew up outside.

"Shit!" I cried.

"Shit!" Ricky cried, his mouth dropping as they entered the building. He quickly checked the new padlock we'd put on the inside of the door, then pulled me down on the floor by the bed. We hunched up together, cringing and cowering at the ring of voices, the thud of footsteps.

There was loud banging at the door. Ricky and I looked at each other desperately, holding hands so tightly it hurt.

Suddenly the bangs were drowned out by the thump of music next door, then more shouting. Perhaps our landlady was in a tussle with the police. Then I froze when I heard a voice, "We have good reason to arrest these two criminals . . ." and Mrs Williams squawking back, "Well, don't look at me, I don't have anything to do with them, never seen them before . . ."

The music suddenly switched off again, leaving an unexpected silence. Another bang made us jump. I stood up but Ricky pulled me back down. I shook my head and gently prised his fingers away, walking slowly to the door. I unlocked the padlock with a strange sense of almost-relief. We couldn't go on like this any longer, it was unbearable . . .

I opened the door, only to see nineteen-stone Nigel, the Hells Angel from next door, pointing to the pay phone, which was dangling on the hook.

"God, what were you two doing in there!" he bellowed. "I've been banging on your door – phone!" With that, he slammed the door of his room and put Nirvana on at top volume.

At first I couldn't discern the voice at the other end. Then, hearing a clipped, smart voice, I thought it must be Henry. Oh thank God, I found myself wilting against the wall, oh thank God, oh please let him forgive me . . .

"Is that Olivia Caldwell?" he seemed to be saying.

"Hang on, hang on, please, just hang on," I banged on Nigel's door and when he flung it open begged, then hissed for him to turn it down. He scowled and swivelled the knob a fraction.

I rushed back to the phone.

"Hello, Olivia Caldwell?" the voice repeated. "Yes, this is Dennis Wimbledon here. I hope you don't mind me calling you at this time but I've just returned from America . . ."

"Olivia!" Ricky burst into the hallway, grabbing my

arm, sending the phone flying. "They weren't here for us!"

"Ricky, shut up – I think – it's –"

"The police were here for the guys – the druggies that live at the bottom! Not for us!"

"Oh Ricky, thank goodness!" I gave him a huge hug, then drew away, pointing desperately to the phone. "I think it's an agent!"

"What!" Ricky jumped on the phone, instantly switching into a smooth business mode that reminded me faintly of Henry. "Ah, yes, I'm awfully sorry about that . . . yah . . . I see . . . well . . . super . . . I'm delighted that you've rung . . . yes . . . we do have a number of other agents interested –" as my eyes widened, he grinned and gave me the thumbs up, "but we are most interested in your offer . . ."

I twisted my curls excitedly around my fingers, mirroring Ricky twirling the phone cord. He seemed to be arranging a time…oh, could it be, could it be that finally after all this mess we had finally, finally . . . ?

Ricky clicked the phone down and for a moment stood with wide eyes and a dropped mouth. Then he jumped and yelled so hard my shocked ears hurt:

"We did it!"

We went out on the town to celebrate. Never had we had so much fun. Ricky drank far too much, despite me telling him off, and also started smoking, despite his recent attempts to give up. He kept walking up to complete strangers and telling them we were going to be the new Shakespeares of the next century. None of them seemed to mind, not even the grumpy barmaid, who even managed a smile when Ricky signed a barmat for her and told her to treasure it because it would be worth a lot one day. Finally, he got totally carried away and ordered the entire pub a round of drinks. As closing time came and the landlord realised Ricky had nothing to pay for them, he was promptly thrown out. The locals, cheering and clapping, picked him up as though he was a rugby hero and carried him down the streets, depositing him in the local graveyard. I followed, laughing and shaking my head.

"I think we'd better go home." I smoothed his fringe back from his bloodshot eyes.

But getting up, Ricky drew me into the deserted little church. I smiled up at the stone angels, my heart leaping over and over with gratitude, oh thank you, Krishna, I love you Krishna . . . Then Ricky turned to me soppily and said,

"Let's get married."

"What!"

"I'm serious! Come on." He looped his arm through mine and then led me down the aisle, tooting the wedding march. At the altar, he pretended to be the best man, doing the most naughty and wonderfully spot-on impersonation of my father getting all pompous and solemn. Then he slipped my old wedding ring off my finger and drew a Budweiser ring-pull out of his pocket.

"I've been plucking up courage to ask all night," he whispered.

"Oh Ricky!" I kissed his lips and face and eyes and hugged him again and again.

This, I thought, as we sat down outside, this is the happiest night of my life. We lay in the grass, listening to the wind in the trees, feeling the caress of the sea breeze and for the first time since that night when we had first made love, I felt calm inside, felt that everything had come good, and everything would be alright.

"If only my mum was here tonight," said Ricky sadly, "she'd be so pleased. I nuzzled my head against him and he kissed me again, then broke off, looking more happy. "Hey, when we get published, we're going to have to go on *The Big Breakfast* you know."

"Have I Got News for You!"

"What shall we wear on the cover? Hey, maybe we can be photographed in black and white, snogging each other, like something out of a Calvin Klein ad."

"We'll have to get a huge house in Notting Hill Gate."

"Next door to Peter Mandelson. Tony Blair will love the book and invite us over."

"We'll become Euro MPs, we'll get voted on without even standing."

"We'll take over the world!" Ricky punched the air, laughing. "Olivia and Ricky strike at last!" he feigned a *Star Trek* voice.

We both started to get such a fit of giggles that we could hardly walk back. Then, on a sudden spur of inspiration, Ricky suddenly dragged me into a phone box and got it into his head that he was going to call Ferras, our old friend from *Vixen*, he was so dying to show off.

"Don't be too long!" I cried, as he put in a pound. "Then I call my mum and tell her!"

"Hello?" Ferras's sleepy voice finally came on the other end.

"Hi, Ferras mate, how are you doing?" Ricky cried. "Guess who!"

"Oh boy, Ricky, where the *fuck* have you been?"

"In Brighton," Ricky chirped.

"Is Olivia with you?"

"Say hi," Ricky passed the phone over to me.

"Olivia, you've gotta get back, you've got to see Henry –"

"I don't need to see him ever again," I declared, buoyed up by Ricky's arrogance. "We're going to be famous and published, we can do whatever we like now."

"No, you don't understand, he's had a heart attack," he spoke very slowly and forcefully, as though he was explaining to a small child. "He's dying, Olivia, d'you hear me, d'you understand? It's in all the papers, about you and Ricky running off and everything – it happened a week ago. He's at Rochester Manor now, just out of hospital –" the beeps cut him off. I hit the phone, punched redial, but there was only the flat dial tone in my ear.

38. The Heart Attack

We finally arrived back at Rochester Manor in the dead of night.

Getting off at the little country station, there were no taxis so we walked to the house in the cold frosty night, silent again.

Going through the big iron gates reminded me of how he had always used to complain about the cracked paint. Then, seeing lights on the house and Agatha's blue Mercedes in the drive, I stalled, but Ricky pulled me forwards.

"Come on, imagine how upset she must be feeling too."

But Agatha was amazingly abrupt.

"What the hell are you two doing here?" She gave us both a look of such disgust that I wriggled my hand away from Ricky's grasp.

"We heard about Henry," I stuttered. "We're so sorry."

"Well, I think it's a little late for that now," she said coldly. She nearly closed the door again, but Ricky stuck his DM boot in. Then, hearing a call from upstairs, she turned back and yelled, "Coming, darling!"

Ricky grabbed my hand but I prised it away and,

dodging past Agatha, scrambled up the stairs. He called again – it was him, it was him! Flinging myself into our bedroom, I stopped short as he said, "Agatha, my Earl Grey is cold –" Then he stopped short.

I stood and gaped. All the way back, I had dreaded walking in and seeing him lying like a fly in a web of wires, eyes closed, skin deadly cold, barely breathing, only the beep of a machine indicating he was still alive. Now here he was, looking awful and yet so normal, sitting up in bed in his stripy M&S pyjamas, a book of Eliot's poetry in his lap, sipping from a cup of Earl Grey tea and wearing his black-rimmed reading spectacles. He removed them and put them rattlingly on the side table.

"Oh Henry!" I flung myself across the bed. "You're okay, you're alive!"

"Careful," he recoiled, just stopping the cup from upsetting. The saucer shook too as he put it down on the side table.

"I'm so sorry," I tried to clasp him but he just froze up, his arms tight against his sides.

"I'm so sorry," I looked up into his eyes, but they were black, unblinking, unforgiving.

Agatha came charging back into the room, red-faced and blustering.

"Will you just get out!" I lost my patience and screamed at her. "He's my husband, I want to be with him, leave us alone!"

Agatha put her hands on her hips and looked at Henry. He gave a brief nod. She left, looking very tight-lipped.

I took Henry's hands in mine; they were warm and dry and wonderfully alive.

"Your hands are cold," he said flatly, gently massaging my stiff fingers. He reached up and caught a tear between his fingers, rubbing the wetness as if as testing to see if it was real. Then suddenly his fingers knotted in my hair, pulling me so abruptly that I yelped. He held me so hard and tight against him, my cheek squashed against his chest, that I could hardly breathe, but I was so relieved to be forgiven I clung back to him just as desperately. Then, as my neck started to ache, I tried to pull back, but he pressed me even harder, rocking slightly, his fingers like steel.

Hearing voices outside, Henry tensed, his finger clawing my cheek.

"Who's that?" he asked with uncharacteristic jumpiness. "Who's there?"

Then, as Ricky sheepishly sidled in, his whole body hardened and I could almost feel his heart seizing up in fury. For a moment they stared at each other, Ricky apologetic, Henry completely vicious.

"Get out of here!" he was so mad he could hardly get his words out. "*Get out, get out!*" He picked up the Eliot and flung it; it banged against the door, followed by the teacup. Ricky backed up, looking at me. He moved his head almost imperceptibly, silently beckoning me to come with him.

I turned back to look at Henry. I was still shocked at the change in his appearance. There was grey in his hair and hollows under his tired, sad eyes, and a hunched, tight look about his shoulders. I could hardly believe what I had done to him. If I go now, he really will die, I realised. I gazed back at Ricky, trying to explain this in my eyes, but he just stared back at me sullenly, then tried to mouth something.

"Get out!" Henry hissed.

Ricky left.

It took Henry a few minutes to recover. His breathing was very fast and hoarse and his eyes were flitting all over the place. The he got out of bed and picked up the Eliot, murmuring, "I think the spine might be damaged."

"I guess I owe you an explanation," I began but he stopped me, shaking his head, drawing me back into bed with him.

With my head on his chest, I watched Ricky walking away down the drive, slightly ziggy-zaggy as though he was stoned. I shut my eyes and opened them again: he was concealed by darkness. I wondered where he would go, where he would sleep. Not back to Josephine, please, I prayed.

Henry locked me in his embrace all night. Sometimes I half fell asleep, only to wake to find him staring at me, as if clinging to me with his eyes. Some time towards dawn, he told me how the heart attack had happened.

"I was standing in the kitchen," he said quietly. It was amazing how calm and neutral he sounded, as though he was speaking about someone else. "It was a few weeks after you left. I read the papers and they had all this rot about you and Ricky. Total bull. And then there was just this overwhelming pain and I thought that I was going to die. I woke up in hospital. No Out of Body Experiences, I'm afraid," he joked lamely.

Then he pulled up his pyjama top and showed me the scars, the red map across his chest like a spreading plant and I tearfully kissed it better.

"When Ricky and I –" I began again; I kept wanting to tell him everything but every time I tried he kissed me, as though he couldn't bear to hear. His breath was acidic and bitter, as though poisoned with his sickness.

"I never meant –" I tried again.

"It's okay, darling, I know it wasn't your fault, I know it was all him. I don't blame you . . ."

The next morning at breakfast, Agatha subjected me to a very long lecture.

"We knew for months that Henry was in danger of having a heart attack. For you and Ricky to run off like that was sheer irresponsibility and selfishness."

"What?" I cried. "I never knew, he never told me."

Agatha gave me a dubious, then condescending.

"Perhaps he felt you couldn't handle it. For the past few months, I've been calling him and telling him to take it easy. It was just the same when we were married. He pushes himself too hard."

She removed a piece of toast from the toaster and started to butter it, then put the plate on a tray.

"Hey," I turned on her, "you don't need to bother, I'm cooking him breakfast."

Agatha eyed my sizzling bacon and eggs in disgust.

"Listen, you silly girl, the doctor warned him about his diet. Food like that is not going to help."

I turned the heat off, suddenly feeling unthinking and stupid.

"But why didn't he tell me?" I was still crestfallen. "I

used to be a veggie. We could have been veggies together." Then I leapt forwards for the tray. "I can take it up to him."

"No, it's fine," she pushed me aside bustlingly, "I can do it."

"He doesn't like toast plain, anyway, he likes jam," I interjected. Then, as she pursed her lips and browsed through the cupboard, I snapped, "You can't take him the pear jam, I made that. I want to take it to him myself."

"I don't need either of you to take it up to me," Henry sighed, entering, looking pale and tired in jeans and a jumper.

"You shouldn't be up!" Agatha cried.

"The doctor said you should rest!" I insisted.

Henry rolled his eyes. "I've got far too much on."

"Henry!" Agatha said in a warning tone.

"Oh, leave him alone," I said, going behind him and massaging his stiff shoulders. "Having you snapping at him all the time doesn't help."

"Oh honestly! I shall go and do the washing now," she said coyly to Henry, as though I wasn't there. In revenge, I picked up the toast and gave it to Henry.

"What's this?" he complained, looking longingly at the stove. "I'd much rather have that lot, thanks."

"Oh well, don't blame me when you – oh, I give up!" Agatha flounced off in disgust. I poked my tongue at her retreating back. Round one to me, I thought victoriously.

I was determined to get Agatha out of the house. Unfortunately, she was just as determined to get rid of me. Nearly every day we fought over who was going to take Henry his newspaper, tea, breakfast, or the never-ending stream of cards and flowers that arrived for him. She read him his favourite Eliot, I read him P G Wodehouse, having read somewhere that laughter was the best medicine. Henry, however, seemed to be in a permanently bad mood since the attack; I don't think I heard him laugh even once.

The more I tried, however, the more I felt I was losing the battle. I spent hours picking plums for Henry, until Agatha joked that she was growing sick of "plum pie, plum jam, plum biscuits and plum crumble".

"Next we'll be having plum and chips," Henry joked back rather cruelly. Then, ignoring me, he turned to her and said, "Have you sent a thanks to Alan Titchmarsh for the flowers he sent?"

"Yesterday," said Agatha; she was managing all his mail with sickening efficiency.

Desperate to try and climb back, I went out and bought Henry yet another tie from Tie Rack.

"Another one to add to my collection," was all he said.

I turned away, curling inside; was it just my imagination, or did he seem to be getting colder and colder towards me? On the other hand, I noted later, he was just as snappy and bossy with Agatha, but she was so thick-skinned, she hardly even seemed to notice.

Things did not improve either when Alicia turned up, taking early leave from boarding-school. She kept ignoring me and asking Agatha how long I was going to stay.

"Not long," Agatha would coo, and then apologise to me. "Sorry, you know what children are like – they don't know what they're saying."

Oh right, I thought darkly, watching a triumphant smile on Alicia's face, I'm sure she's just a little innocent.

But probably her mummy hadn't spent much time with her daddy since the divorce, I thought in an attempt to be more compassionate, and it was true that she was really cheering Henry up.

The next morning, ignoring both Agatha's and my protests, he hid himself in his study. I felt rather privileged when he asked me to join him for 'a private chat'.

I sat down in his big black dentist's chair, spinning round and round in the way that had made him laugh in the past, catch me and kiss me. But he put his hands in his pockets and walked to the window. I couldn't help noticing his corduroy trousers were still loose from all the weight he'd lost.

"There's an e-mail for you on my computer," was all he said.

I sat down frowning, and clicked on the mouse.

Dear Olivia,
I hope you're well and you manage to get this e-mail without that bastard finding it first but I've put our usual password on. I have so much to say to you but I don't know where to begin, but most important of all, I just wanted to say to you that tomorrow I'm going for a meeting with our agent Denis Wimbledon. I really want you to come. I know you have to stay

with Dad and even though I hate him for everything he's done and to be honest I wouldn't care if he dropped dead tomorrow if only I could be with you, I do understand. Well, I admit I was pretty mad with you at first, in fact I hated you but I can never stop loving you, so I'll forgive you only if you come to this meeting (!) You don't have to write under your own name, we can make up some crazy pseudonym and you can send the drafts in secret, Henry will never know. Please come. I know how badly you've wanted to get published for so long, so just consider this a business opportunity, forget all about me and the complications. Just go for it – I know you can be great, Ms Bliss! Stay happy and come, please come tomorrow and we can talk everything through. Just tell Henry you need to get your Xmas shopping in. If you don't reply, I'll assume you're not coming but I left a message with Denise to tell you to check your mail so I hope she passed it on but I have to go now, Emily wants the computer.

All my love, Ricky.

"Oh," I said. "Oh."

"Yes. Oh," said Henry coldly. "Well?" he spread open his palms. "Aren't you going to answer it?" he said sarcastically. "Please feel free to reply."

I turned back to the computer and pressed the *Delete* button. Then I turned back to Henry with a pleading smile, but he was engrossed in the *Oxford English Dictionary*.

"The definition of adultery," he read out loud in a

clear, neutral voice, as though he was giving a literary lecture, "is —"

"Henry, please let me explain."

We were interrupted by Alicia, snivelling because Mummy had just told her off again.

"Why did Mummy tell you off?" Henry ruffled her hair gently, pretending to pet the toy dog she was clutching.

"Because Bonio, my doggie wanted to pretend to be an Andrex puppy and I got a toilet roll all over the landing and she said it was making a *mess* but it was Bonio's fault, not *mine*!" she started to shriek again.

"Can't we ask Agatha and Alicia to go now I'm — well — back?" I pleaded to Henry later that evening as we sat in the living-room, watching TV.

"No." He channel-hopped to the other side, then cursed when he saw his own show come up. A tall man with a glittering smile and a slightly game-show air was hosting temporarily.

"And due to the recent heart attack of Sir Henry Caldwell," he said beamingly, "I shall be temporarily stepping in to review the latest Booker Prize winner and discuss Iris Murdoch's earlier novels with our special guest, Fay Weldon —"

"Bastard," Henry seethed. "He's always been after my job. Ever since Agatha and I went on holiday to Germany in 98 when I had burnt out, he took over for a month, and ever since then — bastard!"

Why does he get so angry about every little thing? I couldn't help worrying. He'll never get better at this rate.

"And," Henry flicked through *The Radio Times,* "the ratings have bloody gone up."

"Well, probably the viewers are just turning on through curiosity." I stroked his arm soothingly, only he shook it if off irritably.

I paused for a while, then swallowed and said, "So, erm, you don't think it might be better if Agatha did go?"

"No," he shook his head, his eyes still on the TV. "I think I would like her to stay," he said. "After all, she was the one who discovered me. I owe her my life – if she hadn't called the ambulance . . ."

"Yes, yes, of course." I pleated the edge of a cushion.

"Besides, I do so like having Alicia around, don't you?"

"Mmm."

He smiled at me intensely, so I smiled back. After that we both watched TV in silence.

I suddenly had a funny feeling that he rather enjoyed us fighting over him, that somehow he was enjoying punishing me. At first it had seemed as though he'd completely forgiven me, and yet we still hadn't had a single discussion about me and Ricky, as though it had never happened. At first I had been happy to avoid the confrontation, but still it lurked beneath the surface, as though he still didn't quite trust me, couldn't bring himself to quite forgive me. Getting that e-mail from Ricky that morning hadn't helped much either.

I was aware of the silent wall between us again as we both got ready for bed and, as usual, he didn't bother to kiss me goodnight. Faced by the wall of his back, I couldn't resist reaching for him, but he merely pushed me away.

"D'you want me to have another heart attack?" he snapped, clicking off the light.

He's never going to forgive me, I sobbed silently, but if he hasn't forgiven me then why hasn't he told me to go? Perhaps he was planning to, perhaps he was just choosing his time. I just felt so unsure and in-secure; being with Ricky in Brighton had had more ups and downs than a roller-coaster but at least I'd never doubted that he loved me...

Hearing me crying, he rolled back over and snapped: "Why are you crying?"

"I'm not," I sobbed.

"Why d'you have to cry about every little thing? What the fuck's the matter now?"

"I just want you to forgive me. I just want to talk to you and talk this all through and have everything out in the open."

He paused for a moment, staring at the ceiling. Outside in the dead of night a few owls called laments to each other. Then he reached out, and, very lightly, almost tentatively, placed his hand on my shoulder.

"Go on then," he whispered roughly. "Talk to me."

So I talked to him. I told him I had never loved Ricky, we had run away on a whim, it had been unplanned and impractical. I told him that I had never stopped loving him and regretted my mistake every day in Brighton. I tried to dredge up all the awful things that had happened; I told him about the terrible house and the debt collectors –

"Typical Ricky," Henry said bitterly. "I remember as a kid he was always borrowing money and never paying me back."

"It was so terrible," I cried, "and then when I heard you had your attack —"

"You felt guilty and came running back, hoping I might pop off soon so that you could inherit all my money."

"No!" I cried, shocked. Was this what he had really been thinking? "I haven't even considered — no — Henry — no. I never had to come back."

"You did. You had no money. You needed me and this big house."

"No, no," I started to cry with the awful truth of his words. "No, I've always loved you, I don't want you to die."

"And there's nothing going on anymore with you and Ricky?" he asked at last.

"Nothing," I insisted.

He rubbed my shoulder very gently, then I winced as he suddenly dug his nails in.

"If you have anything more to do with that son of a bitch, I will kill you and I mean it, Olivia."

"I swear, I won't," I promised. "I swear, I swear."

He let me creep into his arms after that, and it felt so wonderful to feel him holding me again after all his coldness. I felt awful for all the lies I'd told, but then again, surely it was better than provoking more anger and another attack. 'What Henry needs right now,' Agatha kept saying, 'is calm and quiet, no surprises.'

"I love you," I whispered again. But still he didn't reply; perhaps he'd gone to sleep.

*   *   *

By the most wonderful stroke of luck, my prayers were answered and soon Agatha was called away to France because one of her sisters was ill.

"It never rains but it pours," I said, giving her a winning smile. Game, set and match to me, I thought triumphantly as she gave me a sour goodbye.

But instead of things improving between me and Henry, they only seemed to get worse. Perhaps it was because he was getting well again, and more restless.

"But the doctors did say you should rest," I kept saying, until he snapped at me that I sounded like a whingeing parrot.

I tried to cheer him up by suggesting he might do some more writing, but it only seemed to make him worse. He kept writing and then screwing up, slashing out, until at the end of the day he had nothing but balls of paper.

Determined not to sink back into the boredom I'd suffered at the start of our marriage, I decided to start writing something myself. In the past, writing had always soothed me, taking me away from my cares, creating a fantasy world to escape to which was far more colourful than reality. I went back to *Wickham's Memoirs,* the book I had started when I'd first met Ricky. But I found myself stopping and starting, shaking my pen in exasperation as though all the words were blocked inside. Writing, I realised, requires a certain degree of relaxation, and I couldn't stop looking at the clock and wondering how Ricky's meeting was going with his agent. I did hope Henry hadn't called and interfered.

Henry, having screwed up his last sheet of paper, was staring numbly out of the window.

"Erm, would you mind taking a look at what I've written?" I asked Henry tentatively.

It took him twenty minutes to read just the five pages (well, less, since there was so much crossed out) while I fidgeted and played with his paperweights.

Then all he said was: "There's a spelling mistake on page four, dear. Aberration is spelt with two 'r's, as you will note in the *Oxford English*."

"Oh right," I said, hastily taking it back in embarrassment. Obviously, it was so bad it wasn't even worth commenting on.

Henry sighed.

"I've got writer's block," he said gloomily, touching his heart. "I'll never write again."

"Don't be silly, of course, you will," I reassured him, turning him over for yet another massage.

Halfway through, he fell asleep. I shook my tired hands in relief and crept out, whistling for Roberta for a walk. Had it always been this bad between us, I wondered, or was everything coloured by the wonderful time I'd had with Ricky?

Perhaps, I considered, I should suggest to him that we write a book together, but then again, Henry would only pick a subject like Socrates or Ancient Greece which I knew nothing about. Reading back over *Wickham's Memoirs,* I realised Henry was right: it was bloody awful. I tore it all up.

After that, my inspiration dried up totally.

*   *   *

About a month later, Henry was up and about and doing far too much as usual, disappearing off to London for meetings, half the time going without telling me, so that I couldn't tell him off.

It was the start of November and I was making lists for Christmas which I kept losing. Henry was having another fatty breakfast when his hands tightened around *The Daily Telegraph*, then he started to wheeze for air and clutch his heart.

"Oh my God!" I jumped up, knocking over the tea as he doubled up in pain. "Are you okay?" God, why did one ask such stupid questions in emergencies? "Shall I call an ambulance?" He shook his head vehemently so I ran to his side, holding his head against my stomach, rubbing my hands up and down his chest. I could feel his heart pumping like a jumpy rabbit. "Are you sure you're okay?" I repeated. "Your pills? Should you take your pills?"

"I'm fine," he stood up abruptly, pushing me away. "I'm okay, I'm okay." He briskly picked up the paper, folded it in half, and shoved it in the bin.

"Where are you going?" I called after him.

"Just out for a walk. Do I have your permission?" he asked with acid sarcasm.

I mopped up the soggy tea mess despondently. I'm losing him, I thought, I'm losing him again. As I threw away the squelchy napkins, I suddenly spotted a newspaper photograph sticking out of the bin that made me do a double take. Then I pulled it out, feeling the same shocked pain in my heart that Henry must have felt just a few minutes before:

'£600 000 Advance to Two Talented Twenty-somethings'

My eyes flitted to the photograph: Ricky in black tie, grinning wolfishly, with his arm around Josephine, who was wearing black and smiling silkily.

Sitting down very slowly, I took a deep breath before reading on:

Mr Ricky Caldwell, son of the illustrious novelist Henry Caldwell, has received an advance of £600 000 on the strength of three first chapters for a book he has written in collaboration with his wife, Josephine.

But while his father, Sir Henry Caldwell, is famed for his literary novels that have been nominated for awards such as the Booker and the Whitbread, Ricky's novel is in quite different taste. The pair have written a modern-day critique of love and sex in the 90s with alternating chapters. The book is witty, often tasteless, and above all 'wildly outrageous'; in the first chapter, for example, Josephine describes her sexual fantasy is meeting a handsome stranger on a train, spending the night with him and never seeing him again, whilst Ricky gives laddish advice on how Coca Cola can spice up oral sex.

The book, as yet untitled, was going to be published next spring, but it is rumoured that Macmillans are so taken with the selling potential that they may rush to meet the Christmas spending sprees.

How could he? I thought in sick wonder. How could he do this to me? Was it some sick idea of revenge? Then, seeing Henry approaching, I quickly screwed it up and chucked it in the bin.

"Have you cleared your mess up?" Henry asked sulkily. Then he sat at the piano and tinkled restlessly for the rest of the afternoon. Eventually, he got in his car and drove off, refusing to say where he was going, when he would be back.

39. Brief Encounter

Over the next few weeks I did my best to forget about his betrayal, but it was very hard not to.

Josephine had spent the last twenty-six years waiting for her fifteen minutes of fame, and now she was determined to stretch it out as long as possible. She used the book like a model using a beauty contest to climb into the film industry. It wasn't long before she had achieved minor celeb status. Whilst she failed to appear in the real glossies like *Vogue*, I couldn't open a *Woman's Weekly / Realm / World* without seeing her arrogant stare and sparkling smile. She was soon dubbed as a literary equivalent of Emma Noble, which was confirmed when she even managed to swing her own Agony Aunt column in *The Sunday Telegraph* magazine, where preview snippets of the book also filled a column every week.

Ricky, frustratingly enough, maintained a much quieter profile.

I felt mildly better when Henry suddenly announced that my historical romance was to be published that December; I'd actually forgotten all about it.

"So do I get to read what I'm supposed to have

written?" I asked; I couldn't even remember what my ghost writer was called.

"Well, okay," said Henry moodily, "but I'm not having you make a fuss and saying you want it changed."

"I'm sure it's brilliant," I said doubtfully.

"Well, it won't be brilliant," he said. "It's a cheap erotic historical romance aimed at a supermarket readership. But it should sell, which is what counts."

To be honest, I didn't think very much of the book. It was all rampant sex and no plot, written in Ladybird book style, the sort of thing people bought at airports and read on Majorca beaches and then gave away to Oxfam without even bothering to finish. Still, I thought, reassured by Henry's echo, it should sell, and I could do with some of my own money, Henry had been very begrudging recently in giving me any allowance for clothes or Xmas presents.

I thus awaited the publication date with bated breath. It was all rather like waiting for exam results. The week it came out, I flipped through *The Sunday Times* bestseller lists, eagerly hoping it might even have gone straight to number one. That would show Josephine and Ricky, I thought savagely, that would show them. But it didn't feature at all. It was a bit like scanning the exam boards and finding your name wasn't even up there. Maybe it was a misprint; maybe they had left it off. Anyway, I reasoned, it must take time for people to buy it and then for them to collate the info from all the WH Smiths and Dillons and so on around the country.

* * *

A few days later, Henry wanted to drive into London on business. Remembering how enthusiastic he'd been about the book a few months back, I dropped several hints on the way about him maybe arranging some interviews for me but he was snappy and unhelpful.

"If I don't meet you at the car by four, I'll assume you're leaving later on the train," he said edgily, pasting his Pay and Display onto the Mercedes.

"Fine," I said, walking away.

In the local Waterstones, some famous author was doing a book signing and I had to push through the crocodile queue to get to the A-Z Fiction section. C . . . C . . . Caldwell (Henry's, of course) . . . Justin Cartwright . . . Jilly Cooper . . .

The assistant behind the till was not much help, either – one of those permed-hair-nail-filing- types that normally belong in Superdrug. She'd never even heard of *Racing Pulse*.

"Well, maybe you could look on the computer," I offered helpfully; she looked like the sort who wouldn't have heard of Shakespeare if he wasn't mentioned in *Woman's Own*.

After many minutes of tapping away with a look of total boredom on her face, she said she could order it, so I filled out the forms; then she asked for payment in advance.

"Erm, maybe I could just go and get some from a cash machine," I said in growing embarrassment, especially when she spotted my Visa card sticking out of my purse. As I handed over my Barclaycard signed to O J Caldwell, I saw a ghost of a smile on her sullen lips. It was so embarrassing, I wanted to vanish into the bookcases.

"Hiya Olivia, haven't seen you for ages!"

I jumped and turned to see Ricky.

He was leaning against a bookstand, which was filled, I suddenly realised, chocablock with his books.

The assistant suddenly preened her starfish earrings and gave him a ravishing smile.

"Still going like hot cakes!" she exclaimed. "God, we've never had anything like it since *Bridget Jones*."

"I'm doing a book signing," Ricky explained. "I've just had a book published." He looked slightly sheepish.

"I know," I said, giving him a pointed glare and he turned away in embarrassment, looking lost for words. Then he turned back and gave me such a sweet, apologetic smile that all my antagonism melted in a millisecond. God, I'd forgotten what a lovely smile he had, the way it lengthened his eyes and dimpled his cheeks . . .

"Here," the assistant suddenly came into focus, pushing my book towards me. "I found a copy out the back." I jumped and caught myself.

"What did you get?" Ricky leaned over with interest. "Yours," he giggled. "Have you read our – your – well, my book?" he asked.

"Yes," I said, then added in slightly sulky understatement, "I thought it was *okay*. Have you read mine?"

"Yeah." He paused and put his hands into his pockets. "To be honest, I thought it was a load of shit, a kind of spiced-up Mills and Boon."

The assistant repressed a snigger. I stiffened indignantly – bloody cheek!

"I just thought you could do a lot better," said Ricky, more kindly.

"I didn't write it. It was all a ghost writer set up by Henry. You're right, you're right. I've been thinking it myself but not wanting to admit it. It's horrendous. It's just so embarrassing that anyone should think I have written it!"

Ricky started to laugh, and I laughed too and we caught eyes and then looked away. He frowned and checked his watch.

"Erm, I was wondering if you might like to go to a café?" I stammered. "Just for a quick tea – something." Seeing him check his watch again, I added hastily, "Well, obviously not if I'm boring you."

"Oh no, I'd love to," he brightened, "but seriously, I can't. I've got to go and catch a flight. I'm going to America to do a book tour."

"Oh wow, how glamorous."

"Well, why don't you come with me to the station? You can carry my case – it's one of those little wheely ones!"

I smiled, watching him collect it from behind the counter, hardly believing I was here, now, with him. Over the past few months, I'd imagined so many scenarios of bumping into him – shouting, hugging, wild *Gone With the Wind* style embraces, but never this – so expected and yet so unexpected, so bizarrely easy and casual, as though nothing had ever happened.

*   *   *

As he chattered for a moment with the assistant, I was aware at once that there was something indefinably different about him. It was more than just his shorter haircut and change of clothes; for once he'd put on a suit and polished his normally filthy Hush Puppies. There was a new, polite, polished air about him which somehow made him seem more like Henry than ever before.

Outside, it was pouring with rain and the slithery streets were milling with rushing commuters shielding their suits with FTs and disgruntled tourists in shorts cowering in shop windows.

Ricky huddled me up under his umbrella, carefully veering me past the crowds, several times saving me from being ploughed down by hoards of tooting taxis and traffic because I was so busy gazing up at him.

"What?" Ricky caught me looking.

"You're different," I said.

"So are you," said Ricky.

"Oh! Why?"

"You go first," he teased me.

"Well, you're more confident," I said at last. "What about me?"

"Well, I am different," Ricky explained to me as we were swept along by the tide streaming into the tube station. "Getting that massive advance, I've really sorted my life out now. I've even got my own house," he said proudly, slotting his change into the machine, then handing me over a business card with his new address. "In Cheam, with four bedrooms and double glazing and everything, and Jamie lives with me. I work from home now, except when he's not trying to get me to play Twister or hogging my computer playing Dungeons and Dragons."

"Oh, wow Ricky, that's so cool. That's really great," I said breathlessly, tucking the card safely into my purse. "Jamie must be so happy. Oh Ricky, I'm so happy for you." I started as he slotted in more money and handed me over another ticket.

"Come onto the tube with me," he insisted. "We haven't seen each other for so long, just stay with me a little bit longer."

I prayed that there would be the usual delays but with typical Sod's Law, the train sped in with perfect timing. The hot carriages were packed like sardines and I found myself pressed up against Ricky with a pole in my back and a businessman's black shoe on mine until Ricky politely and protectively told him to remove it.

"So how am I different?" I stammered. We were standing so close, I kept staring at the Strepsil poster behind his head to avoid his eyes.

"You just are," said Ricky, quickly ushering me into a seat as it was vacated. He stood above me, hanging onto a black handgrip.

"I just am! Come on, tell me!"

"Well, I guess you're more . . . on edge. More tense."

"Oh right." My eyes flitted back to the ads across the carriage again. It wasn't until we were off the train and sliding up on the escalators that I retorted: "Well, you'd be nervous too if your husband had had a heart attack."

"Sorry," Ricky recoiled, moving his case as a stream of commuters hurried up on the right side. He turned back and caught my gaze and was it my imagination, or was there a faint blush on his face? "How's he doing now?"

"Much better," I lowered my eyes.

Clapham Junction: the train had already pulled in but we had five minutes left. We sat on a red plastic bench, sharing a cup of BR tea.

"I don't know how they manage to make it so scummy." Ricky took a gulp and winced. "It's like Baldrick off *Blackaddder*, the way he made his tea with mud and rats' droppings and what not." Then, as he passed it to me, I recoiled laughing, and he grinned.

"I'd forgotten how much fun you were to be with," he suddenly said.

I stopped laughing and shrugged awkwardly; I'd just been thinking the same about him. It had been a long time since I'd had a good laugh with Henry.

"So," I steeled myself, watching him add more sugars, his hands shaking slightly, spraying crystals onto his linen trousers, "will you be meeting Josephine there?"

"Oh no," he licked the plastic stirrer. "Oh no," he gave a long sigh.

"What?" I asked quickly.

Ricky's eyes darted towards the click of the platform clock.

"There isn't enough time to explain it all. But basically we've broken up again, for the fifty millioneth time, but this time at my instigation. She keeps trying to get back with me but I won't take her back, not anymore. I'm fed up: I've had enough. To be honest, it's been a bit of nightmare working with her on that book. She's supposed to be on the book tour too but we're both so sick of each other we've refused and the publishers are going bonkers – they've had to issue a press release that she's got flu. She's already given them so much hassle. To be honest, she couldn't even write for *The People's Friend* and that's saying something. Not one word of our last book was written by her; our editor had to work very long hours." He looked straight at me. "You should have written it really. I hope you're not too mad at me for using our idea, but I did offer and then . . . well, Josephine just stepped in."

He offered me a sip of the tea; I accepted, then gagged and scalded my tongue.

"The train for Gatwick will be leaving in two minutes' time. Would all passengers please board the train," the female announcer crackled.

"This is so *Brief Encounter*, isn't it?" Ricky suddenly turned to me with a wobbly smile. "Will she stay with her husband or will she get on the train with her true love, the handsome stranger – well, I'm hardly that – only this time will it be for good?" Ricky spoke in a mocking film critic voice and I laughed, relieved and disappointed, realising he was just taking the piss.

Then I saw his face crumple with disappointment.

"I take it that's a no," he said shortly, picking up his case. He got up onto the train. The seats were already nearly full so he stood by the door, gazing down at me. Then a flood of tourists got on, forcing him to retreat back over to the other side of the carriage.

I hopped anxiously from foot to foot, still trying to

assemble what he meant, what on earth he was trying to say.

"Ricky?" I cried at last.

At once, he pushed forwards past a Japanese woman and said eagerly, "Yes?"

"Erm," I said in a low whisper. "Well, maybe, maybe, we could meet next week. Henry's going to Paris." I couldn't help myself.

"I'm not asking you to have an affair with me," he said in a loud whisper, "I'm asking if you want to – oh, forget it." He turned to move his case as another girl got onto the train, then looked back with a cold glance and said, "Our friend Krishna doesn't recommend affairs, you know."

"Well, look, I know it's not ideal," I said, "but I just – I thought . . ."

"No. I can't go through all that again. I'm not interested in lying or sneaking around. I've sorted my life out now and I want someone to be with. And, well, if you don't want me, well, maybe I'll just have to find someone else."

"D'you want to give your dad another heart attack!" I burst out.

"Frankly, I wouldn't care," said Ricky coldly, then, seeing me gasp, he said quickly, "Look, Liv, I think there's something you should know about Dad. He's not . . . exactly . . . look, he isn't being faithful to you."

"I'm sorry?"

"Stand clear of the doors, please!" the guard approached me, waving me away from the edge of the platform. I took a step backwards, gazing at Ricky in bewilderment as the doors started to beep.

"He's cheating on you." Ricky looked at me with complete earnestness.

"I'm sorry?" Time stopped; the station spun; the jazzy Jingle Bells dimmed into muzziness. My ears popped as though I'd just dived into a swimming-pool. "Erm – I – who? Who? What the fuck d'you mean?"

The doors started to close, then slid back as a late arrival jumped onto the train, jamming them back open.

"I don't think I should say," Ricky was looking very sheepish. "Sorry, look, I was a bastard to even say it – it's something you should talk over with him."

"But – you're lying!" I rubbed my forehead. "No, no way. We just – you're just bloody jealous, that's all!" I spat out.

"Olivia!" He tried to push the door open but his sleeve got caught and he tugged it away. As the train shuddered and pulled out of the station, he waved after me but I stood there, gazing at him in shocked disgust.

How could he? I munched unhappily on an almond croissant on the tube back. How could he lie to me like that? Henry would never have an affair, not after all we'd been through, not after taking me back again. Never. I shook my head, shoving my ticket into the machine. And if Ricky was lying about that, how did I know he wasn't lying about Josephine? The machine spat the ticket out and I shoved it in again. It was all so confusing, my mind was swirling like an up-turned snow-shaker.

"Oh God, what's the matter with this machine?"

"You have to insert the ticket the right way up," an American tourist said helpfully.

"Oh right," I said in embarrassment.

4:26, said the platform clock. Henry would have driven back separately by now; I would have to take the 4:40 from Euston. As I sat waiting on the platform, I boiled into such a lather of anger that it was amazing I didn't spontaneously human-combust. I could still hardly believe his nerve. First he steals my book off me, then gives it to Josephine – he ruins, in fact, my entire writing career, without even apologising – it was all very well to say "You would have been better, Olivia!" but it was a bit bloody late for that now – and then, *then* he goes and makes up all this crap about Henry. Like just ruin my marriage too, while you're at it, might as well fuck the whole lot up while you can.

Huh huh huh.

40. The Final Affair

On impulse, I got off the train at Leighton Buzzard and
hurried to the health food shop just in the nick of time
to buy Henry a jar of his favourite Greek sweet: honey
and almond halva. Getting back onto a new train, I
was dying to nibble to silence my tummy, still in post-
Ricky churn. I was cooling down now, but fragments
of our conversation still kept echoing in my mind,
despite the annoying throb of a yobbo's Walkman.
Still, I thought, checking my watch, by now he'll probably be on the plane, flying out of the country. In a
few days, I'd forget about the conversation, lose the
regret. Everything would go back to normal.

Back at the house, there were three large suitcases
in the grand hallway. Henry, striding across the hall,
his large black coat flapping like a bat, stopped short
when he saw me. I hid the jar behind my back,
repressing a smile; perhaps he was planning a surprise
second honeymoon in Majorca . . .

"Olivia, I'm leaving you."

For a second there was an awful silence, shattered
by the crash of the halva jar falling to the floor. I
quickly knelt down, scrabbling to wipe it off the
beautiful pink rug, waiting for Henry to shout at me

for me being so messy as usual. And then I would put my arms around him and nibble kisses over his ears and he would groan, "D'you really think this is going to make everything alright?" and I would look up at him and reply, "Yes," impishly and he would take me to bed and tell me how much he loved me despite –

"Olivia, I'm leaving you," he said very slowly and patiently, as though addressing a small child.

"Well, how long for?" I stuttered. "What if someone calls, a publisher or someone wanting an interview?"

"You don't need to worry about that, Ms French has instructions."

"Can I come?" I stopped trying to clear up the mess and gazed up at him. He came towards me and gently lifted me to my feet, rubbing my shoulders awkwardly.

"Don't worry," he said, so gently it hurt, "I shall look after you. Your mother will be taken care of. Well, I'm not quite sure if I intend to keep her in the Kingston House – I think two bedrooms are a little too much for just her and the baby, and there is a friend of mine, a Japanese businessman, who's willing to pay a huge rent – well, with the view of the Thames, you see. But we can arrange something, maybe a little house in Croydon, or something."

His voice droned out into a radio fuzz. My eyes wandered to the little oak table by the hall. A note was lying on the top. 'Olivia' was written his black spidery ink. I picked it up.

"Ah – that was just an explanation," he had the grace to blush.

"You weren't even going to say it to my face!" I cried, feeling the first burst of anger pierce the still shock.

"Well, yes, of course," said Henry hurriedly, "I was going to come back, in a few days, when you'd read it and settled down and got over the shock."

"'Dear Olivia,'" I read out loud in a high voice. "'It is with great regret —'"

"Oh come on," he snapped, raising his eyes to heaven.

"'It is with great regret'," I repeated in a sharp mimic. "*Great regret!* 'It is with great regret that I have to inform you that I must leave you'." He might have been writing a letter to the bank. "I like the crappy white paper," I noted evenly. "Obviously I'm not worth your nice Basildon Bond letterhead."

"Now come on, Olivia," he said sharply. He tried to prise the letter from my hands but as my eyes flew over the lines, the word *Agatha* leapt out like a salmon.

"Hang on!" I tugged it back, causing a slight tear. "Agatha!" I read it with fierce concentration. 'I am leaving you to return to live with Agatha which is clearly a much more desirable situation for my girl Alicia . . .' Agatha! Why stay with her!"

"I love her," he said stiffly.

"What, you mean, you, you, you like, I mean – love in the sense of *fancy*? But, I mean, when, when – did you – I mean –"

"I've been having an affair with her," he said calmly.

"Having an affair with her. An *affair* affair?"

"An *affair* affair. In the same sense that you had an affair with Ricky."

"No, but that was different, that was different – and that's all over now. How many times do I have to tell you? It's over, you don't need to punish me."

"I'm not trying to. I love Agatha and I am going to live with her."

"But you can't. You can't!" I cried. "She's dreadful. You said so yourself, many a time – to me! She nagged you! I mean, have an affair with anyone but Agatha, she's a complete cow!"

Henry was starting to look seriously cross; his lips had thinned almost to invisibility and there was a muscle going in his cheek like it did when he was interviewing a difficult subject on television.

I gazed back down at the letter. What was somehow worse than the shock was the familiarity. *You've known this*, a deep voice whispered with awful smugness, *you've known this all along, Olivia. I've been trying to tell you but you wouldn't listen. All the signs were there: his moods, his temper, not wanting to even touch you anymore. But you chose to ignore them. Trying as usual to pretend everything was alright.*

"Agatha and I did go through a rocky period," he said, as though he and I had never been married in the meantime, "but we've resolved a lot of differences and we understand each other now. Frankly, Olivia, I just think we are suited. You're far too young for me –"

"Well, that never bothered you when you proposed –"

"I felt pr – look. Look. I need a wife to support my career, entertain my guests, understand my needs –"

"But I entertained your guests! What about bloody boring Bernard! I entertained him. I listened for hours to him bloody droning on about Yeats!"

"Olivia, when you last discussed politics, you thought the ERM was a pop group."

451

"Yes, but a lot of modern pop groups have names like that. Like East 17."

Henry looked completely blank, as though I'd gone completely potty, obviously thinking that East 17 was just a creation of my warped mind.

"But if you never wanted me, why let me come back after Brighton? Was I just some convenient nursemaid to look after you or was it just some sick joke to lull me into a false sense of security and get back at me –"

I had obviously hit a nerve very close to the truth, because he pulled back his expensive sleeve and looked at his watch. "I'm afraid I'm going to have to cut this discussion short. I feel it would be much better to continue this at another time, when your tantrum is over."

"My tantrum!" I shrieked. "What am I, a child?"

"You're behaving like one."

"Well, that's because you always wanted me to be one. You always treated me like that. That was the role – I was the stupid little girl and you got your way and told me what to do. And anyway," my voice caught with tears, "you'd be throwing a tantrum if your partner told you they were going to leave you."

"My partners never leave me," said Henry. "Women never leave me; I leave them."

I opened my mouth to point out I had indeed once left him, then closed it. He was just being a gut because he felt so guilty, just like the more caged he felt, the more formal and distant he became, like a hedgehog putting up spines. I was doing this all wrong, saying all the wrong things, like an actress off cue. If I kept on like this he would make a swift exit and once his foot was over the door I'd lose him. I had to be calm – sweet, feminine!

"How about," I curled a lock around my finger, pushing my wobbling lips into a seductive smile, "how about you stay and I cook you a nice dinner and we talk about this like sensible adults?" I started to unbutton my blouse, slowly, slinkily gliding towards him. For a moment, he froze, caught off guard. Then I tripped on a slither of halva. Henry only just caught me in time. For a moment I clung onto those thick arms that would never protect or caress me again, breathing in one last whiff of his scent, my heart curling with pain. I gazed up at him, silently pleading with his eyes. I saw the regret, felt his hands tightening in weakness, then he gently pushed me away. I stood alone and started to cry. He kicked the glass lightly.

"Get Denise to clear this up," he muttered, then picked up his case and disappeared out of the front door.

I wept and wept – then started, opening my arms as he came back, back for me – no . . . back for the other two cases. He hovered awkwardly in the doorway.

"Come now," he said sheepishly, "you'll be alright." Then he added with a hint of a sneer, "Why not go running back to Ricky!"

"He's gone! He's gone to America!" I cried, tears and snot streaming into my mouth. "Don't you understand, I don't love him, I love you!" But even as I spoke I faltered, knowing I was lying.

"Ah well," he said, with a slight shrug.

"You can't, you can't go –"

"I'm going," he turned his back.

"I'm going to sue you!" I shrieked, my voice echoing throughout the hall like a banshee. "I'm going to break you and get everything from you and then you'll be sorry!"

Henry stood very still, then wheeled back and said in a low, cold voice: "If you dare try – just one thing – I won't give you a penny and your mother will be thrown out of that house and then *you'll* be sorry."

"Oh Henry, I'm sorry, I didn't mean –" I ran after him, "I didn't mean it, I didn't mean –" My words were drowned in the revving up of his new pale blue Mercedes. At the last minute he wound down the window.

"You're the one who had the affair. You're the one who ruined our marriage," he said, then drove off in a spray of gravel.

Back inside the house, Denise was looking at all the mess in dismay.

"I'm terribly sorry," I wiped my tears away on the back of my sleeve. "I'm afraid Henry and I – we had an accident – we are sorry. God," I rubbed my swollen eyes, "my hayfever is killing me."

"Is anything the matter between you?" she asked shiftily.

God, I realised in horror, she knows. Even our bloody char knows. Probably the whole fucking world knows except for me.

"Everything is fine," I said sharply, storming off into the living-room and slamming the door behind me.

I sank down onto the couch. The same couch where Henry and I had made love that time the dressmaker came. I buried my face in the cushions, trying to breathe in the smell of us but it was only mustiness. For a moment I stared out of the window, watching a pair of jolly golfers taking swings. The day was absurdly happy, the sun horribly bright, the joyous birdsong almost mocking. It seemed for a moment so strange and so awful that the rest of the world was carrying on so smoothly when mine was crashing down everywhere.

There was a faint ring in the background. It had to be the doorbell. Henry! Coming back to say it was all a mistake. Or a joke. Was it April Fool's? Yes – I'd forgotten! My heart exploded with hope, then shrivelled. There was frost on the lawn; Henry had been complaining about slipping only that morning at breakfast. It was, it was . . . my brain was in total shutdown, refusing to assemble the data, as though a virus was sweeping through my memory, exterminating all the files. Well, whatever day or month it was, it was winter. Not April. And Henry. My husband. Had left me. For Agatha. And Ricky had gone –

"Ricky!" I said out loud. "Ricky!" Suddenly my brain, feeling as though it had been knocked out of gear, grated into first. I had to speak to him! Explain! Apologise! What was the time? When had he got on the train? Once again, I juddered into neutral.

I ran to the phone, picked it up, then slammed it down. He'd moved. To some palace in Cheam. I had no idea of the number – how many Caldwells were there in Directory Enquiries?

The business card! Of course!

I picked up my handbag, emptied it out, pens,

Tampax, Mars Bars, coins and keys scattering, rolling over the floor.

Where is it? Shit shit shit what have I done with it? Oh God.

I scrabbled about, then realised that it was in my purse. Clicking it open, I rummaged through a wad of receipts and credit-card bills and phone cards and a hundred other silly little stupid things I should have sorted and thrown out months ago – urgh! Useless, useless, Olivia – no wonder Henry's just left you.

I dialled 192, got the number for his agent, Denis Wimbledon. I called up his offices and asked if I could have Ricky's number.

"I just love his books," I said adoringly. "I was hoping I might be able to share my appreciation."

"Well, the agency will forward all fan mail," said the secretary briskly.

"Actually," I changed tack. "Actually, I'm really ringing from a magazine – urm, *Take A Break* as a matter of fact. I was hoping to do an interview."

"Well, perhaps you might like to give us a call next week," she said in a pull-the-other-one voice, and put down the phone.

I punched the air; my fist paused. Oh God, there it was! Staring me right in the face! His business card, with his home number! My hands shaking, I punched in the numbers. It was ringing . . . ringing . . . *oh please, Krishna, please make him pick it up, come on Ricky he's left me, he's just left me Ricky don't do this to me –*

My heart leapt at the click, then fell as a Bruce Springsteen riff twanged and his answerphone came on.

"Oh no!" I slammed down the phone. Maybe he's in the shower, I figured, maybe I should leave a message – oh give it up, Olivia, I snapped, give it up. He's not at home. You saw him get on the train. He's halfway across the planet by now. It's too late, your timing is fucking impeccable yet again.

Without even thinking, I called up my last resort.

"Hello, Josephine speaking."

"Hi, this is um Olivia." Shit, why am I calling her why why *why?* Am I mad? Yes, my husband's just walked out on me I'm mad.

"Olivia!" Her voice dropped several degrees. "What can I do for you?" She was all ultra-bank-staff politeness now.

"I, er – look – I know this sounds like a real cheek but it is a total emergency please have you got Ricky's mobile number?"

A pause. Shock? Hate? Anger? Her voice was neutral: "Sorry. No. I don't."

"Or any number, anything – something from America? Please, Josephine, it's an emergency."

"Why? What's happened?"

"I – oh –" for a moment I nearly made up an excuse about the house burning down, then I broke down, "Henry's left me. For Agatha."

"Well now, there's a surprise."

"What, what d'you mean?" I whispered. Somehow telling someone, out in the open, made it all horribly real. He had left me, it wasn't a nightmare, he had really left me.

"Oh come on, Olivia, surely even you can't be that naïve?"

"What?"

"Everyone knew he was banging Agatha, everyone. Even I knew and I've had nothing to do with you for the past few months. Now," she changed the subject briskly. "I'm afraid the only number I have for Ricky is one for his girlfriend who he's staying with and since America is five hours ahead I don't think it's such a good idea to disturb them right now, okay? Bye."

"But —" But she'd hung up.

I stared down at the phone, then burst into tears. Oh God, oh God. I got up and walked around the room, hugging myself. Ricky's *girlfriend*? Oh, I seethed, I hate men hate them hate them hate them how could he do this to me, what did he want a girl over here and a girl over there for when he travels from place to place? Bastards, all of them. Well, I don't need any of them anyway. But still I cried. I sat down on the rug, knitting and threading the tassels through my fingers. Maybe, maybe he had told Josephine it was his girl-friend but in reality it honestly was just a friend, not a *friend* friend. Olivia, you're mad, I told myself as I picked up the phone again but in my desperation I was beyond caring.

"Hello?" Somehow I knew from the coolness in her tone that she knew it was me again.

"Hi, it's me again, look please don't put the phone down, Josephine. I know this isn't an ideal situation for me to be asking you for a favour like this but I really need his number."

"What for?"

"Because, because — I really need to tell him that I love him," I started to sob. "Please Josephine, please."

"No, I will fucking not," she said in a voice that froze me to ice.

"Alright, alright," I burst out, "if you're going to be like that, fine, there's no need to be such a bitch."

"Me? Me? A bitch. You have a bloody cheek ringing up asking for my husband's number when you stole him off me and ruined our marriage and you're calling *me* a *bitch*?"

"Josephine, please, I'm sorry," I begged her, "I never meant – look – anyway," I said randomly, rationalising with complete irrationality, "it's your karma, I mean don't you remember that time when we were fourteen and you stole my first boyfriend off me, I know he was only Niall but then he was everything in the world to me –"

"*Niall!*" Josephine shrieked. "How can you possibly compare this with one drunken snog when we were fourteen years old and he was off snogging the entire sixth form anyway! You cannot fucking compare the two! I'm sorry, Olivia, but you have just been totally out of order and I never want to speak to you again so don't you dare ever –"

I couldn't bear to hear any more. I put the phone down.

There was nobody left to call, I had nobody left. Only my mother, and she'd only tell me off for being fickle or something. I cried and cried and I tried to pull myself together, knowing I was producing enough to fill a Thames Water reservoir. I started making myself busy, focusing on picking up all the lipsticks and pens and putting them back in my handbag. A packet of Tunes had slipped under the chaise longue. I was reaching underneath for them, when the phone rang. I banged my head in excitement – it was Ricky, it had to be!

"Olivia?"

"Yeah?" I asked, my heart sinking, waiting for Josephine's next tirade. Maybe I should just take the phone off the hook.

"Are you okay?"

"Yeah." Suddenly I felt horribly guilty. After all, she did have every right to be angry; anyone losing someone as lovely as Ricky had a right to be insane. "Are you okay?"

"Not really. Look," she sniffed, "why don't you come over and we'll have a chat. I don't like to think of you all alone in that mansion," she said gruffly.

"Oh, really, can I?" I was so grateful, so unexpectedly touched, that the tears came yet again. Josephine gave a long sigh.

"Don't worry, I've got a whole box of Kleenex here waiting for you . . ."

41. Reunion

"Well, we practically did get through the entire box." Josephine threw the Kleenex at the bin, and missed.

I rubbed my swollen eyes and picked another Skittle out of the big glass bowl in the centre of the crumpled double bed. We were now lying opposite each other, me cuddling an old teddy, Josephine hugging her pillow, both of us completely exhausted. In the last two hours, we had bickered and shouted and screamed and even had a pillow fight as violent as something out of *Gladiators*. A lot had been said, a lot of tears had been shed and I wasn't sure if I had been exactly forgiven or if we were ever quite going to be friends again, but at least everything was out in the open.

"You know, Olivia, I know I behaved like a real slut and you probably thought I was treating Ricky like shit –"

"No, no, not at all," I protested weakly.

"Yeah, come on," she said archly. "I know Leila thought so too. But it wasn't like that, you know. I just didn't want us to end up some boring old couple coming home after work saying 'How was your day?', 'Did you pick up my suit from the cleaners?', 'Did you pick up those little fish fingers from Marks and

Spencers?' I wanted me and Ricky to be different. We all have open relationships, why not an open marriage? So I met some other guys and he met some other – well, he met you."

"Yep, me," I said humbly.

"He is so good in bed though, isn't he?" she said dreamily, cupping her breasts voluptuously, fingering them almost absent-mindedly. "I've slept with enough guys now – I've had rough, large, small, hairy – you name it, I've had it." (I wasn't quite clear whether this remark referred to them or their erections). "But with Ricky it was special. I only ever wanted to sleep with someone else to prove that really I wanted to be in bed with him. D'you know what I mean?"

"Yes," I said uncertainly, thinking: not at all. Once I had been to bed with Ricky I'd never wanted to sleep with anyone on earth ever again.

"Still, I liked the way he talked," she sighed. "He used to tell me how much he loved me, how beautiful I was, how he wanted to make love to me so slowly and tenderly," Josephine sighed up at the ceiling.

Oh God. I wanted to put my hands over my ears. I didn't want to hear this. He used to say all of that to me. I felt my chest tighten in pain. After losing Henry, the one thread I wanted to cling to was Ricky, the one life-belt that might end all this mess. Now it seemed to be sailing off out of my grasp.

I suddenly, uncontrollably, burst into tears again. Josephine propped herself up on her pillow and looked at me with affectionate exasperation.

"You know, Olivia, you shouldn't be feeling bad about him. He's probably not giving you a second thought. He and Agatha are probably screwing away –" she stopped herself when she saw my face, then went to her dressing-table, plonked herself down on the stool and picked up her pad. "Right," she said, her eyebrow pencil poised. "You, Olivia, you are to take revenge. Tell me all the things Henry hates, and we'll get back at him."

"What!" I laughed. "No, really, Josephine, I don't think it's the answer."

"Yeah, but just thinking about it will make you feel a whole lot better," Josephine insisted.

She was right: it did. By the end of half an hour, we'd decided that when I next went home I would put all the central heating on all over the house and leave it running at tremendous cost and cut all the sleeves off his suits and throw his cuff links in the pond and give all his bloody books away to the local Oxfam.

"Now it's my turn!" Josephine cried vengefully. "Well, well, I'd like to smash his computer to bits. Throw it off an eighteenth storey window! And, and – well, basically, cutting his penis off would be tremendously satisfying."

"Oh, don't say that!" I cried, sitting up in horror at the very thought.

Josephine gave me a long look.

"Come here," she beckoned me.

"What?" I said guiltily.

"Come here," she insisted; then, kneeling me down beside her, she frowned at me. "You seriously have to do something about those eyebrows, Olivia, else you really will never attract this phantom Mr Right."

I sniffed, giggled and rolled my eyes.

"What about his American girl?" I said hastily, desperate to cover up. "What about throwing a custard pie into her face?"

"His American girl," she said between gritted teeth, "was just a lie. I just said that to piss you off. Still, maybe when he comes back from America we might try again. D'you still love him?" she suddenly asked.

I gazed past her to the swirl of silver fish mobiles fluttering by her window.

"No," I lied at last. "No. It was just, it was just a way to repair my, erm, crumbling marriage with Henry, and when Henry left I just felt so desperate to speak to him, someone, anyone. I was hysterical . . . Do you still love him?"

A faint pause.

"Yes," she sighed. "Yes, despite myself, I do. But I only just realised. Before, it always used to be me breaking up with him and he'd always take me back. This time he was just so stubborn. And it was only then I realised. You don't really appreciate someone you love until you lose them."

"Oh," I said in a small voice. In that case, I realised, I really seriously can never be with him again. I can't ruin my friendship yet again, I can't do this to Josephine again, not after all her kindness. I saw my life-belt disappear over the horizon, leaving me to drown.

Seeing tears rolling down my eyes, Josephine stroked my hair as I sobbed into her lap.

"I'm really sorry," I said, "I'm so sorry I messed it all up between you."

"It's alright," she said, sounding on the verge of tears

again herself. "To be honest, I don't blame you. It was more the fame, the tensions, the pressure, being in the spotlight. It was the book that did it. When Ricky asked me to join in, I don't think he was prepared for me being the one to get all the attention. I think I'm going to have that difficulty with any man I meet now, that he'll have to be in the background."

Since when was that ever not the case? I found myself thinking, then shook myself.

"No, it wasn't your fault, Olivia, you were just a pawn in a love-hate game we've been playing and I'm sorry you ended up being an innocent victim. It was just his way of getting back at me."

Is she serious? I gaped up at her, then, seeing her face, realised she was. I gulped and nodded gravely too.

Seeing Leila walk past in the landing, we both jumped. She popped her head round the door, looking at me in ill-concealed surprise.

"Hi Livy, long time no see."

"Hi," I grinned awkwardly. "Erm, have a Skittle."

"Thanks – taste the rainbow," Leila imitated the advert and we all laughed.

"Anyway," Josephine put her hands on my shoulders, "Livy's going to come back and live here with us, aren't you?" She gazed down at me. "You will, won't you? You won't go back and hang around in that horrible big old house? I mean, we're putting this place up for sale because I want somewhere bigger but it won't go for ages, I reckon."

"Oh, thank you!" I reached up and hugged her and as I drew away, she hugged me again, very tightly, almost fiercely.

"Well," she said, "we can't let each other down now, not after eighteen years of friendship."

The next few weeks were perfectly dreadful.

Being back with Josephine and Leila was the only thing which enabled me to survive. Especially when my mum was being so unsympathetic. She'd already had enough shocks as it was, with me and Ricky disappearing off to Brighton. When I finally did get the guts to go over and tell her, she was standing with her back to me, changing Kirsty's nappy, and she turned to me and hissed, "You're *what*!" She must have pricked the pin into poor Kirsty's little bottom, who saved me from replying by bursting into floods of tears. Mum picked her up and jiggled her, somewhat vehemently.

"I'm serious, Mum. Don't look at me like that, he's the one who had the affair! Well, I mean, I know I had one too – but he said he wants to go back to her."

"Now come on, Olivia, don't be silly," she said, as though I was sixteen again. "You've just got to accept that that's what men are like! Look at your father! How d'you think I cope, putting up with Jed and Jude and Calvin, d'you think any of them are faithful to me?"

"Well, you're not faithful to them," I faltered.

"Is anyone faithful to anyone? You're just being silly, you've got your head in the clouds."

"It's his idea to get divorced, not mine!" I cried, fighting with Kirsty's shrill screams.

"No, you just go back and tell him that you're not going to let him. Put him in his place. Tell him you'll turn a blind eye if he has a bit on the side. I mean, come on, Olivia, how are you going to cope? You won't last more than fifty seconds in the real world. How are you going to survive?"

"How are *you* going to survive?" I yelled. "This is what it's all about, isn't it? You don't give a shit about me, this is all about you!" Then I turned and ran down the stairs and out of the house. I could still hear Kirsty crying right at the end of the road as I hailed down the bus and jumped on it breathlessly. I'm never going to speak to her again, I brooded all the way home, what kind of mother is she, to let me down when I need her most? Never, never, never.

Slowly, as the days went by, as I mentally unpicked our marriage apart like a quilt, analysing each scene, each square, I had to concede that we had been very mismatched. The gap in age, personality, interests were just a few factors. It really wasn't Agatha's fault – I tried to be reasonable and not have fantasies about killing her – we would have broken apart at some point anyway.

Even so, knowing that all this pain was totally illogical still didn't make it go away. Often it came and went in cycles. Sometimes I would go to bed feeling horribly alone and cold, having to put on three pairs of woolly socks instead of being able to curl up against Henry's warmth in the night. Sometimes I would wake up and think, "Life goes on, things might get better," and even feel happy enough to hum along to the radio and go out on a shopping trip. Only, then I'd find myself in M&S, fingering a jumper and thinking, "I must get that for Henry," – and then realise with a dull thud that there was no Henry to buy for. Once, I went into Barclays to set up an account and we were halfway through the interview and form-filling when I realised I was no longer Lady Olivia Caldwell but plain old Ms Bliss again. The bank manager looked completely distressed when I burst into tears. "We do offer a year with free banking charges!" she called after me as I ran out of the bank and into the nearest portaloo.

Even more confusing, I would sometimes find myself fantasising about Ricky, and catch myself thinking, 'Whatever would Henry say if he knew you were thinking about his son like that?' then realise there was no Henry to tell me off, no Ricky to fantasise about.

Leila once found me crying in the kitchen and asked with a tentative, wry smile, "Erm, which one should I be comforting you about?"

I giggled through my tears.

"Both? Either. This is the awful thing, Leila," I started to cry again, "half the time I don't even know which one I'm grieving for. Sometimes I think it should be Henry, but often I think it's more Ricky."

"To lose a husband is a great loss but to lose one's lover as well might be regarded as sheer carelessness," Leila quipped, making me laugh again. Then she said more sternly, "Why don't you just go back to him, tell him how you feel? What have you got to lose?"

"But I don't think I really do love Henry," I confessed at last. "I've been thinking it all over and I think I was just wanted a father figure, someone to look up to, but I've grown out of that now –"

"I'm talking about Ricky, stupid," Leila said.

"Oh! No!" I cried. "No, no, I can't. I can't do that to Josephine, no! You won't tell her, will you? You musn't say a word, promise, Leila, swear!"

"Okay," said Leila reluctantly.

I was determined to banish Ricky from my mind, especially when Josephine was being so forgiving and supportive.

Our mutual grief made Josephine and me closer than we'd ever been before. We endlessly discussed theories on men and marriage, went out on girly nights, got completely pissed drowning our sorrows, and played the most mean games – making eyes at blokes, then when they came over and offered to buy us a drink, pretending to be lesbians or telling them to fuck off. Josephine once seduced a bloke, took him into a dark shady corner, unzipped his flies and then walked off laughing, leaving him exposed to the whole club. "I think I get a ten out of ten for that one," she laughed with me all the way home. "Did you see his face?"

After clubs, we stayed up in the early hours sharing binges and agreeing that neither of us needed to bother with a sex that spent half its life worrying about the length of its penis and the other half about whether Everton would beat Manchester United. Then we fell asleep together in the double bed, with the Indian doll (the one Ricky had bought on our honeymoon, which he'd called Olivia) as a bolster between us.

For all Josephine's bravado, I could tell she was hurting too. After a few days, a postcard came from Ricky in America.

I'm having a cool time over here. We all crowded over Josephine's shoulder to read his big loopy blue scrawl. *I went through customs and said to the officer, "I have nothing to declare except my enormous penis." Thankfully, there are apparently no customs' rules concerning the size of male or female organs so I was able to arrive in America safely. I have been in several mags and one girl even approached me on the street for my autograph but it turned out she thought I was Rupert Everett (totally different colour hair or what?!) Jamie has also been flown over for an early Christmas treat so I took him to Disneyland. Jamie thought it was all very childish and called Donald Duck a wanker but I got his autograph and had the best time of my life – will I ever grow up?!? And will you ever forgive me, Josephine? Let's talk it all through when I get home. Say hi to Leila. Love R.*

"Oh God," I whispered in horror, then I cried out as Josephine viciously ripped the whole thing up.

"See?" said Josephine, slamming down the bin. "Like we said – penises and football."

I was aching to go and retrieve all the pieces but later on, passing in the hallway, I caught Josephine smearing tomato ketchup off and sellotaping it back together.

That evening Josephine called me and Leila into the living-room for another Exorcise Ex's session.

"We play a game," she handed Leila a pencil and pad, "to think up a 100 reasons why chocolate is better than a bloke."

It sounded fun in theory, but in practice, somehow

we couldn't quite get inspired. For a start, we had a video playing without volume in the background, and watching Leonardo DiCaprio was enough to make men win a long way ahead.

"Chocolate is much harder, especially if you keep it in the fridge?" I offered feebly.

"Oh come on," said Josephine, "come on, you guys, you're not even trying!" Then, as the doorbell rang, she threw down her pen in exasperation, then, as usual, made big eyes at Leila.

"Oh, I'll get it. As usual," Leila snapped and flounced into the hallway.

"It might be someone wanting to buy the house," Josephine said.

"Mmm." I gazed up out of the window as an aeroplane cut a golden path across the night sky outside. I wondered if Ricky was asleep or awake, if he was thinking of me.

"Look who's here!" Leila returned with a flushed face and sparkling eyes.

And there was Ricky. Tall and brown and tanned and grinning, radiating American energy and positive health.

I was the first person he saw as he came into the room, and I was sure, when I analysed this moment a hundred times over afterwards, that his eyes softened and there was love in his smile. He strode forwards and then stopped short, turning instinctively to see Josephine sitting up, gazing up at him in amazement. He looked at her, he looked at me, then paused, as though completely torn who to address.

Go to him! Get up! My brain yelled at my legs! Tell

him! Go on! But my arms and legs just sagged like a dummy's.

"Oh Ricky!" Josephine stood up and fell into his arms, and then he circled his arms around her, smoothing her back and hair just as they soothed me in all my fantasies. "Oh Ricky!"

"You don't mind, do you, Liv?" Josephine asked, after he had gone back to Cheam to unpack and sleep off his jet-lag. "I mean, it's not like he's going to be living here. We're just going to take it slowly, we're just 'seeing' each other. In a way, I prefer it. I know he's wild about me, but I got so fed up, being with him all the time, if I just see him now and again it's a lot better."

"A lot better," I forced a smile. What else could I say?

"I guess it means you'll have to go back to sleep in your own room," she added that evening as we both changed for bed. "Still," she added, prodding the Indian doll which had served as a bolster between us, "you take Josephine with you. Stupid old doll," she tugged a plait affectionately, "I never knew whether to take it as a compliment when he gave it to me as a wedding present and said it was called Josephine."

42. The Beginning of the End

After that, it was as though I went straight back to Square One. As usual, I'd got it all wrong again. With my writer's imagination, I'd twisted and coloured all my memories into thinking Ricky loved me more. I'd been convinced Josephine was the deluded one, but no, as usual – it was me.

Here I was: single, unemployed, and with the man I loved back going out with my best friend, only this time it was Josephine, which was even worse than Leila. Josephine and Ricky were a much noisier combination and thus much harder to ignore, whether they were shouting, throwing cutlery, or making love, like the time I went downstairs on one of my midnight binges and searched endlessly for my Haagen Dazs before I realised they were frozen half naked beneath the kitchen table.

"Sorry, we didn't realise it was yours," Ricky handed my tub back with a very apologetic smile. I turned away shortly; it had gone all gooey and God knows which parts of Josephine's anatomy it had been in. I threw it in the bin.

"Sorry," Josephine echoed as I left. Lying naked on the tiles, she was totally unabashed, almost pleased, I reflected later, that I'd caught them together. Just to prove that she, Josephine, had won again.

Even worse, Ricky was so horribly overly nice to me, convinced I was heartbroken by Henry. One morning he woke me up banging loudly on the door, inviting me to join them on an Xmas shopping trip.

I tried to pretend I was still asleep. I'd no desire to get up and I hadn't washed my hair for six days and all my clothes were in the dirty linen basket, which I couldn't be bothered to wash either. I was also feeling very odd; whether it was hangover, depression or insomniac exhaustion, I couldn't tell.

"Wakey, wakey!" Ricky barged in. Seeing the doll tucked up in bed beside me, he pulled her and proceeded to waltz her around the room. I rolled my eyes.

"My name's Henry," he said in a deep voice, shoving the doll in my face as though I was a kid that needed cheering up, "and I'm a total bastard." Then he punched the doll and threw her to the ground. "Ha, you smiled!" he cried as my lips turned up ever so faintly.

"Come on, Ricky," Josephine came in cleaning her teeth and putting a possessive arm around him. Then she whispered something in his ear which sounded like, "I read in *Cosmo* that if you snog with toothpaste in your mouth you get an amazing sensation."

He slapped her away and said lightly, "Not in front of Olivia, darling."

Christ, there's no way I'm putting up with this, I thought grumpily. I'd rather spend the morning killing myself.

I put my head in my hands and made vague moaning noises.

"What's the matter?" Ricky asked gently, patting my back, making me flinch. "Long hangover or something?"

"I think I have some kind of weird flu," I peered at him through the gap in my fingers. "I just feel so weird and awful – like my body's been torn apart and put back together all wrong."

"You know what the matter with you is," said Josephine, pointing her toothbrush abruptly at me.

"What?" I asked, slightly sullenly.

"You're pregnant."

"I'm sorry?" Ricky and I cried simultaneously.

"You are pregnant," she picked up a copy of *Cosmo,* flicking through. "Okay, here's the checklist. Okay, are you bingeing?" Seeing that the choccies in my advent calendar had been eaten several days too early, she nodded triumphantly. "Yes, you clearly are. Are you sick in the mornings?"

"Yes, but –" But after spending half the night bingeing, surely being sick was quite normal?

"Are you putting on weight?"

"Yes, but –" I'd though that was because of the binges.

"Are your moods swinging?"

"Well, of course, but that's because of R – Henry's gone!" I jumped, caught his eye, quickly looked away.

"You're pregnant, Olivia."

"And hòw come you're so sure?" I cringed in horror. 'Come to think of it, I had missed a period last month, but I assumed that was due to stress.'

She gave me a long look, then nodded. "Intuition. I can just tell."

*   *   *

So I went to see the doctor.

When I returned, I found Ricky in the living-room, watching the cricket, with Jamie on his lap, sharing a Mr Men yoghurt. Oh, what a lovely father he would have been, my heart quailed in disappointment. Seeing me, he jumped and slopped yoghurt down his jumper.

"Well?" he asked with a pale face. "Did – did he . . ."

"The test was negative," I said in a cool voice.

"Oh, right. Well, good," said Ricky.

"Yeah," I said. "Great."

"It's negative," I told Josephine later that evening when she pulled me into the bathroom for a 'private chat'.

"Don't lie to me," said Josephine, folding her arms. "Come on, tell me."

"Okay, okay," I said. "But you don't need to worry," I gulped shakily. "It belongs to Henry, honestly."

In actual fact, I had no idea who it belonged to. The GP had not been able to confirm who the father might be.

"Well, when Ricky and I were in Brighton," I had said, "we couldn't afford to use condoms and my husband didn't like them so sometimes at the end of my period –" I'd caught myself, seeing the doctor's beady eyes flickering in bemusement, "No, look, I'm not a slapper," I'd said hurriedly. "There's just two of them, and Ricky is Henry's son –" As his pen stopped on the page, I'd paused and gulped and made a rapid exit.

"You're sure?" Josephine asked. She almost seemed disappointed. "If it was Ricky's, we could all bring him up together!" She laughed, then, seeing my face, said quickly, "So, are you going to tell Henry?"

"No way!" I cried; for the past few weeks neither of us had contacted each other and even though I was running out of money, there was no way I was going to ring him and crawl.

"Anyway," I said, "can you imagine? Henry would have made me call him Giles and send him off to Eton and turn him into a grand master at the age of twelve." I paused. "You won't tell Ricky, will you?"

"Why ever not?" Josephine asked.

"Because I'm just not sure if I should keep it," I said miserably. "Oh, don't look at me like that. I'm in no state to have a kid, my own life is a complete mess without inflicting it on my child too! And how will it feel, without having a proper dad?"

"Oh, sod that!" Josephine cried. "A nourishing female influence is enough!" She then started on a feminist lecture that lasted several minutes and by the end, I found myself nodding in agreement; in any case, I knew deep down that I would never bring myself to kill my baby off. My baby. God, how strange.

"Okay," I said, "but still don't tell Ricky, okay? Don't tell anyone."

"Well, excuse me for pointing out the obvious," said Josephine, "but I think it might soon start to show."

"Well, I'll worry about that when the time comes," I procrastinated.

I don't know whether it was pre-natal depression, but in the following week I got into a bloody bad mood. Even when a bunch of kids came round to us carol singing, I gave them a one-pence and slammed the door in their faces.

"Touché," said Leila, raising her eyebrows.

"Urgh!" I pulled a face and stomped off.

That was the trouble with a broken heart, I mused miserably, you turn into a first-class bitch. The pain starts to solidify into cynicism, acidify into bitterness. You felt so awful you wanted to spread your pain around and make everyone else share the burden, like taxes.

It was the same the next morning when we finally did all go Xmas shopping. Leila and I trailed after Rick and Josephine, cooing over the His and Hers in M&S.

"Why don't you get this for your mother?" Leila suggested, as she spotted a sparkling leopard-skin dress.

"Haven't spoken to her in three weeks," I said, "and I'm not going to, till she apologises."

"Olivia! 'Tis the season of goodwill."

"Yeah, well, I'm sick of always having to be the one to say sorry to her."

In Boots, Josephine and Ricky dithered over bubble baths, Leila over hairdryers, and me over aspirins. I was dying to ask the assistant how many bottles one needed to commit suicide, but I was terrified she might ring the emergency alarm, so I bought three.

"Obviously you're anticipating a very long Xmas hangover," said Ricky, then stopped when I grimaced at him.

In Dillons several teenagers stopped Josephine and Ricky for autographs and asked if being in love with each other had been the inspiration for their book. I made pukey noises.

"Why don't you write another book?" Leila suggested helpfully.

"Yeah, well, Clare thingummy who published that historical romance rang me up the other day asking for a sequel but I basically told her to fuck off."

"You shouldn't have!" Leila was appalled. "Think of the dosh!"

For a moment I felt a fizzle of inspiration, instantly expurgated by the memory of the time I'd showed Henry *Wickham's Memoirs* and it had been so bad he didn't even comment on it.

"No," I said despondently, shaking my head, "I'm never going to be a writer. It's just never going to happen. It's just not meant to be."

"Bull," Leila tried to rouse me. "It's just your mid-life crisis getting to you again."

As far as I was concerned, my mid-life crisis was over. It hadn't been resolved, it had just fizzled out. There was no way I was going to meet Mr Right or write a bestseller. I wasn't even at the stage where Aspel closed his book and said, "Olivia, you have the most boring life we've ever come across." My life was so dull and worthless I'd never even get invited on the programme.

I decided to commit suicide.

I waited until the house was empty, till Ricky, Josephine and Leila had gone off to yet another Xmas party. Then I turned off the light in my bedroom, lit a few Body Shop candles, swept everything off my dresser and onto the floor. Shit, I swore, as I cracked my best L'Oreal eye shadow. Then I reminded myself if I was dead I'd hardly care.

I laid out all the pills on the dresser. They winked like stars in the night. Well, now for the suicide notes, I gulped.

I proceeded to use up my best writing paper which I was always saving for some special occasion that never came. Half an hour later, I had a callus on my thumb and I was feeling seriously fed up. There were so many to write, and as soon as I'd done one, I remembered another to add to the list, it was worse than Christmas cards, and anyway, I didn't know what to say, so I just limited myself to a paragraph for each, saving myself up for my epic for Ricky.

Dear Leila, Please can I entrust you to look after Roberta. Please feed her twice a day, and please no salmon 'cos even though she'll beg for it it gives her a funny tummy.

Oh God. Somehow the thought of leaving behind my doggie and having her howling all over the place was more upsetting than people's grief.

I paused, steeled myself, took a pill and swallowed it down with a mouthful of Malibu. Normally I never bought Malibu as it's so expensive but I figured I may as well go with a bang.

I wondered how Henry would react. Whether I'd make it to the newspapers: '*Tragic Waste of Literary Talent.*' After all, no writer was appreciated until after their death; look at Ted Hughes.

I took another pill, and another, and began on Ricky's.

Oh my dearest dearest Ricky, I don't know what to say except I love you and I hate writing this now knowing I'm going to die alone I once remember you saying we should be buried together

Oh God. I took another pill, then coughed as it got stuck in my windpipe, so I washed it down with long glugs of Malibu.

Feeling my stomach turn, I suddenly sat up. Was it just my indigestion or did the baby just turn? I wondered if it was feeling the pain? Could it feel? What if, what if it stayed alive after I had died, a floating foetus in my dead stomach? What a way to live and die.

That made me really start to cry. Hearing the phone, I leapt for it, desperate to be discovered, saved.

It was Mum.

"Oh Mum," I wept, "I've taken all these pills, I just got so depressed, I found out I'm pregnant and –"

"You what!" she shrieked, then said in a very still voice, "Stay there. I'll be right over."

While I was waiting, I quickly tore up all the notes; it would be so embarrassing if anyone found them, especially all the bitchy stuff I'd put in the one to Josephine. Feeling the pain like an arrow, I started to sob again.

"Oh Mum," I fell into her arms. Seeing all the pills laid out on my dresser, she baulked and then started to panic, half dragging me down the stairs.

"Oh my God, what have you done, you silly girl, how many did you take?"

"Five!" I wept. "I can't feel it yet but I don't want my stomach pumped – what if the baby comes flying out and I don't want it to end up a vegetable –"

"Five!" she stopped short, staring at me with exasperation and incredulity. "Five! I sometimes take five for a bad hangover!"

"Don't shout at me, it's not my fault."

"Oh come here!" She drew me into her arms.

If one good thing came from the incident, it was being reunited with Mum. She drove me home and cooked for me and we sat up watching *Eastenders* together and even when her admirers phoned, she left the answerphone on. Then she tucked me up in bed and kissed me goodnight, muttering, "Don't you ever do that to me again!"

That night, for the first time in a long time, I slept a good eight hours, and woke up feeling loved and nourished. The sun was shining, nothing seemed quite so bad, and *The Big Breakfast* was certainly worth living for. Sitting on the sofa in my pyjamas, I suddenly felt as though I was sixteen again, before the dreadful divorce, procrastinating about going off to high school in the morning,

My mum also boosted my morale by giving me a pep talk about the baby and my future with men.

"You've got to find a man with a wallet," she said firmly. "Don't worry about looks or love; it's all superficial, passion never lasts. Look," she insisted, seeing my face, "I'm just being practical, Olivia. Even Jane Austen recommended men with bloody big houses, didn't she, hmm?"

"Alright," I said humbly, but I couldn't help thinking: I married a man with a bloody big house and look what happened. And as for money – Henry hadn't coughed up one penny of the so-called phantom 'settlement' I was supposed to be getting; every time I'd dared to call up his Ms French, she'd merely fobbed me off with, "His lawyers are working on it . . ."

The Christmas Eve passion ball at the Hippodrome seemed the obvious answer to finding a new man, rich or otherwise. My mum and I went to the hairdressers, she for a new perm, me for new layers.

Back home, she gave me a makeover and insisted on lending me some of her pulling gear. She dressed me in her high heels, a slinky blue dress, covering my eyelids with glitter and my hair with streaks.

"Oo, don't you look lovely! Doesn't she, Calvin?"

Calvin looked up an inch from his page three of *The Sun* and repressed a smile.

"Too much glitter," he said at last. "She looks like a Christmas Tree."

Instantly I wilted; Henry had reduced my self-confidence to the low of a hedgehog squashed on a motorway; one more rejection and I would probably shave off my hair and become a nun for life.

"Oh, take no notice!" my mother bustled, and even gave me a tenner for drinks.

"Mum, I'm pregnant," I sighed, but she insisted anyway. I gave her a kiss goodbye as Ricky's Beatle pulled up outside.

By the time I came out, both Josephine and Ricky had got out of the car and were standing with arms folded, looking grim. Josephine, as always, had put on just the right thing: a slinky black evening dress with diamonte straps and matching earrings. Ricky was looking equally gorgeous in a tux; they made the perfect, glamorously suited couple.

"We're not going," Josephine twisted her lip.

"We are," Ricky insisted, with an edge to his voice. "We promised Olivia we'd go to cheer her up, and we are going."

"Well, you bloody drive then!" Josephine hissed. She put her hands on her hips, her eyes flashing like sapphires under the glare of the street lamps. "He said he'd drive so I could drink and now he's saying he wants to drink —"

"Look, I'll drive," I said calmly. "Okay?"

"Oh, yes, because you're —"

"Teetotal," I interrupted hastily.

In the back, Josephine and Ricky sat as far away from each other as possible, both staring out of opposite windows. Still, I knew that by the end of the evening they would have kissed and made up. Oh well, at least I was getting used to the pain, halfway near accepting that they wanted to be together. It was time for me to move on to someone new. I could feel my hands slippery on the wheel and a positive aquarium of butterflies in my tummy; I was just like a teenager going out in the hope of a snog and a bloke that might ring me back, that encounter that might just be Love with a big 'L'.

43. Christmas Eve

Arriving, we meet Leila outside and ended up having to queue for hours in the freezing cold. Everyone was in a wild party mood, girls with streaked hair woven with tinsel, the bouncers dressed up in Father Xmas outfits.

"God, I hope I pull tonight," said a pair of Sharons in front who were chewing gum; boobs and bums nearly bursting out of their slinky little black numbers.

"Nah, I'm not going to pull, I'm just going to have a good time," said Sharon 2 snootily, though it was obvious she was completely gagging for it.

Then I shook myself for being such a bitch; I was just as bad, just as desperate.

Inside, we sat up on a balcony sipping Christmas cocktails decorated with berries and holly. Eleven to twelve was the Prowling Hour, as Josephine always called it, where blokes and girls wandered in single-sex groups sizing up the talent. Well, I thought, perhaps, perhaps Mr Right might be here tonight. After all, I never believed in all that stuff about there just being one soul mate out there for you. The trouble was, I'd already found two so the chance of finding a third seemed slim, if not downright greedy.

Even worse, Josephine, who is a worse matchmaker than Jane Austen's *Emma*, perched herself on Ricky's lap as though it was a post from which to view chaps with narrowed eyes over the rim of her glass.

"Wow, get a load of that," she whistled at a group of lads in denim. "I dare you to go over, Livy."

"No, no," I hissed, "I don't know what to say. Don't make me, get Leila to go." I smiled apologetically as Leila gave me a filthy look.

"Be bold!" said Josephine. "Just walk up and say, 'Will you go to bed with me?' The direct approach is always best."

I caught Ricky's eyes and quickly looked away. "You need a drink down you, girl," he feigned Northern heartiness, "to get some guts. Why are you drinking Coke?"

Josephine was about to blurt it all out when I gave her a strong look and she shut up.

Finally, if only to shut Josephine up, I went over to the bar and hovered nervously, ignoring Josephine and Leila's egging looks and Ricky's inscrutable stare. He probably wants to push me off with someone else, I thought miserably, just so he can be sure he's got me off his back and I'll leave him and Joey in peace.

I hardly knew where to begin. I liked the look of the one standing with his back to me, the most gorgeous butt clad in a pair of jeans. Almost without thinking, I pinched it.

He jumped. Spilling his pint all down his white shirt and jeans.

"Oh my God, I'm so sorry!" I cried.

"Alright, it's quite alright," he muttered.

I ruffled in my handbag and pulled out a dirty hanky that was obviously covered in snot. His friends hid their smiles in their pints.

I was about to back away and crawl under a table and wish I was dead, when he held out his hand. "Well? If you're going to throw your drink over me, you could at least introduce yourself."

I grinned uneasily and shook his hand. Golly, he was yummy: Asian, with a shock of dark hair and cheekbones like knives. Then I jumped as Josephine came up behind me.

"Sorry about her," she purred, sticking her elbow into my ribs, "Okay?" she handed him one of her spotless white hankies. "Honestly, I can't take her anywhere."

Our two groups amalgamated. Josephine, caught between five blokes as well as Ricky, was like Queen Elizabeth in a court of adoring suitors. For once, I didn't feel a prick of jealousy, I was so enjoying chatting to Ravi, as I'd discovered his name was. It turned out he was twenty-three (younger man! – so I lied and said I was twenty-four) and in his third year at the St Martin's School of Art. I waited for him to ask me a few 'What do you do?'s but instead he seemed fanatical in talking about his work: huge fifteen-foot-square stretches of canvas with lumps of wood stuck on them. Not just any lumps of wood, he emphasised, but lumps of wood from Canada, to symbolise the plight of diminishing rainforest there.

"But surely if you're using the wood to stick onto bits of paper you're only diminishing it further?" I couldn't resist joking. Ravi didn't smile. He just continued talking about his vision, his plans, the gallery which might take him on.

I took another sip of my Coke. Oh well, I thought, maybe it really is asking too much to expect looks and a sense of humour. But as he continued to pontificate I couldn't help but feel that there wasn't so much an absence of humour as an absence of personality. I couldn't help noticing, as well, that though his dark eyes were very beautiful, they were very bloodshot, and there was an oddly vacant look about them. I got a strange sensation that even if I did get up and walk off, he would carry on talking to the leather seat. Drugs, I thought. Hmm. A scenario floated in my head of my poor baby crying and him mashing up hash in the baby food. Or me giving him a twenty to buy some nappies and him rolling it up to snort cocaine.

Oh dear – this was the trouble with being pregnant, it made one so much more picky. *Am I going to be like this forever after?* I fretted, not able to talk to a bloke for more than five minutes without assessing whether he'd be a suitable role model for my unborn?

By the time the slow dances had come on, Josephine was dragging everyone downstairs and I was thoroughly miserable. If only I had the guts to tell him where to go, then I might just meet Mr Right on the dancefloor at the very last minute. As everyone trailed down, I escaped to the loos and hung around for five minutes, praying that Ravi would just disappear. Then the two Sharons who'd been in the queue earlier came back in, zonking their hair with spray.

Surely he must have gone by now? I opened the

door an inch, then, seeing the Sharons rolling their blue-lined eyes, I eased out. Indeed, the seats were empty. Thank God.

I went to the balcony and gazed down at the couples. There was Leila dancing with one of the lads, bless her; I gave her the thumbs up to say, "Nice one!" There was Josephine dancing with Ricky; he looked up, as though instinctively feeling my gaze, and I quickly looked away, feeling a turn in my stomach; perhaps it was the baby. Oh, oh! And there was Ravi. Dancing with a comely blonde. Well, fine, I thought, somehow feeling furiously gutted. Now it looked as though he'd wanted to get rid of me, not me of him.

Sitting down on a chair, I tried to fight the desperation as the DJ announced "The last smoochy" and put on *Two Become One* by the Spice Girls. Then, suddenly, a tall dark stranger came walking towards me. Oh God, my prayers have come true – there is life after Ricky. He gazed deep into my eyes, cleared his throat and said, "Excuse me, could I borrow this chair?"

"Oh sure, sure," I stumbled. I waved as though to say, 'Take all four.'

"Cheers." He picked it up and walked off.

Oh well, my darling, I whispered silently to my baby, it looks as though it's just you and me. There'll be other clubs, other nights. Still, I felt tears in my eyes. I felt like giving up altogether. What's the point? I thought wearily, by the time I do meet someone I'll be so bitter and cynical and afraid of getting hurt they'll never love me anyway.

Then I felt a presence behind me, a voice in my ear;

"Would you like to dance?"

"Oo, yes please!" I jumped up, then baulked. Oh my God. It was Elvis.

Elvis. Elvis my old Ex, the guy whom I had first got off with in that fatal Spin the Bottle party. Elvis of jeans and psychedelic shirts that made one feel as though one was on LSD. Elvis of smutty breath, slimy hands, spots and greasy hair.

"Ah – well – hi," I said. Before I could say another word, he had his hand clamped on mine and was leading me down. Oh well, I thought, at least it's someone. I feigned a confident, 'All's well – I planned this' smile as Josephine looked over in horror.

Perhaps, I thought, as Elvis squeezed me against him, perhaps it really just is my destiny to end up with a sad loser. Perhaps I am simply trying to fight the course Nature has intended.

Then I looked up and caught Ricky's gaze. He was watching me. I gave him a little wave. He continued to stare. I looked back. A couple moved in front of us, then away. He was still looking. I was still looking. I couldn't help it. I just stared and stared and stared with completely undisguised adoration. What was the look in his eyes? Through the swirl of red-green-blue lights it was impossible to tell.

As Elvis pulled away, the cold air came up between us. All around, couples were necking. Elvis lunged at me and I pulled away.

"It's all your fault!" I suddenly cried. "If it hadn't been for you and me kissing we would be together!"

Elvis blinked like a goldfish; I gave a cry of exasperation and ran upstairs to the loos.

Inside, the two Sharons, sitting despondently on a

couch, looked up in amazement as I dived into a cubicle and burst into tears. I tried to push it shut, then realised the bloody lock was broken. But by now I was beyond caring who saw me. I was just so heartbroken. Why is life so horrible? Why is this all so unfair, so mismatched, me loving Ricky loving Josephine loving anyone who takes her fancy for ten seconds? Why, for once in my life, can't something finally come good, something I really want?

Hearing a rap on the door, I pushed the door, then gasped as it pushed back against me. It was Ricky. I quickly yanked a bit of loo paper to dry my eyes.

"Sorry, just the dry ice, makes my eyes water," I muttered.

Ricky gazed at me, then drew me out of the cubicle and held me against him. I hung on, unable to stop crying, gushing like waterworks, making a complete idiot out of myself.

"Oh God, I'm such a selfish bastard," he muttered into my hair.

"It's not you," I tried to untangle myself in shame, aware of the Sharons watching. Then, something in his eyes made me stop struggling and look up at him.

"D'you think, d'you think?" he blurted out. "I know you're really upset and I swore to myself on the plane back that I'd take a month before making a move and it's only been two days but I love you so much I can't help but say it – there I've said it now. Olivia, I love you."

I was so astonished I couldn't speak.

"I'm sorry," he said, "I don't mean to rush you. I know you've only just started a thing with Elvis –"

"Elvis!" I exclaimed.

"I mean I know you've always fancied him since the party where you got off with him instead of me, but I don't think he suits you," he said crossly. "He looks dodgy to me, way too clingy, you need someone to love you but give you space."

"Elvis! I don't love Elvis!" I cried. "I'm not interested in anyone like that."

"No, I guess you're not ready for a relationship yet." Ricky chewed his lip and turned away. "We'd better meet with Joey, she's gone to get the coats."

"Ricky!"

As he strode to the door, I only just caught him in time. Cupping his face in my hands, I reached up and kissed him with all my love and might. He kissed me back, his eyes wide with surprise, then drew back breathlessly, a smile of pure delight dawning on his face.

"You love me!"

"Of course I love you, you stupid bastard, I've always loved you!" I curled my arms around him, resting my head against chest, closing my eyes in disbelief as he kissed my cheeks and hair and mouth, over and over, not wanting to ever let go again.

"See?" Ricky said a moment later. "Didn't I always say, right from the start, didn't I say in India I knew you were in love with me?" Then he drew back laughing as I tried to hit him.

Sneaking off together was relatively easy. Dear Leila was going back with her new man and Josephine was going back with her five new men, who wanted to play

Strip Poker and watch pornos at some mate's house in Fulham. She begged us to join them, and when we feigned tiredness she told us off for being bores and then went without us.

I got into the front seat of Ricky's Beatle. Getting in too, he slotted the keys into the ignition, then paused.

"I want you to know that I don't love Josephine. I actually came back for you, but when I walked into the room, you just sat there like a lemon and then Josephine came up and —"

"Well, what did you expect me to do?" I cried. "I was hardly going to start ripping off your clothes."

"Oo, that sounds nice," said Ricky with a naughty smile. "We can do that when we get home."

"So you're seriously not in love with Josephine?"

"No. I was just on the rebound again. And then I figured I really shouldn't say a word to you because you still loved Dad."

"No, no!"

"I gave him a right talking to about the way he treated you."

"Oh, you're talking now?"

"Well, kind of. We're getting there. We played golf the other week, which is a start. I think he's getting over it, but you know how it is . . ."

"So what did he say about me?" Then, when Ricky hesitated, I persisted masochistically, "Come on, you can tell me. I can take it, it's over between us now."

"Well, he said he didn't think being married to you was ever going to work because you were too soft and he needed someone hard like Agatha to answer him back. And that he'd only married you on the rebound from her and he'd been happy with you as his mistress but then you'd rushed him into it –"

"Me! Rushed him!" I gasped in indignation. "Huh. Huh. Huh."

"I was also feeling really guilty about doing that book with Josephine, I knew how mad you must have felt."

"Oh, never mind that, I can't write anyway," I said automatically.

"Yes, you can!" Ricky cried.

"Henry says –" I broke off, realising that Henry's word wasn't necessarily law anymore.

"You can write," said Ricky quite fiercely. "You forget Henry, he's such a perfectionist, I once caught him going through a copy of a Shakespeare play correcting with a pencil. We have to write books together," Ricky insisted, taking my hands. "I'm here now, and I swear to you, Olivia, that I'm going to be so good to you and I promise I'm going to make you happy –" He broke off as though searching for the right words. "I just really love you. I love everything about you – the way you laugh, and worry about everything, and all your crazy habits, I love your eyes, and your hair –"

"Urgh! Not my hair!" I protested, feeling so thoroughly overwhelmed I felt I had to tell him to stop, slapping his hand away as he pulled a curl teasingly.

"So tell me what you love about me," said Ricky, drawing me into arms and kissing me again.

On the journey back, we couldn't stop kissing: at traffic-lights, at every stop, every turn. "I just can't wait to get you into bed." Ricky kissed my hair, then veered unsteadily as he nearly collided with an angry Ford coming the other way. "Oops, don't want to kill us both off before we've even begun."

Ricky's house was certainly a wonderful surprise: a huge four-bed-roomer in Cheam, which is a much posher area than Sutton. It was a big white detached house with its own garden. Inside the babysitter had dropped off in front of the TV. She sat up sheepishly but he just grinned, handed her a wad of notes and said, "Have a bonus, Happy New Year. Dear me," he added, when she had gone, "falling in love is going to be very expensive. I feel so careless, as though I just want to give all my money away."

"It's such a lovely, lovely house," I kept exclaiming.

"Not a fraction of the size of Rochester," he apologised, but I shook my head, gazing around at the clean beige carpet and plaid sofa. "No, I like it, it's cosy." I also felt oddly affectionate to see that, despite the plush newness, the tinsel was ragged on the Christmas Tree, dirty plates and sneakers littered the floor, and there was a pair of Boxer shorts hanging from his TV aerial.

"Helps to improve the reception," Ricky caught my gaze and I giggled; how lovely, I thought, it would be to live here with him and look after him and sort him out.

Then I gasped as he came up behind me, circling his arms around my waist, kissing the nape of my neck. I squealed joyously as he suddenly picked me up in his arms.

*   *   *

"You're mine now to do vhat I vant with." He pretended to nip my neck.

Naturally, he had to stop and kiss me on every step. Five steps from the top, he had to put me down because his back was aching, just as his son, Jamie, emerged from his new bedroom in his pyjamas, trailing a stuffed green dragon.

"Daddy, I can't sleep," he said, then he smiled up at me. "Hey, I remember you, you're Olive-a." He laughed.

"Back to bed, Jamie," said Ricky firmly. He put his hands on his shoulders and gently trundled him into his bedroom. Inside there was rose-patterned wallpaper covered by pictures of Wallace & Grommit and Arnold Schwarzenegger. It was very messy; toys and mechano scattered across the floor; my heel caught on a piece of railway track.

"Tell me a story," Jamie demanded.

"Okay," said Ricky at top disc-jockey speed. "There was once a miserable princess and then a nice prince came along and kissed her and she turned into a frog and drowned in a pond and they all lived happily ever after, okay? Now, goodnight." He reached to switch out the light.

"No!" Jamie kicked his legs. "I want a proper story."

"Look, Jamie." Ricky sat down firmly on the bed and I started to slip out through the door. I just caught him saying, "Look, Jamie, you know what it's like when you're playing Kiss Chase at school and then you kissed Elizabeth and then horrible old bag Ms Yates rang the bell for the end of the break and you felt really disappointed . . . ?" He turned and gave me a thumbs up. "Just wait for me in my room . . ."

I shook my head, laughing, and went into Ricky's room. There was a row of little Body Shop candles lined up on the windowsill, so I found his lighter and lit them, shivering – I couldn't believe how freezing it was. I couldn't stop hugging myself with delirious happiness; I couldn't believe it, it was too wonderful, too good to be true . . . Too good to be true.

Henry's pain was making me cynical again. I love you is all very well, I couldn't stop thinking, but what about tomorrow morning, or next week when the thrill of New Year is over. But surely he wouldn't just bring me back here for a one-night stand . . . ? Oh please, no, Krishna, I pressed my hands to my lips, I couldn't bear that, it would hurt too much to go through that pain all over again . . .

"Who-hoh!" Ricky came bounding in, waving a bottle of champagne and some slightly sticky-looking glasses. "I found this in the fridge, leftover from Xmas!"

"Yes, that's lovely, Ricky, but why is it so cold in here?" I asked, taking the bottle and pouring out the champagne.

"Erm, I tried some DIY on the central heating and it went horribly wrong. Oh wow, I feel so happy, I feel like a kid on Christmas Day!" He bounced up and down, then collapsed in a heap, grinning up at me.

I put down the bottle and went to him slowly, my eyes fixed unblinkingly on his. I sat down and took his hand and gazed down at his palm, the strong, confident arc of his life-line, threading my fingers through his, massaging the tips of his fingers. I felt my forehead creasing into worry lines. Ricky sat up.

"What is it? You haven't changed your mind?"

"No!" I turned to him. "It's just – well, you see, look, Ricky, I think you should know . . ." I paused for a moment in doubt. Perhaps a one-night stand with Ricky would be better than frightening him off, just to taste him again, feel him inside me, loving me, kissing me . . .

"What?" he repeated in a quiet, worried voice.

"I'm pregnant." I picked up a glass from the side table and took a nervous sip, fixing my eyes on the bubbles.

"What?"

"I'm pregnant, I've done a test. And I think the baby is yours but to be honest I'm not exactly sure . . ."

"You're kidding!"

His eyes two brown orbs of shock. His warm hands fell away, the cold air rushed up between us, seizing up my stomach. I knew it, I trembled, he doesn't want it, it's too heavy, all he wanted was just fun and a fling. Yet again he has been lumbered with another unwanted child. He won't be able support this one and his son. He'll make me have an abortion.

"But that's marvellous," he breathed, "that's just like so – fucking marvellous – whoops sorry – Christ, I shall have to stop swearing, I don't want our child to grow up with bad manners – but – wow –" He ran his hand over my cheek, between my breasts, resting wonderously on my stomach and womb. "Wow. Our child. My child, or nephew, anyway. But – but – you shouldn't be drinking!" He suddenly put his hand over my glass, frowning at me severely. "Oh God, it's not too cold in here for you, is it? The baby won't be frozen to death, will he, she? Oh, wow, I wonder what it will be. If it's a he, we have to call him Elvis! Oh Olivia, that's the best news ever, this is the happiest night of my life!"

As he hugged me hard against him, I cried out in relief, "Oh thank goodness, I thought you wouldn't want it!"

"Not want it?" he drew back fiercely. "Not want it? As if I wouldn't want our baby! I love you. Look, I'm not going to treat you like Henry, I'm never going to leave you, I'll do everything to look after you, I'd love to marry you even, if you like . . ."

I gaped in surprise. Before I could even digest and compute this most wonderful and astonishing piece of information, he added quickly,

"Well, I don't want to rush you, we can think about that. Look, I really do want to marry you, but if you just want to live together for a while, that's great. Anything. You know, Olivia, marriage doesn't have to be so awful. I mean, I know you've been scarred but I don't have any big ideals either."

"You don't?" I said in relief.

"No, course I don't. I just think, it will be like having a best friend around. Like us being brother and sister."

Hmm, yes, I liked that idea . . .

He leaned over and kissed me.

"That's not very sisterly," I objected.

"Neither is this," he said, pulling off my jumper and then pulling me down on the bed, pulling the sheets up over us so that we were encased in a grey-white cocoon. He ran his hands over me, cupping my stomach, circling the slight bulge.

"Hey!" his face lit up. "I heard him kicking."

"Actually," I laughed. "I think that's just my indigestion after those mince-pies."

We laughed for ages and then gazed at each and kissed each very slowly and gently, drinking in the nectar of our kisses. We started to caress each other, kissing all the time, rubbing noses in an Eskimo kiss. I was so excited to see how much I excited him, so desperate to give to him, and for him to give to me . . .

"Daddy!" Our hands froze as Jamie stumbled in muzzily. "I can't sleep, it's bloody freezing."

"Don't swear," Ricky said automatically. "Go back to bed." Under the covers, he continued to kiss me lusciously, his hands still circling my breasts. I drew in my breath, swallowing back my feverish desire to feel him inside me.

"Daddy, what are you doing!" Jamie pulled up the covers from down below, blasting us with cold air. "I'm tired," he said, climbing up and lodging between us, nestling hazily against his father. He fell asleep at once.

Ricky buried his head in the pillow and groaned. I just laughed and Ricky sighed and gazed down at Jamie.

"I guess we should just go to sleep."

Across the covers, he reached out to hold my hand, making a bridge across Jamie. "We should say our prayers," he whispered, with a loving smile. So we put our hands together and said them together. As I felt his palms warm around mine, all my worries seemed to slip away, as they always did when I was with Ricky. I felt myself again. I swayed gently, my lips moving with my prayer, hearing his whisper, the darkness expanding into infinity . . .

When I opened my eyes, Ricky was looking at me with creased, affectionate eyes. I snuggled up, staring at my beautiful new husband over the hem of my blanket, and now and again he would look back at me and he would smile and I would smile and I would feel my heart bashing against my chest as though it wanted to leap into his body. Then he yawned and slowly his hand slackened on mine as his head rolled in sleep . . .

I lay awake. I felt too happy to sleep. I don't think I had ever felt so blissful in my life, as though my body was just a container to hold the nectar of my love for him like honey in a jamjar.

I lay on the pillow, contentedly gazing at the little candles. They gave the room a holy, happy feel; the flames pirouetting from the white sticks as the draught laughed around them, as if celebrating our love.

More often than not, I looked at Ricky, his face slack in sleep. I kept finding my lips smiling at him, my heart leaping up at my darling, my love, my saviour . . .

My gaze wandered over his blonde head to the window. Outside, the black night sky was celestial with stars. I grinned inanely up at the moon, telling her all the lovely things we were going to do tomorrow. I must wake early and cook him breakfast and bring him a surprise breakfast in bed. Something greasy to start fattening him up. We could take Jamie out to the park – urgh! What a horribly boring married thought that was . . . still, it would be nice . . . I thought of my child being born, and playing with Jamie, and I liked that idea. I started to get excited again – there was just so much to look forward to!

The moon seemed pleased, and reminded me of all that we had been through to come to here. I sighed with that coming-home contentment that makes you wonder why you ever worried or doubted anything. I thought of Michael Aspel and pictured him closing up his red book with a satisfied bang. I pictured Ms Watts sighing in resignation and moving on to another girl. I thought of Krishna, dancing in his fields with his flute, wooing the cows and children and *gopis*, and said a prayer of thanks for bringing me to Ricky, and for our baby and all our future happiness. I closed my eyes and felt Ricky kissing me in his sleep. I felt the universe like a great big umbrella smiling over us, and knew that from now on everything would always be alright.

The End